A Ship of Bones and Teeth

A DARK FANTASY ROMANCE

KARINA HALLE

Books by Karina Halle

DARK FANTASY ROMANCE

River of Shadows (Underworld Gods #1)

Crown of Crimson (Underworld Gods #2)

City of Darkness (Underworld Gods #3) - 2023

Black Sunshine (Dark Eyes Duet #1)

The Blood is Love (Dark Eyes Duet #2)

Nightwolf

Blood Orange (The Dracula Duet #1)

Black Rose (The Dracula Duet #2)

A Ship of Bones and Teeth

HORROR & PARANORMAL ROMANCE

Darkhouse (EIT #1)

Red Fox (EIT #2)

The Benson (EIT #2.5)

Dead Sky Morning (EIT #3)

Lying Season (EIT #4)

On Demon Wings (EIT #5)

Old Blood (EIT #5.5)

The Dex-Files (EIT #5.7)

Into the Hollow (EIT #6)

And With Madness Comes the Light (EIT #6.5)

Come Alive (EIT #7)

Ashes to Ashes (EIT #8)

Dust to Dust (EIT #9)

Ghosted (EIT #9.5)

Came Back Haunted (EIT #10)

The Devil's Metal (The Devil's Duology #1)

The Devil's Reprise (The Devil's Duology #2)

Veiled (Ada Palomino #1)

Song For the Dead (Ada Palomino #2)

Demon Dust (Ada Palomino #3) - coming 2024

CONTEMPORARY ROMANCE

Love, in English/Love, in Spanish

Where Sea Meets Sky

Racing the Sun

The Pact

The Offer

The Play

Winter Wishes

The Lie

The Debt

Smut

Heat Wave

Before I Ever Met You

After All

Rocked Up

Wild Card

Maverick

Hot Shot

Bad at Love

The Swedish Prince

The Wild Heir

A Nordic King

The Royal Rogue

Nothing Personal

My Life in Shambles

The Royal Rogue

The Forbidden Man

The One That Got Away

Lovewrecked

One Hot Italian Summer

All the Love in the World (Anthology)

The Royals Next Door

The Royals Upstairs - coming 2024

ROMANTIC SUSPENSE

Sins and Needles (The Artists Trilogy #1)

On Every Street (An Artists Trilogy Novella #0.5)

Shooting Scars (The Artists Trilogy #2)

Bold Tricks (The Artists Trilogy #3)

Dirty Angels (Dirty Angels #1)

Dirty Deeds (Dirty Angels #2)

Dirty Promises (Dirty Angels #3)

Black Hearts (Sins Duet #1)

Dirty Souls (Sins Duet #2)

Discretion (Dumonts #1)

Disarm (Dumonts #2)

Disavow (Dumonts #3)

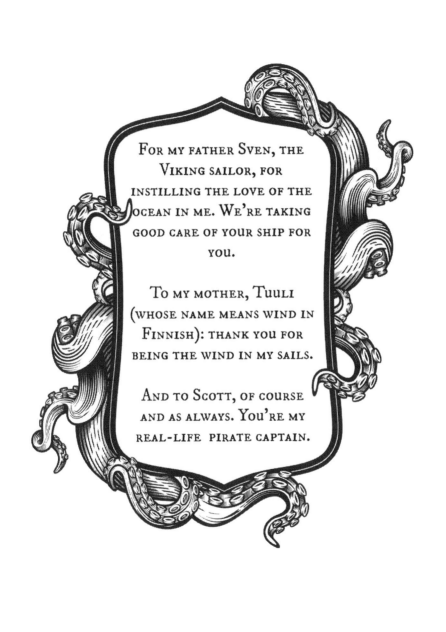

FOR MY FATHER SVEN, THE
VIKING SAILOR, FOR
INSTILLING THE LOVE OF THE
OCEAN IN ME. WE'RE TAKING
GOOD CARE OF YOUR SHIP FOR
YOU.

TO MY MOTHER, TUULI
(WHOSE NAME MEANS WIND IN
FINNISH): THANK YOU FOR
BEING THE WIND IN MY SAILS.

AND TO SCOTT, OF COURSE
AND AS ALWAYS. YOU'RE MY
REAL-LIFE PIRATE CAPTAIN.

First we stand up, then we fall down
We have to move forward, before we drown

— DEPECHE MODE

I descend from grace in arms of undertow
I will take my place in the great below

— NINE INCH NAILS

Playlist

You can find the full playlist on my Spotify here
In the meantime here are some songs featured:

"The Kraken" - Hans Zimmer
"Supernaturally" - Nick Cave and the Bad Seeds
"Mermaids" - Florence and the Machine

"Before We Drown" - Depeche Mode

"Hoist the Colors" - Colm R. McGuiness

"Vivien" - (+++) Crosses

"I am not a woman, I'm a god" - Halsey

"With Teeth" - Nine Inch Nails

"Diamond Eyes" - Deftones

"Always You" - Depeche Mode

"A Drowning" - How to Destroy Angels

"Hurricane" - Halsey

"Gods and Monsters" - Lana Del Rey

"Mermaids" - Hans Zimmer

"La Mer" - Nine Inch Nails

THE NIGHTWIND

ROPE LADDER

AFTCASTLE

MIZZENMAST

WEAPONS ROOM

QUARTERDECK

OFFICER'S QUARTERS

GUN DECK

CAPTAIN'S QUARTERS

CHAIN ROOM

RUDDER

PROVISION HOLD

BILGE

CROW'S NEST

MAINMAST

CREW QUARTERS

FOREMAST

FORECASTLE

BOWSPIRIT

MAIN DECK

JAIL CELL

HEAD

PRISONER HOLD

HULL

GALLEY

CREW QUARTERS

A Ship of Bones & Teeth

Princess Maren is a woman with a secret.

When she was just 16-years old, she sold her soul to the sea witch Edonia, giving up a life underwater in exchange for the love of Prince Aerik on land. But after a decade of abuse and misery inflicted by the cruel prince, Maren wants nothing more than to leave him and her royal role behind and find Edonia to reverse the spell.

An opportunity for escape presents itself when the prince and princess are traveling overseas and are taken hostage by a band of notorious pirates, led by the fearsome Captain Ramsay "Bones" Battista. Maren has heard the sordid stories about the infamous pirate--not only is his ship supposedly haunted and crewed by the damned, but that no prisoners ever survive. Fortunately for Maren, she learns that the captain also has a score to settle with the sea witch. With any luck, Maren may be able to get her old life back, even if it's being held in the captain's wicked hands.

But Ramsay gets more than he bargained for when he learns who--and what--Maren is, and that her appetite for revenge, freedom, and bloodlust rivals his.

Meanwhile Maren finds herself falling for the pirate's dark nature, even as she discovers that Ramsay has a secret more deadly than her own.

When it comes to the high seas, not all monsters lurk beneath the surface.

Content Warning

Hello dear reader! If you are thinking about reading this book, there are a few things you should know before you make the decision to.

One is that though I did a lot of research and did my best to be as accurate as possible with aspects of the the pirate life, old ships, nautical terms, etc, I may have taken a few liberties here and there for this fantasy.

Two, and this is an important one, this book is a dark romance. Let me clarify: If you are a dark romance reader, this is probably just "dark-ish" to you (so don't get your hopes up expecting something deranged).

However, it must be said because if people pick up this book thinking it's going to be like *The Little Mermaid* or *Pirates of the Caribbean* with a bit of PG-13 spice or healthy romance in it, they are in for a rude awakening. *A Ship of Bones & Teeth* is very adult and there's a lot of sex and cursing and a romance that might be considered "unhealthy" by some. In fact, there are some things in the content that I need to particularly warn you about…

The book contains the following triggers: physical and emotional domestic abuse on page (not by the MC), suicidal ideation, death of a loved one, blood, gore, senseless violence, witchcraft, dubious consent within uneven power dynamics, hero who is very possessive, predatory and rough-handed with the heroine (he brands her with a hot iron, just saying) and their romance could possibly be labeled "toxic" (again, he is a pirate and she is a monster), explicit dirty talk, and all characters are very morally gray and flawed in general, of course there's murder, torture, blasphemous cursing and foul language, abuse of power, and graphic sex scenes which feature spanking, ropes, bondage (in chains), being gagged, captive and captor situations, primal kink, and some might even deride this book to be "dark fantasy porn."

I don't want to oversell the sexual content here because it's truly **not** the basis of the book, but I know many people *are* sensitive to gratuitous sex scenes, dark romance themes, and possessive male characters, so I have to make sure this is all spelled out clearly for them so they know exactly what they are getting into when they read this book.

SO…if any of the above annoys you or triggers you in your reading material I suggest you don't read ASOBAT. I'm serious. **Please don't read this book**. I care about your mental health and I also want you to read books you enjoy, not books that will either cause you distress or make you roll your eyes. Life is too short to read a book that you know you won't like.

HOWEVER…if you *are* okay with all of the above…step on board, yo-ho! You're about to set sail on the Nightwind.

Prologue

MAREN

There was no moon on the night I decided to sell my soul. The waters were as dark as octopus ink and, for the first time in a long time, I was afraid. It's as if I finally realized not only what I was about to do, but what I had already done.

A month ago I had left my family behind without a second thought. With just my shark, Nill, as my sole companion, I turned my back on my sisters, on my father, on his kingdom, and swam toward another future. I was always reckless and impulsive, wanting more than the ordinary life in the depths of Limonos, but I'd never done something so rash and dangerous before. I'd never left home.

It's not that I hadn't hinted at it. How many times I'd drifted through the towering green stalks of the kelp forest with Asherah, talking about how all I wanted was to get away, or swam through the coral gardens with Larimar, wishing that my life was more than what my father set out for me. But my sisters never listened to me—I was the youngest and easily dismissed. A princess in name only, never to be queen, never to have any power of her own.

And so one day, I left. I started swimming south along the coast, leaving the sea and the kingdom behind, heading toward waters even warmer, deeper, and darker. Nill swam with me, my loyal protector since I was born, never questioning what I was doing.

Eventually I grew tired and sent Nill to the surface to see if it was safe to take a look. When he assured me it was, I rose up and broke through the swells.

A whole new world awaited me. Instead of the dry and rocky landscape that surrounded Limonos, here everything was lush and green, with parrots flying from the trees, squawking as they went. The sky wasn't as brilliant a blue as it was at home but there was drama and danger in the big dark clouds that rolled in over the surrounding mountain peaks thick with vegetation.

And on the beach was the most beautiful man I had ever seen.

Of course, I had seen men before. Before my mother disappeared, she would often bring them down to the depths of Limonos and offer their organs to us. Asherah, the first born, would get the heart, Larimar would get the liver, and I would usually get a kidney. I had always wanted a man's heart, but my mother said it was something I had to earn. I never got a chance to ask her how I could earn it, since my mother was hauled out of the water by sailors one night, never to be seen again.

As a Syren our first instinct is to lure men to their death. We seduced them, drowned them, and ate them, their body providing us with enough power and nutrients to last us months. They are a rare but much-wanted delicacy. But I had never hunted for a man before, and even though my first instinct upon seeing this particular man should have been to seduce him in order to destroy him, all I wanted was just to seduce him. I was only sixteen at the time, barely an adult, and the sight of him did something to my insides. He made me feel things I had never dreamed about feeling before. I was hungry in a different, more compelling way.

I was such a damn fool.

In seconds I had fallen for him, swallowed up by lust, and this man became my obsession. I spent my days hidden behind the rocks in the shallows, spying on him while Nill circled the waters behind me. The human was traveling with a troupe of people who catered to his every whim. At night he slept in a tent on the beach, the white canvas like a ship's sails, a parade of women disappearing inside, their raucous moans making my body ache with need and envy. During the day he lounged on the sand entertaining guests, gorging themselves on fine food. I found myself wanting to try everything they were eating, but had to settle for clams and crabs and sea cucumbers that lived in the shallow waters around me.

I didn't understand English at the time, but I eventually realized they addressed him as "Prince Aerik."

What I did understand was that I needed him to be mine. Something I could finally call my own. All my life I had felt so fractured and lonely, my father kind but firm and distant, my sisters the light of his life after mother disappeared. But me, I was left with Nill and that was that. No one ever glanced my way or wondered how I was. I was just the third sister taking up too much space in the sea. Even the other Syrens in the kingdom ignored me. Though I was no one within my own family, I was also too different and regal for those outside of it to befriend me.

And so I thought, foolishly, that if I could get this human, this Prince Aerik, to become mine, then I wouldn't have to be alone. But he lived on land and would never survive more than a few minutes below the surface of the sea. He would never be a part of my world.

That's when I knew I would have to become part of his.

As a child, I was warned about the sea witches, beings that possessed magic that let them shapeshift at will, enabling them to live both above the water and below it. Though Syrens were the ones humans feared, us Syrens feared the sea witches. They had the ability to grant us wishes, yet none of their gifts came without a price.

But I was young and headstrong and imprudent. I wanted adventure, I wanted to see what life was like above the sea, I wanted to become something more than I was. I wanted *love*.

And so I set about calling forth a sea witch. My sisters had told me that they liked shiny things as offerings and that they would respond to my Syren call. I spent the evening darting about, finding things that caught my eye like brightly colored coral in saturated hues of red, orange, and yellow, tiny purple starfish, rare glowing azure seaweed and pearls I coaxed from the reluctant mouths of oysters.

Once I had gathered these shiny pieces of the sea, I swam down to a canyon with walls of rock and coral rising up around me, a place with fantastic acoustics. Then I began to sing.

As far as I knew there was no specific song that conjured the sea witches, it was just our voices in general that might draw them to us. All Syrens had enchanting and beautiful singing voices and mine was no exception. I just didn't like to sing since it made me the center of attention (unless either of my sisters were signing, then no one would even hear me).

But there I sang. I sang for the sea witch, I sang about wanting to make a bargain, about wanting a life on land, to win a man's heart, and after what seemed like forever, Nill started doing protective circles around me, signifying that a sea witch was coming.

The first thing to appear were the tentacles. They were giant, slithering ropes with suction ends and puckered purple skin. They didn't belong to the sea witch, but instead to one of the Kraken, the giant sea monsters that the witches controlled.

The rest of the Kraken was hidden in the murky blue depths of the ocean, though I could faintly make out small glowing yellow eyes.

Then Edonia came forward, walking toward me on two legs along the seafloor, completely nude.

She was stunning. I had heard sea witches were ugly hags, but this wasn't the case at all. She was soft and pale, with long flowing white hair that moved around her head like sea snakes. She looked human more than anything and I was immediately jealous of her.

"Sweetheart," she said to me, her voice melodic but low. "Tell me what ails you?"

I was so dumbfounded by her that I couldn't speak.

"You have made a call for assistance from a sea witch, have you not?"

I nodded and she approached. Nill started to come in between us but before I could tell him to stay back, a tentacle whipped toward him, grabbing him. Nill cried out, a sharp sound that very few creatures could hear, and the Kraken wrapped itself around his middle, squeezing him tight.

"No, stop!" I cried out. "Don't hurt him!"

Edonia smirked at me and suddenly all her beauty seemed to vanish. She may have been pretty, but she was cold and ruthless and I immediately knew I couldn't trust her. "A precautionary measure. Depending on how this goes, I'll have him set free. Otherwise…"

I understood the threat. I had called her forth for a favor and now she was the one in control.

"Tell me what you want, sweetheart," she said, sounding bored. "So that we make this deal in haste. I don't have all night."

For a moment I had forgotten even why I had called her, what possessed me to do such a reckless thing as conjuring a sea witch. But then I remembered. The longing inside me, that need to belong to someone and someplace, it was too visceral to ignore.

"I saw a man on the shore," I said as her watchful red eyes narrowed. "His name is Prince Aerik. I want to become a human and I want him to fall in love with me. Can you help?"

She chuckled mirthlessly. "Oh, honey. Yes, I can. But nothing I do comes without a price."

I looked around at the shiny pieces of the sea I had gathered just as the Kraken's tentacle came out and swept them all away. All that effort for naught.

"You think that will do?" Edonia laughed. "So naïve you are. Tell me, how old are you?"

"Sixteen," I managed to say.

"Sixteen. So very young. And you think you know what love is at such an age?"

I didn't say anything to that.

She studied me for a moment. "But I can see that perhaps it is love that you lack at home that really ails you. A sense of discontent. Of not belonging. Yes?"

I nodded. I looked over at Nill to make sure that the Kraken wasn't hurting him but suddenly Edonia was at me, her sharp fingernails at my chin and forcing me to meet her eyes.

"I'll tell you what," she said. I found myself lost in the swirling red of her eyes, like coral in a whirlpool. "I will grant you what you wish for, so as long as I take something of yours in return."

The fact that she could grant my wish had my heart leaping with joy and possibility, so much so that I didn't think any price would be too high to pay.

"What do you want?"

"Your voice," she said simply.

"My voice?"

"It's beautiful," she said with an air of contempt. "We all know that Syrens have the ability to lure men into the sea with their song. I would like the chance to do the same. The Kraken are wonderful pets, but they lack the finesse. They know how to kill and maim and destroy, but they don't know how to lure."

"But you're a witch. Surely you can do that to men already."

"Not all men are created equal," she said sharply. "Some men are resistant to a witch's charms. Your voice wouldn't just be a thing to hear. I will need your tongue."

"My tongue!" I cried out.

"A mermaid's tongue is a missing ingredient for my book of magic."

"Take my tail then if you're to give me legs," I protested.

"Oh, I will be taking that too. Now listen here, my sweet, because you only get one chance to decide. With my spell, I will give you legs. I will take away your gills and your claws and your fangs and your strength and make you a beautiful woman. And you will find your prince and make him your own, should you wish. But you won't be able to become a Syren again. You won't be able to live under the sea. You will be a human through and through. You won't live three hundred years, you will live maybe sixty, if you're lucky." She paused and dug her nail deeper into my skin. "Are you still interested?"

I should have said no. Why didn't I say no?

But instead, I said, "And that's not enough price to pay?"

Her eyes went cold. "You want to become a human and experience that world? You want the love of the prince or whomever you choose?

Then you must know that the human world isn't equal to the Syren's world below. No, it's worth *more*. The human world is a world where you will control your own destiny. To be the person that you, and only you, decide to become. As a human, you can do what you wish, be who you want. You'll be a woman, and a woman has all the power up above. The world will be yours for the taking. Everything you desire, you will find the means to have."

She knew all the right things to say. She was lying through her pointed teeth.

"All I ask in exchange is your tongue," she adds with a shrug, removing her fingers from my chin. "If you're lucky, it won't make much difference to you at all. Humans are adaptable."

When she put it that way, it didn't seem such a large price to pay.

"But I'll never see my father and sisters again," I lamented.

"You swam away from them, did you not? You already left for a reason. You already made your decision before this night. Besides, there's nothing to stop you from taking a boat to your old kingdom one day. Perhaps they'll pay you a visit. The world is your oyster, and you are the pearl, my sweet."

Maybe it wouldn't have to be the end. Maybe I really could take a boat until it was above Limonos and if I dove below, even if just for a minute, maybe I could see them and tell them I was okay.

"Okay," I said to her. "I will do it. But first I want you to let Nill go."

Edonia looked at the Kraken and smirked. The Kraken squeezed so hard that Nill's black eyes started to bulge and I screamed.

Then one of Nill's many teeth popped out, spiraling to the ocean floor.

"Release him," Edonia said begrudgingly to the Kraken.

The tentacle loosened and Nill swam away quickly, heading in the direction of Limonos. I had no doubt that he was going to tell my father what I did.

Edonia walked over to the fallen tooth and picked it up, then came back to me and placed it in my palm.

"There. You can have a reminder of who you used to be. Whenever you regret your life above, you can remember that the only friend you ever had was a damned shark."

"Wait. Why would I regret my life above?" I said, starting to panic.

But Edonia didn't say anything. Instead she grinned, a most malicious smile that still haunts me in my dreams, and grabbed a knife that seemed to be conjured out of nothing.

The tentacle that had been holding Nill shot out and wrapped itself around me, the end holding my mouth open.

I screamed.

Then Edonia took my tongue in her fingers, swiped the sharp blade across it until my head exploded with pain and the water filled with my blood.

The screaming stopped.

PART ONE

The East

ONE

Maren

TEN YEARS LATER

"There ye go, Princess," Daphne, my lady-in-waiting says as she finishes with my hair. "Pretty as always. Fit for all the king's men, I say."

I peer at myself in the mirror, seeing yet not seeing my reflection, and manage a stiff smile. "Thank you Daphne," I say quietly, my fingers going to Nill's tooth hanging from a dainty silver chain. I'll remove it in a moment, knowing how irate Aerik gets when he sees it on me.

"I wish it wasn't so drab and dark in here so we could get a better look at ye," she says with a sniff, looking around my chambers. "Just the fire and a couple of sconces expected to light the whole room. I suppose not all royal palaces are the same, are they now? This is nothing like the one back home, Yer Highness."

Prince Ferdinand's palace might not be as grand as the one Aerik and I occupy at Vemmetofte, but this place is on the other side of the world, and not only that, the prince doesn't even live here most of the time. Aerik and Ferdinand have far too much in common, both of them spending their years gallivanting around the world and wasting money instead of having anything to do with their prospective families, other than asking for more funds.

In Ferdinand's case, he's settled here in Butuan for a few months out of the year, the rest of the time he's in different corners of the empire belonging to King Philip V, his father. Aerik and I have been on our royal ship, *Elephanten*, our journeys not too dissimilar. The only difference is that we are expected back home this year by order of our King, Prince Aerik's father, Frederick IV. I had been expecting us to continue our journey around the globe, following the trade winds up and across the ocean to the colonies, but duty finally called for my husband, and in turn, for me.

To say I'm disappointed is an understatement. I had hoped that when the ship reached land on the other side of the mighty ocean, I might be able to find my way back home, even though it would be useless for me as a human. Still, I spent days and nights dreaming of diving overboard, swimming deep down into the depths until I entered the Kingdom of Limonos. Even if I could only be under for as long as my lungs would let me, I just wanted a glimpse of my father and my sisters again. A chance to tell them that I'm sorry, that I had made a grave mistake, and that I loved them and would do anything to be with them.

At the very least I could find Edonia and make her reverse the spell. If she didn't, I was prepared to kill her. Oh, I imagined killing her many times over the last ten years, especially after a row with Aerik, when I felt helpless and trampled by my own bad decisions. I imagined what it would be like to have claws and razor-sharp teeth again, to sink them into her jugular and tear out her pretty throat, the water filling with blood.

"Are ye all right, Princess?" Daphne asks as she peers at me. "Ye look a little flushed. Hard to say in such a dim room," she adds with a grumble.

"I'm fine." I clear my throat and focus on my face in the mirror, finally allowing myself to take a look at my reflection. I hate mirrors, hate the emptiness I always see in my eyes. When I was a Syren, I would often admire my reflection in broken mirrors and glass my sisters would salvage from shipwrecks, but I don't look a thing like I once did. My eyes used to be a bright blue that would change from the pale turquoise of shallow shoals to the luminous color of glowing plankton, all depending on my mood.

Now they're just the shade of the endless sea, and the woman who stares back at me is someone I don't recognize, especially not with my hair pinned up in various curls at the top of my head. It's the look of the moment among all the ladies, but I would rather my hair be down and loose, like waves of ink, would rather the stiff stays at my waist be loosened. Feels utterly wrong to have them made from whalebone, animals I considered friends.

The only thing that remains from my old self are the faded imprints of my gills, three faint lines on either side of my neck, so faint that you can only see them under certain light. A symbol of my life underwater, before I traded it away.

"Well, don't ye look lovely, anyway?" Daphne murmurs as she adjusts a few strands of hair on my head. "A sweet sight for yer last night on land. I have no doubt the princes will miss each other when we set sail again."

My stomach twists at the thought. Aerik will miss Ferdinand, a kindred spirit in debauchery, and perhaps more. He'll miss the freedom that the ship has given him. He's been kinder to me for most of the journey, less violent and critical. He's only happy when he's exploring, when he's far away from his family's watchful eye, and I worry what returning home will do to his mood.

Throw yourself off the ship, I tell myself. *Let the seas claim you. Better to drown and die than live with that man and the man he'll become again.*

I swallow hard and rub the shark tooth between my fingers. "Daphne," I say quietly. "When you were younger, did you ever do something so ill-informed that you've regretted it ever since?"

Daphne blinks at me in the mirror's reflection. She's been my lady-in-waiting ever since I married the prince, and she's been there through thick and thin, keeping the darkest secrets close to her chest To protect the prince more than me, I'm sure, since they would only reveal him in a bad light, but she's still the closest person to me. And yet there's distance between us, a friendship that can never really deepen because of my standing as a royal figure, and a life built on lies.

"Oh, that seems to me a tough question," she says, humming to a tune in her head for a moment. "I may have to think about this a bit. Perhaps when I was a child, I may have stolen some candy, *lakrid*, from my brother at Christmas. I never told him." She places her hand at her chest. "Please don't think poorly of me."

I give her a quick smile. "I never shall, Daphne." I should have figured it would be something so minor. She would never understand. I don't think anyone on this earth would.

"And, if I'm not being too bold, may I ask the same of ye?" she says.

I stiffen.

"I have my regrets about many things," I tell her carefully. Since Daphne has seen the way my marriage has crumbled, she doesn't have to think hard about what I might regret. "It's hard to live a life without wondering *what if,* isn't it?"

A life that's a lie. My entire backstory is a lie, one I've told myself and others so many times that I've almost come to believe it. Ten years ago, I woke up washed upon the shore of the very beach that Aerik had been staying on. His manservant Hodges found me completely nude, bloodied and unable to speak, not just from the fact that my tongue had been cut out and I was still choking on my own blood, but from the trauma of it all. Being on land, having legs, breathing air in underused lungs—I knew within seconds of waking that I had made the biggest mistake of my life.

Which is probably why I've tried so hard to make my mistake worthwhile, even though it's come at so many costs.

But I digress. In reality, Aerik saw me carried in Hodges arms and, because of Edonia's spell, I was able to charm Aerik despite not being able to talk. Or perhaps it wasn't the spell or my charm that won him over, but the fact that I was beautiful, nude, and silent. Something he could both show off to the world and manipulate to suit his whims.

It wasn't until much later that I was able to understand English and learned how to write it that I was able to tell Aerik and the others my story, one I had spent a long time creating in my head. I had been kidnapped from a faraway land called Limonos by pirates, who had cut out my tongue and threw me overboard, leaving me for dead. With pirates already terrorizing the seas and shipping routes at that time, my story was wholly believable, and most of the world contained faraway lands that no one had ever heard of. What else could have explained it? From what I had gathered, Syrens were called mermaids and were stuff of myths and legends, things that only the crusty old sailors seemed to believe. They would have labeled me insane had I told them the truth about where I'd come from.

Turns out, I'd soon push my luck within the realms of what's possible. Within a year of being unable to talk, my tongue started to grow back. It slowly regenerated, just as a Syren's tail would if it got sliced off, until one day I was able to speak again. By the time we reached the continent, Aerik's doctor considered me a miracle, and I was able to slip into the royal family with nary a blemish to me. Edonia may have taken my voice for her own, but she didn't prevent mine from coming back.

"All that wondering won't do much for ye except bring ye sorrow, I say," Daphne laments. "Better to accept the lot that god gave ye." She pauses and gives me a pitying smile that fills her round red cheeks. "No matter the hardships."

And yet all I've done for the last decade is accept it. I don't want to accept it anymore. I want to fight back, fight my way to freedom. But this world above the seas is cruel to women, no matter their rank, and it's a world that isn't my own. I will never fit in here among the humans because, at the heart of me, I'm not one.

Yet I'm not a Syren either. I just exist in this space between the worlds with nowhere to belong to. My soul is adrift.

All because I believed Edonia's lies.

Suddenly the door behind us swings open and in the mirror's reflection I see Aerik stumbling into the room.

"There you are," he says to me, his words slurring, his black periwig askew. Obviously drunk. My pulse starts to race, thrumming in my veins, my hand going over Nill's tooth and clasping it tightly. "My split-tongued she-snake," he says with a snort. He eyes Daphne with a disdainful jerk of his head. "Go along now, I need a word with my slippery wife."

Please don't leave me, I think, my heart sinking as I watch Daphne scuttle out of the room. I already can't breathe.

"You're late," he says, stopping a few feet away and peering at me in the mirror. "Ferdinand and I have already been through a bottle, waiting for you. Food is getting cold."

Oh, damn it.

"I was told the dinner was at seven," I say, trying to keep my voice steady and calm, but submissive. I give him the softest smile that I can and relax my gaze so I don't seem like I'm challenging him.

"I highly doubt you were told that," he says with a sneer. "You were told the correct time, but your pea-sized brain couldn't comprehend it, could it now?"

My smile falters slightly and I fold my hands demurely in my lap. He's already stepped back into the bitter man he was. "My mistake. If it pleases you, I'm ready now."

He frowns at me in the mirror, his eyes going to my chest. Before I have a chance to cover my necklace his hand is shooting out and grabbing the shark tooth.

"What have I told you about this foul thing?" he says, ripping it off my neck, the chain snapping in two. "I've told you not to wear it, it's what a savage would wear, not a bloody princess."

I cry out in horror, twisting around to try to grab it from him. My fingers curl around his hands, trying to pry his fingers open. "No, please don't, you know that's special to me, you know it's all I have of home, I—"

"Oh, sod off," he says and I know he's about to backhand me seconds before he does it. The crack sounds like dynamite, my face thrown back and erupting in flames from the sting of his palm, but if this is all he'll give me, then I'll take it.

But then he's storming over to the fireplace and throwing the necklace in and I'm yelling, staggering out of the chair, running clumsily to the fire to save it.

He holds me back, his breath hot and smelling of alcohol.

"You know I liked you a lot better when you couldn't talk," he whispers, leaning in and the fire reflects in his dark eyes, black as sin. "Even better when you could barely walk. Yes, I reckon I liked you much better then."

With a grunt he kicks at my left shin and I yelp as my leg falls under me and I crumple to the floor. He knows how weak my legs are naturally and always goes for them.

He gives my side a firm nudge with his boot and I curl into a ball to protect myself further. "We set sail tomorrow morning," he says to me, and I'm too afraid to say anything, I just keep my hands over my head, my chin tucked into my chest, lying at his feet. The shame I feel runs deep.

"I wanted my last night here to be a good one." His voice is wistful now, but I don't dare let my guard down. "All I'll have of my time with Ferdinand is fond memories. That's what you don't understand, my Maren. You are too daft to ever understand what it's like to be a man like me. To have the world at your fingertips and then have that world taken away. Never allowed to be who you yearn to be."

I hear him turn and sigh, and only when the floor shakes slightly from his footsteps do I raise my head.

"Don't bother with coming to dinner," he says without turning around. "You could do with skipping a few meals from the looks of you."

His insult does nothing to me. I rather prefer it when he finds me revolting.

I wait until I see him leave, then I'm getting to my feet, my leg sore but stable, and run over to the fire. The necklace is on the log, the tooth blackened. I grab the poker and fish it out, dropping it on the wood floor where I hear a slight hiss from the heat.

The metal of the chain doesn't seem to have melted and the tooth is charred but intact.

The only reminder of who I truly was still remains.

TWO

Maren

T he sun is relentless and the air, smelling of salt and tar and
incense, is becoming thicker and more humid as the morning
stretches on. The faint breeze that ruffles the palm fronds
doesn't seem to reach us down at the docks and things are already
running behind schedule, the crew and our royal troupe cranky from
the heat.

Aerik is especially cantankerous. He's red-eyed and pale from last
night's festivities with Ferdinand, who is here helping to see us off
from the port at Butuan City. I've been avoiding my husband as much
as I can. I'm lucky that he didn't leave a mark on me last night but
even if he had, everyone would look the other way, as they always do.

"Alright, let's get underway for god's sake," Aerik says with a
scowl, pushing past me and onto the gangplank that leads to the ship.
It's been a month since I last stepped foot on the *Elephanten*, a ship of
the line that belongs to the monarchy, which was lent to Aerik for his
adventures. As much as I love being at sea and the ship's size makes
living on it fairly comfortable, the idea of being in confined quarters
for such a long time makes my palms feel clammy.

His manservant Hodges follows, along with the cook and the rest
of the troupe, and some of the crew who also look a little worse for

wear. Their month or so on land seems to have lent itself to drinking by the looks of it.

"Always a bit chaotic when we're casting off, ain't it Yer Highness?" Daphne says, holding a parasol above me to shield me from the sun and taking my arm as we walk along the gangplank and onto the broad deck of the ship. "Though I don't like the look of those clouds."

I follow her line of sight to see a mass of dark clouds in the distance above the green peaks of the nearest islands.

"We should be fine," I tell her. "That's north, we're heading west to the Sulu Sea."

"Didn't ye hear?" she says. "Plans changed. We're making a stop at Manila to get supplies. North it is."

"Manila?" I repeat. A surge of hope warms my chest. Even with wind in our sails and following seas it will take at least a week for this ship to get to Manila, but once there we'll be going on shore. There's a chance I might be able to sneak off and lose myself in the city. I could escape. Part of me wonders if Aerik would put out much of a search for me. He hates me, I know that much, but even after all these years I can't tell if he needs me despite it.

"Yes," Daphne says. "I reckon it will be a nice slow start to the voyage. Come along now, we must get yer trunks in yer quarters."

We head down below to the officers' quarters where we stay, the servants bringing the chests with all my belongings. Buried at the bottom of the trunk, inside a silk pouch, is Nill's tooth. I insist to Daphne and the servants that I'll put everything away myself, but the truth is I just need the proper hiding place for the necklace.

Fortunately, I don't have to share a bunk with Aerik, who is in the cabin next to mine, which means I'm allotted a bit of privacy. I decide to hide it underneath the thin mattress and hope he never comes across it.

I wipe the sweat from my brow, my chemise already sticking to my skin as the temperature below deck starts to rise. I wish I could go up top to experience the breeze and see us cast off, but I know Aerik would say I am in the way. So I remain below, putting my items away until the sweat is rolling down my chest and arms, then I lie back on the bed.

I must have drifted off to sleep because the next thing I know my room is shaking and rain and waves are lashing at the window. I sit up, the air no longer smelling of resin and sweat but of fresh sea air and the kind of delicious electricity that comes with a storm.

I adjust my dress and hair, then exit my quarters and quickly make my way up to the deck of the ship, passing by crew and servants who bow to me as I go, until my face is met with a lashing of rain.

"Your Highness, it isn't safe for you to be up here," Miguel, one of the crew, says to me as I step on deck.

But I'm not even listening. I feel like something is coming alive. The crew are yelling at each other to adjust the sails and there's chaos all around me, but I'm enthralled. The rain is warm, the wind is blowing my hair loose, and I actually find myself smiling as I tilt my head back to the sky, which is growing darker by the second. Dusk has descended, deepened by the blackened clouds above and when I look to the west, I see the last light of an orange sunset hovering around the silhouette of the nearest islands.

"You really should go back down below, ma'am," Miguel says, taking me by the elbow. "This is no place for a woman, much less a princess."

I glance at him, the rain streaming down my face. "Where is Aerik?"

"He's being sensible and staying down below."

"No one ever said I was sensible, did they Miguel?" I say, feeling my spirits returning. I pull away from him and walk carefully across the deck—it doesn't matter how many years I've had legs, walking has always been a bit of an issue for me and I have a slight limp that I can't hide. I go all the way to the forecastle deck where Ivan, our quarter-master, is standing with the pilot, a local man they'd hired to help navigate the area at night.

"Your Highness," Ivan says to me in surprise. "You best—"

"Yes, go down below, so I've been told," I say. "I just wanted some fresh air."

"Be plenty of time for fresh air in the months ahead," he says, giving his hat a shake before slipping it back on. "But a storm isn't the best time for it."

"How bad is it going to get?" I ask, peering out in front of us. Sailing at night, especially between islands where there are lots of reefs and hazards, is always a risky venture. Add in a storm and things can get tricky.

"Shouldn't be too bad, I reckon," he says. "We're passing under, it's passing above."

I grip the railing as the ship cuts through the waves and I suddenly wish I was alone up here. Just me and the sea and my thoughts. It feels like my soul is being pulled to the surface of the water.

I fix my eyes to the faraway lights that dot the shoreline on the other side of the dark waves, fires and lanterns of the people who live on these islands. I find myself wondering what their lives are like, if they have any worries. If I could trade my life for theirs.

I blink, my eyes trying to adjust. Some of the lights start to move, as if separating from the island.

Then, silhouetted against that last grainy light of dusk, a giant mast and sails come into view and I realize it's actually a ship. A big one, gliding right toward us. I frown, trying to figure out how it's possible for them to approach considering they shouldn't have any wind in their sails at all from that direction, yet they do.

The ship begins to fade before my eyes.

One by one, the lights on the ship go out until I can barely see it anymore.

"There's a ship," I say in surprise, pointing in the direction. "I saw a ship."

"Where?" Ivan asks, and both he and the pilot come to my side, staring out at the darkness.

"It was there. Then it just went dark, as if all the lanterns were snuffed out one by one." I look over at them. "Why would it do that? Don't they want us to see them?"

The pilot's eyes go wide and he shakes his head fearfully. "No," he says, his accent heavy. "No. No, it can't be, not now."

"What?" Ivan asks brusquely. "Tell me now, who is it?"

"It is…the Brethren of the Blood."

I exchange a look with Ivan. "The Brethren of the Blood?" I repeat. "You mean pirates?"

"Yes. Pirates!" the pilot cries out.

Ivan swallows hard and gives me a stern look. "Princess, I insist you go back inside at once. Tell the Prince to hide the valuables and hide yourselves."

"But the Brethren are just tall tales, aren't they?" I ask. "They aren't really a ship of the undead and damned."

"Whatever they may be, Princess, they are most definitely pirates," he says gravelly. His eyes focus over my shoulder, his jaw tightening. "Now get going!"

He grabs my arm and practically pushes me along toward the steps then yells at the rest of the crew. "Pirates! Pirates spotted, ghost ship at portside! All hands on deck! Get the captain!"

Every soul on deck starts panicking and yelling, running back and forth, and their energy is contagious. I find myself nearly slipping down the stairs and across the deck, trying to stay out of their way until I'm down below.

"Aerik!" I yell down the corridor. "Where's Aerik!?"

"What is with the blasted yelling?" Aerik says, coming out of the galley, wiping his mouth on a cloth.

"Pirates!" I tell him. "Ivan said for us to hide ourselves and our valuables."

He frowns. "Pirates? Are you sure?"

"Yes, yes, I saw them myself. They were sailing just out there and then all their lights went out as they approached."

"Pirates don't attack in the night like that."

"The pilot says it's the Brethren of the Blood."

He snorts. "A fairy tale is all they are, straight from Brothers Grimm."

"That's what I thought too." But I saw the fear in both Ivan's eyes and the pilot's. The Brethren were supposed to be a crew of vicious pirates rumored to be undead, their ship built in the bowels of hell. There have been countless stories of them attacking the Spanish galleon fleet coming in and out of Manila, the ships ransacked, treasures taken, and everyone on board either left for dead or kidnapped. At the heart of them is their leader, Captain Ramsay "Bones" Battista, a man deemed so evil that even the devil didn't want him.

"Fairy tale or not, they might be coming aboard," I add fearfully.

Aerik opens his mouth to say something, probably unkind, then there's a loud BANG that seems to blow out my ears and I'm thrown to the ground.

"Cannon fire!" someone yells from above as I try to push myself up on my elbows. Aerik is leaning against the wall, making no motion to help me to my feet.

"What the heavens is happening?" Daphne cries out as she comes out of her room. "Princess Maren!"

She comes over and helps me up.

"Pirates," I tell her, gripping her arms. "We have to hide."

"Remember where the captain told us to go," Daphne says quickly. "Down in the sailhold."

She starts pulling me and Aerik along toward the steps leading to the decks below, but I manage to break away just as another cannon fires into the side of the ship, this time blasting all the way through to the galley where people scream in horror, shards of wood flying like shrapnel.

I'm thrown against the wall but I manage to regain my balance and start running for my cabin.

"Where are ye going!?" Daphne yells after me. "Do come back!"

"Don't waste your life on her," I hear Aerik say to her. "Your duty is to me first."

"Go! Hide! I'll follow!" I yell, the ship shuddering again, this time cannons are firing from our side. I manage to make it to my cabin and then throw back the mattress on my bed, grabbing the pouch with Nill's tooth. I quickly take the necklace out, my hands shaking, and tie it around the strap of my stays underneath my bodice. I start heading back to the door when I hear more screams, this time from the top deck, and with a sinking sense of horror I realize the pirates have boarded.

I could go down into the sailhold with Aerik and Daphne and whatever royal servants are left, hide myself under a molding cover and hope that the pirates don't find me. Perhaps Aerik and Daphne and I will be the only ones left alive on the ship.

But the idea of that is almost as worse as the idea of pirates, particularly a notoriously wicked man such as Captain Bones, killing us here with no mercy, or taking us on board their ship to torture us. And I'm sure what's in store for me is much, much worse than I can imagine.

I pull the necklace out of my bodice. My fingers tighten around the shark tooth and I bring it to my trembling lips, kissing it. "Give me strength, Nill," I say softly.

Then I tuck it back in and turn and grab the chair from the corner of the cabin. I pick it up, holding it above my head, then I throw it at the window with a yelp.

The chair shatters the stained-glass, rain and sea water spraying inside. I pick my way carefully along the floor, avoiding the broken shards, then grab the end of my dress, the petticoats providing enough padding as I wrap it around my fist. I punch out the remaining sharp shards stuck in the window's frame until it's relatively safe, then I stick my upper body out of the window. A few wayward spikes of glass stab my skin, but I manage to ignore it.

Above the wind and rain and waves I hear splashing, people falling or jumping overboard, plus the occasional scream or hollering for god and mercy. As I stare down at the surface of the water, lit only by the lone lantern above that hangs at the aftcastle, I realize *Elephanten* has stopped cruising. The pirates must have taken down the sails and mast, disabling the ship. If I jump, I have to make sure I swim as fast as possible to shore so I'm not detected. The pirates might not even know I exist, unless they targeted our ship on purpose.

I don't have time to think about it.

I pull the rest of my body up, wiggling through the window, then turn around and slowly, carefully lower myself so that I'm dangling above the sea, my hands holding on to the windowsill as tight as they can.

I close my eyes and take in a deep breath.

Better to risk drowning and swim to shore than to spend a minute with whatever the men on this ship have in mind for me.

And that includes my husband.

I let go.

I fall through the air, my gown flapping around me as I twist my body away from the boat so as not to hit the rudder.

The water meets me like a slap to the face.

And everything goes dark and very, very cold.

THREE

Ramsay

"They're Danish, Cap'n," my bosun, Crazy Eyes, says as he walks over to me, folding up the spyglass. "Looks to be a navy ship from the Dano-Norwegian line, a big-un at that, but she's a bit too quiet than she oughta be."

I look around, my eyes scanning the waters in front and behind of the vessel that serendipitously crossed our path this evening. "For a supposed ship of the line, there looks to be no one else in her line. I'd wager she's easy pickings."

"Think she has anything worthwhile on board?" the bosun asks.

I shrug and give him an encouraging smile. "We'll have to find out, won't we, bosun?"

He laughs and looks through the spyglass again as I turn the wheel enough to bring the *Nightwind* closer to the mystery ship. She's a beauty all right, and I can see with my own eyes now that she doesn't have the crew of a naval ship in service. Either they're transporting precious cargo, or precious people.

"What do you think, Captain?" Sam asks as she runs up the stairs to me in the forecastle. "Do we hold back?"

I give her a tepid look. It's not often that Sam shows any restraint.

"I think we're going to politely ask the Norsemen to surrender whatever it is they have—and then themselves."

She snorts. I am quite polite, but only after I've slit a few throats.

"Do you think that's the *Elephanten*?" she asks. "You heard of it, the one that the Danish prince and princess are on. They've been spotted about these waters on their travels. Could be their ship."

"A prince and a princess?" Crazy Eyes says. He looks delighted. "Mayhaps they have treasures we'd never even imagined. A crown I could fix on me head!"

"Possibly," I muse. In all my years sailing the high seas, I'd never intercepted a royal ship before. Our usual route across the Pacific only had us overtaking Spanish galleons and the occasional Chinese junk ship. "They might have jewels and crowns on board. Or they might have something more valuable than that."

"What's that?" he asks.

"Themselves."

Sam smacks me on the arm. "Careful, Bones. We don't need to bring any more people on board than we usually do. They start to smell after a while."

I give my mariner another wry look. "My dear sister-in-law, this would be a *real* hostage. Not the ones you discard, but ones you can hold for ransom and negotiations. For money. You don't think the King of Denmark will want his son and daughter-in-law back? He'd have to pay a hefty price, mark that."

"So, this has turned into a legitimate kidnapping operation," she says with a sigh. "You know I hate having to hold myself back."

"You'll manage." I clear my throat and look across the ship at my crew, who are awaiting my instructions.

"Listen here now, lads," I boom. Sam stopped rolling her eyes at being called a lad a long time ago. "A bit of a different approach for tonight. That pretty ship there, she's up for grabs and she's a Danish navy ship at that. If the lady here is correct, there's a prince and a princess on board."

"Ooooh," the crew says with a laugh.

"And I've taken a notion to them being worth more alive than dead.

Sure, we'll take their loot if they got 'em, and we'll do our best with some of their crew, but when we take the royal couple aboard, I don't want a hair on their heads touched. Well. Unless the prince is wearing one of them periwigs. Then feel free to toss it overboard." I look down at Sterling McCoy. "You best get the cell ready for them."

He nods from the quarterdeck, jangling the jailer keys at his side.

"Still and patient, lads," I tell the crew, keeping my hands steady on the wheel. "We should be able to take this ship with our eyes closed." I glance up at the Greek on the mizzenmast above me, hanging like a monkey. "Drakos, bring in the mizzen. Soon as we're close I want you and Lothar swinging aboard. Take out their mast and rigging. They won't even see you coming in the dark."

Drakos grins at me and nods. He's always such a happy-go-lucky lad, but nights like this light him up like the fireworks we saw over Malacca.

"Deck to be cleared fore and aft!" Thane yells as he storms down the middle of the deck, hands behind his back. "Hammocks up and chests down!"

"Bring small arms up to the quarterdeck and every man to his post," I add, making sure my voice is louder than my brother's. Though he's the quartermaster, I am the captain, and he often seems to confuse the two. Doesn't help that the crew tends to listen to him more than they listen to me. "And snuff the lights. It's time we go dark!"

A small cry of enthusiasm goes up, followed by the silence we need by going dark. Henry and Lucas, two of our page boys, run around snuffing out all the lights on the *Nightwind* until I know that we're invisible to the other ship. But the other ship isn't invisible to us.

"Hoist the colors?" Cruz, my first mate, asks me.

"Aye. They won't see them in the dark but I like the formality."

"Hoist the colors!" Cruz yells as Sam starts hoisting the red flag affixed with a white skull up the mast.

Thane comes up beside me. "You verily sure this is a good idea, *Captain*?" As always he exaggerates the word captain.

"This might be one of the last ships we see before we hit Los Pintados. We need supplies for us and for Lucas and the boys, and we need money."

"We have enough money."

I scoff. "Money for today, but what about tomorrow?"

"And you reckon holding a prince and princess hostage for months will result in anything? Might take that long before the king hears of this, and then what?"

"I haven't thought that far ahead, brother, but like you said, we have plenty of time for thinking. We'll just make sure we keep one crew member alive long enough to kick them overboard. They'll swim to shore and spread the word just as we leave the islands. Maybe we'll leave a few survivors here as well. Be merciful for once."

Thane's golden eyes narrow thoughtfully. "It's a gamble. By the time we get to Acapulco, they might be old news."

"Then we kill them. No harm, no foul."

"There is something to be said for keeping things simple. First you wanted to go hunting, which will lead us on a daft chase around the ocean, now you want to add people to our crew."

"We're not press-ganging them," I remind him. "Now, if you please, I'd like my quartermaster to pick up the slack."

His jaw tightens as it always does when I order him about. Something to do with him being born first and expecting his brother to cower at his feet.

I turn my attention back to the royal ship. Judging by the yelling from onboard, they've spotted us despite the cover of night, which means they'll be going on the defensive any moment now. It takes a lot of round shots at close-range to damage the *Nightwind*—any good ship can take a real beating from the guns and come out fine—but even so I'd rather she come out unscathed.

"Set fighting sail!" I yell. "Prayers and rums up!"

The pages run around giving everyone a shot of rum while Drakos, our only religious fella, recites his prayer in a furious blast of Greek.

"Steady gunners! Get the chain shots in there! Bowsprit to boarding!"

The mariners take in the sails enough so that the bow of the ship is now going to collide with the lowest part of their ship and I give the wheel enough of a push to set it on the right course.

"Bosun take the helm," I say, stepping away from the wheel to give it to Crazy Eyes. "Let me be the first one off." I run down the stairs and sprint to the bow. "Gunners, fire round shot, then chain it!"

I hear an "aye, aye," from down below and then one cannon goes off, sending the ball flying into the wooden side of the navy ship. It doesn't blast clean through, but I know that was enough to maim anyone standing nearby.

I make sure my cutlass is secure before climbing up onto the bowsprit, running carefully to the very end of the mast. I may have good balance, but one wrong slip and I'll be in the water.

Once at the end, I stand and I watch as the other ship comes closer and closer and I'm locking eyes with one of their crew members, a portly man with a mustache.

"God Almighty," the man says, his mouth open in fear.

"Not a god," I tell him. "More like a devil."

I turn and make a signal with my fingers for another round and the cry goes out, another cannon firing. This time the whole boat heels to one side and I know that hit did some real damage.

Then I leap off the bowsprit and onto the ship. The crew member tries to grab his weapon but I'm at him in a second. I immediately run my sword across his neck, slitting his throat, the blood spilling out and splashing onto my boots. I ignore the sight. We've all become desensitized to the sight of blood during battle so that it doesn't have an effect on us anymore.

No point in wasting any time, though I know Thane is grumbling to himself about my lack of mercy. He may want to keep things simple, but keeping things simple means killing as many as we're able to. The less people to deal with, the simpler it gets, I say.

One of the crew lets out a cry of vengeance for his fallen mate and starts running for me, a hefty broadsword drawn, and I know it's a matter of time before someone fires a musket at me. Then I'll really be peeved.

I block his lances with ease, doing a delicate dance for a moment before I knock his sword away and run my blade right into his stomach. The man spits up blood in a pitiful cry, then collapses to the deck.

"Bones, we'll need *some* alive," Cruz says with amusement as he jumps down from the bowsprit beside me and looks over the man.

"I'm doing my best," I tell him. "Kill a few more and maybe they'll all surrender peacefully."

Thankfully, by the time Drakos and Lothar swing on board, pistols and swords ready, the crew on deck has fallen to their knees and given surrender. Sterling comes aboard next, his massive frame keeping the new prisoners in line, and Thane follows, hunting down the captain with Cruz below deck.

While they rummage for the people below, I take stock of the crew that have surrendered. We always take prisoners, indeed we need to before a big crossing, even with magic up in *Nightwind's* sails, but selecting the right prisoners is an art. Whoever is the most fruitful will usually do, but women tend to last the longest.

Alas, I don't see any women thus far. I decide on six of the strongest men, then order the lads to kill all the rest save the two youngest. The two youngest are instructed to deliver the message and our hostage negotiations before they're hauled to their feet and thrown overboard.

As the slaughter for the rest of them commences, Thane and Sterling come up with a round-cheeked older lady in one hand and, judging by his wig, the prince in another. Both the lady and the prince look terrified, but the lady has a toughness about her that the prince doesn't possess, something I appreciate.

"This isn't the princess," I say, gesturing to the woman. "She may be pretty, but she's much too old." I take a step toward them. "Where is the princess? We had heard she was traveling with you, Prince?"

I don't even know the names of these royals, but it doesn't seem to matter.

"I don't know where she is," the prince says, a hint of resentment in his voice, as if he wanted and expected us to find her.

I look to the lady and she gives her head a fearful shake.

"Take them aboard *Nightwind*," I say to Thane, then I brush past them and run down into the lower deck. There are moans down here from fallen men and small fires caused by the cannons, the gangways a mess of splintered oak. I quickly search through the ship, trying to pick up on the scent of anything floral and feminine above the smell of destruction that lingers with the smoke in the air.

I follow my nose into one of the cabins at the aft and am met with sea air and broken glass. I rush to the shattered window and look out.

Sure enough, there's a woman in the water below, her pale yellow dress floating around her like a dampened sail, black hair spooling like ink. Her head keeps dipping underwater like she's unconscious or close to being so.

"Not so hasty, Princess!" I yell from the window.

She doesn't stir. Still, I should save her while I have the chance. She won't be much good to me if the sea claims her.

I stare at her for a moment longer, something about her making me pause. From this height, her features are obscured and yet I'm strangely compelled by her. It's like she's not even trying to stay afloat, like she wants the sea to swallow her whole. She wants to give up.

And I'm here to ruin it all for her.

I squeeze my frame through the window feet first then drop down into the water, managing to do a twist into a swan dive part-way through. The water is cold but refreshing and I glide through the waves with case, popping up right beside the woman.

"Princess?" I ask, and the woman stirs, her eyes widening, as if she's suddenly aware that she's floating in the ocean. "I've come to rescue you, milady," I tell her, flashing her a grin and spitting out sea water.

I expect her to scream for help or try to swim away.

Instead, the princess punches me right in the face.

FOUR

Maren

I thought I had died.

Once upon a time, when I was young and probably being a pain to my sisters, my mother told me that if Syrens were bad they never achieved immortality in the afterlife, and instead they became the sea foam on the waves. I was certain that the moment I hit the water that I had dissolved into that very foam, punishment for trading my tail away for legs that don't even work well half the time, for turning my back on my family forever, for forsaking what the gods made me.

I'd had thoughts of letting go for a long time prior, of course. Sometimes the thoughts were truly suicidal, other times they were desperate wishes for a different life, for an escape. But when I thought I was dying I realized how easily I succumbed to the idea of death.

I forgot about the ship and Aerik and Daphne. I just thought of my family. I thought of starting over. I thought of all my regrets.

There have been too many regrets.

The water was so very cold and dark and my dress was so heavy and I thought maybe instead of swimming to shore, I'd just sink to my own watery grave and finally be done with it.

I wanted to become sea foam.

And then I heard shouting. Yelling.

A strange male voice, a vaguely Scottish accent.

I opened my eyes to see a man swimming toward me, grinning as if we had both gone for a swim together.

He called me *Princess*. Told me he was here to rescue me, but from the triumphant and devilish look on his face, I knew he wasn't my rescue.

He was a pirate.

So I did what I always yearned to do to Aerik.

I punched the man in the face, feeling the satisfying snap of bone under my knuckles, and started to swim away, as fast as my dress would let me.

I didn't get far.

The man was taken by surprise by my hit (as was I, quite honestly) but it did nothing to slow him down.

Instead, he grabbed me around the waist and wrapped his arm around me, as if we were lovers going for a stroll, and started swimming toward the ship, so fast and strong that he caused a ripple of envy through me, for once upon a time, I was able to swim that way as well.

It shouldn't have been possible for a man to be so strong, and that's when I knew what I know now. This was no ordinary man.

This was the notorious pirate, Captain Bones.

And I was doomed.

"I have the princess," the captain announces as he drags me on board the ship. I don't know how he was able to hang on to me, despite my kicking and squirming and the fact that I weigh a lot in a soaked dress, and pull me up the rope onto the deck of his ship, but he did it like I was only a cumbersome sack of potatoes over his shoulder.

I fall to the deck in an unceremonious heap, splinters going into the heels of my palms as I break my fall. Someone snickers and I look up, my hair half-loose and falling over my face and I know I look like a madwoman.

There are three pirates gathered around me. To my surprise, one of them is a pale woman, wearing her stays laced on top of a billowy men's shirt above wide petticoat breeches, and her red hair in a braid down her back. For a moment I think that maybe she's another woman that's been taken and ravaged by this gang of devils but from the amused gleam in her eyes, I don't think that's the case. She's the one that snickered.

The other two pirates happen to be the roguish captain, and a very tall Black man. There's something about the two of them that are catching me off-guard, and it takes me a moment to realize what it is. I had been expecting the pirates to look like dirty dogs wearing stained and ragged salt-bleached clothing, and yet they don't look anything of the sort. Granted, the captain is soaking wet and they're wearing an eclectic assortment of clothes, yet they're clean looking, the clothes could be tailored.

"You sure she's the princess?" the Black man asks as he peers at me curiously, his accent sounding Spanish or Portuguese.

"I'd wager so," the captain says, reaching down and grabbing me by my arm, his grip tight and bruising as he hauls me up to my feet. "Care to refute that, Your Highness?"

I stare at the captain, refusing to be intimidated by him. Strangely, I thought I'd see his nose broken, bruised and bloodied from my fist, but there isn't a mark on him. I'm shocked at how disappointed I feel, as if I was needing to draw blood. How quickly my morals have descended.

"Where is Daphne?" I demand, raising my chin and meeting the pirate captain in the eyes. It's dark so it's hard to discern, but they seem colorless.

"Who?" the woman pirate asks.

"Daphne?" the captain repeats. He frowns. "Are you asking after that lady with the years on her? Apple-cheeked and hefty?"

I barely nod, afraid of his answer.

His frown deepens. "She's already been taken below. You're an interesting piece, aren't you? Asking about her and not a thought for your dear husband, the prince?"

"She could be my mother," I suggest, only feeling a smidge of guilt for thinking of Daphne's well-being before my own husband's.

"Ah," he says with a curve of a smile and a sharp jab of his finger into the air, "but she isn't now. I'd wager she's your lady-in-waiting.

Unfortunately, I don't know much about royalty, in fact you're the first royal I've ever met, if you can believe that. I don't even know your name."

I press my lips together, refusing to give it to him.

"It's Princess Maren. Mark my word," the woman says proudly. "And the Prince goes by Aerik."

"And Daphne, the lady-in-waiting," the captain surmises. "Glad to formally meet you. I'm Captain Battista." He nods to the woman. "This little flutterin' dove over here is Sam. And that's Cruz, my first mate."

"I don't care who any of you are," I say, trying to keep my voice steady. "You can all go straight to hell."

I try to shrug out of his grasp but it's fruitless even as he bursts out laughing. "My oh my. Listen to the mouth on this bit of fluff. Is that how you talk over in Copenhagen, or have you been on a boat too long? You sound like a bloody sailor."

"Where are the rest of the crew?" I ask, looking over at the other ship. The noise from earlier has died down and though I can't see much in the darkness beyond, I can hear talking and laughing but the screaming has stopped. That makes it even worse. My blood runs cold at the silence. The smell of burning fills the air.

"We've taken some of your crew into the hold," Cruz says.

"And the rest of them?" What about the servants who have been loyally at our side for years?

Cruz raises his brows. "They're dead," he says simply, like I'm daft.

The words are an arrow to my heart.

"You do know what ship you've found yourself on," the woman pirate says, "don't ya?"

I do my best to seem strong, though I'm afraid I'm crumbling inside. "Yes. They call you the Brethren of the Blood."

The captain snorts and gives me a wry look, tilting his head just so that the shadows under his high cheekbones seem to combine with his scruffy facial hair, making his face look like a skull. "So, our reputation precedes us."

"I always thought we should be called the Ancient Brotherhood," Cruz muses, running a hand over his chin. "Or the Devil's Brethren."

Sam, the woman pirate, clears her throat. "Though they both mean the same, I prefer brethren to brotherhood, if you get my saying. And I reckon it was Troop of Desperados."

"Ah yes, Desperados," the captain says appreciatively. "That one I'm quite fond of. I know that's what the Spanish merchants have so affectionately termed us." He looks to me, the shadows deepening more, so that I swear I'm looking through his skin and at his skeleton underneath. It must be a trick of the light.

Or all the legends you'd heard about them being a ghost ship are true.

My blood runs colder still. Whoever these men are, they killed the rest of the crew with no mercy.

"Either way, you don't seem afraid enough," the captain says, smiling unkindly. "Perhaps I've been too hospitable. I'll thank you to come now and we can reunite you with your dear prince."

He tugs at me hard enough that I nearly fall down. I'm stopped by his arms, his motions dizzyingly fast.

"And Daphne?" I ask as he pulls me along the deck, my wet dress dragging behind me.

"As Cruz said, she's in the hold," he says. "But that's not fit for a princess. No darling, I have a special spot for the royal couple, reserved just for you."

Oh blast.

"Are you taking us all prisoner?"

He leads me down the stairs into the ship. It's so dark below, with not a single lantern lit or a fire in the galley. My night vision is better than most, a holdover from being a Syren, but even so I can't see a thing.

"I'm going to take you and your husband prisoner," he says, yanking me roughly down another flight of stairs. With my balance off even on my good days, I nearly tumble again.

"Why?" I ask, trying to pick up the ends of my wet dress so I don't trip on it.

"Because I wager you're both worth a lot of money," he says. In the darkness he feels bigger somehow and more imposing. The captain is a fairly tall, large man, big arms and wide shoulders but, now that I can't see him, can only feel his presence, he seems larger than life, more powerful and deadly. I fear he's going to do something to me and I won't see it coming. The idea makes my pulse quicken, my chest growing tight.

"I'm not worth anything," I tell him and the minute I open my mouth I regret it. If he thinks I'm worth nothing, then there's no reason to keep me alive.

He pulls me to a stop and even in the dark I swear I see his eyes glow for a moment, a flash of gray-blue, like the sea during a storm. "You think I'll let you go now? You're worth something. Perhaps the prince is worth more than you, but you still count. No king will leave a princess out to rot, not with the world watching."

"How will he even know? Who will tell him you have us?"

"You see, luv," he says, his voice taking on a raspy quality and I feel him lean in closer to me, his breath hot on my cheek, "we didn't actually kill your entire crew. We do have *some* morals. We let a few go and told them to spread the word to your dear king. I have no doubt that by the time we reach Acapulco, there'll be money waiting for us."

"Acapulco!" I exclaim. "In New Spain?"

"'Tis a long voyage, yes, but the *Nightwind* has made it countless times. I dare say we'll get to know each other pretty good by then. You may not even want to disembark."

The voyage across the Pacific, which I've heard takes months upon months for the Spanish galleons that frequent the route, isn't what first struck me. It was the fact that Acapulco is close to Limonos. Closer than I'll ever have been to home since I first left.

If I can somehow make it alive across the ocean, held captive on this godforsaken ship for months, there's a chance that I'll be able to return to Limonos. It depends on me escaping when we get close to land, but I'll gladly take that chance and risk death if it means seeing my family for even just a second.

"Come now, and get used to your new home," the captain says to me, yanking me forward until I feel we've walked into another cabin.

"Maren?" I hear Aerik's voice, sounding small and weak in the dark.

"I've got your princess here," Captain Battista says, and then I hear the rattling of keys. "If you try anything, you'll be made to suffer, mark my word as god."

I hear the creak of metal, a cage door opening, and I'm pushed in until I'm stumbling against Aerik.

"Enjoy the privacy, you little lovebirds," the captain says, and I hear the lock shut. "For I'm sure there will be chaos come the morning."

I hear him walk off, his boots echoing in the ship, then hear the cabin door close.

"You're soaking wet," Aerik says, stepping back from me. "What happened to you?"

"I tried to swim for help," I say. I didn't expect him to be crying with joy at my return, but I didn't think he'd be so cold so soon.

"Liar," he seethes and even though I can't see him, I know his eyes are doing that thing when the pettiness and anger overtakes him. "You weren't going for help! You were trying to escape. Leave me for dead."

"I wasn't," I say but I stop myself. Because I am a liar. I *was* leaving him for dead. And I was trying to save only myself.

"Fine," I add, finally feeling resolve in my nerves. I can't be afraid of him anymore, not here, not now, not after all of this. "I was just trying to survive. I—"

CRACK.

He strikes me, fist against cheekbone and my neck snaps back from the force of it all.

Everything goes dark, as if it wasn't already so black.

FIVE

Ramsay

The dream always starts the same.

The sea is calm as glass, not a cloud above, and the horizon is a thin straight line of blue that nearly blends in with the sky. At this point it is hard to differentiate what is a memory and what is a dream. My memories tell me that there was nothing off or ominous about that particular day, not even the threat of becoming becalmed (not that it would matter when it comes to the *Nightwind*).

But my dreams feel different. The air feels heavy and oppressive, all the wind sucked away, and the heavens above seem frightening in their scope. In the dream it's like we are just a ship in a bottle, watched over by some mythical overlord who decides when we live and when we die.

Then the first hit happens just as it did in real life. That horrible thud that still echoes through my brain on days where I've had too much sun and ale and too much time to think. The strike shakes the entire ship and while most of my crew didn't know what it was, I knew. I knew what it was and why it was here and what it wanted to do.

It was one of the Kraken.

Which meant the sea witch was here too.

She wanted the book, the one that belonged to my wife, Venla.

I just wanted to grieve and hold on to the one piece I had of her left.

But while the dream always starts the same, with that blasted thud and that god-awful heaviness and the dread that follows, it doesn't always end the same.

Tonight I am helpless in the dream, knowing it's not real and yet knowing it's already happened, and I watch, I watch as the tentacle flops over the side of the ship, watch as it reaches for Hilla, and I scream. So fucking loud that my throat feels torn out.

"Hilla!" My voice envelopes the thick air and she turns to look at me, big blue eyes, a smudge of chocolate on her cheek from the treat I had given her just minutes before.

I'm lucky this time that I don't wake up screaming. The crew has gotten used to it over the years, but I haven't. You don't get used to something like this.

I open my eyes and stare at the ceiling. My heart is on a rampage in my chest, my body reliving the trauma. I take in long deep breaths until my heart calms, then I sit up in my bed.

It takes a moment for the dream to fade and for memories of last night to come into my mind. I welcome it, welcome my past being buried by the present.

The *prince* and the *princess*. What good fortune that was to stumble upon that Danish ship just before we set out across the Pacific. The Spanish galleons leaving Manilla and heading across the Pacific were leaving in convoys now to prevent attacks from the *Nightwind*, much like the merchant ships had to do when they crossed the Atlantic. For as unstoppable and powerful as my crew and ship are, we are not enough to take on a fleet, especially one that's on the watch for us.

Or at least, we aren't that powerful yet. There are rumors about a mermaid kept in a glass tank on board the skeleton crew's ghost ship. It was enough for me to chart course for Los Pintados and Nan Madol the famous "Reef City"—for their ship is always bound to return there.

But now with the hostages on board, there's at least a little reward for when we reach New Spain, in case our detour isn't as rewarding as some may think. I only hope that when the crew were jettisoned over-board with the message for the king, they actually survive long enough to deliver it.

Perhaps you should have let them all survive.

But thoughts like that never do me any good. I've had too many regrets in my past, I don't let myself entertain them anymore. Yes, I could have let them all survive, but the truth is that killing is part of my nature, no different than a jaguar in the jungle. People never want to admit to themselves that they're bad, wicked, made in the devil's image, not god's. Everybody on this green and blue earth thinks they're perfect, and that's no way to live. I think there's a bit of peace given to you when you accept who and what you are.

Like the princess. I don't know her from Eve, she's but a stranger and comes from the stock of people I abhor the most, the ones in charge of society. Yet there's something about her nature that appeals to me. Perhaps it's that she struck me in the face, or that she cursed openly, or doesn't seem all that concerned about the prince. All of these moments showed me who she really was and she wasn't afraid to show it.

With thoughts of her on my mind, I get up, my cock at a stand. Naturally it wasn't just her attitude that warmed me to her, but how damn desirable she looked in that wet gown. With her long black hair, wild and free from the hair pinnings, full tits and gleaming blue eyes, she looked like she belonged to the darkness, like a goddess of some forgotten religion.

I don't have time this morning to do anything about the stiffness of my cock. Instead I look out the clear section of the stained-glass window of my chambers. Dawn is breaking and the night watch will be ending soon, and it looks like they've kept the ship going at a steady clip. Judging by the land to starboard, we should be through the San Bernardino Strait by late afternoon. After that, we can breathe a little easier. It's not unusual for navy ships to be lurking in the island coves, but once we hit the Pacific we should be clear of them.

My heart beats faster at the thought of the open ocean, the unyielding horizon and the freedom it represents. If it were up to me, we'd never make landfall at all. But though I am captain of this ship, this ship is a democracy and most of the crew get a little funny when they haven't seen land for a while. It's my job above all else to keep them healthy and happy.

I get dressed and do a quick wash in the freshwater basin before heading out. I should go up top first and check in with the night watch before it ends but I'm curious to see how my prisoners are. I can hear the ones down in the hold from here, moaning and crying and begging for release, but I have no interest in them at the moment. Instead, I head down a level to the gun deck and to the cell where the royal couple is kept.

I open the door to their cabin and brace myself, expecting to be hit with flying excrement or something of the sort. That's happened a few times before when I've taken a special interest in a prisoner and kept them behind bars here.

Instead, I find the lovers on opposite ends of the cell. The princess is sitting on the floor, her hair in her face and looking down, the prince is leaning against the bars with a pitiful look on his face.

"I demand you to release me!" the prince says the moment he locks eyes with me, gripping the bars of the cell until his knuckles turn white. "By order of King Frederick, IV, of the Danish Realm! I am Prince Aerik, and you have no right taking me hostage."

"And yet here you are," I say to him. "I'd ask how you slept but judging by your foul mood and complete lack of gratitude for not being killed on sight, I'm going to assume it wasn't well."

I glance down at the princess, eager to see if she has a rebuttal. But the woman I see before me is completely different than the one I met last night. She doesn't even raise her head to look at me and, if anything, she seems to be cowering. Perhaps she suddenly remembered I am to be feared. Either that or she's in shock.

"And what say you, Princess?" I walk to the cell, keeping out of reach enough just in case the prince decides to do something stupid. Knowing me I'd end up killing him, and I really don't want to ruin a good thing. "You're awfully quiet this morning. Could barely get you to shut up last night."

At that Aerik turns to look at her, giving her a cold look. "Yes, that is an issue with her."

Finally she raises her head to look at him, fire in her eyes. Her hair moves back just enough for me to glimpse purple bruises along her cheekbone and edge of her eye. I know I was rough with her last night but I'd never hit a woman. It might be expected, especially among pirates, but I find it to be rather a sloppy and inelegant show of violence.

"What's this?" I ask, peering at her. "What happened to your face?"

She wiggles her jaw together and avoids my eyes.

"She must have hit her face on the bars in the night," the prince says, and I immediately know it was him that did this to her. I feel a twinge of guilt in my gut, a feeling that I've rarely felt over the years.

"She's clumsy like that," he adds, tone more spiteful now. "Like a graceless newborn foal."

The last thing I want or need is to complicate the matter and get involved in whatever marital trouble they seem to be having, and yet there's a part of me that thinks I need to get the princess alone for a bit. I need to investigate this further, because if this weasely prince is a danger to her in any way, then I'll be losing a valuable asset.

"I'm going to open the door," I say, taking out my keys. "Either of you try anything, I'll remove your head. You get that?"

I spring the lock and open the door, quickly reaching down to grab the princess by the arm. As I'm pulling her up, the prince makes a go for the door, as I knew he would. In a blink of an eye I have the princess pulled tight against my side and with my other hand I remove my dagger from my holster and push the prince back. I pin him against the bars, tip of the blade pressed up against his chin.

"I told you I'd remove your head," I tell him roughly, leaning in close so he can see the wildness in my eyes. "Might cut off a few pieces of your face first. With your fine royal breeding, you'd make a bloody good snack."

He growls at me, a pathetic mewling and I push him back before swiftly exiting the cell, pushing the princess out of it and to the floor while I lock it. Aerik launches himself at the door but it's too late.

"I'll come back later," I tell him, hauling the princess to her feet again. "If you behave, I might bring you some water. It might even be clean."

I take her out of the room, keeping the door open. If any of my crew feel like tormenting the prince a bit, I'd look the other way.

"Where are you taking me?" the princess asks impatiently.

"Ah, she speaks again," I say to her as I pull her toward the stairs. "First we're going to get some fresh air and I'm going to ask the crew if they had anything to do with your black eye there."

I glance back at her and she clamps her lips shut, looking away so that her hair falls over her eye.

"Unless," I go on, "you want to tell me it was your husband."

I know that no one on the crew would manhandle her like that (other than Sterling, but his impact packs more of a wallop, so to speak), but I want to hear her admit that it was Prince Aerik.

She still doesn't say anything as I pull her up the stairs, passing through the main deck where I can hear some of the crew stirring from their quarters at the foredeck, and the smell of fresh coffee is now wafting from the galley. The princess makes an agreeable sound, almost like a moan that causes my cock to twitch, and I realize I might be able to use coffee as leverage with her. I save that information for later and continue to bring her up to the main deck.

The sun is bright, though there's a haze in the air, cutting down its strength. Even though we've all spent years on this ship and many others, the sun is something that never ceases to be an annoyance. In my haste this morning I had forgotten my hat, so I'm squinting at the light as I bring the princess up to the quarterdeck and over to the helmsman.

"Princess, may I introduce you to Conner Benedict, our bosun, though you may wish to call him Crazy Eyes."

Crazy Eyes look at her and widens his eyes so that the whites take over, leaning into his moniker. "Pleasure to meet you, Princess."

She swallows. "How do you do," she says unsurely, a greeting rather than a question.

"She's a pretty one," he says, looking her up and down, his eyes resting on her chest. Her dress is still damp from last night's swim and her hair is a mess but her physical attributes still shine even under the daylight. As does the bruise on her face, which Crazy Eyes notices. "You rough her up, Captain?"

I shake my head. "I was wondering if you knew who had."

"Don't know of anyone who would have been down there by the cells."

"Not even Sterling?"

He nods at the forecastle. "Sterling's been up there all night, mumbling and moaning about this and that. That man sure has many a complaint about ya."

I growl as my gaze goes to Sterling at the bow of the ship, his bald head shining under the sun. I know that the sun bothers him, as it does the rest of us, but he believes he is more of a man for never covering his head.

"Well, he can complain all he wants, things ain't ever going to change for that bilge-licker." I bring the princess close, her face just inches from mine. She stares at me wide-eyed. "Are you going to tell me who laid their hands on you?"

"What does it matter? I'm your prisoner," she practically spits out.

"But that's why it does matter, luv. I'm not concerned out of the goodness of my heart, for I don't hold any good in my heart at all. But you are precious cargo now, and as valuable as gold. If it be your husband that beats you, I need to know. Two months is an awful long time to be caged with someone like that."

Her black brows raise. "Two months? That's not possible. I know it's at least four to cross the Pacific heading to New Spain. My husband is close with Prince Ferdinand. He talks about the Spanish galleons crossing all the time."

"Ah, the Spanish Prince. What a waste of breath that boy is. Figures your husband would fraternize with the likes of him."

"You didn't answer my question," she says and Crazy Eyes chuckles in amusement at how bold she is.

"I suppose I didn't," I say, grinning at her impudence. "What if I were to tell you that there's magic up in these sails. What say you then?"

She looks up at the sails billowing then looks around her, her focus going to the islands we're passing by. "We are moving awfully fast for a ship. How many knots?"

I'm vaguely impressed at her nautical knowledge, half expecting her to be the sort of woman who would stay below deck for all her travels and never learning a lick of the lingo.

"Ten knots," I tell her.

She shakes her head. "Not even the fastest ship in the royal fleet can go that fast."

"But you've never been on the *Nightwind* before."

"I would have heard about it."

"There's very few that have been on board this vessel and live to tell the tale of her speed—or other things. But believe it or not, that's how fast she goes. We have wind even in the middle of the doldrums. When we cut across the Pacific, we cut straight across. No need to sail up to Japan and across to the colonies when we can go right to New Spain. There's a chance that we'll get to Acapulco before we get word from your father-in-law, but no matter, darling. I'm a very patient man."

She remains skeptical, as she should. You mention magic to any landlubber and they're quick to dismiss you and label you insane. It's only the seafaring folk that are more open-minded when you talk of the strange and mystic.

Then something else crosses her face, her expression turning cunning for a moment. But she doesn't express it with words, leaving me in wonder.

"Bones," Cruz says, stepping up onto the deck. "You get any sleep?"

"Enough," I say and turn the princess towards him. "I don't think she got any, judging by the looks of her. Know of anyone in the crew that may have roughed her up?"

Cruz appraises her as he puts on his hat. "I don't. Probably her husband, no?"

"That's what I'm thinking," I say, and I lead the princess away from the helm as Cruz replaces the bosun for his shift. "Perhaps you would be safer caged in my chambers?"

She blinks at me. "Why do you have a cage in your chambers?"

A good question. "Let's just say I like to collect beautiful things. You fit the bill, luv. Come now and see."

I take her down to the main deck and to my quarters at the rear of the ship. Naturally, as befitting a captain, it's the most spacious room on board, with my bed tucked away to the side and the rest a large library, with shelf upon shelf of books and other curiosities I've picked up on my travels. The stained-glass windows run down the entire length of the cabin with a door leading to a balcony, and there's a large table in the middle for crew meetings or when I feel like drinking alone.

And then there's the cage in the corner, human-sized.

"I'm sure it's not as nice as your quarters on the royal ship," I tell her. "But they do me just fine."

I let go of her arm and she seems so enthralled by the books and curios I have on the shelves that she's completely ignoring my collection of weapons to the side. Or maybe that's what she wants me to think.

"I've never seen so many books," she says breathlessly as she looks around.

"I doubt that. Surely the king and queen have libraries upon libraries in their palaces."

She gives me a wry look. "Those books don't count. They're unreadable." She slowly walks around, trailing her fingers over the cloth and leather spines. "These are real books. Ones that tell stories, not just someone's boring lineage."

I fold my arms across my chest. "I'm glad you're impressed."

That makes her features harden. Somehow that look makes her even more beautiful. "I'm only impressed because you're a pirate," she says.

"And you think the lot of us are illiterate imbeciles?"

"Yes," she says.

"Fair enough. And that might be true for most of the rogue marauders you may meet, but the crew of the *Nightwind* is more intelligent than you'll ever give us credit for."

The skepticism remains on her face. "If you think intelligence is some sort of virtue for a man who has a cage in his room, you're more daft than I thought."

I chuckle and head to the windows, peering out. "Darling, you'll find that we're all unhinged on this ship. They don't call us the Devil's Brethren sometimes for—"

But before I can finish my words, I realize the mistake I've made. I hear the blade of a sword being unsheathed and no doubt pointed in my direction.

SIX

Maren

I have the cutlass pointed straight at Captain Battista. There's a table between us but even so, it feels good to have a weapon in my hand. I may not know how to fight well with a sword—I'd only been indulged in fencing on a few occasions and by none other than my father-in-law the king—who was rather tickled by my interest in combat—but I feel I could do some damage if it came to it.

The captain turns around slowly and eyes the sword, acknowledging it with a raise of his dark brow.

"I figured all the fawning over literature was a ruse."

"It wasn't a rouse," I say, gritting my teeth as I grip the handle of the cutlass harder. "But I'm also not an idiot."

He folds his arms across his chest and leans back against the windows. Despite the size of the room, he's a commanding presence in it. Dressed in black breeches and boots, a crisp white shirt, and a dark brown leather holster that crisscrosses over his chest and back with lots of weapons and buckles, he looks like he belongs here. He looks the type that would spend the evening flipping open the tomes with his large silver-ringed hands and blasting people's brains out with the twitch of a pistol. He also looks like a man who would have a cage in his chambers fit for a human, but he'd probably offer them some food and drink from time to time. Maybe even read to them.

Then there's the other things in his quarters that I find intriguing. The crystals. Jars of herbs and salt. Collections of shells and bones. Black candles. The artifacts that only a witch would have. Why does he have them? Does he use them? Does he possess magic too? He admitted outright that there is magic in the *Nightwind's* sails to account for how she goes so fast. How did he get that magic? Is he a witch of sorts? It would explain so much.

"So, what are you planning to do, Your Highness?" he says, with a feigned bow. I flinch at the movement, the sword vibrating in my hand, but he doesn't make a move for any of the weapons on him.

My plan is simple and made up on the spot. "I want you to let me jump off the ship. I'll walk the plank, I don't care, so as long as you let me go."

He snorts. "Walk the plank." He gives me a dry look and tilt of his head. "We don't *do* that here."

"I don't give a damn what you do here," I seethe, finding courage from deep down. "But if you don't let me go so I can swim to land, I'll end you."

The corner of his mouth quirks up and if I didn't want to drive the sword right through the middle of him, I'd think he was almost handsome.

He throws his arms wide, displaying the wide breadth of his chest. "Then end me, darling. I'm not going to fight you."

"You're a most infuriating pirate," I say gruffly, taking a step around the table.

He doesn't even move, remaining right where he is.

"And you're a most infuriating princess," he says. "All this talk, no action."

"I'm warning you," I tell him.

"You want to go, go."

I narrow my eyes at him, trying to figure out his game.

"All I offer you is my protection," he adds.

"From who?"

"From your husband."

"And from you?"

"I never promised any protection from me."

"I figured that much."

It didn't matter. It was better the devil I knew. As much as I hated the idea of being caged up with Aerik, especially for a couple of months, I at least knew how he operated. I didn't know this pirate at all. So far, he's proved to be wholly unpredictable and I don't buy this chivalrous act for a second, not when he's the same man who slaughtered my whole crew and help without a second thought.

I start backing up now, heading toward the door. If I can get there in time, I can run to the top deck and throw myself overboard. He's right in that the ship is sailing far faster than seems possible, but even so it's worth the risk. If I survive the fall, I'll swim to shore.

"I know you want to return to your royal life as quickly as possible…" he says.

I let out an acidic laugh. "Is that what you think? Perhaps I'd rather disappear into the jungles, never to be seen again. It would be better than staying here with the likes of you, and better than anything my role might bring me."

Another brow raise. "I see. Well, in the event that your wishes aren't attainable, my offer is still on the table."

I jerk my head in the direction of the cage but don't dare take my eyes off him. "You mean to keep me in that? If you really want to separate me from Aerik, then put me down in the hold with the others. At least let me be with Daphne."

He gives his head a sharp shake, his eyes shining. "Oh, I'm afraid you wouldn't like that, luv," he says huskily.

I want to ask why but I don't dare. I'm afraid that if I show any more concern over my lady-in-waiting, he might purposefully hurt her. Instead, I back up further, almost to the door now.

"I suppose this is goodbye then, Princess," he says, his stormy sea eyes mocking me with faux sadness.

I feel for the handle, still keeping the sword pointed at him, readying myself to throw the door open and hoping I don't trip on my dress when I make a run for it.

"Meow."

I glance down to see a tabby cat padding toward my legs, tail raised and waving, not a care in the world.

Before I can even register my surprise, I see the captain leaping over the table. He moves soundlessly, not even rattling a chair, and so fast that if I blinked I would have missed him moving at all.

He comes at me with the power of twenty horses, pressing me back against the door, his hand enclosed over the blade of the cutlass, stopping me from driving it into his chest. He has no weapon drawn, he's just using his brute strength to keep me in my place.

His face comes close and I'm nearly swallowed up by his eyes that seem to shift between gray and blue. "Let's not fight, shall we?" he murmurs, his voice low and raspy, and for some reason I feel a shiver run down my back. The intensity of his gaze drops to my lips and I feel it burn there. "Even though I rather like it."

He pushes his hips against mine and I can feel how much he likes it. My first instinct is to be repulsed by his apparently large lust for me, but I'm not. Instead, I'm distracted by a dripping sound, and when I glance down I see blood running down the sharp edge of the cutlass and dripping onto the floor. The orange cat that surprised me comes over and starts lapping up the blood from a small puddle that has formed.

It's the captain that's bleeding, not me, and yet he doesn't let go of the blade.

I take in a shaking breath, trying to swallow. I'm afraid to look up at his eyes, as if I'll drown to death in them.

"You can drop the sword now, luv," he says softly. "It won't do you any good. I'm not going to let you get away, no matter how much you beg. And believe me, I would *love* to hear you beg."

My hand starts to shake. I'm afraid, yes, but more than that, I'm angry. I hate how helpless I feel. If I was still a Syren, I would be tearing this man apart with my bare hands, my claws ripping out his insides and I would eat them and make him watch as he slowly lay dying.

But now I am just a woman. Powerless and weak and everything this human society has made me become. I'm everything I hate.

He tilts his head and frowns, studying me. "Don't waste your tears on me, Princess," he says, and that's when I realize I'm crying silently, my cheeks wet. "Let's get you back to where you belong."

With one smooth and sudden movement he rips the blade back and throws it across the room, causing the cat to bolt with a yelp, its hairs raised as it runs for a corner.

Then the captain grabs me by the bicep, the blood from his hand smearing on my gown, and opens the door, pulling me along and down to the level below.

In moments I am back in the room that holds the cell and before I know it, the cage door is unlocked and I'm shoved back inside with Aerik.

"What happened?" my husband asks me.

"She tried to escape," the captain says, showing his bloodied hand. "I was starting to feel sorry for her for a moment, if you can believe that. You've got your work cut out for you, matey."

"It's Prince Aerik of the Danish Realm to you!" he yells at him, and he's never sounded so pitiful before. What in damnation did I ever see in this sorry excuse for a man?

"Actually, to me, you're a half-masted arse with a boot for a face," the captain says, turning on his heel for the door.

Aerik lets out a cry of indignation, then the anger flares in his eyes as he turns to me. "So, he's the one hurt and you don't have a mark on you? What are you, a whore now? Their spy?"

He's raging now, not of his right mind, and he raises his fist to strike me.

But everything happens so fast.

There's a *crack* that seems to part the air and a cat-o-nine tails whip appears from out of nowhere, the leather coils reaching through the bars and snapping around Aerik's forearm before he has a chance to touch me.

Captain Battista yanks the whip back and Aerik's arm is pulled right through the bars, his face and body smashed up against the cage.

The pirate flicks the whip again causing Aerik's arm to twist at an ungodly angle. Aerik screams and Battista twists his arm even further as he saunters over to him.

"You aren't to lay a hand on the princess," he says in a low, steady voice, words brimming with menace. "I know you figure that's your right as the husband, but you have no rights to anything anymore and especially not to her. She's my property now, as are you, and if I catch you leaving a mark on my property again, I'll eat your balls for breakfast. Savvy?"

Aerik is still screeching in agony, enough that I have to speak up.

"Stop," I tell the captain. "He understands."

The pirate gives me a furtive look. "You sure about that? Because on your word, I'll do a lot worse than this."

I nod. I don't need to tell him that if I ever get half the chance, I'm capable of doing the same as him.

He nods slowly, just a hint of a smile curving his lips. He knows.

"Alright, Princess," he says. He steps back and, with a quick flick of his wrist he uncoils the whip, freeing Aerik who collapses against the bars. He sinks to the floor with a pitiful moan and the captain puts the whip back against the wall. "Have it your way."

Then he leaves, closing the door behind him. The room is windowless and without the light from the rest of the ship, Aerik and I are plunged back into darkness, the planks on the ship so airtight that not even a speck of light gets in.

"Fuck," Aerik curses from at my feet. "And fuck you, you doxy bitch."

I'm so damned tempted to kick him in the side, same way he's done to me when he's laid me down on the floor. But I don't.

Instead, I threaten him.

"You can curse me out all you want," I tell him. "But the next time you lay a hand on me, I'll make sure you lose it at the wrist."

"Oh, fuck off."

I don't say anything to that. I don't need to. The threat is there.

I just hate that I have Captain Ramsay "Bones" Battista to thank for that.

A erik spends the rest of the morning whimpering in pain. I do what I can to tune him out. The more I listen to him, the more I feel sorry for him, and right now he's not someone who deserves an ounce of my pity.

At some point one of the crew, a young sweet-looking boy around the age of ten, comes to give us a bowl of water like we're a pair of dogs, and a couple of pieces of hardtack to nibble on, placed gently just outside the bars.

If I were in a better frame of mind, I would try and talk to the young lad and convince him to set us free. I'm sure it wouldn't do much good with him being a pirate-in-training, possibly press-ganged into service, but it would have been worth a shot.

As it was, I was too tired from the morning's ordeal and didn't say a word. Aerik, who also normally would have tried to command the boy, stayed silent too.

The boy left and we were plunged back in darkness again. Only then did I help myself to a few leaking palmfuls of water, for the bowl wouldn't fit through the bars, and a piece of the hardtack bread, which tasted like heaven having not eaten since breakfast yesterday.

With my belly somewhat full, I sleep on and off and I wake only when the ship is filled with screams. Screams from the hold beneath us, screams of our crew and servants that are being kept below. A most hair-raising unnatural sound.

One of the screams belongs to Daphne.

SEVEN

Ramsay

"What say you, boy?" I ask Henry as he climbs the stairs to the stern deck where I'm sitting on top of a bench, spyglass at my side.

Henry reaches into his burlap sack and tosses me an apple which I catch without even looking at it. "That all?" I ask, examining the apple's surface, red but peppered with bruises. "She's seen better days."

He starts looking through the bag but I quickly wave him off. "No, no. The apple is fine. Something to pass the time until we cross the strait. What I mean is, how are the prisoners?"

"Which ones? The ones in the hold are screaming."

"To be expected. What about the couple in the cell?"

He shrugs. "They seem fine, I guess."

"Did they speak to you?"

He shakes his head. "Nah. I don't think the fella even looked at me. The lady did but she didn't say anything, just watched. She's pretty."

I find myself smiling. "She is, isn't she? And not just a lady, but a princess."

"Maybe she should have better clothes. And someone to change out their bucket. It's starting to smell in there."

I wrinkle my nose. I forgot how prisoners can get. The ones in the hold will smell much, much worse. Eventually only those with noses made of steel will be able to go down there to tend to them. We differ from others in the cruising trade, for cleanliness is one mainstay of the Brethren and our crew keeps their hygiene levels high, bathing regularly from the rainwater barrels we collect on deck and using the head at the bowsprit. I have my own tub, and a privy located outside my quarters, though I let the higher officers like Thane and Cruz use it too when they request privacy. Oh, and Sam, since she's a woman and all. She's in there more often than not, to our annoyance. Sometimes I think she just wants a break from us, and I can't blame her for that.

"I'll make a note of that, Henry boy," I tell him. "We'll get someone to change out their bucket, perhaps get the lady a new dress. Have we gone through the trunks we've looted from their ship?"

"Remi and Horse are doing that right now."

"Good. Tell them to put the princess's things in my quarters. Then tell them to return to their posts." I look around at the land we're passing. "I want our gun men to be at the ready until we're in the open ocean. That goes for Matisse and Sterling too. Then get Lothar to change out the royal's bucket."

Henry nods and turns to leave.

"Also," I call out and he stops and turns to face me, awaiting my order. "If you can get Sedge to put on another pot of coffee and bring me a mug, that would great."

"Rum in it, sir?"

"Not until this evening." I tap the side of my head. "I need to stay sharp."

He gives me an impish smile. "Do you think I could finally have coffee? With sugar and milk?"

"If you think you deserve it," I say. "Perhaps you'll work through some vocabulary exercises tonight and we'll call it." He nods so earnestly I nearly laugh. He hurries off down the stairs with an extra spring in his wee step. I have a feeling the lad isn't going to like coffee unless Sedge, our cook, makes it so it's mainly hot milk. Much like Hilla was, Henry's affection for sweets knows no bounds.

Henry came aboard the *Nightwind* when he was just five years old. He was the son of a pirate woman, Elizabeth, who had joined our crew when we were holed up in Fragrant Harbor Village in China. She had heard about us and deserted the English ship belonging to the East India Trading Company that she was on. We folded them into our family, always happy for more Brethren of the Blood, and Henry became the best of friends with Lucas, who is Thane and Sam's boy, only two years older.

Then tragedy struck, as it often seems to do on the *Nightwind*. Maybe it's the nature of the game, of this life we chose, the way our service to the devil can cut our lives very short. But we were in the process of looting a merchant ship when one of the officers captured Elizabeth and sliced her head clean off. It was an act of ferocious violence, even to our eyes, though perhaps our reputation of us being hard to kill led the officer to take such gruesome measures.

It worked. Elizabeth died, her head held high like a prize, then all of us swarmed the officer and made sure the same was done to him. Henry came under the care of the ship and I've taken an affection to the boy. In so many ways he reminds me of my Hilla, sweet and thoughtful but with a mischievous quality. He keeps me on my toes and his presence, along with Lucas, and the other pages, eighteen-year old twins John and Bart, give the ship a boost of youthfulness—much-needed since the Brethren can get tired and stuck in their ways.

I've even taken to helping both Henry and Lucas with their reading and writing skills when I can, my library of books turning into a study a couple of times a week. Sam and Thane teach them things like math and history the rest of the time. Growing up on a ship is no excuse for not having an education.

Speak of the devil.

"Ramsay," Thane calls out, heading up the stairs to my deck. As usual, my brother is dressed in all black, from his shirt with the sleeves rolled up to his biceps, unbuttoned to show off the layers of necklaces over his chest, to his wide black petticoat breeches. On any other man, the outfit would give him the appearance of being halved and stocky but my brother and I share the same genes that give us height and width to our shoulders. I dare say Thane might be able to pull off anything, especially with his hair cut neat and short under his hat, unlike mine which is unruly and falls to my shoulder, often pulled back with a black band.

I tip up my hat and bite into my apple. "Yes, Quartermaster?" I say, my way of reminding him that he didn't address me as captain.

He frowns at me as I eat the apple. "You seem awfully cavalier, considering all that's about."

"It's the apple, brother. Anyone eating an apple looks like they've got nothing better to do." I observe him for a moment, the set of his jaw and the hawkish look in his eyes. "Have you ever considered dabbling in levity every now and then? Might lead you on the road to having a sense of humor."

He makes a gruff sound in response. "If I *dabbled in levity*, as you suggest, we'd probably run aground." He clears his throat. "Look now, we may have a problem on our hands."

"When don't we?"

"Ramsay," he says sharply. "I've gotten word that the navy might be in these waters."

I get up and saunter over to the rail, chucking the eaten apple overboard and gazing about for any sign of ships. "You've gotten word you say? From whom?" I ask, though there's only one way to have word travel when you're under sail. We've tried passenger pigeons but Skip, the ship's cat, ate them more times than not.

"You know who," he says, an edge to his tone.

"From your crystal ball? You know, the sooner you admit that magic exists, the sooner we can just come out with it."

"I obviously know it—look here, it doesn't matter. Yes. I used the ball."

"And?"

"And I asked if there was any danger ahead and that's when I saw the navy ship."

I think about that for a moment. The ball isn't always accurate. Yes, it can show you the future, but the images are often hazy with no time or space attached to them. Thane might have seen a navy ship, but to know when in our future we'll come across it is harder to pin down.

The crystal ball itself was a gift from my wife Venla to him when she first married into the family. She was a witch, and she knew that my brother and my parents would be hard to win over. Indeed, it took me a very long time for them to even agree to meet her. Witches aren't the most liked creatures in my family, or really anywhere else for that matter.

So Venla gave Thane a large crystal ball, a translucent quartz that turned an opaque shade of purple and pink when you used it with your own energy. Venla told Thane he could use it for manifesting what he wants, or that he could ask it to show him the future.

I have to admit, I was jealous when she first gave him that. It sounds petty, but I was so used to my older brother getting everything and it bothered me that he could use the ball and I couldn't. Even if I held the ball and asked for the same things, it would never show me anything.

Venla would laugh when I complained about it and told me that marrying a witch gave me the upper hand. It did in many respects, including the wind in the sails, but now Thane has something of Venla's and I don't. It's been a long time since Venla died, and I have come to terms with her death, but to have a part of her still would have been nice. I had Hilla, I had the book, but the sea witch took all of that from me.

"Ramsay?" Thane says, bringing me back on track.

"Do you know if any of the vessels you saw are Smith's?" I ask, my voice automatically lowering over his name. The same name causes my brother's nostrils to flare, his posturing stiffening even more than it was before.

He shakes his head. "If I knew, I'd have told ya."

"Well, then we have no choice but to be prepared. I've already told the gunmen to go to their posts, Matisse and Sterling too."

He nods and adjusts his hat, scanning the area. The sky is still a little hazy, the humidity clinging to my skin, and the air smells earthy and sweet with flowers as we pass close to land. On either side of the ship are islands, lush with palm trees that line the sugary white-sand beaches, the sea shifting through shades of azure and turquoise before it meets the shore. It's a tropical paradise, a million miles away from the cold wet Scottish highlands that Thane and I grew up in. And yet people from our past, like Captain Ed Smith, can follow us here. They say the world is large and endless and uncharted, but in my opinion it's very, very small.

"I heard you were asking if anyone had laid a hand on the princess," Thane says.

"Who did you hear that from?"

He gives me a knowing look. The role of the quartermaster is to not just be second in command, ahead of the first mate, but to be the one the crew goes to for anything. Though Thane's grizzled personality could make a crocodile seem charming, his studious and thoughtful nature invites others to seek his counsel. "Sam told me."

Sam and everyone else, I'm sure.

"I didn't actually expect any of the crew to have touched her, except for Sterling of course. I was just playing a game with her."

"And what game was that, exactly?" he asks with a raised brow.

I chew on that for a pause. "I'm not sure, to be honest with you, brother. She compels me."

My eyes are scanning the nearest coves as we pass but even so I can feel my brother's focus on me. "It was your idea to take them hostage, mate. No good can come of this if this woman *compels* you."

I shake my head. "Nay, it's not like that. There's just something different about her and I don't know what it is. And the fact that she stays with an arse like the weasel-faced prince…"

Thane lets out a huff of dry amusement. "As if you are a true gentleman yourself and not a dirty pirate."

"Dirty?" I scoff. I hold out my hand. "You see these nails? Not a speck of dirt under them. We're the cleanest group of pirates anyone's ever met."

"Yes. Perhaps we'd get a reputation if only we'd let people live long enough to spread the truth." He leans back against the rail and tilts his head. A grave expression comes over his face, causing the lines around his eyes to deepen. "You know, one of these days there's going to be a reckoning for us. For what we've done. For what we are. It ain't going to be pretty."

I glance at him sharply. "A reckoning? Don't think I've already been reckoned with? Don't you think I've already paid the price when I lost her? I was *good* when I still had a daughter."

"You were never good, Ramsay," he says gruffly. "Neither was I. How could we have been with where we came from?"

"So then the reckoning is for the sins of the father," I grumble. "I still think I've paid my fair share of the price."

I pay the price every morning when I wake up and realize Hilla is gone.

"We can't keep doing this forever."

"But we can," I tell him adamantly, trying to escape this sinking feeling inside me, like I'm being tied down with bricks. "We *can* do this forever. There's no other life for us, Thane. How could there be? We are safest here, together. We don't belong in the old world or the new, so we have to create one of our own. This is our home."

He gives his head a shake while gnawing on his lip. "It's no place to raise a child."

"It's the only place to raise your child. That's why our father did it with us."

"And he made us into this. Into killers. Into—"

"Into men of fortune, doing what they have to do to survive," I interrupt him. "This life we chose, this ship, this crew, we're doing what we can to live another day. I'll admit that maybe the senseless killings have gone too far and my bloodlust gets the best of me and maybe it doesn't have to be that way. Maybe I need to be reined in before I become a real madman. But this is the only life, the only path, that lets us be who we really are. I won't give that all up for a life on land where society would destroy us, not in a million years."

He sighs heavily, running his hand down his face. "It's a rousing speech but I've heard it all before. It's time you remember to use it on the crew. It's been a while since they've had any purpose. You need to give them a purpose, Ramsay, or there will be a mutiny on your hands and I don't think I'm important enough to them to stop it."

The word mutiny is a kick in the gut. "Who is talking mutiny? Sterling?"

Sterling has always been throwing *that* word around, ever since he was demoted from first mate to gunner, after I had taken control of the *Nightwind* when my father was killed. He wanted to become captain, not me. Suffice to say, his attempt for control didn't go well. I don't trust him and if this were any other ship and I was any other pirate, he would be gone. But Sterling is a part of the Brethren and for now, he stays.

"Not that I know. And not anyone in particular. Just a feeling."

"Did your ball show you this?"

He manages to grin. "My balls show me lots of things."

I laugh at that, about to point out that his sense of humor may be immature but at least it's present, when suddenly Drakos shouts from the crow's nest above.

"Navy ship! Three hundred yards portside!"

EIGHT

Maren

I f I were a proper lady, I probably would have been insulted that
Aerik and I were being treated like caged animals, but when the
quiet pirate with the dark menacing stare and calm movements
came to collect our bucket of waste and replace it with a clean one, I
was nothing but grateful. It was starting to smell awful and any sense
of humility disappeared long ago.

But Aerik, despite his dislocated arm, decided to provoke the pirate
who reacted swiftly with a knife to Aerik's cheek. Luckily he left just a
scratch but the pirate seemed to enjoy it a little too much.

"Bastard," Aerik says under his breath as he wipes the blood from
his cheek and the pirate leaves the room. This time he doesn't close the
door, leaving us with some light to see by.

*Maybe if you weren't filled with so much foolish pride you wouldn't
get as banged up as you are*, I think to myself, staying silent on the
matter. I know the captain threatened him with more harm if he laid a
hand on me, but since Aerik doesn't seem to learn from his mistakes,
I'm not taking a chance.

With the door open now we hear the pirate that was just in the
room with us go elsewhere on this deck and start talking to other

pirates which he addresses as the "gunmen." Something about being ready if the situation arises.

Suddenly the ship erupts with shouts from above deck, very different from the screams we've been hearing on and off from the hold. This one reeks of panic and for a moment I'm feeling hopeful. If they're panicking, it means there's been another ship spotted, an enemy, and with any luck it's some sort of authority. Whether they were sent to rescue us or sent to take down the pirates, our freedom might be moments away.

Aerik glances at me, his fingers pressed against his cheek. "What do you think that is?" he asks. "Are we under attack?"

"It might be our rescue."

For a moment the anger fades from his eyes and they're filled with hope instead and he looks very much like the boy I fell in love with ten years ago. Back then he was softer. A fool still, brash and selfish, but I honestly did love him and I know he did love me. It's just that Edonia never mentioned how human love can wear many disguises and can change over the years, becoming sour and corrupt as spoiled milk.

BANG!

I hear the cannon fire first, sounding far away and muffled, coming from the other ship, and I grab the bars bracing for impact.

There's a loud CRASH and the ship sways and I hold on tightly as Aerik falls to his knees, the commotion upstairs increasing and I hear the captain yell, "We're broadside! Fire roundshots!"

Cannons go off inside the ship. We must be on the gun deck because it sounds like it's happening right next to us; I can feel the ship shudder as the cannons roll back, the smell of the powder, and fire, followed by the manic laughter of the gunmen.

BOOM!

Another loud shot, this one sounding closer and when it hits this time it feels like it's done some damage to the *Nightwind*, the ship tipping violently and I'm thrown to the ground beside Aerik. Screams sound out from below, not much different from the ones we heard earlier but I know this is because we've been hit. And if it hit close to the waterline, where the hold is, there's a chance now we could sink.

I'm about to voice this to Aerik when I hear Daphne's scream coming closer and closer to us, followed by footsteps and the screams of others.

"Daphne!" I shout out, hoping she can hear me among the chaos.

"Princess!" she yells back from somewhere on the deck.

"The prisoners are escaping!" I hear one of the gunmen cry out.

"Let them," growls another one. "Boy, swab the barrel and load!"

Suddenly Daphne appears at the doorway. With the light coming in from behind her she looks the same as always, her silhouette familiar.

Then she stumbles inside and I gasp in horror. She's covered in blood.

"You're hurt!" I cry out, my heart breaking to see my longest companion in such a state of disarray. Her hair is matted, her wrists bandaged as if all she's been through has led her to attempted suicide.

"Monsters!" she howls, her voice raw and she grabs the bars of the cell, her eyes looking positively mad. "They're monsters, the whole lot of them. You must get off this ship, Princess, you must! They'll do to you what they've done to the rest of us!"

"Calm down," Aerik tells her. "What happened? Are we sinking?"

She only blinks at him like she doesn't know who he is. "This isn't a normal ship. This isn't a normal ship. She can't sink if she was built in the bowels of hell!"

Her words make my stomach flip with terror.

"Get a hold of yourself woman," Aerik snipes, "and get us out of here!"

She opens her mouth to say something when suddenly there's another explosion, so loud and deafening that it feels like it's coming from inside my brain and blowing out my eardrums. Through the sound of splintering wood and twisting of metal I'm thrown backward against the other side of the cell, smacking the back of my head against the bars before I collapse to the ground in a heap.

Everything goes black and my ears are ringing, the world beyond that is muffled. I can hear my heartbeat in my head which at least tells me that I'm still alive. I pry my eyes open but my vision is a little hazy, my head feeling full of cotton balls.

What just happened?

I cough and push myself up onto my elbows and look around. Aerik is groaning on the ground beside me, though he looks no more injured than he was before. The cannon ball came in hard enough to destroy the corner of the cell, knocking out two of the bars, right in front of where I was talking to Daphne and…

Oh my goodness, no.

Daphne!

She's lying motionless on the ground, face down, blood pooling around her.

"Daphne?" I say softly, my voice shaking.

She's alright. She's going to be alright.

She *has* to be alright.

"Daphne?" I say, louder now, so terrified that she might not answer me.

Oh please gods, don't let her be dead. Please, please, please.

I manage to crawl over the wood splinters and metal that have been destroyed by the cannon shot and reach through the newly opened space in the bars, dragging myself through them toward her. Once I'm through the bars, I put my hands on her shoulders and roll her over.

And I scream.

A large piece of metal is stuck straight into her chest, blood spilling out. Her eyes have rolled back in her head, her mouth open.

She can't be dead. This can't be my certainty.

"Daphne?" I say, my voice weak, a whisper. I tap the side of her face gently. "Please wake up. Please."

But she doesn't stir.

Maybe if I take the shrapnel out of her…

I run my hands over her chest, over the metal, but I can't seem to pull it out. It's lodged in too tight, and my nails are broken and short from the last few days. If only I had the claws that I had as a Syren, I'd be able to pull it out. Maybe I can use my dress to stem the bleeding?

"What are you doing?" Aerik says and I look over my shoulder to see him free from the cell and standing over me, blood running down the side of his head. "She's dead. We're free."

I shake my head, glancing back down at her. Already the pink flush that she always had in her full cheeks is fading away.

She's fading away.

Maybe she was gone before I even touched her.

I don't think I've ever seen anyone die before. Even when my mother would bring home sailors for us to eat, they were dead a long time before they got to the depths of Limonos.

But Daphne...she's been like a mother to me, if not a friend. The only friend I've had these last ten years.

I can't lose her. If I lose her, I lose the only good thing I had in my life above and I'm cursing myself for never telling her this. I'm cursing myself for never telling her the truth about me. Maybe she would have believed I was once a Syren, maybe she wouldn't have, but it would have been nice to have someone know my secret, someone I trusted.

Now I'm truly alone.

"I can't leave her, Aerik," I say, the tears starting to burn under my eyes. "I can't."

"Then you're on your own," he says and staggers out of the room and into the rest of the ship.

I'm aware that there is chaos all around me. There are screams from above deck and below, shouts and more gunfire, muskets now, and guns on the top of the ship, and the cannons on this level going off again and again. There's smoke and there's the smell of burning and tar and though the ship has stopped shaking so violently, it's still shuddering with each blast from the cannons.

And yet my world is all whittled down to just one thing: my lady-in-waiting.

Dead.

Aerik may have gone but it feels so wrong to leave her like this. I don't know what death means right now. I don't understand how she can just cease to be.

But she isn't moving. She isn't breathing.

She has ceased.

And if Aerik ends up escaping and I don't, then I'm going to regret it forever. Daphne would want me to at least try.

It takes time for me to do something about it. I just can't seem to move. Minutes stretch on and I'm holding my breath hoping, praying, wishing that she will open her eyes and come back to life. What if I walk away and then she comes out of it? What if I could have saved her but I didn't? How can I just leave her like this?

But she doesn't come back.

So I lean down and close her mouth and press my lips against hers, as is the custom in Limonos, and with tears streaming down my face, I get to my feet unsteadily. Syren's have the ability to rejuvenate people with their kiss and though I never knew anyone who had done it, the elders said that a kiss could even bring a drowned sailor back to life.

But Daphne remains dead.

And I have to flee. I'd say I'd wasted so much time already, but none of these last moments with Daphne could have been called a waste.

I turn and stumble out of the room, into smoke that obscures the cannons. The gun deck seems to be empty now, the cannons have ceased firing on all ends. I feel my way to the stairs and then up to the second level, looking for a window out, when I'm suddenly accosted by someone, hands taking a rough hold of my elbows.

"Where do you think you're going, strumpet?" A tall bald-headed man has a hold of me. He's built like a bear and his breath smells of beer and pennies. "Thinking you might escape during a little fight, did ye now?"

"Let me go!" I growl at him and try to get out of his grasp but it's useless. His fingernails are sharp and they dig in hard enough to pierce my skin. I grit my teeth.

"No, I won't be doing that. Let's take a stroll, shall we?"

"Sterling!" someone yells from above. "Don't leave your post!"

"The winds is in the sails!" Sterling yells back. "Can't you see the ship will be in our shadow before long?"

Then he pulls me up the stairs to the top deck and the sun is so bright after all that time beneath that I can barely see. By the time they adjust, I expect to see bloodshed and mayhem on the deck.

Instead it's a different scene entirely.

The enemy ship looks far behind the stern, so far that I can't even tell what flag they're flying. They aren't retreating but instead the speed of the *Nightwind* has picked up several knots and we are leaving them in our wake, causing my heart to sink even further than it already had.

And all of the *Nightwind's* crew has gone completely still.

They're all focused on Aerik, who has his arm around the young boy that brought us water and bread, holding a marlinespike against his temple. His hand is shaking, no doubt due to the fervor that's masking his damaged arm but he still looks like he could kill the boy in an instant.

"Give me the ship's boat," Aerik sneers. "Or I'll drive this spike right into this little boy's brain."

My gaze goes to the captain. For once he looks completely worried, his dark brows furrowed, his jaw tense, and a faint sense of anguish in his eyes. I wonder if this is the captain's son?

And while I never give Aerik much credit—he's often more bark than bite, except when it comes to dealing with me—he looks positively deranged now and unpredictable. I wouldn't be surprised if he followed through with his threat.

"I said, give me the ship's boat and let me find my safety, or this child is dead. Do you understand?"

"If the child is dead, your wife is dead," Sterling grunts, his breath raspy and wet in my ear.

"I wasn't planning on taking her with me at any rate," Aerik snipes. He looks back to the captain. "Do we have a deal?"

All eyes are on the captain now.

"I don't make deals," the captain says gravely, his eyes focused intently on the little boy, as if telling him a message. "And you're not leaving this ship, Prince Aerik."

Aerik's eyes go wide with surprise, then rage, and I fear he's about to kill the little boy. And after that, Sterling might kill me. What use am I if the prince is gone? His survival means my survival.

My eyes are glued to Aerik's grip as it tightens on the rusted spike and he makes the motion to stab the boy and I can't help but cry out "No! Aerik, stop!"

But the words barely leave my mouth as a small man leaps from behind Aerik like he's part monkey, and tackles him from above. Aerik is knocked to the ground and the boy manages to escape his grasp, running over to the captain's side who ushers the boy behind him.

Aerik grapples with the man, still wielding the spike, and somehow manages to get the advantage for just long enough to drive the spike right into the side of the man's head.

I gasp while Sterling goes, "That one hurts," and yet no one else in the crew seems all that bothered by the fact that their mate has a spike sticking out of his temple. Instead, two of the crew members start walking to Aerik, who looks in shock at what he just did.

He looks even more in shock when the man he just stabbed suddenly reaches up and pulls the spike out of his head and tosses it to the deck. Just a thin trickle of blood comes out of his head and he staggers to his feet, staring down at Aerik.

"You want to kill me, you're going to have to try harder than that."

NINE

Ramsay

Drakos kicks the marlinespike away as he walks over to the rail, one palm pressed against his temple. Poor cunt, I know he must be in pain. I'll have to give him extra rations later as a way of saying thanks. While the entire crew is strong, no one has the spritely agility that Drakos has, leaping from mast to mast, balancing on thin rope, doing twists and rolls in the air like a god damned acrobat. In hand-to-hand combat he is a most formidable asset and he'll do it with a smile on his face.

Except now the Greek isn't laughing. That wound might take longer than usual to heal. Best he stays out of the game to heal for a bit.

"What should we do with him, Captain?" Horse asks as he holds onto a struggling prince, Matisse on his other side. "I seen the cell, she's taken a beatin' from the roundshots."

I nod at Lothar. "See what welding you can do on the cell and if there needs to be reinforcements in the hold, if anyone is still alive down there. And the ship might need some repairs in the hull from the rounds." I look to Horse and Matisse. "In the meantime, put him in the chains. At least that will keep him in one spot."

"Chains!" the prince cries out and he looks so indignant that I feel myself losing control. He can't deal with chains and yet he was prepared to kill Henry before my eyes?

I move like the wind and I'm at the prince in a second, pushing him against the rise of the quarterdeck, my pistol drawn and pressed up against his chin.

"I don't know how many times I have to hurt you, Prince," I practically growl at him. "But it's starting to eat into my time. Still, if you ever, ever threaten Henry again, I will cut off your cock and feed it to you with a spoon."

"That's a good one, Captain," Horse chuckles.

I remove the pistol and slip it back in my holster and nod at them to take the sniveling prince away. They do so, Matisse twisting his bad arm even further, making him howl all the way down through the decks.

Good. I've barely had that prince for a couple days and he's already becoming more trouble than he's worth. If we don't end up getting our weight in gold for him, I plan to torture that royal bastard for a very long time. Might end up doing that anyway. I'm not always fond of patience.

I turn to focus on the princess now. She's in Sterling's grasp and the sight of it makes my chest tighten, just a little. She doesn't look frightened per se, just watching the scene unfold in front of her, her blue eyes taking it all in, but with that powder-brained ape having his hands on her, I'm feeling a sting between my ribs and I'm not sure what to do about it.

"And you," I say, slowly sauntering over to her. "I have to decide what to do with you, darling. It's my lack of foresight to think we wouldn't need two sets of chains."

"I say I take her down to the hold," Sterling grunts. "Put her in with the others. If she's worthless to the prince and he doesn't care if she lives or dies then let her provide for us in other ways."

I stare right into Sterling's void of a soul. I know exactly what he means about her *providing*. "You're not taking her anywhere. You're handing her over to me." He bristles and I cock my head. "I damn well mean it, baldy."

His lips open and he bares his teeth at me like a fucking animal. I know the rest of the crew is watching closely to see what I'm going to do. Is this when he's going to declare his mutiny? Will any of them follow his lead?

"First rule of the ship is that the captain gets the best of the goods," I go on and gesture to the princess.

"Actually, the rule is that all the treasure is doled out equally," I hear Thane say from behind me and I could kick him in the fucking shin for that.

"*After* the captain gets first pick," I remind them. "And I've already picked her as mine. Be happy with the vermin in the hold, Sterling. This one has my name on it."

Sterling snorts. "I don't see your name on her."

I know what he means. He's not being figurative and now I'm not either.

"You will," I tell him. I look to Lothar. "Before you start your welding, better get the iron ready." I turn to Cruz. "The rope please."

He tosses me a spool of rope while the princess stiffens under Sterling's grasp.

"Iron?" she asks, the fear finally finding her again.

Sterling just scowls while I motion impatiently for him to hand her over to me. "Mark my words," I tell him. "I'm marking *her*."

He growls at me, beady eyes flashing in contempt, and after a delay, shoves her toward me until she's falling into my arms.

"Hello, luv," I purr as I stare down at her. "Rescuing you once again."

I grab a tight hold of her and bring her to the stairs and down to the main deck below.

"How is this rescuing me?" she practically snarls, squirming under my hands.

"Believe me, darling, I'm the better option," I tell her. "And there's no one else here to save you. Your lovely prince certainly won't."

"The ship that attacked us, they were coming for me."

"The navy? Maybe they were, maybe they weren't. Doesn't matter now when we've left them far behind. Their ship will have to be scuttled soon and our ship can sustain a lot more than that feeble little show they gave us."

I pull her toward my quarters when she sticks her foot in between my ankles and I nearly trip, my grip loosening just for a moment, just enough for her to yank herself out of my grasp.

The sight of her scampering away awakens an instinct inside me and I can't help but smile to myself, always loving the chase.

She's at the foot of the stairs when I catch her. She falls onto the stairs with a cry and I'm flipping her over so she's on her back.

"You're a monster!" she says, struggling against me, but I quickly pull her arms up over her head, securing them with the rope that I've already attached to my waist. Can't be too careful now.

"A monster?" I repeat, pressing my body against hers until she can't even move an inch. "Tell me more, darling. I always fancy a compliment."

Her eyes flare with outrage, flashing to a luminescent teal for a moment. She's mesmerizing up close, the milky quality of her skin, the freckles across her delicate nose, those radiant eyes of her framed by thick black lashes, eyes that don't hold anything back. I swear I could read her like a book just by staring in her eyes. And right now, all she wants is to kill me.

I don't know what it is about a woman that wants me dead, but I swear nothing gets me harder.

"I saw what you did to Daphne! She's dead!"

Her eyes water for a moment and I almost feel sorry for her.

"I didn't kill her," I say calmly. Her anguish radiates outward, enveloping us.

"She said you were monsters! She looked like cattle waiting for the slaughter."

"I still didn't have anything to do with her death."

"But you would have, wouldn't you?"

I don't say anything to that. I get up and pull her to her feet and drag her along to my quarters, her hands now bound at her front. "I'm very sorry you lost your lady-in-waiting, Princess. I had no idea the bonds between the upper-class would be so strong."

"That's because you know nothing!"

"Aye, that's what my father used to say," I concede and bring her into my chambers, kicking the door closed after us.

She's looking around wildly for an escape, her gaze going to the windows, then to the weapons, but she's not getting very far this time.

"You do realize that even if you escape, there is no hope for you," I say as I pull her towards the cage in the corner. "This ship is going at a clip to leave our assailants behind. Soon you won't be able to see land. Nowhere to swim to, lass."

She plants her heels, trying to stay in place but it's no use. I'm forcing her in the cage and then, before she can try anything, I'm fastening both her hands and her feet to the bars with more rope.

"You're tying me up *in* a cage?" she cries out, pulling at the restraints.

"There's a point to it," I grumble. "You're going to want to stand as still as possible."

She turns her head to face me, wild-eyed. She's breathing hard, her chest heaving against the bars. "You think ravaging me is rescuing me? Just because it's by you and not that other man?"

I bite back my smile and come around behind her. I press myself against her backside until she's pressed against the cage, my cock already stiff against her arse, and I brush her loose tangled black hair from her shoulders and lean in until my mouth is at her ear. "You say *ravishing* as if it's a bad thing," I whisper, my voice thick. "Apparently you've never been ravished properly before."

Then I pull back. "Alas, you need a hot bath and some time with a bar of soap before I'd even think about ravishing you. You smell something awful, Princess."

The gasp of shock that comes out of her mouth makes me chuckle. Nothing will insult a lady more than telling her she smells.

"Then what are you doing?" she asks, and I lean down and gather the hem of her dirty ragged gown pulling it up until it's gathered at her waist. She gasps again, her legs now completely exposed.

"Marking you as mine," I tell her. Then I yell for Lothar. "Lothar, I'm ready!"

"No, no," she starts to say.

"I told you you're my property now. Do you think that word means nothing to me? I have to claim you if you want to be safe."

"Safe?!" she cries out.

"Aye, you may not understand our world much, but when something is yours, it belongs only to you. I have a special brand for occasions such as these."

Lothar appears in the room holding out an iron poker. At the end of it is my brand, not quite red-hot but it will do the job.

"Thank you," I tell him. "You mind coming in here and holding up her dress?"

"No, please," the princess pleads, yanking again at the restraints to no avail. She doesn't understand why I'm doing this and that's fine with me. It's not just a matter of possession, it's for her own good.

Lothar's usually impassive face twists into a wicked grin as he comes into the cage and hands me the poker. It's hot on my palm, burning into my skin, but I enjoy this particular pain. Perhaps she will too.

He goes behind her and holds her dress up gathered around her waist and now I take the iron and aim it at the fleshy part of the side of her hip.

"It will only hurt for a moment, luv," I tell her before pressing the brand into the skin.

She lets out a howl as it sizzles and I promptly remove the brand to admire my handiwork. Her skin is burned a bright red where my mark has been left behind: a skull and crossbones with my initials RB. Crude but elegant, in my opinion.

The princess is still whimpering so I tell Lothar to grab me a bottle of rum from the galley, as well as some apples and hardtack. While he goes, I head over to the trunk that belonged to the princess and rummage through it for a dress. They're all fancy, each composed of many layers which will need to be pinned on, none of which will do her any good on a ship. I pick a light blue one that has the least amount of frivolity. We like to dress well, but you still have to be practical at sea.

"Here," I say to her, bringing it over, along with new stays and a chemise. I toss it at her feet. "You'll want to change into something clean, I reckon."

"Go to hell," she seethes.

"Been there already," I tell her just as I see Lucas walking past on the main deck. "Lucas!" I yell after him. "Be a good lad and bring me a bucket of water, soap, and a washcloth."

He nods and runs off.

I turn back to the princess. "You can drink the water. Piss in it. Bathe in it. It's all up to you."

She just scowls at me, her features contorting into something fearsome and for a moment I almost see her as someone else. No, not someone else. *Something* else.

Unhuman.

I stare at her, trying to grab hold and dissect this curious feeling that sounds alarm bells in my gut. There's something not right about her. There's something inside of her that she keeps buried out of fear and I'm starting to see that whatever it is that lives in her and gnaws away at her bones is dying to come out and play.

"What?" she snaps.

I know I'm still staring at her openly and I don't give a wit.

I tilt my head. "Curious creature, aren't you? So much rage for such a small woman."

She frowns. She's short, but she's by no means a waif. She's got a lot of meat on her bones, which I appreciate heartily.

Lucas comes into the room, breaking my gaze.

"Here you go, Captain," he says placing the bucket of water at my feet and holds out a washcloth and a bar of soap.

"Thank you, nephew," I tell him and nod at him to run along. He does so, passing Lothar who has the goods from the galley gathered in a sack.

"Put the bag in the cell for the lady," I tell him.

Lothar puts it inside, giving the princess a leering look.

She snaps her teeth at him which surprises him and he's a hard fella to shock.

He turns to me and jerks his thumb at her. "She might be unhinged, this one."

"Aren't we all," I say as I dismiss him.

When he leaves, I take the bucket, soap and washcloth and put it in the corner of the cage beside the bag. Then I step out and lock the cage behind me with one of my skeleton keys that hangs from my belt.

"There," I tell her. "You have everything you could possibly need. You're mine now and you're safe."

Her eyes flash wildly in response to that. One day she'll understand.

I walk around over to the side where her legs and hands are tied to the bars. I take out my dagger and make quick work of cutting her loose from the bars so that she's entirely free.

"If you don't wish to use the bucket, I can always escort you to the privy. Perhaps you've had enough of humility for now."

I turn to leave my chambers when I hear a scraping sound and as I turn around to see what it is, I'm met with a bucket full of water right to my face, drenching me.

I close my eyes and let it cascade over me, spitting some out. Then I wipe my sopping hair off my face and give the princess a pointed look. She's holding the empty bucket in her hands, eyes wild, chest heaving with breath.

"Perhaps I needed a freshening up too," I tell her, spitting out another bit of water. "I thank you for that."

Then I give her a little bow, droplets of water coming off me as I do so, before I turn on my heel and leave my chambers, locking the door behind me and leaving her to stew.

TEN

Maren

I wake up to something licking my hand.

I lift my head, my body already stiffening, expecting to see one of the pirates on the ground beside me, about to do who knows what.

But what I see instead is the orange tabby cat from the other day. It stops licking my hand once it notices that I'm awake and sits back on its haunches, giving me a curious stare. Its eyes are the soft green of sea glass.

"Hello," I say to it.

"Mew," the cat responds.

"I suppose I should get up, shouldn't I?" I say to it, to which it meows again.

I groan and push myself up halfway, surveying the scene.

I'm lying on the floor of the cage, the bag of food still in the corner. The ground has dried from where I tossed the water through the bars and soaked the captain head to toe. I should regret it since I would have liked to have cleaned myself up and put on a new dress, but the look on his face was worth it. At any rate, if he deems my smell intolerable, then I'm going to revel in it out of spite.

That said, I do feel more filthy than I ever have before and I find myself gravitating toward the clean gown. I sit back, being careful not to put any pressure on where he branded me.

I can scarcely believe he did that. Or I can, it's just that his method of cruelty took me by surprise. I'm so used to being beaten and battered and called names, that to be branded with a hot iron was something that took me off-guard. Frankly, I was expecting something worse, especially when he humiliated me by taking up my dress and baring my bottom and legs to him. And yet, even though I felt his lust for me once again, he didn't act on it. I suppose my current state of uncleanliness deterred him and saved me from that type of savagery.

Though he seems to think that by branding me and keeping me in a cage, he's the one saving me. I don't understand it. He's the captain and it's clear that everyone on the ship, save that Sterling beast, respects and listens to him. Surely Sterling would know to keep his hands off me if the captain told him to. And yet it seemed like branding me was the only way to "claim" me.

It doesn't really matter though. The way that pirates do things are different than what anyone civilized might do. They act according to their own code and there seems to be cultural differences within their own Brethren. Perhaps by the time this voyage is over I'll have learned a thing or two.

The thought depresses me. I pull my blue dress toward me and hold it up to my face, feeling the clean fabric, pressed by the servants right before we left on our travels. The dress smells like Ferdinand's palace, like linen and florals and the incense the locals would light.

Daphne.

The smell brings forth the image of Daphne as she was, always pleasant and smiling and terribly funny at times.

Then the horror of seeing her dead hits me like bricks and I blink back the tears this time, determined not to cry. The salt from my tears reminds me too much of home and all I've lost since then.

I breathe in deeply, keeping the dress pressed to my face, wishing I could be somewhere else.

But where would I even go? What is there for me?

Home. Keep your head on Limonos. Keep your focus on getting across the Pacific alive. Let Limonos be your compass.

"Mew?"

I bring the dress off my face to see the cat staring at me.

"You think so?" I say, giving the cat a bit of a smile. Once upon a time I could communicate with all the creatures that lived under the sea.

Which does make me pause.

What if I still could?

"Mew," the cat says and seems to nod.

I am most definitely imagining that.

"Can you understand me?" I ask it, my voice barely a whisper. Even though I'm alone in the captain's quarters, I still feel a tad silly for talking out loud to a cat.

The cat raises its paw.

I still don't believe it.

"Could you go and..." I look around the room for something. "Knock that crystal off the bookshelf."

The cat cranes its head and looks at the bookshelf where the captain has a row of crystals displayed like some fortune teller's shop. Then it looks back to me with an unimpressed look on its face.

I hold my breath and wait. Even if the cat could understand me, it is still a cat and they don't listen to anyone. The queen had a pair of Siamese cats that ruled the palace and terrorized everyone. I didn't see them often and I never got the impression they understood me. Then again, I never tried to talk to them. Humans would deem that crazy.

"Meow," the cat says lazily, then turns around and pads over to the shelf and jumps up on it. It goes right over to first crystal it sees, a black tourmaline tower, and with a tap-tap-tap of its paw, it pushes it off.

The crystal clatters to the deck but doesn't break on the wood planks.

The cat does understand me!

I look over to the row of weapons the captain has. The cat follows my gaze. It couldn't bring me a pistol or a sword but maybe it could take a small dagger in its mouth and—

The sound of the door unlocking interrupts my thought and the cat jumps down from the shelf and scampers away to the corner, hiding behind a chair just as the door swings open and the captain steps in.

I want to ignore him. I want to look away. But he has this strangely compelling and commanding presence about him that I find it hard to keep my gaze away, even when I'm filled with hatred for him.

It doesn't help that he's handsome. He doesn't have the refined blue blood of Aerik which shows in his smooth skin and stiff posturing, but what the captain has is both rugged and shadowy. Enigmatic. His jaw is sharp under his beard, chin strong, his nose distinctive but doesn't overpower his face. Lips that are full and expressive. His low dark brows give a brooding quality to his dusky blue eyes, yet even though he looks dangerous—even though he *is* dangerous—there's always a twinkle to them. Though it speaks more to his wickedness than to his frivolity.

The most mysterious thing about him is the lack of scarring he has on his face. He doesn't have the weathered sea face of a sailor, or the marks and blemishes of someone who has no doubt been involved with many skirmishes. The pirates I've heard stories about all have missing eyes covered with eye patches and scars running down their faces or missing limbs. His crew all seem very intact and rather fresh-looking.

Because they're monsters, I hear Daphne's voice in my head. *All of them.*

And yet I was a monster once too.

"And how are we this morning, your ladyship?" the captain says as he strides over to me.

"This morning?" I exclaim.

A corner of his lips curls into a crooked smile. "You mean you don't know how long you slept for?"

I blink. The last thing I remember was sitting back down in the corner of the cage after I threw the water at him. I must have fallen asleep but I didn't think I'd slept *that* long.

"And you haven't even touched your food," he says, eyeing the bag. "Well, if you don't mind, I might have to take the rum back. I thought it would help you with the pain, emotional and, well, otherwise," he nods at me, alluding to the brand, "but…"

He crouches down and reaches through the bars for the bag, sifting through it for the bottle, and before I know what's happening I'm launching forward, my finger splayed out and I dig my nails into his forearm, deep enough to draw blood.

He yelps and withdraws his arm, holding it to his chest.

"Aye, alright, Princess, you can keep the rum."

"You deserve that and more," I tell him.

The truth is, I acted out of a much older instinct. It was as if I had claws again. My fingernails are short and stubby and only did minor damage, but still I'm surprised that I was able to even break the skin.

I almost apologize.

Almost.

I swallow it down instead.

"I'm merely claiming what's mine," I add.

His brows raise, wrinkling his forehead. "Me? Or the rum?"

"The rum," I say coldly.

"It's all yours then," he says, gesturing to it. "My apologies for even thinking otherwise."

I narrow my eyes at him. "So are you saying that I was asleep all night here in the corner of this cage and you were in your bed over there?"

Another hint of a smile. "Aye," he says.

"And I'm to believe you just stayed there and didn't…"

"Come over here and pester you? No. You were knackered, Princess, but I don't doubt you would have awakened and plunged your little claws into me had I even the thought of touching you. Which I didn't."

I mull over that for a moment. I believe him. I was tired but I'm also so on edge that my instincts would have woke me had he come near me at all. At the very least, I would have heard the cage open.

I guess I had been through so much that I slept like the dead.

And he's still watching me, that intense look in his eyes ever-present.

"Need an escort to the privy?"

"I don't need an escort," I retort. But the moment he mentions the toilet, I realize I really have to use it. I know most sailors use the "head" at the front of the ship, which affords them no privacy at all, but on the royal ship, Aerik and I and some of the servants had private toilets to use. I'm hoping this ship isn't that much different.

Regardless, I'm not going to do my business in a bucket with him here. I may have lost a lot of pride, but I still have some.

"But you'll have an escort nonetheless," he says. "I'll stay outside the door and keep you on a leash. Just in case you decide to go out the window. Just remember we are very far from land and I've seen you in the water. You're not very good at swimming."

He has no idea how much that last sentence irks me.

He goes to the table in the middle of the room where a spool of rope is and notices the knocked over crystal. He stoops down to pick it up and gives me a curious look. I don't say anything.

"Skip," he says by way of explanation. "Always up to trouble."

"Skip?"

"The cat," he says as he puts the crystal back on the shelf.

"You named the cat Skip? As in the skipper? Not the most original name for a cat on a ship."

"Listen, we were calling him *Cat* for a few years there. We aren't always known for our originality."

He comes over and unlocks the cage door with his set of skeleton keys he has clipped to his breeches. "Now do I need to tie you or will you—"

Before he can finish the question I wind up and punch him right in the face again. For the second time, the feeling of my knuckles smashing into his nose sends a murderous thrill up my spine.

He gives out a cry of pain and surprise and while I make a feeble attempt to run past him, he reaches out with his one hand, taking a firm grip of my elbow, while his other covers his nose.

"Did you really think you'd have any chance of escape?"

"Not really," I admit. "I just wanted to punch you again."

"Feel better?" he asks, wiggling his face around, grimacing in discomfort. He notices the small smile on my lips. "I guess you do. Well, Princess, perhaps we can be considered even now."

I give him an incredulous look. "You going to let me brand you on your rear, then?"

He gives me a salacious grin. "If that's what tickles your fancy."

Oh, rats. He'd probably just enjoy it, wouldn't he?

He removes his hand and wipes a bit of blood from under his nostrils.

"How is my nose?"

"Still there, unfortunately," I mutter.

"All this sleep seems to have put some pep in your step. That's a good sign, darling. You'll be one of us before long."

"I'll never be one of you," I tell him in an icy tone, my gaze matching it.

"But why be a princess, when you could be a pirate?" He pauses, bringing me so I'm pressed right up against his chest. His chin dips as he peers at me, his voice becoming rich and husky. "Think about it, luv. No society to adhere to, no rules to be beholden to. You'd be a free woman, free to do what you want, when you want. Act any way you wish. No matter how…dark or depraved."

I feel myself falling forward into his eyes, like a maelstrom at sea.

I have to close them forcefully, severing whatever strange pull he has on me.

"I've fallen for lies once before and I'm still paying for it," I admit, keeping my eyes shut. "There is no freedom for a woman, especially a woman like me."

"A woman like you? The very one that's struck me in the face twice, tripped me up, and driven her nails into my flesh so hard that she's drawn blood? I think that woman is a force to be reckoned with. She just needs someone to set her free."

"And it won't be you," I whisper, because he's right. He's so very right. I feel my past clawing up through me, wanting more than anything to be set free again. Free to become what I once was. I may not be a force to be reckoned with now, only because he doesn't know the monster I was before. That Syren, she's the one he's talking about. He just doesn't know the half of it.

"Well," he says, clearing his throat, his grip loosening slightly. "Whoever sets you free, I hope I'm around to see it."

I can't help my acidic smile as I open my eyes and gaze up at him. "If you are, I'll be sure to kill you first."

He nearly beams at that, as if I've given him the greatest compliment. It makes his eyes dance. "Even over your husband? Yo-ho, I consider that high praise. Now come on before Sam decides she needs to use the privy too."

He pulls me along, though not as roughly as before, perhaps because I'm not being as obstinate as usual. I do have to use the facilities, badly now.

He takes me out of the quarters and to a room just outside. It's built into the side of the ship and consists of a seat with a hole in it. There's a row of narrow windows that are open, the sea breeze flowing inside and I'm trying to calculate if I can break through them and escape. I believe him when he says there's no land around to swim to, but it might be worth the risk.

But the individual windowpanes are too small to fit through, especially with my ample chest and rear, and fastened by metal bars that I'm not strong enough to break.

The captain closes the door behind me and leaves me to my business and I wish I could stay inside here all day and just hide and ponder, but I know the captain is waiting outside, giving me as little privacy as possible by rapping on the door every few minutes.

When I finally emerge he gives me a look of exaggerated impatience and grabs my arm just when someone runs halfway down the stairs and yells, "Bones! You better come look at this!"

He looks at the door to his chambers, probably calculating how long it will take to put me away, then decides against it and brings me over to the stairs and up them to where Cruz, his first mate, is.

"What is it?" the captain asks as he brings me up to the deck and Cruz hands him a spyglass.

"We spotted them," he says.

"Spotted who?" I ask, but no one is paying me any attention. Instead, most of the crew are all huddled on the foredeck passing another spyglass around.

The captain takes me over there and the crew parts for him. They all give me a passing glance as we slip through, not unkind, just curious. I'm suddenly very aware of how awful I must look, dirty and smelly, apparently, and how clean and well-put together they look by contrast.

"Where are they?" the captain asks the man already looking through the spyglass. He lets go of me and rests his elbows on the rail beside the man and puts his own spyglass to his eye.

"Straight ahead," the other pirate says.

I look around them, scanning the horizon and trying to see a ship but I don't spot anything. The horizon is an unwavering line, the sea calm and as blue as the sky above, only deeper.

"I see," the captain says.

"See what?" I ask. I'd wager I have better eyesight than anyone in the crew but no spyglass can make a ship appear where there isn't one.

"The princess asks too many questions," one of the crew says, which makes another one laugh.

The captain lowers his spyglass and looks to the man beside him. It's only now that I realize how similar they look. They could be brothers. In fact, he did call that boy from earlier his nephew.

"We should be able to catch them at the islands, providing they make a stop," the captain says.

"You know they have to stop there," the man says gruffly. "The sea witch always keeps them on a short leash."

"Sea witch?" I say my heart nearly stopping.

Finally the captain looks at me. "Are you going to stop?"

I raise my brows. "Now that you've uttered the words sea witch, no I don't think I will. What sea witch? What's her name?"

The captain balks as he eyes me. "Her name? What a strange question."

"It's Nerissa," the woman pirate speaks up. "The island is her home. It's how she controls the skeleton crew."

I turn to her in gratitude. "Thank you," I tell her emphatically. "Nice to be on the same page."

She shrugs. "I've been in your shoes, lass," she says. "This lot of pigheads love to ignore a woman, even when they're balls deep inside her. Or especially so."

Both the captain and the other man turn around to stare at her aghast.

"What?!" the woman exclaims with a heavy sigh. "It's true. Except for you, luv." She gently taps her boot against the other pirate's calf. He rolls his eyes in response.

"You don't seem too surprised about sea witches," the captain comments. "Or a skeleton crew, for that matter."

"I've heard of sea witches," I say carefully. "But I'll admit I don't know what you mean by a skeleton crew."

"It's a long story," he says. "And a story the likes of you would never believe."

"You should try me," I say.

"I like the mouth on her," the woman pirate says, her admiration obvious even to me, and I glance at her pretty face. "Look here, lass. There's a lot that you won't believe while you're on this ship, the least of which are witches and skeletons. But they aren't even the most fantastical things you'll hear of. There's one thing that they have that this crew wants more than anything else."

"And what's that?" I ask.

"A mermaid."

ELEVEN

Maren

"A mermaid?" I ask dumbly. If my heart stopped at the idea of sea witches, I feel like I'm going to drop dead at the mention of mermaids.

"Like I said, lass," the woman says, "it's all fantastical. But time will prove to you how much magic really exists out here at sea, once you know how to look for it."

A mermaid.

A *Syren*.

"What...why do you want a mermaid?"

Silence fills the air. There's only the sound of the bow sluicing through the water and the steady beat of wind in the sails.

Finally the captain clears his throat and turns to face me, looking relaxed as he leans with one arm on the railing. "Mermaids are valuable, darling. Very valuable."

"To the world at large or just to you?"

He barks out a laugh. "Astute. The world at large doesn't believe in mermaids, don't you know that?"

"But you do."

"Aye we do. It's not a matter of belief, you'll soon see to that. They exist. But I'm not about to argue the points of nature with you," he says, giving me a dismissive wave.

"I believe it," I say quickly, and he lifts his chin as he glances at me. "Tell me more."

He exchanges a glance with the other man. "What do you say, Quartermaster? Should I tell her more?"

So the other man is the quartermaster.

The quartermaster shrugs. "No point asking me when you're clearly going to do it anyway."

The captain narrows his gaze at him then looks back to me, grabbing my arm and handing his spyglass over to the woman. "Let me know when we're close to the islands. I'll be in my chambers."

He pulls me along and I wish my legs weren't so unsteady in general. Right now they barely work at all, my gait uneven. He glances down at me in quick look of a concern. "You hurt your leg?"

I shake my head. I most definitely wouldn't explain it to him now.

"So, tell me more about the witches and mermaids," I say as he leads me down the stairs to the main deck.

"So you can humor me?" he asks.

"No. Because I want to know more."

"How about we discuss it over dinner?" he asks, his voice dipping down to something low and gravelly. It makes the hairs stand up at the back of my neck. He pulls me to him just outside of his chambers. "No apples and hardtack. I'm talking a proper dinner. Hot food. Wine."

I want to stay strong and say no but I'm already drooling at the thought and my stomach pinches hungrily, overriding anything that I want to say out of spite.

"What kind of food?" I ask, unable to help it.

"Boar," he says. "Fatty crispy boar with all the drippings. And any fish you could desire. Grilled, poached, you name it. We could finish off with a nice cup of coffee."

I let out a quiet moan, imagining the taste, the feeling of a full belly.

"Don't let your pride deprive you of this, Princess," he says to me. Then he brings me inside and over to the cage. "I'll get you another bucket to bathe with. You'll have all the privacy in the world, and if you want to throw it at me again, be my guest. I rather enjoyed it. I imagined it was a…release of sorts for you."

I don't have to read between the lines to get what he means. I don't think I ever need to do that. What he means is always clear on his face, the heat in his eyes, the part of his lips.

I swallow hard and nod as he puts me back in the cage. The thought of bathing and putting on my clean gown wins.

Once I'm locked inside he comes back with a full bucket of water and puts it back in the cage with me.

"I'll return this evening," he says with a wink and then he's gone.

Water had never felt so good.

It wasn't just about cleansing myself of the dirt and blood and filth—though the soap that was made from olive oil and ash and a sprinkling of herbs worked divine—it was that my body physically feels weaker without water. It's as if despite not being a Syren anymore, the blood in my body remembers that I once lived under the sea and had water over my skin at all times.

When I was finally clean and smelling of the fresh herbs and oils that fragranced the soap, I slipped on the dress. My stays were dirty so I washed them in the leftover water. I made sure to keep Nill's shark tooth necklace close by, sticking it in an inner pocket in the dress's bodice. The clean material over my clean skin made my head feel clearer, like I could think for the first time.

And I have a lot to think about.

There's a sea witch. Not Edonia, but one called Nerissa. She lives at some island that controls a skeleton crew, whatever that may be. And she, or the crew, have a mermaid, which is somehow valuable to the crew of the *Nightwind*.

But valuable in what way, I don't know. All I know is that they want her. Or him. When they use the term mermaid they're always talking about women, but us Syrens consist of both genders as well as a third one, which is a combination of both.

Even though I'm absolutely starving for meat and proper food, the thing I'm looking forward to the most with this dinner is the fact that I'll have the captain one-on-one in a (hopefully) equal setting for some time. Time enough to get answers to all my questions.

The captain keeps me in suspense, which I'm starting to believe is on purpose. It's only when my stomach is really eating itself and I'm growing a little desperate that he comes into the chambers.

He stops in front of the cage and looks me up and down.

"Well, well, well. There's the princess looking lovely. Feel better?"

"I'll feel better when I have something to eat," I tell him.

He looks at the apples and hardtack on the floor. "Beggars can't be choosers, I suppose, though I guess you're not begging now. I rather liked it when you did. Now if you'll excuse me, I'm going to put on a new shirt. A seagull shat on this one."

I start to laugh at that but then he pulls his shirt over his head and the laughter gets caught in my throat. Though I'd noticed the shape and build of the captain's body before, absently noted down in the back of my mind, seeing him bare-chested in front of me brings my focus entirely to his form. Though I was only sixteen when I stopped being a Syren and my feminine urges were just starting to explode, our whole species revolves around hunting men—for food and for more lustful purposes. I may not know much of this world, but in the underwater world, no species can match ours for our sexual appetite. From the way my sisters would gossip rosy-cheeked in hushed tones, from how certain elders would describe it with salacious details, it wasn't just that we hunted men for their hearts and organs—we used them for our own sexual gains before we killed them. We seduced them, bedded them, ate them. Our lust was only matched by our hunger.

So the sight of the captain shirtless makes my blood run hot, a tightness forming at my core that wasn't there before. My eyes can't help but dance along his form, drinking him in like a potent ale. His muscles are lean and sinewy and yet there's a density to them that hints at his true power, power I've felt before as he's handled me. His shoulders have considerable breadth to them, hard rounded muscles leading to thick biceps and firm and wide chest, making his tightly muscled abdomen narrow to his hips like an inverted triangle.

My admiration for his body catches me by surprise and I'm both angry at myself and embarrassed for noticing, for even finding him enticing. I avert my eyes.

"Never seen a man in his birthday suit before?" he asks.

"You're not quite in your birthday suit," I say, staring down at the hem of my dress.

"Say the word and I could be…"

I glance up at him quickly, in time to see a wicked grin flit across his lips before he turns his back to me.

Again, confronted with such an expansive plane of muscle and bare skin, my instinct is to stare. No, it's to do more than just stare. My fingers twitch like I want to touch him, run my fingers down his back.

Gods, I chastise myself, pinching my eyes shut. *This man branded his bloody name into your skin. Finding him attractive is the worst idea you've ever had. Nearly as bad as trading in your fins for the love of a blasted prince.*

I feel steely cold resolve flood through my veins. The thing about being a Syren, even a former one, is that though our hungry appetites can lead us astray, we also have unflinching detachment when we need it.

And I need it.

It doesn't take much to remind me that men are nothing but devils and the only thing he's good for at this point is information.

When the captain has slipped another shirt back on, this one black and half-unbuttoned, my composure has been regained. I stare at him impassively, waiting to be released from the cage like a patient bird.

He saunters over to me, his movements languid and steady. I've always noticed he's moved with a lot of grace, a surprising amount for a man of his size and stature, like he glides just above the floor, even though his boots give a hard echo with each step. He fishes out the keys and unlocks the cage, opening it wide with a flourish of his arm.

"Your dining room this evening," he announces, even though the table is bare. "I see your disappointment. My apologies if I don't have all the proper tableware out. Though I do consider myself to be a gentleman, our standards for pomp and decorum have taken a dive since going rogue."

My eyes flit to the weapons again but he just makes a disagreeable noise deep in his throat. "And don't tell me you're thinking about attacking me with one of my own swords again. It's a game you will not win, Princess."

He's right. If my legs weren't so unstable, perhaps I could make it there before him, but he is exceedingly fast and strong and doesn't think twice about grabbing sharp blades with his bare hands. I've learned my lesson before.

Though perhaps if I got close to him when he least suspected it, with a bottle of rum or wine within reach, I could get him over the head with it.

And then what? So I knock him out? There's nowhere for me to go. In the end, no matter what scenario I pull from my head, I'm trapped.

"Sit," he says, pulling out a chair for me beside the head of the table.

I give him a discerning glance. He really insists on such a charade, doesn't he? As if he has any real manners at all.

"If you please," he adds and I sit down reluctantly, gathering in my dress, and he takes his place beside me at the head of the table.

The door to his chambers opens and a very tall gangly man steps in, long blond hair swept back in a braid and a softness to his eyes that the other pirates seem to lack, marred only by a long scar down one side of his face. He's carrying a roasted boar on the plate, or at least the bottom half of one.

The man sets it down on the middle of the table while the boy from earlier, the captain's nephew, runs in with bowls and forks and dishtowels, placing it beside the boar before he runs back out of the room.

"Sorry it's not the boar's head," the captain says to me. "That's Drakos' favorite, and with the way he dislodged your husband yester-day, he more than deserves it." He nods at the man. "Sedge, make sure you have your fair share, too. No rationing tonight. We need to keep up our strength for what's to come."

Sedge nods and motions with his hands quickly.

The captain eyes his hands and then says, "Yes, a bottle or two of the Madeira wine, thank you."

"Can he not speak?" I ask as Sedge leaves.

The captain reaches over and hands me my plate and fork. "No. Never could. Can write some and talk using his hands. Just a little…I wouldn't call him slow, he's quite bright, but lucky."

"Lucky?" I repeat, the bitterness coating my tongue as I remember what it was like to go without a voice.

"Aye," he says, spearing a piece of meat with his fork and putting it on my plate. "Maybe not so much being a mute, but in that the way he looks at the world reminds me of my…well…" he clears his throat and drifts off, now spooning some cooked tropical fruits onto my plate, a sauce of sorts.

Reminds you of your…? I want to ask. From the sudden darkness in his eyes, I can tell it's something he doesn't want to talk about.

Sedge comes back in with a dusty bottle of wine and two goblets, placing them in front of the captain. He stares at him with an expectant look and though Sedge doesn't look childish in any way, there is that softness in his eyes I saw earlier and the slightest hint of a smile above a round chin.

"That will be all Sedge," he says and Sedge nods, going out the door and closing it behind him.

"How did he end up as part of the crew?" I ask, gingerly picking up my fork as if I hadn't held one in years.

"I killed his family," the captain says it so simply that for a moment I don't think I'm hearing him right.

"Oh," I say, putting my fork back down.

He gives me a quick smile. "You're disappointed in me, luv. You shouldn't be."

"Because you're a pirate."

"Because sometimes we do what we must to survive."

"You don't have to kill people…" but the moment I say that, I stop and think of what I am. A killer like him. Maybe I never took a life when I was a Syren, but I eventually would have. I was raised to be one.

"But sometimes you do," he says. "And anyway, I killed them and regretted it when I discovered him, still alive and hiding from me. So I took him. He was my first brand."

My fork clatters against the plate. "You took him and *branded* him?"

He shrugs. "He became my property."

"He's a human," I implore him.

"Yes. He is a human. And the world is changing, Princess. If I hadn't taken Sedge, he would have died. There would have been no one to look after him. Society shuns those that are different. They refuse them any care. So I took him on the ship. We had no need for a cook but it turns out he was rather good at it, something he was allowed to do in his life before. He took a shine to it and to us. Perhaps because we treated him like a normal human being and not a child."

"But you still branded him like he's livestock." I'm unable to keep the disgust out of my tone.

"I told you that you wouldn't understand. But it was for his own safety too."

My eyes go big. "You have men ravishing each other on this ship?"

"Ravishing?" He lets out a large bark of a laugh. "Oh. Well. Yes. There's some of that. Wanted by both parties, mind you. We don't think about things like that too deeply here."

Men bedding men. Though we had such in Limonos, I knew how taboo it was to even speak of the sin of sodomy in this human world.

But clearly this was a ship of sin.

"Now eat up," he says, tapping his fork on my plate. "Or you aren't getting any wine."

The conversation stole my appetite, but it doesn't take long for it to return, especially as he uncorks the wine and pours it into the goblets. I eat forkful after forkful of the crispy pig meat with the juice and fat inside, the fruit sauce a wonderful complement. Seems Sedge is just as good or better than the cooks the royal palace employed.

For a moment I remember Aerik. He's not eating like this tonight.

"Where is Aerik?" I ask, my voice going quiet as I swallow.

The captain pauses, a forkful of meat halfway to his mouth.

"He's back in the cell," he says, a dry twist to his lips. "That man never stopped complaining about the chains. Lothar is quick with welding, thankfully." He pauses, studying me. "If it pleases you, I can make sure your prince has a good meal tonight."

"It wouldn't please me," I say slowly. "But it's probably the right thing to do."

"Right by whom? That man deserves everything he's getting, you know that, don't you?" His voice drops to a low murmur and I'm surprised to see anger flickering in his eyes.

"He took care of me when I needed it," I say and give him a warning look to just leave it at that and grab my glass of wine, suddenly wanting to get drunk.

The wine is just as good as the food, dry and sweet at the same time, flowing down my throat with ease. I drink up and up, my taste-buds coming alive, my thirst insatiable, until I remember the company I'm keeping.

The captain is staring at me with an expression that is both tense and eager, like he's waiting for something...more.

"Sorry," I say, forgetting who I am for a moment and I put the wine down, using the cloth to wipe my lips.

"Don't be," he says. "I think you forgot I was in the room for a moment. I like that uninhibited side of you."

My stomach growls, wanting more, but I have new questions now on top of the ones from earlier.

I take a deep breath, trying to hide any sense of stakes related to the question.

"Tell me about the mermaid."

TWELVE

Ramsay

Mermaid.

Say the word and most people will laugh, lumping the idea together with unicorns and griffins. Say the word to a sailor and that laughter will take a nervous slant. Most sailors, whether they be pirates, part of the navy, merchant crew, or an old man pulling up crab nets outside a shanty town, won't entertain such nonsense until you get them drunk. Until they're sailing through uncharted waters in the dark and they hear the siren's call, until they're shipwrecked on a shoal and feel eyes watching them from the depths. Then they might tell you a different story. They might tell you that mermaids are real. They might tell you that they're demons, no different than the Kraken. True monsters of the deep.

And yet here is the princess, lips colored red from wine, staring at me with desperate curiosity in her eyes. She either wants to believe in them…or she already does.

What has she seen during her voyages at sea? Mermaids were more commonly found in the Pacific, not the Atlantic, if you believe all the tales, which I do. But while the world feels small at times, each unexplored corner slowly becoming colonized, the ocean is forever a mystery. The surface doesn't even hint at what lies below. Much like the company I'm keeping.

I finish chewing and put my fork down, then swallow a gulp of the fine wine before pouring her another glass. Sedge better come back soon with another bottle.

I gaze at her eyes, that impossibly bright blue shining beneath dark lashes. They remind me of something, the sheen that the water takes in certain areas at certain times of night, glowing with luminescent particles. They're so enticing that they keep my focus on them and not the full swell of her breasts in that gown. Her hair is still wet from being washed, in thick coils around her shoulders, shining like ink and if I didn't know any better I'd say she looked taken from the sea herself.

But that is a ridiculous notion. Mermaids don't have legs, they don't walk on land. She is something else, I'm sure, I just don't know what. What I do know is that by the time we reach Acapulco, I will have her figured out in every way possible.

"What would you like to know?" I ask her, adjusting my seat as I try to will my erection away. My damn cock is always speaking up when she's around, and she looks especially stunning tonight.

"You said mermaids are valuable. How? Do they end up in fish tanks?"

"They do in a way. They have gills to breathe through, like a fish, but they also have lungs like us, letting them stay above water for long periods of time. But we have found that when you take them out of the water, they need to be kept wet or they'll dry out and die. A very grisly-looking scene."

Her eyes are wide and she's gone so completely still that I fear she's had a stroke.

"Princess?" I prod.

She swallows hard. An odd look of indignation comes over her features. "You've captured them before?"

"I thought that was apparent. It's what we do."

"You're pirates!"

"We're the Brethren of the Blood and we plunder the high seas. We take what we can and we use it or trade it. No different than any other pirate."

"But what do you need a mermaid for?" she cries out.

"I reckon you ought to calm down, your ladyship," I tell her. "We aren't hunting kittens and puppies. Mermaids aren't the delicate beautiful women of the sea that you've heard about. They're predators. They eat the hearts of men. They seduce them, fuck them, and tear them apart. I've seen it with my own eyes. You'd find more mercy with a lion."

Her nostrils flare as she breathes heavily. "You've seen it?" she asks, her tone strained. "You've seen them kill?"

I nod, not particularly wanting to talk about it. "Only once, but it was enough. Comrade of mine slipped into the sea while we hauled one on board. The mermaids that had been trying to free her attacked him. In only seconds he was shredded finer than this meat." I tap my fork on the pork on the plate.

She doesn't look disgusted in the least. Instead she still wears this look of passion on her pretty face. "Why do you hunt them? That's...barbaric."

"They're barbaric if you ask me."

"It sounds like they kill in order to survive!"

I shake my head. "No. I know the difference between killing to survive and killing for fun, believe me. There are plenty of fish in the sea, as they say. There are things for them to eat. Instead, I think they hunt men out of sport, much like men hunt the fox with their hounds."

"So you take them out of revenge."

"We take them because they are valuable."

"But *why*?"

I'm not sure how best to answer this. I guess the truth is often the easiest.

"Mermaid blood is potent. It's magic. It gives you magic, for lack of a better word."

"You drink their blood?"

I grin at her. "Does this displease you?"

She scrunches up her nose, looking disgusted, then that disgust levels out into fear. Silence falls between us and a strange thread of tension dances in the air. Oddly enough, I don't want her to think any different of me, but it's inevitable when you tell a human you drink mermaid blood.

Sedge breaks up the tension by coming into the cabin with another bottle of wine, very much-needed too.

He leaves and I uncork the new bottle, pouring us both a glass. I push hers toward her. "Here. Drink up."

She gives me a sullen look in response.

"You might hate me less if you're drunk," I add.

"I couldn't hate you more," she says stiffly.

"Good to know there's a threshold," I say. I drink down half my glass before I turn my attention back to the pig. I don't need to eat anymore, I wasn't hungry to begin with, but the taste is too good to abstain.

"So it gives you magic," she finally says. "Like a witch."

"Something like that," I tell her.

"What about this Nerissa? The sea witch. What can you tell me about her? And the skeleton crew?"

I'm grateful she's dropped the subject of mermaids since it bothered her so.

"Sea witches roam the seas the same as the mermaids do. I believe sea witches are the only known enemy to them. I suppose you could say they're our enemy too. They're a lot more duplicitous and monstrous than the normal witches you find on land."

She tilts her head curiously. "And you've dealt with both types of witches?"

I nod. "Aye." I lick the wine off my lips and debate whether to tell her more. She compels me even when she's angry. Maybe even more so. "I was married to a witch."

Her hand shakes and she nearly spills her wine. "You were married to a witch?"

"It was a long time ago."

She lowers her goblet. "What happened?"

I take in a sharp breath through my nose, hardening myself for the response. "She died during childbirth. Even witches can't save themselves sometimes. They're just human in the end."

Her fingers go to her mouth, pressing against her lips and she gasps softly. "I'm so sorry."

"Yes. So am I. So was everyone. Venla was well-liked, despite what she was. She was a good witch. And she made a dauntless pirate."

"And the child?" she asks quietly.

My heart twists in my chest and I try to smile over the pain. "She lived. Hilla. She was a beautiful little girl."

"Oh." Her eyes shift to a soft blue, a sad blue, no doubt picking up on the past tense.

"Yes," I say, clearing the thickness from the back of my throat. "She died when she was eight. I raised her myself, well, with the help of the crew, much like we've done with Henry and Lucas. I did the best I could for her and she was such a happy child here despite never knowing her mother. But looking back, I know I shouldn't have raised her on this ship, not with the world the way it is."

"Was it the navy or...?"

"A sea witch," I tell her, my tone taking on a razor edge. "A sea witch that controls a great beast."

Her eyes widen slightly. "What beast?"

"The Kraken."

She gasps in response.

"Before you ask, yes they are real too," I tell her. "They are horribly real. And they killed my little girl before my eyes. Now all I want is my revenge."

"On this Nerissa?" she asks, her voice rising. "Or on the Kraken?"

"As far as I know, Nerissa didn't have anything to do with Hilla's death and can't control the Kraken. What she does control is a curse that she inflicts on sailors who sail too close to her islands. The skeleton crew are victims of her unfortunate curse. Humans turned into skeletons for eternity. The only way they can ever appear human again is by finding magic of their own..."

"Mermaid blood."

"Exactly." I have another sip of my wine. "So they hunt them too, even though the magic doesn't last very long for them. They're a mad lot, you see. You would be too if you'd been reduced to a walking corpse for the rest of your life."

She thinks that over for a moment, then asks in a low voice, "So what witch does control the Kraken?"

"Her name is Edonia."

The princess's eyes go frightfully large then quickly back to normal, her face turning blank.

"You know her," I surmise.

She gives her head a shake. "No. I don't know any witches."

"Then why did your skin pale like you'd seen a ghost?"

"Perhaps all your tales are spooking me."

The lady is lying. I've been around her enough now to know that nothing seems to spook her. That's fine. She can save her secrets. I'll uncover them sooner than later.

"So what is your plan then?" she asks, straightening up in her seat and taking on an air of false dignity, eyes focused on her plate.

"We spotted their ship yesterday for a brief moment. They are being pulled back to the islands." She frowns in confusion and I go on. "Nerissa keeps them on a leash, letting them cast off only when she feels generous. Eventually she will pull them back to the islands, like a magic rope. Their ship moves as fast as the *Nightwind* when she's controlling it and the crew are at her mercy. It truly is a ghost ship."

"But if we're going to the islands, where this sea witch is who curses humans, isn't she going to do the same to us?"

I shake my head. "No. She won't. She can't touch us."

"Why not?"

I run my tongue over my teeth. "Magic."

"From the last time you killed a mermaid and drank her blood?"

"From my wife, if you must know."

"She gave you magic."

"Once upon a time. She even wrote me a book of magic. Some might say we wrote it together. But it was made for me and my crew.

She knew how truly dangerous these seas were." I pause, sucking back on my lip for a moment. "She knew how spiteful her sister was."

"Sister?"

"Half sister. Edonia is Venla's half sister. And oh did she hate that her blood got together with the likes of me."

"So…" she trails off, her lips downturned.

"So killing Hilla was her revenge, I suppose," I say. "Edonia took my girl. And she took my book. The one that Venla made for me."

The princess's mouth opens for a moment, then shuts. She presses her lips together for a second before saying, "I'm sorry."

I don't want her pity, though I can feel her empathy. It rises out from her like a warm embrace. It's a nice feeling.

"Yes. Well. Suffice to say, I want my revenge now too. On Edonia. And with only scraps of magic left behind from the book, we need mermaid's blood to truly defeat the sea witch and survive the Kraken. You understand now, don't you?"

"I do," she says solemnly.

"And while we have had luck in the past with hunting mermaids, we haven't seen any for a very long time. It's like the species is becoming sparse. I'm not sure why that is, they don't have any predators."

"Except the sea witch."

"Aye."

"And you."

"*Aye.* And us, but not for a very long time. Hence why we are going after the skeleton crew. If they have a mermaid on board, it will be easy pickings for us."

Her gaze darkens. "How do you know the mermaid is still alive?"

"I don't. But only fresh blood will do. Doesn't work if they're dead."

"So you're going to attack the skeleton crew and steal their mermaid and bring her aboard the *Nightwind.*"

"Precisely."

"Easy pickings you said."

"In a way. I know the *Nightwind* has been called a ship of the undead but it's actually the *Norfinn*, that's the ship's name, that suits that moniker. If they're already dead, they're impossible to kill. It can get dangerous. But you'll be safe in your cage."

"I can fight."

I laugh. "You're a feisty one, I'll give you that. But if you can't overtake me, you certainly can't overtake the undead."

"I've trained with a sword."

I raise a brow, biting back my amusement. "Where? When?"

"The king liked to indulge me. I learned here and there."

"I've seen you handle a sword and, I'm sorry to say, you're not very good at it."

"I can hold my own."

"And yet you let Aerik treat you the way he did."

Her eyes blaze. "I did not *let* him do the things he has done!" she snaps. "You have no idea what it's been like. And he is no different than you with your hot iron."

Fair enough. I can't pretend I know what it's been like for her.

"My apologies," I say. "I didn't mean to sound so crass."

"You're nothing but crass."

I shrug as if to say, *pirate.*

"But maybe you can teach me," she goes on.

I grin. "Teach you how to wield a sword in combat? Why, so you can stab me at the first chance you get?"

"I don't think stabbing you will do any good," she mutters.

"You're right. I find being stabbed to be highly annoying."

She chuckles at that, a light melodic sound and I realize it may be the first time I've heard her laugh. Suddenly I want nothing more than to make her laugh again.

But then she catches herself, like she remembered that she hates me, and her face goes sullen again. Moody but still beautiful. God Almighty, I would take her in any mood and be happier for it.

"When do you think we'll reach them?" she asks, averting her eyes, perhaps because I'm staring so blatantly at her.

"Tomorrow evening," I tell her. "We'll pull back a little as we get closer to the island. Let them get settled. Then we'll plan an ambush."

She finishes her glass of wine from the goblet and turns the stem between her fingers. "Can I ask you something?"

"Anything, luv."

"Have you ever killed a mermaid that you knew was a mother?"

A most peculiar question. This woman has a bleeding heart underneath.

"Not that I know of," I say. "It's hard to imagine any of those vicious creatures as mothers, but I suppose mermaids have to come from somewhere. Just figured they came from the devil himself."

A look comes over her eyes, one that harkens to storms at sea that would swallow a ship whole. "Maybe they did," she says blankly, and I swear I see a hint of a smile.

PART TWO

The Islands

THIRTEEN

Ramsay

"How is the princess?" Cruz asks.

The sun is beginning to set in the west, a brilliant display of corals and purples that dance with the burgeoning stars. I feel a hit of guilt at the mention of her, the fact that she's kept down in the cage when she could be up here taking in nature's wonder, the sunset and the fresh sea air that has a slight floral scent to it, hinting at our proximity to the islands.

"She is surviving," I tell him, the wind in the sails a steady drum above us.

"And how long are you planning to keep her in her cage?" he asks, levity in his voice. "After I heard you had dinner together last night, I assumed she'd be a part of the crew by now."

"I don't trust her not to hurt herself," I admit. "She's reckless and rash. She'd jump into the open ocean if given half the chance. When it comes to the islands, she'll swim for them."

"I see. And you don't want to keep her with her husband because you want her all to yourself."

"Her husband *beats* her," I say, giving him a sharp look.

"And you don't want to keep her with her husband because you want her all to yourself," Cruz repeats with a grin.

"I'm keeping our asset safe," I grumble, leaning against the rail.

Cruz just chuckles and takes a swig of his rum before passing the goatskin canteen to me. "You mean, *your* asset, since you claimed her as yours."

I consider the rum for a moment then wave it off, needing a clear head for tonight's attack. "Aye. My asset."

"You are still planning to trade her off for ransom, aren't you?" he says, scrutinizing my expression.

I give him nothing. "I am."

"It's just that when you first brought dear Sedge aboard this boat you never had any intentions of letting him go, not after you branded him."

"You knew why we couldn't let him go."

"He can't talk, Bones," Cruz says. "No one would have known what goes on here, and no one would have believed him anyway."

"You can't be too careful. At any rate, Sedge has proved himself valuable. The princess will do the same. But the real money-maker is the prince. Unfortunately. I really would like to kill him."

"I'm sure you will at some point," Cruz says with a laugh, slapping me hard on the back. "I know your temper."

"Aye, it's almost as bad as yours."

He just grins at me and tips back the canteen, more rum pouring into his mouth. Most of the crew drinks rum before we get into any battles and skirmishes because it helps with courage and, in their words, makes things more fun. But even though we have battled the skeleton crew before, it's not always easy. Our crew may be inhumanely blessed, but we aren't the undead. You *can* kill us, but you can't kill them. Our only luck in this situation is the fact that even if we're taken prisoner, we won't become doomed to their fate. The curse can't touch us.

Well, most of us.

Cruz turns and surveys the crew. It's the calm before the storm. Normally Cruz would start up the violin—he's a talented musician in his own right and music always gets the crew ready and excited for a fight. But tonight we need stealth and quiet if we are to have an actual ambush.

"Quartermaster!" I call out once I spot Thane on the deck below talking to Sam and Lucas, probably reminding Lucas to stay below and out of trouble and for his wife to do the same, even though he knows she won't listen a whit.

He comes up the stairs to join us on the aft deck. "What's the word?" he asks, sounding grumpier than usual.

"Just figuring out our plan of attack. What's gotten into you, brother?"

He lets out a deep grumbling noise. "I don't like this."

I frown. "What do you mean? Did you see something in the ball?"

"No. But after the attack from the navy ship, I feel things are a wee precarious at the moment. If you want to trade your prisoners for money from the king, I am all for that, but to detour to these blasted islands, no," he gives his head a stern shake, "I feel it's becoming too complicated. We need to stick to one task at a time."

"The navy attack was nothing," Cruz says. "Lothar did all the carpentry and repairs in a day. *Nightwind* was never in any danger, you know that."

"But our food supply sustained damage during those hits."

"That's why mermaid blood is the answer."

"Mermaid blood is only the answer because you want your revenge, not because you want us all to survive."

I glare at him. "You know I would do anything for this crew. My revenge is everyone's revenge. You were Hilla's uncle."

He glances away, only a hint of shame on his face. "It's not just about Hilla. It's the book. You need to let it go, Ramsay. You're holding onto the past too much. Venla, she—"

"I have made my peace about my wife," I sneer at him, taking a menacing step toward him. "I have let go of the past. But that book has magic, magic that we need if we wish to survive in this world. You said so yourself, how long can we keep doing this? How long can we go on? We need this to survive. All of us. Now if we get the mermaid, we get the blood, then we can destroy that sea bitch once and for all and get all the magic that Venla created for us. And at the very end, if we end up fetching a high price for the prisoners, then that's just the icing on the cake."

He raises his chin, peering down at me with amber eyes. "I don't think you understand, *brother*," he says. "It's the prisoners that are proving to be the complication. So far the prince has rendered Drakos incapable, and the princess, well you're spending time with her that you shouldn't be. I just hope I'm wrong about all of it." He punctuates that with a scowl.

"Look at you, with a face only a mother could love," Cruz says jovially to him, always there to defuse the tension between us. He pats Thane on the chest. "Now that you're done telling off the captain, perhaps we can turn our attention to the plan of attack so that there aren't complications."

Cruz pulls out a rolled-up chart from his back pocket and unfurls it out flat for us to read. "Now, we've been to Los Pintados before," he says, slipping into his role of navigator with ease. He points to the crudely drawn chart with his canteen. "They will most likely anchor in the bay here where they are protected. If we come up on the other side of the island, where the ruins of the Reef City meet the sea, we'll have the cover of the island. We can go across land."

I'm nodding. "And then slip into the water on the other side, swim to the ship, crawl up the sides and the anchor. Get the captain and dispose of him."

"They'll be on the lookout for anyone approaching by sea, not by land," Cruz adds.

"But what about the sea witch, Nerissa?" Thane asks. "If she's not below the water then she lives near those ruins, does she not? She won't let us pass."

"Why not? She doesn't have any business with us and we don't have any business with her."

"But we're stealing a mermaid from her cursed crew," Thane points out.

"Yes, but that mermaid gives her cursed crew magic. Believe me, she would want the mermaid gone."

"In fact, the mermaid might already be gone," Cruz says quietly. "If Nerissa finds it on board before we get there…"

"All the more reason why we need to do this as quickly as possible," I tell them. "Quartermaster, inform the crew of the plans. We'll need at least five others to come with me to secure the ship. The rest will bring the *Nightwind* around so we can bring the mermaid aboard."

"You're making this sound too easy," Thane grumbles.

"That's my job, isn't it?" I snipe. "I make it sound easy, you make it sound impossible."

He runs his hand over his jaw, the stubble scratching audibly. "Fine. I'll tell the crew and get the teams together."

He walks off toward the rest of the ship.

"Going to get the mermaid are we?" Crazy Eyes says to us from the helm.

I turn and go to him. "Aye. We'll need you to bring the ship around the moment you drop us off at our starting point."

Cruz comes over with the map, showing the bosun the plan.

"What are we planning to do with the mermaid?" he asks with a waggle of his bushy brows after he glances at the chart. "Will ye let us all have her or will she belong to ye like the princess does?"

"She will be evenly distributed amongst the crew," I assure him.

"I can't wait," he says excitedly. "I've heard they have the tightest holes imaginable."

I give him a look of disdain. "Bosun. You know that's not what she's for."

"Bah, what do you think the skeleton crew been doin' with her?"

"Conner," Cruz says to him, trying not to smile. "They're skeletons. They have no cocks!"

"But I sure do," he hoots.

Figures that's where his mind would go. We only left port last week and yet he's thinking with his cock already. Granted, I have been too but only because I've got a delectable creature caged in my room.

Which reminds me.

I leave the deck and head down the stairs to my quarters where I find Skip running across the room and hiding under the table, while the princess is looking sheepish in her cage.

"The cat bothering you?" I ask.

"Just making friends," she says. "You may not believe this, but it's getting rather boring being in here."

"I can put you back with your husband if you want some excitement."

Her eyes narrow icily. "You wouldn't dare."

"Actually, I'm a very daring fellow," I tell her. I stride over to my wardrobe and start taking off my clothes.

"Do you mind?" she asks, covering her eyes.

"I do not mind. But I can turn around if it pleases you."

"Please do."

"Interesting, I could have sworn you enjoyed the sight of me shirtless the other day." I smirk at her, shaking my head, then step out of my breeches and shirt, placing them on the back of a chair, and into a set of darker clothes that dry fast, perfect for being stealthy while swimming. I need the least amount of restriction and accessories as possible, just a dagger and a cutlass and that's it. A flintlock wouldn't fire if it were wet.

I turn around once I'm dressed and as I'm buttoning up my shirt she peers at me through her fingers. "Can I ask, if the crew is already cursed and dead, how you're going to go about defeating them?" she says.

"Slice their heads off. Dismember them. It won't kill them but if they don't get ahold of their bones, they can't be put back together."

"Fascinating," she says under her breath, though she sounds sincere. "But they'll see you coming, won't they?"

"Not if me and a few mates sneak on their ship first. We're getting dropped off at shore, then the *Nightwind* will sail around the island to pick us up. Meanwhile we'll have dismembered the captain. Take out the captain, you take out the crew."

"I'll keep that in mind," she says idly.

"You stay here, luv," I tell her. "It will all be over in no time."

I leave her, locking the door to my chambers behind me. It's only when I'm on the ship's boat and being lowered to the water, along with my crew of Cruz, Matisse, Lothar, Remi, Horse, and the page, John, that I remember I left my keys to the princess's cage behind in my other trousers. I shake it out of my head. She can't get out of the cage and no one else can get into my chambers. She's safe.

I turn my focus to our plan and our surroundings. A heavy fog has settled over the water and islands, coating it with an eerie mist. We silently row the boat to shore in the dark cover of night, taking in the reverence of the area. Nan Madol is a city of half-submerged ruins by the water's edge. Columns of basalt rocks rise up along built canals, giving the abandoned site the name "Venice of the Pacific."

I have been to Venice and the nickname is a stretch, but even so it's an impressive place with the residents, who were the elite members of the tribes, living here until a hundred years ago. In that time since the city was abandoned, the vegetation has taken over, vines stretching over the ruins, the sand and water swallowing the rest.

Our boat glides soundlessly along the stone walls of the canals built up on the coral reefs and rising up through the mist. If it were daytime and the sun were shining you would see down through the clear blue water to where old stones had sunk to the bottom, but in the fog and under a moonless sky it looks like we are slicing through ink. Above, statues peer down at us, big gaping eyes giving silent judgment. It's the type of place you don't even want to breathe for fear of pissing off some god that you don't believe in.

Eventually, we reach the shore and we quickly step off while John turns the boat around and starts rowing it back to the *Nightwind*, the ship looking ghostly as it sits there in the mist, barely visible.

I take the lead and Cruz brings up the back and I lead my crew through the thick jungle, past the ruins. It's even darker in here, the fog reaching through the trees like fingers, and I have to use my cutlass as a machete to slice through all the overgrowth. Strange creatures make growling noises in the pitch, and beady eyes watch us from the tree-tops. Every now and then I swear I hear a girl crying but I know it's just a trick. After all, this place was completely normal until Nerissa decided to take over. Now it pulses with her witchcraft.

"Captain, I'm pretty sure there's something following us," Remi says, his voice shaking. Remi is the youngest of the full-fledged Brethren and isn't used to being pulled away from his post at the cannons.

"It's just me," Cruz says. "And...something else. But the more you talk about it, the more it will follow us. Let's keep moving with our mouths shut."

Remi whimpers and his lover, Horse, utters some comforting words to him, and we continue on, our breathing heavy and quick, the sound of my machete echoing through the darkness over and over again.

Eventually, I see a bit of light through the trees, and I raise my hand for us to slow down and stay quiet. I get down onto my stomach and everyone else behind me does the same and we crawl through the jungle until the dirt turns to sand and we find ourselves on the beach. The thick fog parts just enough so that we're staring right across the water at the ghost ship.

FOURTEEN

Maren

"Skip?" I ask softly, looking around for the orange feline.

When the captain entered the room earlier the cat ran under the table. I don't get the impression that the cat is afraid of the captain, rather that he's afraid of being found complicit. In that sense I have to wonder if the captain is able to communicate with the cat too. He may not be a Syren, but it wouldn't surprise me.

But there's no sign of the cat. Perhaps he ran out of the room earlier and I didn't see it.

I sigh and lean back against the bars of the cage and slide down until I'm on the floor, my mind still tumbling over everything that was said at dinner last night.

The pirates hunted mermaids for their magic blood.

Edonia killed the captain's daughter and stole a book of magic.

The captain was once married to a witch.

The captain may or may not have been the ones who stole my mother from the depths of Limonos. Was my mother hunting them or were they hunting her? Or was it some other sailors or pirates that dragged her from the water, never to be seen again? I don't need yet another reason to hate the captain, so I'd like to pretend he was never involved with her death.

I've been trying to make sense of it all and my mind keeps coming around to two key points:

Mermaid blood is magic and they kill for it. More than that, they seem to view mermaids as monsters, which isn't wrong. But if they were to ever find out what I truly am, I believe all bets would be off. I'd wager the captain wouldn't hesitate to drain me of my blood in hopes that it might give him magic. Maybe it would, or maybe my magic was drained when Edonia was finished with me, but he would try.

The reason he needs the mermaid blood is because he needs it to help defeat Edonia. Which means that once he has the magic, he will go after her and possibly before he gets rid of me. If he does that, that means *I'm* one step closer to Edonia. He's going to try and get his book back, but if I somehow got the book back first, I could use it to barter with Edonia and get my fins back.

So now it seems that everything has a purpose, and a plan could possibly fall into place. I just have to accomplish two things: keep my Syren identity a secret, and keep on the captain's good side for as long as I can. That last one will be harder than the first since there's something about that man's face that makes me want to strike him with fist and nails. But if I can accomplish that, if I can help him get his book back, then double-cross him and steal the book and use that to get back to Limonos and life as a Syren, then that will solve everything.

For the first time in the last ten years, I can see everything I want in plain sight.

My freedom.

My return to my true self.

I'll be going home.

It makes me pause. I suppose if I want to stay on the captain's good side, that means I have to stay on his ship. That means I need to obey.

And yet I can see his breeches on the back of the chair, see the keys to my cage hanging from them. If I could find the cat and convince him to give me the keys…

And you think that will win you his favor? I think to myself.

I sigh and lean back against the cage. The ship has started moving again, which means that the boat must be back from dropping the men off on the island. The rocking movement and the thick heady smell of night air in the tropics lulls me off to sleep, for when I wake up there's a terrible racket up above.

The sound of us under attack.

But there's no cannon fire, no roundshots slamming into the ships. Instead there's yelling and shouting along with the clang of swords, rattling sounds that might only be described as skeletons being dismembered, and the occasional shot of a musket.

And it all sounds like it's coming from our boat above.

If any of the skeleton crew get down here, they could blow the captain's lock off with a blunderbuss. I might be a sitting duck.

"Skip!" I call out again. "Time to make haste and free me please!"

Suddenly the cat appears, this time coming out from near the captain's bed, and stops right in front of me, in no rush at all.

"Thank the gods," I say, kneeling on the floor next to it. "Please, if you can understand me, I need your help. We are under attack. Your captain would like you to set me free so that I may defend myself."

Skip tilts his head as if questioning me.

"I swear to it, Skip. And I promise if you free me I will find Sedge and the rest of the pork from last night. Or the fish, we barely touched the fish we were so full. I'll give you as much food as you want." I'm starting to feel ridiculous pleading with a cat but I go on. "If those skeleton people get in here, they'll attack me and I know the captain would be very mad at you if you let that happen."

The tabby opens his mouth in a big yawn, canines showing, then turns, showing me its rear, and pads its way across the room and over to the chair where his breeches are. I didn't even have to tell him, he's already jumping up on the chair and fishing out the keys. I hear metal being unclipped and then the jangling of the keys and the next thing I know Skip is leaping off the chair and trotting toward me with the ring of keys in his mouth.

I watch in awe as he drops the keys right outside the bars of the cell.

"Mew," he says plainly.

I reach through and take the keys. "Thank you, thank you. Good kitty."

Then I get to my feet and fumble with the lock awkwardly. With the way it is on the outside it's hard to get the key in but I eventually succeed. It happens at the same time the fighting from above sounds like it's escalating with more muskets and pistols going off, the air smelling of powder.

I quickly open the door and step out of the cage and into the room, then go for the door out of his quarters. Naturally that's locked from the outside, so I can't get out either and none of the keys I have on the ring seem to work with it.

Blast, I swear. But then I think about what the word *blast* actually means.

I look over at his row of weapons and eye the flintlock musket. The king let me handle a musket once during a target practice outing. I understood the fascination with guns but to me it was far too impersonal to use. If I had to kill something, I wanted to do it face-to-face and with my bare hands.

But I do remember how it works and how to use one. I pick it off the wall and peer at it, unsure if it's loaded with gunpowder or not. I jam the end of it against the ground just in case, so that if there is powder it will go back into the vent to take the spark from the striking flint.

Only one way to test it. I glance over at Skip who gives me a loud "meow" and then I aim it at the lock at the door, close enough that I shouldn't miss.

I pull the trigger and the flint strikes.

The bullet fires, the sound of the blast filling the room followed by the door's lock being blown off and clattering to the floor in pieces.

I don't have time to reload the gun and I wouldn't know how anyway, so I run back to the weapons, grab a knife, and then go back to the door, opening it to the chaos on the other side.

Except that at the moment, all of the skirmish seems to be happening on the top deck. I look behind me at Skip, gesturing with my head to follow me but he only goes under the table. Probably a smart move.

But me, I feel I must be on the offensive.

I step out, looking up the stairs to see a skeleton walking past, skin half-rotting off its horrible face, waving a sword around while Thane knocks it out of its hand with his cutlass.

"Looks like the pretty princess got out of her cage," a gravely voice says from behind me. The sound of it makes my stomach turn.

I turn around to face Sterling who is leering at me.

"You should be upstairs fighting," I tell him, searching for bravado.

"I think I'd rather be fighting you," he says, smiling to show strangely perfect teeth. He reaches out and grabs my arm, trying to pull me away into the dark depths of the ship but I dig my heels in.

"You can't touch me," I tell him, trying to yank my arm away but to no avail. "I belong to him. He branded me. He claimed me in his name."

Sterling frowns. "He did not."

"You want to see?" I ask and then I reach down and gather my dress, pulling it up to show my hip.

His expression goes from wanton lust to one of pure disbelief, then hatred.

He actually steps back from me.

"That bastard claimed you," he says with a wet growl. "I didn't think he'd have the nerve."

"He did," I tell him, feeling emboldened now. "I belong to Captain Ramsay Battista and no one else. That's his name in my skin. I'm his property."

He snaps at me like he's a mangy dog. "It's your funeral then, poppet. You don't know what you've signed up for." He shoves me aside with a meaty hand so I go flying against the railing of the stairs. I can't believe that Ramsay was telling the truth when he said his brand would keep me safe. "I've got to go help bring in a mermaid."

Mermaid? My attention swings back to that. *Do they have her? Is she alive?*

I debate whether to hide somewhere in the ship or to go up top but curiously gets the best of me. I need to see the Syren before they kill her or torture her or whatever they're going to do. I wish I could save her, but now that I know my reaching Edonia relies on the captain and crew getting their mermaid blood, I don't think I can.

The fact that I would be choosing myself over another Syren's life breaks me a little. But already sacrifices are being made.

I slowly creep up the stairs to the deck, poking my head up just in time to see a most preposterously chaotic scene unfold.

It seems that most of the *Nightwind's* crew are here now, each of them fighting one or two rotting skeletons dressed in baggy clothes, armed with rapiers and broadswords. *Nightwind* seems to be winning despite the disadvantage, though I look just in time to see one of the skeletons jab their rapier right into the stomach of the pirate who cut Aerik's cheek.

But though the pirate doubles over in pain, he still manages to slice the skeleton's legs off at the shins, then brings down the side of his sword into the skull, crushing it into fragments.

"Here's a fair maiden."

A twirl around to see a skeleton face gaping at me a foot away, about to stick his sword through me.

"Here's a headless bastard," says Sam as the woman pirate comes in from out of nowhere.

I scream as she swings her sword and cuts the head clean off. The skull goes bouncing along the deck, the mouth still open in a holler.

I stare at the woman, shocked that she saved me. "Thank you," I say breathlessly.

"You're most welcome," she says. "Figured Bones would have my own head if I let anything happen to you." She looks at the knife in my hands. "I'd tell you that you should be below deck where it's safe, but I reckon you're a woman who doesn't listen to most."

"You'd be right about that," I say, my gaze going to the rest of the battle unfolding around us. "Are we winning?"

"We?" she says with a grin. "I'm glad to know which side you're on. Aye, I say we're winning. Takes a lot to get these cursed men down but once they are..." She jerks her chin at the man she had decapitated.

The body is slowly crawling back toward the head. She goes over and reaches down, grabbing a hold of one boney arm and ripping it off, then whips it around so it goes flying off the deck of the ship and into the water. "You can keep them down for a while."

She looks over the rest of the scene, at the fighting skeletons and the thick eerie fog that's creeping over the ship, and frowns.

"I have a bad feeling about this," she says to me as she comes back over, her cutlass at her side, pulsing with the need to stab something.

"What?"

Her gaze is steady on the other boat which is mashed up right beside the *Nightwind*. Some of the *Nightwind's* crew, including Sterling, are bringing aboard a long box of sorts. It reminds me of a coffin except that it's covered in a muslin sheet. "That's the mermaid in there."

My mouth drops open and I let out a sharp gasp. "They have her?"

"Or what's left of her," Sam says, disappointment in her tone. "You see how the cursed men are more or less skeleton? Mermaid blood would have given them the appearance of human for a short time. The fact that their humanity and skin has faded into shreds means that the mermaid isn't giving enough blood. That or she's already dead."

"Aaaaaaargh!" a skeleton man cries out and starts running toward us with his broadsword raised.

Sam quickly turns to fight him, her swordplay an even match for his, and though I want to stay and maybe help her, she doesn't look like she needs help from the likes of me. Instead, I want to follow Sterling and the Syren to wherever they go.

I step out of the way, hiding behind a barrel of tar, then watch as they take the long box down the stairs and into the lower deck. I wait a bit and then go down after them. They aren't on the main deck, not near the captain's or officers' quarters or the galley, so I sneak down the next set of stairs to the gun deck.

They step out of the room where Aerik's cell is and I duck behind a post, watching as they run back up the stairs to join the fight against the cursed crew, singing a sea shanty together as they go.

They left the door to the room open, thankfully, and I scurry toward it. They had lit a lantern and placed it in the corner of the room, illuminating the covered box and Aerik who is staring down at it from his jail cell in weary confusion.

He looks over at me and blinks. He really looks worse for wear. His face is bruised and bloodied, looking like skin-and-bones already. I almost feel sorry for him.

"You're still alive," he comments, his voice raw and hoarse.

"Sorry to disappoint you," I say as I take a step closer to the coffin-sized box.

"What is that?" he asks.

"This?" I say, reaching for the sheet that's covering it. My hand is starting to tremble, my nerves all over the place. "This is a mermaid."

"A mermaid?" Aerik says in contemptuous disbelief.

I nod and take in a shaking breath.

I hold it and pull the cloth off the box.

And I scream.

FIFTEEN

Maren

My screams echo around the room, deafening even to my own ears.

This can't be real. This can't be certainty.

The coffin is actually a glass tank, half-filled with murky, bloodied water, and inside the glass is a Syren. I can't tell if she's alive or dead by the emaciated look of her, by the way she's partly-submerged with her eyes closed, a hand at her chest, her gray hair floating around her.

But what I do know is that this isn't any ordinary Syren.

This is my oldest sister.

It's Asherah.

It has been ten years since I last saw her. But then she had purple-black hair, not gray, with shimmering tawny skin, not this deathly white pallor. Her scales at the time were a gleaming silver and pink, not this dull, flaking ash, the length of her tail coated in algae film. She was beautiful and now she has wasted away to almost nothing, like she's aged 300 years over the course of a decade.

"God Almighty, Jesus!" Aerik curses. "That's a mermaid."

I ignore him and press my hands on the glass. "Asherah. It's me. It's Maren."

"Asherah?" Aerik repeats from behind me. "Maren, I think you've been with these pirates far too long."

But my sister stirs. The tank is too short for her full tail to unfurl so it's curled up beside her and the tips of her translucent decaying fins twitch.

I quickly tap at the glass, hope rising in my throat.

"Asherah!" I cry out.

Then I remember that beneath the surface we didn't talk like this.

I go inside my head and speak there, for only she will be able to hear me.

Asherah. It's Maren. Please wake up. I plead.

She stirs again and this time she opens her eyes. Her once violet eyes, the same color as our sister's, have now faded to a pale pink. But it's her. It's her all the same.

M-Maren? she asks inside my head. *How is this possible?*

I can't help but smile, tears spilling down my cheeks. *I don't know but it is. It is. And I have to get you out of here.*

Where am I? she asks. She attempts to look around but can barely move an inch, her muscles trembling with weakness. *What has happened? Why are you here?*

I don't know why, I tell her. I need to hold her hand, to let her feel me. I push at the glass on top of the tank but it's heavy. It takes a lot of shoving with all my strength for it to slide off and drop loudly on the deck beside us.

She gasps, needing the air for both her lungs and her gills. I watch as the gills along the side of her neck open and close, trying to take in the dirty water.

I'm going to get you out of here, I tell her. I reach into the water and grab her hand. Her bones feel brittle and her claws have all broken off. The webbing between them has been shredded like a worn flag.

Maren, she says quietly. *Do not do anything to endanger yourself. You're the reason I'm here.*

I blink at her, my grip on her hand tightening in surprise. *What do you mean?*

Her eyes blaze with fire, the most energy I've seen her give so far, and she fixes me in their gaze. *Don't you know what happened? When Nill came back and told us what Edonia did to you, father sent the whole kingdom out to find you.*

I can't believe it. *He did what?* He would do that for me? That's what I want to say. *But he knew I was above water not below.*

She manages a weak nod. *We were looking for Edonia too, to get her to bring you back and reverse the spell. Nill told us how she tricked you. You were only sixteen, you weren't of sound mind and she knew it. But no matter where we went, there was no trace of you. None of the Syrens to the south or north of Limonos had seen you when they watched the shore and for passing ships, and none had found Edonia either.*

She takes in a deep breath through her gills and nose. Then, she goes on, her eyes closing. *So I decided to come this way. We had never explored what was to the west of us. This big ocean. Larimar came with me but we got separated when I was caught. They didn't catch her, she tried to save me but couldn't. She's okay, don't worry. She's out there still.*

I swallow the lump in my throat. *And father? Is he back in Limonos? Is he…is he well?*

Asherah's eyes open, filled with sorrow, and I know. I know in my heart that he is gone, just like my mother is.

"No," I say softly, out loud. "Please, not him."

"What are you doing, woman?" Aerik moans. "Talking to a fish?"

"Shut your mouth or I'll shut it for you!" I snap at him viciously before turning back to my sister.

Please tell me father is okay, I can't bear it, I plead.

She gives her head the subtlest shake. *He died. A broken heart, some said. After losing our mother, he couldn't stand the idea of losing you and he lost the will to live.*

Oh, gods. No.

The tears are rolling down my face like a river.

So many of the Syrens are gone now, she goes on, giving my hand a faint squeeze back. *We are a dying breed, Maren. We have been for a while. I shudder to think how many are left. Soon they will be less one.*

No! I cry out, holding her hand to my face, her skin clammy and cold. My tears roll over it. *You are not going to die. I will protect you from them. I will pick you up and take you to the water and you will be free.*

But how free can I really be without my dear sister? she says sadly, giving me a soft smile. *You were so reckless and selfish and brave, and I have missed you so.*

"I have missed you too," I say through a sob, ignoring Aerik's mockery behind me. *But I will free you, I promise. You will live.*

I am dying, Maren. They captured me many moons ago. They've been slowly drinking my blood ever since. Her gaze moves to her wrist and I hold it away from my face to see a deep wound that looks like it's been scarred over and over again.

Monsters, I growl. *I will kill them all.*

They are already dead, she says. *I only helped them feel alive but it's something they will never be. I may be in pain, but I will die and my pain will be over. Their pain will never be.*

I don't care about them, I care about you!

And I care about you, so much, she says. *I know you have a new life here, but from the looks of it,* her gaze goes briefly to Aerik, *perhaps it's not all that you were promised it would be. I am so glad to see you alive and I hope to the gods that they don't discover what you really are.*

I practically growl. *Is that so? Because now I hope they do. Now I wish I had your power to rip everyone's heads right off. Let's see them try and take my blood.*

She manages a smile, showing just a hint of translucent pointed teeth. *That's my sister. That's my Maren. So much anger and rage for such a small creature. That's the Syren I love so dearly.*

She reaches up with her hand, pressing it against my cheek and I lean in, briefly pressing my closed mouth against hers. But instead of feeling her dry lips, there's a faint buzz of electricity passing from her mouth to mine and I pull back to stare at her.

Perhaps a Syren's kiss even works while she's dying, she says.

I go still. Did my kiss give her the power to rejuvenate herself, like the elders spoke of reviving drowned sailors?

But she doesn't seem any stronger.

If anything, I'm feeling stronger. My heart is racing fast and I feel my blood starting to boil white-hot, a not unpleasant feeling, considering.

Your rage will free you, my dear sister, she says to me faintly.

I'm contemplating what she's said when I suddenly feel another presence in the room.

"What in damnation is going on here?"

I turn to see Ramsay standing in the doorway, staring at me aghast. I must look quite odd kneeling beside a mermaid in a tank, her hand in mine.

"Stay back!" I tell him, getting to my feet. "I can't let you hurt her! I won't!"

He shakes his head, utterly befuddled. "Did I not just tell you all the stories about what vicious beasts they are?"

"Vicious beasts or not, she is dying, can't you see? How cruel of a man do you really wish to be? You want to drink her blood and torture her further?"

His dark brows come together and he walks over to me, staring down at my sister in the tank. "She's dying," he agrees quietly, his words little more than a noise in his throat.

"She'll be no good to you," I tell him. "She can't give you what you want in this state, there's nothing left inside her. The right thing to do would be to let her go."

He nods slowly, running his hand over his jaw as his eyes flit over her Syren form. "You're right, Princess."

My heart swells with hope and I look back down at my sister adoringly.

You're going to be okay, I assure her. *He's the captain of this ship and he might be a good man at heart.*

The corner of her mouth twitches weakly. *There are no good men, sister. But there are no good Syrens either. We are all just trying to survive.*

Her gaze goes to the captain's now, meeting his eyes. She gives him the slightest nod and I don't know what it means.

Until I see him pull out his knife.

"What are you doing!?" I scream, trying to grab his arms.

But he moves to the other side of the tank and says, "I'm letting her go."

Before I can stop him he takes the knife and plunges it right into my sister's heart.

For the second time the room is filled with the deafening roar of my scream, the sound so high and awful that cracks appear on the glass tank and Aerik and the captain have to cover their ears.

I love you, Asherah says to me as her eyes close and she chokes on her last breath. *Be free.*

"Why?!" I cry through a wailing sob, staring at the captain in blinding horror. "Why did you do that!?"

I reach into the tank and try to stop the bleeding but there's barely any blood coming from the wound. I reach down for her hands, holding on tight, hoping this isn't the end. But much like it was with Daphne, there's nothing left in her to hold me back.

"She was at death's door," Ramsay says, straightening up. Through my blurry tears I see him wipe his knife on his shirt and stick it back in its holder. "I was putting her out of her misery."

"You said you were going to let her go! You could have let her go into her home, into the sea!"

"Do you honestly think she would have just swam away? She could barely move, barely breathe. She's been drained of all her blood."

"You don't know! You could have tried."

"So she could be picked off by a shark? I know we have differing opinions on what constitutes cruelty, but that's cruelty to me."

"Captain!" someone yells from in the ship.

"Be right there!" he barks. He looks at my sister, then at me, and finally at Aerik. "I'll be back. Don't do anything stupid."

I can't tell who he's talking to, but it doesn't matter.

I watch as he walks off and then I attempt to climb into the tank, trying to move my gown and body next to Asherah, until I'm in the water and wrapping my arms around her.

"What the devil is wrong with you?" Aerik says derisively from his cell. "You're mad. You've gone absolutely mad."

I ignore him, the tears still flowing, the sobs shooting through my lungs until I feel they might shatter. I kiss the top of Asherah's head, smelling the same sweet scent that she's had since we were young, like the coral gardens we would play in, where she would teach me the names of the animals that lived nearby, and I feel like I might just die here on the spot. All I wanted was to be with my family again, and I was reunited with my sister only to have her taken away so brutally.

And she was here because of *me*. She came looking across the Pacific for me. This is my fault that she was captured and tortured, my fault that she's in my arms dead. My fault that my father died. I have ruined everyone and everything.

"I'm so sorry," I cry, the water sloshing from how much I'm shaking as I hold her tight. "I am so sorry I chose this life when I should have chosen what was right. I never wanted to hurt anyone. I love you. I love you and I wish you didn't love me, because if you didn't love me you never would have come here. I never would have lost you."

I continue to cry, letting it all come out, my sorrow and grief swirling together with vengeance and rage, like a maelstrom forming inside my soul that's growing deeper and wider and more destructive by the second.

"You really think you know this *mermaid*? Do you think you are one?" Aerik sneers, his hands on the bars and his ugly face pressed through. "Have you concocted all of this in your head to make up for all your shortcomings? The fact that you have come from no family, that you have no one that loves you, that the only thing you have going for yourself is a pretty face and a nice pair of tits and a tight cunt that I'm sure you're doling out to the captain whenever he wants." He pauses. "And so now you pretend to have feelings for this overgrown piece of rotting salmon."

My rage goes white hot. It blinds me. Overcomes me.

Your rage will free you, my sister said.

Ramsay said something similar to me, too.

And now, now I'm letting it go free.

Whatever energy Asherah passed through her lips and onto mine I feel coursing through me, changing my structure, making me become primal fury.

I feel my teeth sharpen in my mouth, look down to see my finger-nails extending and curving, growing into hard claws, feel strength building in the marrow of my bones, giving me power I hadn't felt since I was sixteen.

Aerik makes a sound of horror and surprise and my gaze shoots to him, pinning him in place. I growl at him, baring my razor teeth, and before I know what I'm doing, I'm jumping out of the tank and landing right in front of the cell.

"From this moment forth, I will never have to listen to you again," I grind out, my voice sounding less human, more monster.

More Syren.

His mouth opens to say something but I cut him off.

Forever.

My arm shoots out through the bars with my claws extended and I pierce his skin with them, reaching through muscle and fat and bone until I feel his beating heart under my palm. I snarl and close my hand around his heart and pull it back out of his chest and through the bars.

While he's still looking at me, while he's still alive for just a few more seconds, I take his still beating heart and shove part of it in my mouth, biting down with needle sharp teeth as ravenous, monstrous hunger takes over.

I make sure it's the last thing he sees.

SIXTEEN

Ramsay

It takes me a moment to comprehend what I'm looking at. At first I reckoned the princess was offering some type of meat to the prince just outside the cell.

Then I realized she was holding not meat but a pulsing heart.

Then I came to see that it wasn't just any heart, but it had come from Aerik himself, and I watched as the princess brought the heart to her mouth and started eating it gleefully.

Aerik's dead body teeters on its feet for a moment, the sight of her eating his own heart no doubt the last thing he will ever see, and then he topples over, his head smacking the bars as he slumps to the floor. Dead.

I stand here flabbergasted because I still can't figure out what's happening.

Princess Maren just pulled her husband's heart out of his chest and is currently eating that heart like she's never eaten anything before. She's eating his heart with more gusto than she did the roast boar the other night.

She's mad. This woman is pure madness. She needs to be locked up. She's dangerous and wild and unsafe.

And yet, how is it that I've never been so delighted before?

"You have a monstrous little soul, don't you my dear?" I whisper.

She whips her head toward me and sees me standing in the door-way. She's literally caught red-handed, her mouth smeared with blood that also drips down her arms and hands and onto her dress, which is partially wet when it wasn't before.

"What on earth am I supposed to do with you?" I muse to myself.

She just stares at me and finishes eating the heart. I don't make a move for her, not until I have a plan. She's clearly deranged and, more than that, clearly not human. She has to be a witch or magicked in some way. Perhaps a demoness. That would explain a lot.

Or maybe she's just like me and has adapted to this life...differently.

She swallows down the rest of the heart, wiping the back of her hand over her lips and I notice her claws, how they slowly shrink in size before my eyes, until they are just fingers and nails again.

"Are you a sea witch?" I ask carefully. "Have you been sent by Edonia?"

She only scowls at me.

"You know I told you not to do anything stupid."

"I haven't done anything stupid," she snaps. "I only did what I've been dying to do for the last ten years."

"Aye, well, you killed my hostage."

"You still have me."

"Do I? Princess, I don't know what I have at this point. What in god's name are you?"

"A monster," she says and smiles. Sharp teeth slowly fade back into her regular ones. Once again she looks like her normal self, though now I'm wondering how normal that self is. Has she been wearing a mask this whole time? Has this creature always been under her skin? I've touched her, briefly, but the only thing I noticed was how soft she was.

But I need to take her at her word. She is indeed a monster and if she has the strength suddenly to rip the heart out of her husband, then she has the strength to do that to me, and that's something I wouldn't survive. No one with a heart would.

This woman is now my equal.

And therefore, she can't be trusted not to kill me.

I approach her like I would a predator. If I were swimming and saw a shark, how would I react? I would normally display brute force in hopes that the shark would swim away, not wanting the fight, but the princess seems to be reveling in her wild side a little too much. Luckily for me, my wild side likes to come out to play, and I don't back down until I win.

"If you could help me to understand what just happened," I say, walking toward her slowly, my palms displayed in peace.

"I had enough," she hisses, giving Aerik an angry look, as if she expects him to say something back to her. Instead, he is staring up blankly at the ceiling, blood pouring out of the hole in his chest.

"And the mermaid?" I gesture to the dead creature in the tank.

"Your lack of compassion has spurred me." Her eyes meet mine and narrow. Though they were always an ever-changing brilliant shade of blue before, now they positively glow like there's a light shining from behind them.

What kind of witchcraft does this woman possess? Venla was a witch and a powerful one in her own right, but she did not radiate power and otherness like this creature does. Venla had a temper, but she did not rip the hearts of men from their chests and devour them like steak. Venla kept me on my toes but she wasn't so thoroughly unpredictable and rash that I couldn't see her coming.

"You are a stunning abyss of a creature," I tell her. "One that I could spend eons swimming in and never get to the bottom of."

She frowns. "I am not that complicated."

"You are a mystery, Maren," I tell her. "I can call you by your name now, can't I? With your husband gone, you are no longer a princess."

She opens her mouth to say something, then purses her still bloody lips. "You've always called me whatever the hell you wanted."

My mouth twitches. "That be true."

Her shoulders relax a fraction of an inch, imperceptible to most but not me. It's enough to make me move.

I'm on her in a second, moving like a flash of lightning and grabbing her wrists, pulling them behind her as I go behind her back, my hand at her throat and holding tight. I'm not foolish enough to attempt to put my hand over her mouth, not with those needle teeth that could reappear at any moment.

She squirms and she's stronger than she was before but I'm still stronger. No matter what she is, I still can overpower her, and I'm faster too.

"I'd like to make this as easy on you as possible," I say to her, my mouth at her ear. "But with how I've seen you behave, I…"

I trail off. Dear lord, her smell is overpowering and in the most aggravating way possible. She's sweet and musky and it screams sex to me, overriding my senses and making me want to fuck her something fierce, more so than normal.

I have to shake it out of me. That's not what I'm doing here.

"What about how I behave?" she says, her throat moving against my hand as she speaks. The vibration gets under my skin, making my cock harder than ever. What is she doing to me? Is this part of her spell?

"I can't trust you not to kill me or my crew," I manage to say to her, my voice thick. "So I have no choice but to lock you up."

"Put the bird back in her cage," she comments sourly.

"Oh, you're not going in the cage. You're going in chains."

"Chains!" She cries out and tries to struggle.

I hold her tight. "Quiet. You sound just like your insufferable husband." I pause. "Or should I say late-husband. You know I'm going to have to answer for a lot now that the mermaid is dead and so is the hostage."

"You're the one who killed the mermaid," she spits out.

"Mercy kill," I remind her. "I'll thank you to come along now."

With my grip vice-tight, I bring her out of the room with the dead bodies and down the stairs to the hold. At one end is the place where we hold the prisoners and livestock if we bring any on board, the rest is storage for dry provisions, powder and shot stores, water and provisions in barrels, plus a hold for any treasure we plunder. At the opposite side of the ship from the prisoner hold is a small room where we keep a set of chains for certain events. This is where I bring Maren.

It's pitch black in here but I can do this with my eyes closed. I quickly put her hands above her head, chains running from a beam in the ceiling to the cuffs around her wrists, then I do the same to her feet on the ground, keeping her legs far apart enough to keep her from trying to move but not so much that she can't stand.

"You bastard!" she cries out, squirming and twisting. "You can't do this to me!"

I chuckle and fumble for matches nearby and strike one against the wall, lighting a nearby lantern. I put the lantern over to the side and out of the way and look her over as the flames dance along her features, illuminating the room in light and shadows.

She's sneering at me, her face contorting into hatred but just like before, the more she hates me, the more I seem to desire her.

"Let's see what you really are, luv," I say to her. I step over until I'm right in front of her and I place my hands at her chest, my fingers taking a hold of the edges of her bodice, the fabric still wet with the blood from Aerik's heart. With one defiant tug I yank the dress apart, ripping it down the middle.

She cries out and I'm staring at her naked body like I'd just been slapped by god himself.

She is built like a goddess, a creation of the divine. Her breasts are full, large, heavy, her nipples turning into small pink peaks in the exposed air, her skin a smooth white that erupts with gooseflesh under my gaze. Her stomach is soft and round and begging to be touched, her thighs wide, her calves quite thin in comparison, and short. At first I think I see what I'm looking for, some sort of hint at the creature she is. If she was a type of mermaid that could trade fins for legs, would she have scales? But there is no sign of scales, just the natural lines of white and pink that stripe along her fleshy thighs and stomach, all perfectly normal on a woman.

I come around to her back and do the same thing to the dress there, ripping it down the middle so that it falls away to the sides, the fabric only held on by the arms. I expected to see perhaps a fish-like spine or maybe a divination tattoo linking her to witchcraft but instead there is nothing but smooth skin and a firm, supple arse and…

Her back. I squint to see various lines and scars running over her back. But these aren't from growth spurts or from having supernatural origins. They're from being flogged.

A low grumble sounds in my chest like a warning. "Do I need to ask who did this to you?" I manage to say.

"I've taken care of it," she says coldly and there's nothing more to say. The prince she married, the prince who ridiculed her and beat her throughout her marriage, is now dead, and at her hands. Literally.

I come back around to her front.

"Did you find what you were looking for?" she asks. Her voice is a touch lower now, sounding like silk. Something about her tone sets me on edge.

"Figured it was only fair since you saw me nude, it's time I saw you," I tell her. I'm close, quite close, but the more I stare at her lips, at the dried blood on them, the more I want to kiss her and I know that's what she wants. I need to keep my distance. There's no telling when those teeth might come back.

I step back an inch to where she can't bite my face off. But still I'm unable to unhook myself from her gaze. I don't want to. I need to keep my focus on her at all times. Her eyes are absolutely hypnotic.

"Do I look acceptable to you?" she asks, and the seductive slant of her eyes softens slightly, a touch of vulnerability coming through her voice.

"Do you mean your body?" I ask her dumbly.

She nods and the sweet honesty, such a juxtaposition to her earlier, makes my cock strain uncomfortably against the buttons of my fly.

"Darling, your body would bring any man to their knees where they would be in the right position to worship you. It's a body carved by god yet meant for sin, and it would become anyone's salvation."

"Then why aren't you on your knees?" she asks, her lids growing heavy again.

God Almighty, she is the moon and I am the tides. I feel my resolve begin to slip away as her eyes pull me in.

"Because I don't trust you not to knee me in the face," I admit. "I don't want to end up like your husband."

"So the big bad captain finally fears something."

"I fear many things, luv. And from the start, I have always feared you."

She gnaws on her lip for a moment and my cock twitches again, hot and swollen and begging to be freed.

"Touch me," she whispers.

I swallow hard. I am not sure I will survive this.

"Touch you where?" I ask, my voice husky with pure red lust.

"Everywhere," she says softly. Her eyes close. "Please."

This is a trap and you know it, my mind reasons. *Leave her where she is and go tend to your crew. Break to them the bad news about the dead prince and mermaid.*

But though my mind is right, I can't.

I've dreamed about doing this too much and my cock is always in charge.

I reach out with both of my hands and gently cup her breasts.

She immediately lets out a low moan that leaves me weak at the damn knees.

Her breasts are heavy and sink into my palms, her skin sinfully soft and warm and I want so badly to take my body and press it against hers, take my cock and find the heat inside her. But even though I'm obliging her wishes, I can't play into her hands. This is a game, after all, and it always has been.

Instead, I slowly run my thumbs over her nipples, feeling them harden more until they're round pebbles, and the gasp she lets out makes me moan in response. Her head goes back, long black hair unspooling down her back, her neck exposed as she writhes under my touch.

I can smell her blood under her skin, smell how addictive she would be. I want nothing more than to just take her, bite her, have my way with her rough and hard. I have always been a man of restraint when I need to, an important lesson to learn when you're at sea, but even so it takes all my effort not to let loose.

I bring my eyes back to her beautiful tits, so weighted in my hands, working her nipples again and again until she's starting to buck against the restraints.

Keeping my eyes glued to her, watching for any sudden movements, I bring my head down until I'm pressing the flat of my tongue against her skin and lapping up around the deep curve of her breasts.

"Ramsay," she says through a broken gasp, and it's not lost on me that this is the first time she's addressed me by my name. It sounds reverent when it comes from her lips.

With my gaze locked on her wanton expression I suck her nipple into my mouth, my tongue swirling around the tight peaks, her pulse thrumming beneath the skin. She tastes heavenly, feels like sin, and I know she has the power to pull me to the depths and sink me. Yet it's a risk I'm willing to take in order to get her to say my name like that again.

With her moans increasing, one hand releases her breast and roams down over her stomach, through her curls and to the meeting of her thighs, which the leg cuffs are already holding apart for me.

I slide my finger between her and find her drenched with desire for me, my breath hitching in my chest and how silky she feels.

"Christ, woman," I swear gruffly. "You could drown a man."

She lets out another breathy moan, this one deeper and so desperate that it shoots straight to my cock. I don't know how much more of this either of us will be able to take. She wants me to bed her, I can tell, but that would be a misstep on my behalf. As long as I'm standing here and feeling her then I'm in control. The moment I stick my cock inside her, I know I'll let my guard down and that can't happen.

But, heaven help me, I want it to happen.

Instead I slip my finger along her wetness, circling her clitoris with easy rhythm until she's trembling in the restraints. From the sound of the chains, I know her wrists must be eaten up by the cuffs, enough so that I'm tempted to stop and see if she's alright, but when I pull back just for a second she lets out this ravenous cry that belongs to an animal in heat and so I plunge two fingers inside of her.

"Gods!" she calls out, the sound echoing around the room as her walls squeeze my fingers.

I can't take any more of this.

While I'm fingering her with one hand, I'm reaching into my breeches and pulling out my cock with the other. It's already so thick and hot and heavy in my palm that I know I won't last long. Luckily I don't need to in this case.

With my gaze fixed on her expressive face, I stroke myself from root to tip, my length pulsing hot beneath my grip, while my other hand fucks her, the sound of her slickness loud and lewd in the room, mixing with the groan of the chains.

I've been with plenty of women in my life but never like this. No, never like this and never with a woman like her. I don't know what snapped inside her, whether it was freeing herself from her husband for good or welcoming her monstrous side, but whatever it is, I'm under its spell now. All this time she only hinted at the vivacious creature underneath, someone I had wanted to set free, and now that she's loose and wild and dangerous, I don't know how I'll ever be able to leave her side.

But you'll have to, eventually, my mind reminds me.

Be that as it may, tonight we're coming together.

"Hell," I cry out, my hand jerking faster now and I can feel my release around the corner, almost there, almost fucking there.

"Come inside me," she urges breathlessly, her hips bucking to meet my hand, her eyes closed, her head arching backwards. "I want you inside me."

Those are the words I'd been waiting to hear, the words that send me over the edge, even though I know I won't obey them. But to hear her need for me, her want for me, overriding her *hate* for me, there's nothing more wicked than that.

I come with a roar, my seed shooting out in thick ropes to land on her belly, her breasts, even up onto her collarbones. She gasps, staring down at the mess I left on her, another physical way of claiming her as mine, and I quicken my wrist to bring her to release, my fingers thrusting in deep, my thumb sliding over her wet swollen heat.

"Ramsay!" she yelps, her hips bucking uncontrollably against my hand like a wild horse. Her body trembles violently, her walls squeezing my hand with python-like strength and, damn, do I wish it was my cock now that was being punished this way.

With my breath still ragged and my heartrate returning to normal, I tuck my spent cock back into my breeches and remove my fingers. She lifts her head up to stare at me through sated eyes and I lock eyes with her as I slide my fingers along my lips, tasting her sweetness, letting it coat my tongue.

Then I lower my head and lick up the seed I spilled on her body before it can drip to the floor, the two flavors mingling, the taste of what our union would be. One could get addicted to it.

"Captain!"

I jerk, startled at the interruption and turn to see who has intruded on this intimate moment between a captor and his captive, a captain and his monster.

Page John is standing in the doorway looking at me with worry but when he finally notices Maren hanging naked from chains, her body glistening in the lantern light from the wet passes of my tongue, his eyes nearly bulge out.

"What is it?" I snap. "I'm a wee bit busy."

"It's Sedge, Captain," he says, bringing his eyes back to me. "He's missing."

This is news to me. Bad news. My gut sinks. "Missing? How can you be sure?"

"They've checked the whole boat, Captain."

"They can't have since you're the first person we've seen down here."

"He was last spotted on the deck."

"The deck!?" I exclaim. That's the last place Sedge should be.

"Yes sir. He wanted to help fight the skeleton crew."

This isn't good. This isn't good at all.

I glance at Maren and there's a softness in her eyes, a concern for Sedge, and yet I know I can't trust it.

"John boy," I say as I walk over to him and put my hand on his shoulder, leaning in to stare at him dead in the eye. He's young, only eighteen, and a long ways off from becoming a full member of the Brethren, but I trust him all the same. "I'll go see what's happening but I can't leave her alone. She's dangerous, do you understand? She's not who you think she is."

"Okay sir," he says unsurely.

I give his shoulder a hard squeeze. "I need you to watch her. You don't need to do anything but stand in this doorway and watch her. Don't even think about getting close to her. Do you understand me, boy?"

He nods, shoulders going back. "Yes. Yes, sir."

I glance back at Maren. "You be a good girl," I warn her. "Good girls get rewards."

Then I slap John on the back and head out of the room to find out what happened to my dear Sedge.

SEVENTEEN

Ramsay

"What do you mean Sedge is missing?" I yell as I step onto the upper deck.

Thane comes storming toward me, hands behind his back. "He was last seen up top. He said he wanted to help Drakos, knowing he was still injured."

"The damn sweet fool," I curse. "Did anyone see him taken? Killed?"

I look around at the crew who shake their heads. The entire deck is a mess of bones, most of them crawling about. I see a twitching hand near my boot and I stomp on it, shattering the fingers.

A frustrated noise sounds in my chest and I go to the rail and look behind me at our wake, the sky and sea black as onyx, the fog sitting in the distance like a blanket. The moment we got what we wanted and the mermaid was brought on board, we pushed off from the *Norfinn* and began to sail away. Not all of the skeleton crew were defeated, and I never even saw the captain, but since we stole something of theirs we had to make quick work of escaping, otherwise the battle would drag on for days, as it often does when you're battling the undead.

Could the cursed crew have taken Sedge? Retribution for stealing their mermaid, as useless as she was? I try my best not to think of it. Sedge is part of my crew, but he isn't part of the Brethren. The curse that befalls them would befall him if he became a part of theirs. We could lose him forever.

"Fuck," I growl, my hands gripping the rail. This is my fault. I was so damn distracted by Maren that I didn't even do a head count to make sure everyone was here before we sailed away. I blindly assumed that Sedge would have stayed in the galley as he always does, just as Henry and Lucas are ordered to stay away during battles, the three of them the most vulnerable on the ship. Pages John and Bart are also vulnerable, but they at least know how to fight.

At the thought of John, I make a silent prayer to whoever the hell is listening up there or down below for him to keep his wits about him. The last thing this ship needs right now is a monster like Maren on the loose. I doubt she could do much damage to the Brethren, but the Brethren could do a lot of damage to her and they wouldn't hesitate. I don't want to lose her.

And I don't want to lose Sedge either. He belongs to me just as she does, and I have made an oath to protect him the same way I have to protect her.

"Belay! Turn the ship around!" I bellow.

"What?" Thane snaps.

I twist around to face my brother. "We're going back to the skeleton crew. If Sedge is with them, we're taking him back."

"But if he's with them he's part of the crew," Thane argues, his golden eyes flashing. "And there will be no hope for him if he's cursed."

"We don't leave any of our crew behind, you know that, it's part of our creed."

"But he'll be as good as dead and you'll be leading us all back into battle! What about the crew you have now?"

"Quartermaster, you think the rest of us are a bunch of pussies?" Cruz barks out in a laugh. He looks at the rest of the crew. "We are here to fight!" He punctuates that by raising his cutlass in the air. "Are we not?"

Sam grumbles at that, a pussy in her own right, while everyone else erupts into cheers.

I give my brother a triumphant look. "We're turning around, Quartermaster. We're getting our Sedge back. Dear god, of all of us to take, he's as vulnerable as your own son and no doubt we would do the same for him."

Thane breathes hard through his nose, his lips pressed together in a firm line. Then he nods. "Aye. Captain."

"Bosun, bring us round! Back the way we came!" I holler.

"Aye, sir," Crazy Eyes says, and Cruz runs up to the aft deck to help him turn the wheel. Meanwhile Thane starts barking orders for the rest of the crew to adjust the sails. As the boat turns, the hull creaking as she goes, the wind appears now from behind, pushing into the flapping sails.

Thank you, Venla, I think. Her greatest gift to me was Hilla. After that, it was this wind.

I go to the forecastle, grabbing a spyglass along the way. Though it's night, I'll be able to spot when we get close, as long as the fog clears some.

I lean against the railing and look past the bowsprit to the ink-black horizon. Their ghost ship won't have any lights, which makes things trickier, but the islands around the Reef City are still inhabited by natives. The fires from their camps will be the first things to appear.

"You did the right thing," Sam says quietly, joining me at my side.

I glance at her. "You're siding with me instead of your dear husband? I never thought I'd see the day."

She gives me a faint smile. "Don't get used to it, Bones." She smacks me lightly on the arm. "But going back for Sedge is the right thing to do. I know he's not truly one of us, but I consider him as part of the Brethren all the same. You're doing what a good, fair captain would do."

"And you're saying the quartermaster isn't any of those things?"

She sighs and tucks the windblown strands of red hair behind her ears. "You know how Thane is. Stubborn as the devil made him. I have no doubt he would go back for any of the Brethren, but you know how distrustful he can be of others. Even someone as harmless and helpful as Sedge, someone who is truly part of the crew. You can't really blame him or any of us for possibly feeling that way. Not in this world."

I know what she means. "Humans can be nice."

She chuckles at that, giving me a wry smile. "Humans can be nice? This is coming from *the* Captain Ramsay Bones Battista, who slices heads off first and asks questions later?"

I shrug. "We all have the capacity to do monstrous things."

I think of Maren. She might not be "human" in that sense, or perhaps she is, but she's a good example, nonetheless.

Sam must pick up on an expression on my face because she says, "You know, the princess would make a fine pirate."

"Aye," I agree with a nod. "Though she's not a princess anymore," I add quietly.

She frowns. "What do you mean?"

I can't help but wince as I tell her the truth. "The prince is dead. The mermaid too."

"The mermaid and the hostage are dead!?" Sterling suddenly bellows from behind me.

Fuck. Why does he have to overhear everything?

I sigh heavily and turn around to see Sterling standing behind me. The rest of the crew has frozen in place, staring at me in horror.

I run a hand down my face, wishing I didn't have to say any of this.

With another loaded exhale, I address my crew, ignoring Sterling entirely.

"Unfortunately, the mermaid was dying." Everyone gasps. "She didn't have any blood left in her to give and whatever she had probably wouldn't have worked in the state she was in. She was a decaying fish in a tank, that's all. So I killed her out of mercy."

"You could have at least let us try!" Sterling growls. "We still could have fed from her! She had a hole we could have fucked."

I glare at him. "It was the right thing to do."

"And you killed the prince too?" he adds, spitting as he talks.

I hesitate. I don't want to throw Maren under the keel, but I don't want to lie either.

"The princess killed him. She had enough of his abuse," I say.

"Then the princess is to be put to death!" Sterling yells.

"The princess, Maren, still belongs to me. Body if not soul. You know how it works, Sterling. I claimed her as mine and that is a bond that doesn't break for any member of the Brethren."

He lumbers toward me, trying to look intimidating. He reminds me of a rhino.

"A brand doesn't mean she's yours," he ekes out.

"What about her orgasm?" I say, running my fingers under his nose, knowing the smell of her desire still lingers.

His nose wrinkles, his face going red hot.

"Our food supplies are non-existent!" he yells, giving his head a shake. "You killed the one thing that would have helped us, and you let the princess kill our source of income. What are we all doing this for if not for those things? You are leading us to poverty and starvation. You are not fit to be captain!"

I refuse to back down, pressing my chest right up against his and staring into his beady eyes. "Are you declaring mutiny?" I challenge. "Out with it then!"

"Captain!" one of the crew yells, and the warning tone of his voice causes both me and Sterling to look. Remi is pointing at the bow with terror in his eyes.

I whip around to see a waterspout forming on the dark surface of the sea, the column of water drawn higher and higher into the sky. I don't know what to make of it, its creation doesn't seem natural.

Then something shoots out of the top of the waterspout and with the way its wings are spread I think it's a great gull or albatross, until I realize the wings aren't feathered but slick and rubbery and belong to a giant manta ray.

The ray comes falling toward the deck and is about to hit when suddenly it starts changing forms in mid-air. The wings fold in to become human arms, the tail elongates and widens to become legs, and the manta's mouth shrinks to become lips.

Standing before us, her feet gently touching the deck, is a sea witch.

"Nerissa," Sam says softly from the side of me.

Nerissa fixes her gaze on Sam and gives her an impish smile. "You're still here, Samantha Battista. I thought you would have died by now." Then her focus comes to me. "And here's the man I wanted to see."

I swallow hard, summoning nerves of steel. Nerissa, like most sea witches, is a stunning woman, a human put together with dangerous magic. She's as tall as I am, her body lush with curves that are accentuated under her gossamer thin gown made of pearlescent oyster shell which moves around her like liquid. Her hair is long and a perpetually wet dark-green that morphs into shiny kelp near the ends. Her skin is brown with a metallic pink sheen that shifts under the light, her eyes a bright glowing copper.

She has everyone on this ship mesmerized. I wish Maren could see her for herself since she was so interested in sea witches. Though now I'm wondering why.

I push that thought from my mind and clear my throat.

"Good evening, Nerissa. What brings you to the *Nightwind*?"

She chuckles softly, twirling a piece of kelp hair around her finger. "Loving the formality, Bones," she says to me. "No time for idle talk, aye?" Her gaze sharpens. "I'm here because your crew has stolen something from my crew."

"We didn't steal it, we borrowed it," I tell her. "And the mermaid is below deck if you want her back."

"She's dead," Sterling spits out.

I shoot him a hard look. "Thanks for that. Very helpful."

"Dead, is she?" Nerissa asks, her voice low, rich and melodic. "Well, I shouldn't be surprised, she had been dying for some time. Her blood didn't even help my crew in the end, but they are a stubborn bunch as you know. So attached to the idea of becoming something they will never become."

"Yes, well it's your crew now that has something of ours," I tell her. "Sedge, our cook. He's useless on your ship. They don't eat."

"Neither do you," she says.

"Of course we do," I scoff.

She raises her chin. "Right," she says. "I forget sometimes." She makes a face of disgust. "Regardless of who has what and how important that is, my crew won't be giving you your cook back unless you give us something in return."

"Well, you can have the fair mermaid," I tell her. "Be my guest."

"Alive. We want something *alive*."

"Why do you care what the crew have or don't have? You're the one that cursed them."

Her nostrils flare contemptuously. "I'm sure you can understand, Captain, that no matter what you've done to your crew or how they feel about you, they're still your responsibility. I may have cursed them and their ship, but I do care about their well-being. Didn't you ever have a pet while growing up? Perhaps eels or barracuda?"

I frown. "No…"

"Give her the princess then," Sterling says. "That will call it even."

"Yes, give her the princess," Thane says and oh, I could kill my brother right now, my hands curling into fists.

Nerissa's watchful eyes notice this. "Princess? Do tell."

"He's been sticking his cock in the princess," Sterling rasps. "She was captured for ransom but now her husband, the prince, is dead and none of us, save the Captain, have any use for her."

"I have not been…" I start, then close my eyes and give my head a shake. When I open them I give Nerissa an imploring look. "You don't want the princess. She's not even a princess anymore. She's worth no money and she'd be a lousy member of any crew. All she does is talk back and look pretty."

"Is she a human?" she asks.

"Possibly?" I answer with a shrug.

"*Possibly?*" Sam repeats under her breath.

"Hmmm," Nerissa says, her lips pursed. "I suppose this might make a fair arrangement. Though I am a little confused by her possibly not being human."

I lift a shoulder. "It's hard to tell sometimes."

"Yes. Well, let me lay eyes on her," she says taking on an air of command. "Take me to this princess."

Oh, hell.

My head spins and I'm trying to think of what to do. I need Sedge back but I can't let her take Maren either. I can't let her take any of our crew.

"Is the captain seriously considering not trading a useless cunt for one of his own crew?" Sterling challenges, noticing my hesitation.

I glare at him. "Not at all. Let's go."

I lead them down to the quarterdeck and to the stairs below, my mind desperately trying to figure out how to get through this. Could I offer myself to the witch? Nerissa would probably like that even though her curse would never work on me.

We pass by Thane who is looking at me sharply, perhaps not believing what I said I would do.

Nerissa pauses by him for a moment and runs her finger over his chin. "You and I have destiny together," she purrs at him then continues following me.

I lead her and the rest of the crew down to the hold and over to the room where Maren is locked up.

Only to find Page John unconscious on the ground, half-naked, and the chains empty.

Maren is gone.

EIGHTEEN

Maren

I don't care if he made me see stars and shot his seed all over my belly, I don't trust the captain not to kill me. He's one step closer to finding out what I am and I won't have my blood siphoned to feed him and his crew, even if it brings me closer to Edonia. I won't let what happened to my sister happen to me.

You could have thought about that before your desires got the best of you, the voice of reason says. *Before that pirate stuck his skilled fingers inside of you and made you buck and moan like you never have before.*

I ignore that voice. I had a plan and it didn't exactly unfurl as I had hoped. Part of me thought that perhaps I could seduce the captain into letting me go. The other part of me *wanted* to seduce the captain, but for my own pleasure. The moment I felt the Syren energy flow through me I knew my blood was changing, the moment I ate Aerik's heart the urges I had were inevitable.

But now I have only one thing I need to do, and that's escape. I may not be able to control my monstrous features at will, which is proving to be most unfortunate thus far, but I can still seduce a man, especially one that isn't the captain. With a young strapping boy like that Page John, it was easier than I thought. The minute he admitted he was a virgin and I promised I would let him see heaven with his own eyes, he was unlocking my restraints as quickly as he could.

The damn fool didn't see me coming when I knocked him out with the butt of his own sword. Then I made quick work of things, taking his shirt and putting it on me, then his holster which I tied around my waist, the shirt long enough to cover my thighs and rear. Before I could leave I went to my torn gown and fished out Nill's shark-tooth necklace and tied it back on around my neck. With Aerik dead, I was free to wear what I wanted and do what I wanted.

And what I wanted now was to escape.

I run out of the room with the chains, leaving an unconscious John behind, and start looking for a way out. I can't go above deck and from the way the boat is suddenly turning, causing me to stagger off-balance, I have a feeling we're turning around, no longer heading in the direction we should be going in.

But it is the direction back to the islands. Now if I jumped overboard, there's a very good chance that I could get my ability to swim well. Perhaps my legs would morph together into a tail the moment I hit the water. At any rate, I finally have a chance to swim and I'm going take it.

My sister wanted me to be free.

I run toward the opposite end of the ship, a place I've never explored before, hoping to find a weapon of some kind but there's nothing. Nothing but some faint moans coming from the hold.

The prisoners! Dear lord, were some of the servants and crew of the *Elephanten* still alive?

I go toward the sounds, my heart in my throat and before I can even reach the door I'm overwhelmed by a revolting smell, simultaneously sour and sweet and rotted. With one hand on my nose and one on the handle I open it. In the faint light of the deck's lantern I see a row of dead bodies propped up on the ground, chained to a beam above them. Excrement, blood, and gore fill the area and I start coughing violently, fighting the urge to vomit.

"Princess," I hear a voice weakly say.

No. No, no one can still be alive.

But I did hear a moan and now I hear my title and as I step forward among the bodies, recognizing the gaunt and pale faces, their bodies seemingly drained of blood, I see Hodges. Hodges, Aerik's manservant and the man who carried me from the sea all those years ago. Fitting that I would see him before I went back into its depths.

"Hodges?" I say softly, trying not to cry. If he wasn't talking I would have thought he was dead.

He opens his eyes, completely red with blood. "Kill me, Your Highness. Make it swift and quick."

I shake my head as panic seizes me. "No. I can't do that. Tell me what they are doing to you in here? Why do they keep you?"

"One of the crew called them..." he licks his lips but he has no saliva to spare, "*Mandurugo*."

"What does that mean?"

He just stares at me. "Please. Don't make me beg for my end. Please."

Hodges lets out a raspy weak breath and eyes the knife in the holster at my waist.

I can't actually kill him, can I? I killed Aerik, yes, and I would do it again. But while Hodges was never overly kind to me, he was loyal and never cruel.

"I can't suffer any longer," he manages to add. "Let me go home to God."

I find myself reaching for the knife and pulling it out, the blade trembling in my hand. Where has all my bravado gone? Earlier I had no problems killing Aerik, eating his heart, and asking the captain to touch me. Now I find myself feeling sick and weak at the idea of killing an innocent man. What happened to the Syren inside me?

Perhaps my humanity has decided to stick around.

"I will have my vengeance for you," I tell him, holding the knife above his heart.

"Forget your vengeance," he says. "You need only to escape. Be merciful, Princess Maren. Let me go. God will forgive us both."

I take in a deep breath, hoping that whatever gods there are will indeed forgive me for this one, and plunge the knife down into his heart.

It sinks in to the hilt and kills him instantly and I feel the air calm with his passing.

But I don't have time to mourn him or ponder the horrors that have happened in this hold. I have to save myself.

I leave the hold and run to the stairs and go up to the cannons at the gun deck. I pick one and swing my leg up over, straddling it, the metal cold on my inner thighs and not totally unpleasant.

I ignore the way my feminine urges keep springing up at inappropriate times and shift myself along the cannon barrel until I'm popping open the gun port at the end, fresh sea air meeting my face. I'm about to slide off into the sea that's moving quickly below when I hear the crew start coming down the stairs and the voice of an unfamiliar woman.

I don't want to stick around and find out who it belongs to.

I take in a deep breath and let go of the end of the cannon.

Wind rushes past me as I freefall, trying to move my body away from the edge of the giant ship so I don't get sucked under the keel, which is much easier to do when you're not wearing a weighty gown.

I hit the water feet-first, the impact rattling me, and immediately start swimming away from the ship as quick as I can. The water is cold at first but soon feels like a second skin and I'm swimming with my legs pressed together, hoping beyond hope that they'll fuse together into a tail.

But before that might possibly happen, as I move through the dark water, I realize I'm actually breathing it in. It's not coming through my nose or mouth, but my *gills*. I reach up to touch the side of my neck and the faint scars I once had there to symbolize them are now actual working gills.

I let out a cry of delight and look back at my legs. Even though my eyesight is excellent in the dark now, I still can't make out every detail. What I do see is that my legs are just that—legs. There might be a pearlescent tinge to them that wasn't there before, a faint impression of scales, but other than that they haven't turned into a tail.

It doesn't matter. I can swim fast with them together as one, and with working gills, I can stay under the water for as long as I like.

Still, I need to swim to land for now before I decide what to do next. I tilt my head up and back to look at the ship, its lantern lights growing fainter and fainter. Though we are both heading in the same direction, the *Nightwind* is so much faster than me. I just have to make sure that I don't end up where they're going.

My heart pangs a little at the thought, a tightness in my chest.

What if I don't see Ramsay again? With this plan, I probably won't. After all, not seeing him again *was* the plan. I hate to admit it, but I think I've grown some sort of attachment to him. The man is a mystery. A monster perhaps, but that only makes him a better match for me. Never in my life had I had someone that showed such a degree of possession and protectiveness over me, like I was a treasure to be guarded.

He killed your sister. He would have killed Daphne. And for all you know he killed your mother, too, a voice reminds me. *You promised vengeance and nothing else.*

I swallow the lump in my throat and strengthen my resolve before I twist around and keep swimming. I'm popping up my head above water every so often to make sure I'm headed for land and now that dawn is breaking it is easier to see.

Finally I spot the hazy silhouette of an island lit behind a violet sunrise and relief floods over me. I dive back down under the waves, not going too deep, when I see what seems like faint twinkling lights coming from the dark depths beneath me.

What is that? I think, slowing down as the lights get brighter and brighter.

I realize what I'm looking at are two angler fish rising toward me, a lit ball hanging from the protrusion at the front of their heads. Though their eyes are ghostly white, and their teeth are formidable, I know they aren't that fast and they're certainly a lot smaller than me.

Then I notice they aren't alone.

Behind them, emerging from the darkness of the deep are two skeletons.

No. That's not quite right.

Two *Syren* skeletons.

I gasp, water flooding through my mouth.

The Syrens grin up at me with sharp teeth, their eyes empty sockets as transparent weedy hair flows from their skulls, their arms outstretched and reaching for me.

I flip around and start swimming as fast as I can. I don't know if these Syrens are remnants of the curse or what, but I'm not waiting around to find out what they want from me.

But even though they're just bone, they have tails and they move frighteningly fast. They let out a high-pitched screech and grab hold of my arms, one on either side of me.

I scream, trying to thrash, but I'm helpless in their grasp as they start swimming at top speed, pulling me through the water.

What are you? I ask. *Where are you taking me?*

They don't answer but it doesn't take long for me to figure it out.

They're taking me back to the ship.

The question is, which ship?

NINETEEN

Maren

I find out which ship quickly enough.

The dead Syrens drag me right back to the *Nightwind*, the very ship I just tried to escape. We break the surface and I stare up at the boat to see a woman looking over the railing, her hair green kelp. I immediately know her aura—she's a sea witch.

This must be the infamous Nerissa.

"Is this the princess you were talking about?" Nerissa asks, her voice low and hypnotic. Beside her Ramsay's head appears, staring down at me.

I meet his eyes. *Please let me go. Please don't bring me back on board. Let me be free*, I say inside, hoping he can somehow hear and understand.

His eyes soften at the corners and he gives me a blasé look as if to say, *I'm sorry?*

Then Nerissa gestures with her hands, raising them and the skeleton Syrens start to climb up the side of the ship, hauling me up with them. Their bone claws hook into the side of the wood and I watch as Ramsay winces at the damage they're doing to the ship. Naturally, he doesn't look all that concerned about me.

Finally, they reach the top and shove me onto the deck before they turn and dive back into the sea. I crumple to my hands and knees.

Nerissa walks over to me until her feet stop right in front of my face, her toenails silver and affixed with tiny pearls.

"Princess Maren," Nerissa says to me and for a moment I'm terrified that she knows who I am, that us Syrens, even former ones, have a certain look or smell to us. "On your feet."

I know better than to disobey a sea witch. I carefully press myself up until I'm on my feet, artfully arranging my hair over my shoulders. I'm aware that the water has caused John's shirt to become semi-transparent on me, so I drape my tendrils over my breasts as if I'm being modest, when I'm really covering up the gills that must be visible on the sides of my neck.

"Do you know who I am?" Nerissa asks, a coy smile on her lips. Her cheeks are round and high when she smiles, glinting iridescent pink in dawn's light. Her eyes glow like burnished copper as she takes me in under her thick lashes.

"A sea witch," I tell her. "I've heard a great deal about you."

"All good things, I hope," she says demurely.

"Not if you ask the skeleton crew."

She laughs. "That is verily true, my girl. Now, do you know why I brought you back on board after you tried to escape?"

I glance at Ramsay, but his eyes give nothing away, his face irritatingly blank.

I look back at her and shake my head. The only reason I can think of is that she heard somehow, perhaps from Ramsay, that I had Syren or witch-like tendencies and that was enough to fetch me.

"Because the crew here has decided to hand you over to me in exchange for one of their own."

"Sedge," I whisper, thinking back to what John had said when he came across me and Ramsay, how he had gone missing.

"Yes. The dear Sedge. He is most beloved by the crew of the *Nightwind*, despite not being one of the Brethren. And you, who are also not part of the Brethren, are not."

"Listen now," Ramsay speaks up, clearing his throat. "We can come to some sort of deal."

Nerissa smirks at him. "Is that so? And what deal is that?"

He opens his mouth and I cut him off. Truth is, I might be better off with her. Especially if she does what I ask.

"I'll go with you," I say quickly. "But only if you help me with one thing."

She folds her arms across her ample chest. "And what is that?" she asks, a brow raised.

"I want you to take me to Edonia."

Nerissa's other brow raises in surprise. "Edonia?" she asks.

"Why Edonia?" Ramsay says, stepping toward me. He grabs my elbow. "Maren, what are you doing?"

I give him a deadly glare and shrug out of his grasp.

"Stand back until the deal is complete," Nerissa commands him, the air seeming to sizzle with electricity of her own doing. He lets out a low gruff sound and reluctantly steps away from me. "Now, Maren, what do you know about Edonia, and why do you want to see her?"

"I heard she's the most powerful sea witch there is."

Nerissa rolls her red-gold eyes. "Pray, I think you've heard wrong. For I am a witch of equal or greater value to Edonia. Whatever you wish to go to her for, you can come to me. So do tell, my ink-haired child, what is it that you seek?"

I rub my lips together, tasting the salt. I have to think fast but carefully. If I lay my cards on the table and tell her what happened with Edonia, then I have nothing left to hide—and no mask I can continue to wear. The crew will know I'm a Syren and they'll want me for my blood. I'll end up back in chains, bleeding on demand. I'll end up like Asherah and I can't trust that Ramsay will put me out of my mercy. After all, it seems like he needs my blood the most.

Furthermore, if Nerissa is anything like Edonia, she might have qualms with me being a Syren as well. Sea witches are our only real enemy, aside from man, and she may not feel like bargaining with me or granting me any favors. She may wish to flat-out kill me, and I would be completely defenseless.

"I wish to become a mermaid," I tell her.

She laughs in surprise, as do a few of the crew.

"A mermaid?" she says, pressing her hand to her chest. Her nails remind me of Nill's tooth, which is thankfully still around my neck. "Why would you ever want to be one of them?"

I try not to show offense at her tone. "Because I saw the one that they brought on board. She was so magical and special and I love the sea. I would love it if you could turn me into one." I make my voice lighter and breathier, as if I'm some idiotic child who wishes to believe in fairy tales.

"What game are you playing, luv?" I hear Ramsay utter under his breath.

I keep my focus on Nerissa, smiling with put-upon hope. If she thinks Syrens are so awful, she may just grant me the wish to teach me a lesson about getting what you wished for. A lesson I've certainly learned before.

She lets out another mirthless laugh. "You are quite naïve for a princess. Though I suppose most born into royalty are. A mermaid is something no woman should want to be. Savage creatures of the deep they are. No, I'm afraid that unless I am given a better deal, you are to come with me to *Norfinn*. And I will return Sedge to this crew."

"What about the captain?" Sterling speaks up in a belligerent tone. "I was about to declare a mutiny on him anyway. I think this ship has been under poor management for far too long. This is no longer a democracy but a dictatorship! Our food is gone, our money is gone, and now he's thinking of keeping some dumb cunt instead of trading her for one of our own!"

I suck in my breath, expecting to hear the crew side with Sterling and call for Ramsay to be replaced, but there's only silence.

"Well?" Nerissa says to Ramsay. "Are you willing to take her place?"

"Will they get Sedge back?" he asks, and I can't believe he's considering it.

She nods.

"Then aye, I will."

My heart drops.

Now a cry goes up amongst everyone.

What on earth is Ramsay doing?

"You see!" Sterling shouts. "He's willing to abandon his crew for her! *Her*! What kind of captain is that!?" He comes at Ramsay, and I get out of the way just in time. "Here, I'll help you get rid of him," he snaps.

He tackles Ramsay at the waist, pushing him back until he's pressed back over the railing and Ramsay bashes his forehead against his and then knees him in the groin, which causes Sterling to double over just enough for Ramsay to slide out of the way of Sterling's over-sized body.

Ramsay raises his arms in peace as he staggers toward Nerissa. "I'll go willing, I—"

Suddenly Sterling rights himself and picks up a musket from beside him and raises it above Ramsay's head.

"Ramsay!" I yell, trying to warn him but by the time Ramsay whips around, Sterling swings the gun and it makes contact with the side of Ramsay's temple with a *THWACK!*

Ramsay spins around, his eyes rolling back to his head and falls straight down to the deck. He doesn't move.

"Sterling!" Thane commands as he pushes through the crowd toward him. "Stop at once or you're going in the hold!"

But Sterling just sneers at the quartermaster and picks up Ramsay, taking him right to the railing before chucking the unconscious captain overboard.

"No!" I scream running to the rail and looking over to see Ramsay fall straight into the sea with a hefty splash. Thane and Sam run to either side of me and stare down into the water.

"He can swim can't he?" Nerissa asks curiously from behind me.

"Not if he's knocked unconscious!" Thane snaps at her.

Before I know what doing I'm climbing over the railing.

"Princess!" Sam yells at me, trying to grab my leg but I'm already launching off and swan diving off the railing. Out of everyone on deck, aside from Nerissa, I'm the only one who can breathe underwater, the only one who can save him.

I hit the water more gracefully than I did when I hung off the cannon, perhaps having the confidence that I can swim almost as well as I used to, that I'm no longer just a human.

I dive deep, down and down I go, the water a crystal-clear shade of turquoise thanks to the rising sun. It's not too deep now that we're closer to the reefs and shore, but it's still a hundred feet down and the light gets further and further away the deeper I go. Eventually I see Ramsay on the sea floor, his dark form a blot against the white sandy bottom, the dark blue stretching out into the fathomless void behind him.

I swim faster knowing that time is of the essence. How long has he been under? He must be drowning already.

He might be dead already.

Panic seizes me, gripping my heart and I push on, my heart racing faster now with the fear that I may not get to him in time. I can't watch another person die, I can't.

I'm close, so close, when the angler fish and the skeleton Syrens appear again coming right out of the deep dark blue, the high-pitched screech of my ilk creating waves across the water. They swim at me fast, their claws extended, and now that I think they're somehow cursed like the crew is, I know exactly what to do.

For once I'm grateful I have legs and not fins.

As they approach, I pull my knees to my chest and then push out my leg like I'm doing a kick. Even underwater I'm able to do this move fast, my body having more grace and balance down here than up on land.

My foot connects with one of the Syren's skulls and crushes it completely before knocking it clean off the vertebrae. I watch for a moment as it floats away, rendering the Syren useless before I quickly get in position and do the same to other one.

Crunch.

The other Syren's head is kicked clean off and it too starts to sink

toward the bottom while the rest of the creature made of bones floun-
ders in the water, unsure where to go.

I don't have time to watch what happens. Instead I start swimming
down again, following the sinking heads down, down, down, hoping
and praying that I get to Ramsay in time.

Finally, I reach him. With his black shirt and dark hair flowing
around him he looks like a fallen angel, one that belongs to the devil,
the image made even more significant by the sight of the Syren's
decapitated skulls bouncing along the bottom beside him.

Please be here. Please be okay.

I press my fingers to his face, debating whether I should kiss him
or not. My kiss didn't bring back Asherah, but her kiss did something
to me. Do I have that power now? Or is he too far gone?

Because he has to be dead. He's drowned. No one could survive
that long underwater.

I continue holding my fingers against his jaw, wishing I could tell
him one last thing but I don't even know what that would be.

I guess if it weren't for him, I would have never escaped Aerik.

I would have never been set free.

And even though I'm not quite a Syren anymore, I'm more than I
have been in a long time, and I feel like he saw that in me from the
beginning.

For all that he's done, for all that I hate him for, in the end I think
he really saw me for me.

And more than that, he *liked* it.

I swallow the lump in my throat and decide to give it a try.

I lean in to kiss him but before my lips can get close to his, he gives
me the biggest fright.

His eyes open.

Ramsay's eyes open, the blue of them matching the blue of the
dusky water, and he stares directly at me.

"Ramsay?" I ask, the sound muffled as bubbles rise from my
mouth.

He frowns and slowly tilts his head to look at me, then looks up at the surface that's so far away. When he looks back to me, a small, satisfied smile turns up the corner of his mouth.

"You came for me," he says, bubbles floating from his mouth now.

I nod, overjoyed that he's alive but before I can ask him how he's still alive and seemingly not needing to breathe under the sea, he leans in, grabs my face...

And kisses me.

TWENTY

Ramsay

S am had always said that I'm a man that attacks first and asks questions later, and that's certainly true when it comes to the opposite sex (or the same sex, depending on the decade). I had many questions for Maren after Sterling clobbered me over the head and I found myself at the bottom of the sea, one being why she seemed to come after me—I assume to save me (unless she swam down to make sure I was dead, to which I would not be surprised).

And two, that she had swam down to get me at all. Looking up at the surface it seemed it was a long way up and she seemed to be doing just fine holding her breath, her dark hair flowing around her in such a way that it was hard not to imagine her as a mermaid.

Either way, those questions are quickly shoved to the back of my mind when I see her face so close to mine, her fingers pressed gently on the side of my face, her gaze focused on my lips. It doesn't matter that we are at the bottom of the sea, all I want, all I need, is to kiss her once and for all.

I grab her face hastily, fingertips digging into her skin, and my mouth finds hers, claiming it with intent. Her lips part in surprise and she lets out a groan at the contact that seems to echo through the water. Her lips are as soft as honey and just as sweet, and my tongue plunders her mouth in the very same rough manner in which I am known to fuck. I taste her, savor her, want to sink deeper in these depths until she is my only obsession.

I have wanted to kiss her like this since the moment she first punched me in the face.

My fingers go into her hair, pulling it back and she suddenly stops and moves back, her hands brushing her hair forward over her shoulders, a look of fright in her eyes.

Then she starts swimming toward the surface, her legs pressed together and moving as one for a second before she abandons that and starts moving her arms and clawing her way to the top.

I watch her rise above me for a moment, remembering what she had said to Nerissa. She wanted the sea witch to turn her into a mermaid. Why would she want that? Is she living out some fantasy here at the bottom of the sea? And how on earth is she able to hold her breath for so long?

With the feeling of her lips still lingering on mine, my cock at a stand, I go after her, swimming up and up with powerful kicks of my legs until the sun beams though the water get brighter and brighter, the deep blue fading and then I'm breaking through the surface.

I take in a gulp of fresh air and look at Maren treading water beside me, her eyes focused warily on mine, droplets gathered in her dark lashes.

"What are you?" I ask.

"What are *you*?" she counters.

I press my lips together. Hmmm. Seems we are at a crossroads.

I whirl around, looking for the *Nightwind*, and my heart sinks.

She's nowhere to be found. All I see is the cursed crew's ship back in their cove between islands. The *Nightwind* is gone.

"Damn it!" I yell, smacking the water with my fist. "They've taken her."

"That ship means a lot to you, doesn't it?" Maren says quietly.

"Aye," I reply sharply, as if that wasn't obvious. "She does, and so does the crew. I can't lose either of them."

"They're your family," she comments, sounding rather wistful.

I frown. "That they are." I look to the nearest land, which of course happens to be the ruined Reef City. Figures that we'd be back on Nerissa's territory so soon. "Come on, we have to get to shore and think of a plan."

She doesn't say anything to that. She doesn't need to, I can practically hear her thoughts, which is something that is possible between the Brethren at times. She's thinking she doesn't want anything to do with whatever plan I come up with.

We start swimming for the shore. We're a long ways off and even though I'm in peak physical form, and she's demonstrating the same, by the time we finally find our footing on the reefs and sunken basalt columns of the city, we're both exhausted and out of breath.

"Don't stand on the reef," she chastises me. Her haughty tone irks me, like she's back to acting like a princess again.

"And pray tell, why not?"

"Because you're damaging them."

I stare down through the clear water to my boots. "Who?"

"The coral are living creatures. You're hurting them."

I want to ask her how she knows that because this is the first I'm hearing of it, but I know her answer will be infuriatingly vague and I'll have to chalk it up to her being royalty and having a finer education than me.

"Fine," I grumble and step off the reef, swimming a few more yards until I'm staggering onto the shore. I walk away from the water until I find a patch of short coarse grass and plunk down. I rest my elbows on my thighs and drop my head, trying to get my brain back in order.

I hear Maren follow, sitting down beside me, close but still distant enough. She's breathing hard and when I give her a side glance my eyes go straight to her chest which rises and falls with each heaving breath. If it weren't for her hair covering her nipples she'd look nude with how transparent her shirt is. A jolt of hot lust thrums through my veins, knowing how good she looks in her birthday suit.

"Stole that shirt from Page John, didn't you?" I ask, my mind going back to how she felt as she came on my fingers, the sounds she made. Christ.

She doesn't look at me, just stares at the ruins of the city and the reef beyond. "I didn't kill him," she states.

"I never said you did, but you knocked him out cold. Poor fella, I should have known he'd be powerless against the likes of you."

Her brow raises and she eyes me. "What about the likes of me?"

I gesture with my hand. "Your feminine wiles. No one can resist."

"You resisted."

My mouth parts for a moment. This woman drives me to madness. "Is that so? I resisted?"

"You took me with your hands, not your staff," she says.

"Would you have wanted my cock inside you while you hung from chains?"

The heated look that comes over her eyes, similar to the one she had while I was making her come, says she would have readily taken it.

And now, no surprise, my cock is stealing the thoughts from my mind, my skin growing tight and hot with need. As much as I want to take her right here and now, my ship is still gone and I'm surrounded by a mystery.

I decide to try and get some answers.

"Are you very good at holding your breath or something to that nature?" I ask, nodding at the sea.

"Are you?"

"Answering questions with questions is not answering the question."

"That's because I have no plans to answer the question." She pauses. "Did Nerissa really send her dead Sy—dead mermaids after me because you wanted to do a trade?"

I sigh, pushing my wet hair off my face. My skin already feels scratchy from the drying salt. "*They* wanted to trade you for Sedge."

"And you were going to let them."

"No, I wasn't."

"You were. I know it."

"Okay, maybe at first," I admit.

She glares at me. "I knew it."

"But if you didn't happen to notice, I offered to take your place. Me. Captain Battista, of the good ship *Nightwind*, offered to be traded to the sea witch and her skeleton crew so that the likes of you wouldn't have to. If that isn't a noble sacrifice, I don't know what is."

"Oh, how very honorable of you," she says, sarcasm dripping. "But you're the one who told me that the curse can have no effect on you. You knew you'd come out unscathed."

"Unscathed? You don't understand sea witches. They are still witches, and they are our natural enemy. I may have had good luck with one in the past, but witches will always find a way to make your life a living hell."

Her eyes flit over my face, trying to read me. I widen my eyes at her. Not sure if I can be more sincere.

"So then, why did you do it? Why offer to take my place?"

Oh, she is daft at times. "Because of that mark on your hip, luv. Because you belong to me. You're my property."

She flinches at that. "I don't care for being called anyone's property."

"You were property of the crown before."

"And I hated it," she seethes.

"Yes, well you tend to hate a lot of things," I mutter.

"With good reason!" she cries out. "There are many things to hate."

"Especially me."

"Especially *you*."

"And I suppose I'm about to hear all the reasons why you hate the captain, aren't I? Alright, have at it then." I gesture with my hand for her to unleash.

"You're crude," she says, crawling toward me, her breasts swinging under the low dip of her shirt and it takes all my effort to pull my eyes up to meet hers. They rage with glowing blue fire. "You're barbaric. You're a murderer."

I give her an acidic grin. "So are you, darling."

"A monster," she spits out, crawling even closer. Maybe too close for comfort considering what a monster she can be.

"If the boot fits. They fit us both."

"A heathen," she says, her eyes now on my lips.

"Being a saint is so fucking boring."

"You torture people."

"Not for fun," I say, though that is a bit of a lie. "Unless they deserve it," I clarify.

Her eyes flash. "I saw the hold. I saw where you kept the crew and my servants. What you did to them."

Blast. I didn't want her to see that.

"We didn't torture *them* for fun," I try to explain. "That's not what we do...that's not what we're about. The Brethren has a strict moral code."

She barks out a sour laugh. "Oh, I've heard all about your pirate's code."

"No. Not a pirate code. The code of the Brethren. We happen to be pirates, but not all pirates are part of the Brethren. All the ones that are you'll find on the *Nightwind*."

"So then you're some kind of devil-worshipping cult."

"That's making us sound organized. We only do—"

"What you must to survive," she finishes. "Yes, I've heard it all before."

"Then by now you should know it to be true." I wait a beat, waiting to see if I should provoke her or not. I know she can be dangerous but at the same time I want that. I want to tussle with her with her claws out. "But at least we have a code. You don't. I caught you eating your husband's heart like you were a stray dog."

She lets out a roar and pounces on me like a lioness, her claws sharpening, teeth turning into sharp slivers. "Damn you!" she growls and she's on top of me, my hands holding her back with a tight grip around her wrists, her mouth snapping, her fingers trying to claw the air.

"My little monster has come out to play again," I say, grinning up at her. "Don't you know this only excites me?"

Her nostrils flare as she seems to take in the sight of her claws, the way they extend from her fingers like eagle's talons. Then the surprised look in her eyes turns to one of pride and satisfaction. She eyes me. "I could eat you right here."

"So could I," I counter. "Only I'd make it worth your while."

"You already kissed me." Her eyes glint. "I wasn't that impressed."

I snort. "My apologies. I thought you could handle it."

"I can handle it."

"Then I'll probably do it again. I can't help myself around you."

"Because you're unhinged, getting your prick up by a creature like me."

"A gorgeous creature," I correct her. "And a dangerous one. I'm a fool for a strong woman, a free woman, one who goes by her own rules, one who does what she wants and doesn't care what the world says. Don't you think you fit the bill?"

She stops squirming for a moment and I lower her toward me an inch, the tips of her thick wet hair tickling my face. She's breathing hard and her eyes look away from my face for a moment, as if thinking over what I said.

"Oh, just take my cock so I can fuck you and be done with it," I say.

She blanches, a venomous gaze darting back to mine. "Be done with it?"

"Aye. So I can make you see heaven before you go back to hating me."

"Perhaps I'd rather fuck you and hate you at the same time."

"Anyone ever tell you how immoral your mouth is?"

"Never. I suppose I've been saving it for you."

I give her a crooked smile. "I think I'd risk those teeth along my cock for the mere promise of what your lips and tongue can do, but the honest truth is I'd rather be using my mouth on *you*."

"I'd like to see you try."

I give her a look that says, *oh really?*

With a grunt I flip her over, slamming her back against the grass and she lets out a yelp.

"You going to fight me or fuck me?" I growl at her, pinning her clawed hands above her head and straddling her hips. "Let me know so we can have some rules."

She snarls in response, baring her teeth and showing no signs of wanting to play fair. If I'm not careful I'll come out of this missing the tip of my nose.

Or worse.

"Fine," I say. "Guess I'll have to take my chances."

With one hand still affixed to her wrists, I bring my other one down to her thighs, parting them roughly. I slide my hand up to her womanhood and I'm not all too surprised to find her bare and wet.

A gasp gets caught in her throat and for a moment she gives in, her eyes fluttering, mouth parting, then her neck cords and she snaps her head toward me.

"Remember what I said before," I tell her as I quickly pull my head back from hers just in time. My fingers then slide along her clitoris and toward her cunt. "Good girls get rewards."

"What do the bad girls get?" she asks through a growl.

I grin at her. "Bad girls get punished thoroughly. I reckon you deserve both."

"Then get on with it," she says.

"Yes, Princess," I say with mock reverence as I plunge three fingers deep inside her.

"Gods!" she cries out, panting while she squeezes snugly around me.

"I need to know if you're able to take me all the way in," I murmur, my fingers curling inside her walls until she's bucking her hips up for more. "I've got a thick cock and you have a tight little cunt, luv."

I watch as pink blooms across her cheeks. I've made the lady blush.

"I'll tell you what," I say, my face coming closer to hers, enough that I can count the freckles across her nose, "you keep the biting and scratching to a minimum, and I'll fuck you with my tongue next. Savvy?"

"Yes, Captain," she groans.

I let out a harsh breath. Devil Almighty. The term captain never sounded so sweet.

I take her at her word and let go of her hands, my heart a beating drum against my ribs. Part of me is wondering if she's going to maim me, the other wants to be maimed. But more than anything I just want to lick her senseless.

TWENTY-ONE

Maren

I lie back in the grass, finding it hard to completely surrender to him. My body is a firestorm of feelings, heat licking up my skin and making me burn for him. I want to fight him, want to argue, but I also want him like I've never wanted anyone before. It's like all those feminine and ungodly urges that were kept at bay after I turned human are coming out in full force now and taking control of my body.

So I decide to submit.

I let out a sharp cry as I squeeze around his fingers, wanting more of him, all of him and I know he's grinning at me with that self-satisfied smirk of his. I don't care. Let him smile all he wants. I suppose he deserves to for making me succumb to him like this, parting my legs for him with ease.

"You're a greedy little monster, aren't you, lass?" he murmurs. "Deprived of a good cock for too long."

I blush again, his words a constant surprise. Some might say he speaks straight from the devil, but I'm discovering I like what the devil has to say.

He starts moving down the middle of me and I'm acutely aware of how large and hard his body is when it's hovering inches above mine. I can feel the heat coming off him, his hands bringing flames to my thighs as he pushes my shirt up further until it's bunched around my waist.

My heart catches so high in my throat as his face lowers between the soft skin of my thighs and then, and then…

My gods. I let out a breathy cry as I feel his lips press against my delicate flesh, followed by a wet pass of his tongue.

My mind is blown open.

I've never had a man down there before. Aerik hadn't touched me in a sexual manner for years, but even when things were frequent and physical between us, he was quick and never cared if I came to completion, and certainly never thought to put his mouth on me like this. He would have said it was immoral.

But Ramsay…he's lapping me up like he loves the taste of sin, the flat of his tongue firm and slick, the sensations becoming too much to handle.

And yet I must watch. I lift my head to see him between my legs and, dear lord, he's looking up at me now, those stormy eyes staring right at my soul while his tongue tastes, savors me, me over and over again.

It's so jarringly intimate, this connection that now simmers between us, my submission into his mouth and hands and anything else he wants to use to take me over the edge.

"You like this, luv?" he asks, pausing to blow air along my wet skin.

I yelp, my head going back to the grass as my limbs jerk from the sensation. He lets out a low, rich chuckle, like he's enjoying this as much as I am. "Want me to keep devouring you like the dessert that you are?"

"Yes," I whisper harshly.

"Yes *please*, princess," he says to me. "Or have you forgotten all your manners already?"

"Yes please," I say, panting now.

"Ask me for it, Your Highness."

I raise my head to give him an incredulous look. But he isn't joking.

"Devour me," I say. "Please."

His full lips, shiny with my desire, curl into a grin and then he attacks me savagely with his tongue, swirling and sucking me into his mouth.

"Gods!" I can't help but moan.

My hips are bucking, my hands gripping the grass and I let out a sharp groan as his mouth moves lower, his tongue pushing into me and I feel like I'm breaking apart. My body starts to tremble, my mind going numb and I let out another cry as my hands reach down and grip his hair.

"Ramsay, I'm...I'm...I'm going to—"

"Let go of yourself for me," he murmurs against my skin, the sensations rocking through me.

My hips start moving of their own accord, pushing my sex against his mouth and his tongue delves deeper into me until he's all I feel.

Gods, it's too much. I'm going to break apart.

His strong large hands hold my thighs, keeping them apart and I'm exploding, neck arching back.

Colors flash behind my eyes, my body goes rigid and I feel as if I'm shooting light out of my fingertips as I come undone. He is consuming me whole.

My screams are loud and raw, my throat burning like fire, and I'm sure any animals that had been in the surrounding area have scurried away by now, but I don't care. I feel primal, a creature in the throes of heat. My head is spinning, my mouth is dry, and my limbs are completely useless.

But in the aftermath there's a contentment that I've never felt before. I feel powerful and yet sated at the same time. There's a thread of vulnerability that wants to tighten around me, remind me that I am lying here naked from the waist down, bare for him to see, touch, and taste, and yet this feeling of bliss overrides it.

"That was..." I manage to say, licking my lips. "That was..."

"What it was is not over yet," he says gruffly, and I raise my head to see him yank down his breeches. He takes his cock into his hand and while I'd seen it when I was hanging from chains the other night, right now it's closer and so much more impressive in the morning light. Thick, long, and very hard, it makes his large hands look small in comparison.

I gulp with fear. I really don't think it will fit inside me. I give him a look of trepidation, wondering how much this will hurt.

He reads that look. "You can handle me, can't you luv? Maybe your prissy princess cunt would cower, but you're a monster at heart. You can take whatever I give you."

My face goes red again at his words and a flame is stoked inside me. He knows I like a challenge.

"Why don't you show me instead of talking about it?" I tell him.

He laughs, giving his head a shake before a molten look hardens his eyes. "Don't mind if I do," he says, his voice rough with desire. He moves over me, his arms braced on either side of my head, and I brace myself too.

I feel his cock press against my opening. I'm so wet from his ministrations but my body instinctively tightens up.

"Relax," he says, one of his hands going to my hair, brushing a strand off my face in a startlingly delicate gesture that is at odds with how his cock wants to treat me.

"Relax, luv," he says again, more firmly this time and I nod my head faintly.

He breathes in deep through his nose, those stormy blue eyes intense as he searches my face. Then he moves closer to me, lips just inches away from mine, and he pushes in slowly.

I try to hold my breath. His girth is stretching me and my body is a hurricane of sensation and I'm gripping the grass harder as I try to make room for him.

"Hold on to me," he whispers, running the tip of his nose over the tip of mine. "I've got you."

I nod again and I reach up, feeling along the hard, flexing muscles of his back, my nails digging into his shirt as he goes deeper, pushing in inch by inch until he's fully seated inside me.

I gasp for air, completely breathless. I don't know where he ends and I begin. I feel completely and utterly fused to him, hips to hips, skin to skin.

He doesn't move right away. One hand is in my hair, the other bracing himself by my head, his face hovering inches above mine as his gaze drifts over my features, taking stock of me.

"How does it feel, luv?" he asks quietly.

I try to move my hips, experiment with the feeling. "Full," I manage to say.

"Good," he says, his eyes dark with need.

I feel full, yes, but it's a good full. It's a full that brings with it heat that seeps through my veins and into my bones.

A kind of full that makes me realize how empty I had been before.

His arms are starting to shake on either side of me and I can tell he's struggling not to move, his breath in short bursts through his nose, his eyes hazy with lust. My body is on fire, it clenches around him and the longer he stretches me like this, the more I grow hungry for him.

"Such a good little creature," he murmurs, leaning down and sucking along my jaw. "You're making me see the heavens already."

He starts moving his hips, so slow that it's almost like torture. I can feel every inch of his cock as it pushes into me, my wetness making the way easier but my body is fighting to not be taken by it. His lips almost touch mine and I open my mouth, needing to take in air, but he isn't going fast enough. I can't breathe.

"More." I gasp, my hands going to his chest, needing something to break the suffocating heat that is accumulating inside of me.

He gets the hint, pulling back, his cock just barely inside of me before he plunges back into me, sending a shock of pain across my hips.

The pain knocks the breath out of me and I shudder for breath, my eyes squeezing shut and my body clenching around him.

"Relax," he says again, his voice a growl this time. "You can take all of me."

He moves again, this time his cock retreating completely and then he plunges into me again. This time I don't gasp for air. This time I moan, my hips bucking against him of their own accord.

It's slow and agonizing and I want more.

"You like that, aye?" he rasps, his accent growing thicker with pleasure.

I nod, clutching at his shirt desperately as he begins to pick up the pace, his hips slapping into me, making the pain a distant memory.

I'm filled with him, his cock stretching me, his body so heavy on top of me that I can barely function. His lips find mine and he kisses me fiercely, his tongue forcing my mouth open and dancing with mine, his teeth nipping at my mouth and his growls sending vibrations through me.

How is this even happening? I think to myself as I feel a knot start to form inside of me. *Was this inevitable between us from the start? Is it fate or destiny or just another one of my mistakes I'll come to regret?*

But my thoughts quickly dissolve as the rhythm of his hips continues, impaling me to the ground. His cock is pounding into me and I'm totally enraptured by it, to this meeting of our bodies. He's a pirate, he's been my captor, and yet I'm craving him, wanting him as if he's something so much more than that.

Is it possible that the man who kept me in a cage is the same one to set me free?

"Look at me," Ramsay says, bringing my focus back to his face, to the fierce determination in his eyes. "Keep looking at me while I fuck you. I don't want you to be imagining anyone else but me."

"I couldn't even if I tried," I admit through a breathy moan.

His mouth curls and he leans in and takes my bottom lip between his teeth, giving it a tug while he slams his hips in deep, his shaft into the hilt.

I let out a hoarse cry as the sensation blinds me, then I roll my hips under him, pulling him even deeper.

"Fuck," he grunts. His eyes blaze, mouth falling open and he throws his head back for a moment, trying to catch his composure. I can see it slipping; want him to let loose inside me.

"I'm going to fill you with my seed, luv," he says, his voice low and gravelly as he brings his lips back to my neck. "Not that pathetic prince, but me. I'll claim you in every way that I can, my essence so deep inside you that I'll become a part of your blood and bones."

He's thrusting deep and hard now and I'm helpless against it, my breath rushing from me in short bursts as I fight to keep my eyes open, to keep looking directly into his. His brow has come together, his face growing red and strained with the physical force of his actions and he's working me like he'll die if he doesn't. I've never been looked at like that before, never been the utter focus of someone like this, like I'm the only thing that exists in Ramsay's world.

It makes me realize what I've been missing all along.

The pleasure inside of me is starting to unravel now and I feel like I'm going to detonate, like I'm going to shatter into a thousand pieces scattered throughout the waves.

"There it is, luv," he rasps thickly. "Right there."

His hand goes to my hair, making a fist, and he kisses me again, hard and fierce as I feel the tension break apart and my fingers dig into his hips as I come. I'm awash in ecstasy, shuddering against it and my hand goes to his shoulder, bucking against him to ride out the wave that crashes over me again and again.

The orgasm pulls me into an undertow, my body bowing away from him as my muscles contract, fluttering around that heavy cock that has worked me so well.

Then he's brought to the edge of the precipice with another hard pump. He lets out a savage growl, his neck cording and shoulders straining as his cock pulses hard inside of me, his body completely out of his control, shooting what seems like an endless stream of his seed into me.

His hips stutter against mine, bucking me up against him. Then his movements slow, riding it out to the very end, his body trembling against me, his breath harsh and ragged.

He dips his head so his damp forehead rests against mine, his chest rising and falling with each breath and his lips brush mine tenderly He's looking at me with warm, satisfied, half-lidded eyes.

A bead of sweat rolls down the side of his face and I reach up and wipe it away. He grins at the gesture, his face still flushed and the veins in his forearms standing out as he slowly pulls out of me. I can feel the tension leave my body until I'm hollow inside without him there.

I swallow hard, trying to get my mind to think clearly again. He may have just pleasured me in countless ways with his body, but he is still my enemy, still a man that would do me no good if I felt anything but hate for him.

He tucks his cock back inside his breeches and then sits back down on the grass beside me, chest heaving. "See," he says, eyeing the expression on my face. "Now you have no reason to keep fighting me."

All the wonderful, blissful feelings I had moments earlier abruptly fade away. "Yes, I do," I say, my voice hard.

"Still?" he asks with wide eyes, indignant. "Why?"

I pause, feeling venom in my veins again.

"You killed my sister."

TWENTY-TWO

Ramsay

I stare at her beautiful face, completely dumbfounded.

"What do you mean I killed your sister?" I ask, my brain going over all the people I've killed over the years. There's so many, I wouldn't even know where to start, but because of our trade, we're usually taking merchant men and naval sailors on board the *Nightwind*, not women.

She glowers up at me through her lashes, pulling her shirt back down over her body. "The mermaid."

"That mermaid was your *sister*?" I blink. She's joking, is she not?

Then she lifts her hair off her shoulders, gathering it into a knot behind her back and turns her head so that her neck is exposed. She points to the three faint lines I only recently noticed on the side of it.

"Scars?" I ask. "What about them?"

She gives me a pointed look, like I'm supposed to figure this out. I think back to the gills on the mermaid's neck and...

"You're a mermaid," I say slowly.

"A Syren," she corrects me, raising her chin.

I give my head a shake. Though it all makes sense, it still remains unbelievable. "But you don't have a fishtail. I would know, I was just between your legs."

She averts her eyes, gazing over the horizon. "It's a long story."

"Well, lucky for you, we have a lot of time."

"We don't," she says. "You said yourself you have to make plans."

"I have time for you, luv," I tell her. "I have time for this."

I mean, a mermaid. She realizes how valuable she is, doesn't she?

Think of what you can do with her blood, the devil on my shoulder hisses.

I'm trying not to.

"Do tell your story, Maren," I encourage her before my mind gets carried away on me and I do something I shouldn't.

She lets out a low breath and closes her eyes briefly.

"When I was sixteen…" she begins, trailing off. I stay silent and give her space to find her words. "I left my home. The Kingdom of Limonos. I was tired of being overlooked and undervalued. Really, I just felt ignored. Looking back, I don't think I was any of those things, but I was young and I had all these big feelings inside of me that I didn't know how to explore, how to let loose. My mother disappeared when I was young and I couldn't turn to my father or sisters with anything. I thought the best way to deal with it would be to leave home and start anew somewhere else where I would be appreciated, where people would see me for what I really am. Not just a Syren, but what I am in here." She presses her hand against her chest.

Then she takes in a deep breath, still searching the waves, as if they're helping her to remember. "I traveled far with only my shark, Nill, to protect me." My eyes drift to the shark-tooth necklace I noticed on her earlier. "And one day I looked above the surface and found myself in the bay of a strange land. On shore there was a strange man and something possessed me at that moment. The need to make him mine. I wanted him, something to call my own, and I wanted him so madly that I swam to the canyons in the sea and I called to the sea witch to answer me."

"Edonia," I whisper, the realization dawning over me.

Maren nods, sucking on her bottom lip. "Yes. It was Edonia. We were taught to fear the sea witches and to revere the sea witches, and I knew she could grant me my wish. I wanted to be able to be on land, as a human, and make the man, the prince, fall in love with me. I wanted a life that didn't seem attainable in Limonos."

My eyes widen. So that's how she met that pathetic prince.

"She granted me my wish but not before I had to pay the price. She cut out my tongue because she believed it would help with her book of magic."

My heart stills. Not only because that witch cut out her tongue, a grotesque act of violence even for me, but because it was for her book. For *my* book, the one that Venla wrote for me, the one that Edonia stole right after she killed my daughter.

"She also told me that I could never return to the sea again and would be destined to be human forever," Maren goes on. "And it all sounded so fine to my ears because she tricked me. She told me that women were revered on land, that we had all the power, that I would never be under the thumb of a man. She lied to me, and it was that lie that sealed the deal because that's all I wanted. I had no idea that what waited for me on the shore was what would condemn me to hell for the next ten years."

She clears her throat, her eyes welling with tears, and presses on. "Hodges, Aerik's manservant, found me…naked, missing a tongue, unable to talk, barely able to walk. He brought me to Aerik and the prince fell in love with me. Or should I say lust. Of course he did. Because I was mute and I was pretty and I was weak. He loved all of those things but he never loved me. I don't need to tell you that."

"So that's how you came to be a princess," I say thoughtfully.

"I was a princess in Limonos," she says with a raise of her chin, her tone defensive. "My father was the king. But I traded that crown for one I had no right to, in a world I didn't belong to."

I should have figured. There is something about Maren's posture and the way that she carries herself that hints to a royal past, even when her monstrous side is coming through. "And how were you able to get your tongue back? I know firsthand you have one from the way you kiss."

She shrugs, giving me a quick, shy smile. "It grew back. You know when our tails get chomped by curious shark or we lose one during battle with a neighboring kingdom, they grow back. Same happened with my tongue. But other than that, there was no way that anyone would ever believe what I was. In fact, there was no sign of it at all except for the lines on my neck. I didn't get any of my old self back until I saw Asherah on the *Nightwind*, and only then did I feel a partial return to my Syren state, or whatever I am now."

She looks down at her hands, her fingernails normal again. "Aerik never knew the truth about me, neither did Daphne. They all believed my story about being kidnapped from a faraway land by pirates."

"Pirates?" I chuckle. "I should be so honored."

"Well, you did kidnap me, Captain Battista," she reminds me. Her gaze darkens. "And if I'm not mistaken, I believe I'm still kidnapped by you."

I swallow. "Aye. You are."

"You could just…let me go," she says, her tone slightly pleading, eyes soft. "You could find your way back to the *Nightwind* and you could just leave me here."

"On Nerissa's island? I think not."

"Then you could take me to the nearest safest port and I could finally be free."

"You are free, my dear. But you also belong to me."

"That's not freedom."

"It is if you want me."

"But I don't want you," she snaps.

I've experienced rejection here and there, but this is the first time it's actually hurt, like a knife between the ribs, finding my soft spot.

"Whether you do or not, I claimed you," I tell her stiffly.

"But what does that even mean? So you branded your name on me. It's not magic." Her eyes slowly widen. "Is it?"

"Some might say it is," I answer carefully. "Regardless, my name on you means that you belong to me. It's not just in a spiritual or soulful or sexual manner. It's keeping you safe from others. It's a code of the Brethren."

"You mean to say that had you not branded me with a skull and your initials, I'd be passed around and violated by all your crew? You act so proud of them and yet they're all a bunch of madmen and rapists."

I give my head a shake, knowing why she's confused. "Some may be madmen and some might have been rapists. I don't keep tabs on them at all hours of the day and I don't judge what they did before they joined my crew. But there are other ways of harming you, luv, and they don't all involve things of a sexual nature. There are other, more deadly natures at stake."

"Such as what?"

"The nature of survival."

She throws up her hands in frustration. "You and your incessant excuse of survival. What in sodding hell does that even mean?"

"It means if I didn't protect you, the crew would try and *eat* you."

I let the truth hang in the air while Maren's brows draw together.

"Eat me?" she repeats. "W-why?"

"Why did you eat your husband's heart?"

Her frown deepens. "Because I…because it was my revenge. I wanted vengeance for the way he treated me for so long. I wanted to show him what I really was."

"You could have ripped out his heart. You didn't have to eat it."

She swallows uneasily, a flash of shame coming over her expression before it turns cool. "I ate it because that's what we do. We are vicious beasts, you said so yourself. We eat the hearts of men, not just because it tastes good—believe me it was the best thing I've ever tasted—but because it's in our nature. It sustains us, more than the liver or the kidneys of men, or the brains or heart of any fish."

She says all of that with defiance, as if daring me to be disgusted by her.

Naturally, I'm not disgusted in the slightest. I only call her kind vicious beasts because they are, and in my eyes it's the highest compliment you can give a woman.

"What if I were to tell you that me and my Brethren are the same?" I venture. "What if I told you that your blood provides us with the same things."

"Blood?" she says, bristling. "You mean mermaid blood? Yes, I know, it gives you magic."

"No, luv. I mean any living creature's blood. Human's preferred."

"What, you mean like a lamprey?" she asks, her mind going to our underwater equivalent.

I give her a quiet smile. "Lamprey. Bats. Mosquitos. Every village in every corner of the world has a story about creatures like us, creatures that must drink blood to survive, just as they have stories about creatures like you. The thing is, both of us are so easily dismissed by a world that doesn't want to believe in the supernatural and magic, and yet we exist. We exist very much."

"What do they call you?"

"They as in the humans?" I say, appreciating her otherness. "They call us many things depending on where you're from. Around these parts we've been called Mandurugo. Back home we were called Dearg-Diulai. But we call ourselves the Brethren of the Blood."

"But I've seen you eat food."

"We can eat food," I tell her. "Some of us enjoy it too. And rum and wine, of course, we couldn't do without that. We just don't need food to survive. Though I suppose that's not exactly true since we can't die."

"You can't die?" She looks aghast.

I lick my lips. I certainly don't want to tell her how to kill me, however I don't wish to lie. Not when she's been so honest with me. "As you've noticed, we don't need to breathe all that much. We'll grow weak without blood, and it would be pure torture for our bodies, but going without won't kill us. The only way you can is if you remove our heads or hearts, light us on fire, or blow us to smithereens. Other than that, though," I cluck my tongue against my teeth and grin at her, "we're immortal."

Her brows go up, eyes wide as blue moons. "You mean you'll live forever?"

I lift a shoulder. "That's what they say."

Her mouth carefully forms the next question before she says it. "How old are you? When were you born?"

"Not in this century." I wait a beat. "And not in the last one either."

"So you were born in the 1500s?"

"Just made it. 1596," I tell her.

She whistles. "That's mighty impressive, Captain Battista. Us Syrens live for about three hundred."

"And how old are you?"

"Twenty-six."

"Nearly too young for me."

She gives me an unsure smile which quickly fades and touches her necklace. "Your daughter. Was she not…one of you?"

I knew that question would come. "Aye. She was. As long as one parent is, they are part of the Brethren. But the problem lies in how we become one. Females don't turn until they're twenty-one. Males turn when they're thirty-five. After that, we are immortal and frozen in time. But before that we are human and, tragically, we can die like them too."

"So is everyone on the ship the same creature as you? The boys?"

"All the pages are, but they are vulnerable. We won't even let Page John or Bart fight until they're thirty-five. It's not worth the risk of them dying if they don't have to. They certainly want to, and they have the skills to do so, but I don't think it's necessary."

"And Sedge…"

"I had told you before Sedge is a human. I meant it. And because he's human, he'll fall victim to Nerissa's curse. Which is why we need to go back on their ship and save him. Then after that, we'll take over the ship and sail it after the *Nightwind*."

"You'll never catch the *Nightwind*, you've said so yourself."

"Ah," I say, displaying my flexed fingers and moving them around in the air. "But the magic that Venla granted me isn't tied to the *Nightwind*. It's tied to me. I'm the one that controls it. They may be under Nerissa's control right now, but I can put wind into any ship's sails."

She swallows, her throat bobbing and she looks down at the grass. "You must have really loved her."

Her statement surprises me. "My wife? Of course I did."

"She seems like a hard act to follow. But I suppose you have until the end of time to find someone else."

"I haven't been looking, to be honest with you," I admit slowly, wondering if Maren's words hint at anything at all. "It's been thirty years and there have been women and men here and there since she died, but I haven't found another to share my heart with. And yes, before you question it, I do have a heart."

She slides her eyes to mine. "Do you think you ever will find someone?"

"I'm not sure," I muse. "It's hard to find one that doesn't hate me."

That brings a smile out of her, followed by a soft laugh, and for a moment I feel like going over to her and pulling her toward me, kissing her soft lips, and telling her that maybe one day, in another world, in another century, she could learn to love me instead of hate me.

But then I think about what she is and what I have to do still, and I know I will only end up making her hate me more in the end. Our destiny is suited for monsters.

She can sense the shift in my thoughts because her smile falters and her posture stiffens. My preternatural sense of smell is always strong, too strong at times, hence why I run such a clean ship, and I can smell the metallic tang that blood takes when prey catches wind of a predator.

"I can help you get Sedge back to the *Nightwind*," she says quietly. "If you promise to let me go after that."

I shake my head, giving her a sad smile. "I'm sorry, luv. But I can't let you go."

"You've claimed me in front of your crew, you said they won't touch me now. You said I'm safe."

"Aye. Safe from them. But you are not safe from me."

Her hand starts to tremble and she lets go of her necklace, her eyes scouring the jungle behind me, looking for an escape path. "Why not?"

"You know why, Maren. Your blood. Your mermaid blood. I can't defeat Edonia without it. You, my dear, are the answer to all of my prayers. You are the key to my revenge."

"So that's it then?" she asks, her chin contorting, her features turning hard. "So you bed me and use me to bleed me and kill me?"

"I promise I won't kill you," I tell her. "I'll keep you alive. I have to keep you alive."

"Alive down in the hold where you kept the others? Where I'll be left to rot while you siphon my blood and drink and I end up like my sister? So I can beg you to end my life?" The pitch of her words gets higher and higher.

"It doesn't have to be that way," I assure her, though I don't think she's going to believe me. "You can go back in my cage. It will only be me who drinks from you, I won't let anyone else, I—"

I almost don't see her coming. Suddenly she's flying at me, her claws extended, aimed right at my heart.

I knew I shouldn't have told her how to kill me.

I raise my arm and manage to deflect her, even though her claws slice right through the muscle and fat of my forearm, straight to the bone.

"Fuck!" I roar, the blood flowing from my limb as she gets to her feet and starts running through the jungle. I hold my shredded arm to me, trying to stem the blood even though I know it's pointless, then I stagger to my feet. By tomorrow my arm will have fully healed and I'll be fine, but until then it's going to be a pain the arse to deal with.

I let out a low growl that rumbles from deep in my chest.

Then I begin the chase.

TWENTY-THREE

Maren

I run like I'm running out of hell. Perhaps the thought isn't too far off.

When Ramsay finally admitted what he was, that he wasn't your average human being, that he wasn't even human at all and was instead a monster like me, I suddenly knew what I was up against. While I had long suspected that he wasn't normal or even human, I didn't know what kind of creature he was. I figured he and the entire crew were hard to kill, that they had superhuman strength and reflexes, and that they enjoyed torturing people. I didn't know that they actually drank people's blood.

I think back to Daphne, the way she said they were monsters. I think about Hodges and the rest of the crew and servants who were drained of their blood. I think about how often the crew talked vaguely about rations and provisions, how many times they referred to Sedge or me as "human," about all the chains and cages and cells. Transporting hostages across the Pacific wasn't a normal thing for them. What was normal was to raid ships, steal their treasure, and then steal some of their crew so that they could feed from them across long voyages. They harvested humans like humans would cattle, keeping them alive in order to eat them.

The idea that the crew of the *Nightwind* are bloodsuckers, much like the lampreys that attach themselves to poor unsuspecting fish, fills my stomach with dread. But try as I might, I can't be disgusted by it, for I'm no different than they are in many ways. Perhaps I don't drink the blood of a man like a mosquito would, but I do eat their organs and I suppose some might argue that's worse. I know Aerik would.

But regardless of how I feel equal parts kinship and admiration for Ramsay and his Brethren, I also feel fear. Because I realized that though I am a Syren, I am still on land on two legs and I am not the apex predator of this world. No, that would be the Brethren. They have the brains, the strength, the appetite, and the fact that they are immortal all going for them. Until I get my fins back, until I'm fighting any of them underwater, I don't stand much of a chance against them here. Syrens may have long lives, but we can easily be killed.

Of course, I tried to fight back. I tried to kill Ramsay. Part of me wonders if I really would have sunk my claws around his heart and pulled it out on the spot like I did to Aerik, or if I would have just maimed him, rendered him incapacitated. I don't want to kill the captain, not if I had a choice, and yet my own Syren instincts were to do exactly that.

Perhaps he should be as afraid of me as much as I am afraid of him. Yet I am not going to stick and around and find out.

I run through the jungle, my legs stronger than they've ever been, but they still don't possess the same strength as my arms and the rest of my body does. I have to be careful as I leap over fallen logs and try to dodge hanging vines and trees. The light beneath the canopy of leaves is dim despite the bright morning sun beyond and I have to keep focused or I'll trip. It doesn't help that around every corner I keep thinking I see a pair of glowing eyes watching me.

Could it be Nerissa? A wild animal?

But before I have the chance to contemplate it even further, suddenly my world gets turned upside down. The ground moves out from under me and I'm falling, caught by thick ropes that press roughly against my cheek, and then I'm being hauled straight up into the air.

A fishing net! I'm caught in a fishing net on land! This is exactly what we think happened to my mother, what the elders say has happened to other Syrens in other seas.

I cry out, struggling against the rope. I start trying to filet it with my claws, shredding at net until I'm almost free.

Someone lets out a holler from below. "She's escaping!"

I look down through the net to see the skeleton crew on the ground beneath me, staring up at me through their empty skulls. Oh, blast.

I work faster now, until the rope starts to stretch and snap and I'm slipping through the hole I created, only to land directly on the skeletons, smashing their bones.

I get to my feet ready to run again for my dear life but I only get a few feet before two other intact skeletons reach out and grab me.

I snap my teeth at them hoping to scare them, but they're made of nothing but bone and they'll never die, no matter how hard my bite is. Thank goodness none of them seem to know I'm a mermaid or I'll be put in the tank like my sister was.

"Look at what we have here," one of the skeletons. "Captain Mahoney will love this."

"Finally, a lady to join us for eternity in our curse," says the other one. "Though she is a rather strange looking lady, isn't she?"

"Her teeth are so pointy. Her nails too. Perhaps she's French," one jokes in his British accent.

Both of them start laughing at that.

I elbow one of them in the ribs, shattering the bone.

"Fucking bitch," the skeleton growls, his hard grip tightening on my arm. "You're a dead woman now."

They drag me through the forest with more of their skeleton crew coming to get me. The *Nightwind's* crew is small and I've grown accustomed to it, so I've forgotten how large a normal ship's crew is. Even though *Nightwind* won the battle against the cursed crew, I suppose a lot of their bones came back together after all.

Finally, the canopy opens up and we come to a white beach and their ship just off shore. They take me along to the ship's boat on the sugary sand and shove me inside it. I take a hard fall, my reflexes not as quick as I'd hoped, though that doesn't stop me from scrambling to my feet and attempting to dive off.

But there's ten of the crew now surrounding me and their boney hands grab my ankles and calves, pulling me back on the boat, my teeth clacking together so hard that one of them falls out.

A skeleton laughs and picks up the pointed tooth. "I got me self a souvenir. What are ye, part shark?"

I snarl at him, hoping that tooth comes back like it would when I was a full Syren. I'm still not sure how my body is working, it seems that my claws and teeth only come out when I'm enraged and ready to fight, and that my gills only detach from my neck when I'm underwater. Still, my vanity hopes that I didn't lose an actual human tooth for good. Funny how you can worry about such frivolous things when your life is on the line.

All I know is that I can't end up like those skeleton Syrens. Is it Nerissa that passes the curse onto me, or is it the crew themselves? Is it the ship?

The questions have me panicking and trying to battle my way through the crew on the boat every couple of seconds until a bunch of them have to sit on me to keep me in place and one ties ropes around my wrists and ankles, binding me the same way Ramsay once did.

Fortunately, I have something now that I didn't then and that's sharp teeth. I start gnawing away at the ropes, making progress so that I'm almost free by the time I'm hauled up on the deck of their ship like a freshly caught shark.

Until one of them notices what I'm doing and they run around trying to find a solution, which comes in the form of an actual rusted chain being shoved between my teeth and fastened at the back of my head like a gag.

I scream, the sound gargled by the chain but high enough still to make them cover their ears. Rust flakes off into my tongue, making my whole mouth salivate at the metallic taste and I start coughing hard.

No. This can't be my fate, after every single thing I've been through.

I refuse to submit to it.

With a bellow I pull up from my lungs, I start fighting them the best that I can, thrashing around, smashing their bodies with mine until their bones break. I have a lot of meat on my bones and they have none.

This is all Ramsay's fault, I decide. *He could have just let me go instead of making me run.*

But whether that thought is true or not it's the last one that I have before something hits me over the head and the world goes dark.

I wake up to someone shaking my shoulder.

My eyes slowly flicker open, wincing at the bright light coming in through a window. Blood pumps noisily in my head, my brain feeling like it's too big for my skull and my mouth is aching from being wedged open with the rusted chain.

I groan and try to move my head to see who's shaking me, letting out a sharp gasp of pain when my head feels like it's been shaken to pieces.

A kind smiling face looks down at me.

Sedge!

Except once I see past the familiar soft eyes and rounded chin, I realize that he's already been inflicted by the curse. Parts of his face are peeling off, revealing jawbone and teeth underneath, and whatever skin is left is stretched tight across his face.

"Oh, Sedge," I say to him, lifting up my bound hands to touch his shoulder, too afraid I might do further damage to his face. "Did they get to you already?" Of course, he can't quite understand what I'm saying with this chain in my mouth, but he seems adept at reading people.

He gives me a sympathetic smile and raises his hands. I see that they are bound too, skin being flayed from the ropes at the wrist. He may only be human, but he's a big man and I have no doubt he tried to do some real damage to the crew.

Where are we? I think, looking around carefully so that my head doesn't explode from the pain. There's a small porthole window and that's it. The room is narrow and empty except for the two of us.

I manage to get to my feet and hop over to the closed door, the ropes tight around my ankles. I try the handle but naturally it's locked. No doubt Sedge would have tried to break it down before he decided it was no use.

When I look back he's shaking his head to tell me not to bother. There's a look about him that I hate, one that seems resigned to his fate now.

I can't think that way.

"Listen," I say to him, trying to speak as clearly as possible even with the metal in my mouth and my throat parched. "We are going to find a way out of here. I know you want to give up, but you mustn't. I have put up with too much for far too long to just wave the white the flag and surrender. We aren't going to stop until the both of us are free, alright?"

I worry he didn't understand a word of my mushed speech but a look comes across his tired face. I've seen that look before. Ramsay looks at me like that sometimes, like he's both amused and in awe.

"I know I'm stubborn," I add. "But the fight in me isn't over."

He nods, even though I can tell he doesn't share my optimism.

And it's not that I'm obtusely optimistic. I'm aware of what's at stake here. I understand the fate that is laid out for me by the gods. I know that the chances of us getting out of here alive are low, not to mention further unscathed, but I don't have a choice. If I sit back and submit, I'll die hating myself. I've spent too much of my life hating myself for the mistakes and choices I made in my past, repeatedly beating myself up over the same moments. It's time for me to forgive the girl that I was and accept the path that my life has taken, no matter how hard it's been. We can't go back and fix what was, but we can use it to make sure those mistakes don't happen again.

And I will never hide who I am or betray my true spirit.

I will have agency until I die.

I let out a growl of determination and hop over to the porthole to see where abouts we are. To my surprise I'm looking out at a familiar looking jungle and a beach that still has ruts in the sand from where the ship's boat was launched. We haven't left the bay at all. Is Nerissa's pull keeping the ship in place now, no matter what?

I cup my hands on the salt-flecked glass to get a better look when suddenly a pair of stormy eyes shoots up into my vision.

I yelp and stumble backward in shock, falling on my rear.

There at the window is Ramsay.

"How on earth?" I attempt to say, and he frowns at me, perhaps noticing I've been gagged with a rusted chain. Then his attention goes over to Sedge and Ramsay grins at him, giving him a little wave.

Sedge waves back, happy to see his captain.

When I look back to the window however, the captain is gone.

"Huh?" I go to the porthole again to look out and see nothing.

Then I hear the muffled sound of glass breaking elsewhere in the ship, the sound of footsteps, and then a soft rap at our door.

My heart leaps into my throat and I exchange a worried look with Sedge. I don't really want it to be Ramsay, but I definitely don't want it to be the skeleton crew.

I'm about to tell whoever it is to come in or something ridiculous to that end, when suddenly I hear the door unlocking.

I suck in my breath and wait.

The door opens and Ramsay steps inside, his larger-than-life presence filling the small space. Even though I still hate the monster, part of me is absolutely relieved he's here. There's comfort in my disdain for him.

"Here you are," he says softly.

"How did you get here?" I cry out in a muffle.

"It's helpful to have a key that can open any lock." He displays a key which he puts back in his pocket and then frowns at the metal in my mouth. "The crew may lack brains in those skulls, but I admit that's a smart way to shut you up."

"Flog off," I swear, hoping he understood that too.

"I will," he says. "But first I'm here to rescue my dear Sedge." His gaze goes to Sedge and I watch the captain's flippant expression crumble in real time. "I thought I saw this through the window, but I didn't want my eyes to be telling the truth."

He goes over to Sedge and kneels by his side, placing his hand on top of Sedge's blond hair, ducking his head down to stare intently into his mate's eyes. "I will fix you. I promise you that."

Sedge nods, believing it.

Honestly, I believe it too. The look of devotion and determination in Ramsay's face would make any crowd rally behind him.

Yes, he does this for Sedge. But for you? He'll drain your blood.

I know that voice is correct. But at the same time my heart feels a little too big for my chest, as if part of me wants to imagine that he would do the same for me. That I *want* him to do the same for me.

I swallow it down and remember what I told myself.

I will have agency until I die.

Ramsay swings his gaze to me now.

"Did they hurt you?" he asks, his jaw going tight.

I give my head a shake and show him my bindings, trying to say, *they did this.*

He tilts his head as he considers me, his features relaxing, that damn infuriating twinkle back in his eyes. "I can't say I blame them. Do you, luv?"

Then he straightens up and looks at the both of us. "Don't worry. I have a plan." He starts walking to the door.

"Hey!" I cry out, trying to reach for him. He stops and I gesture to the chain. "Take it out of my mouth!" But of course my words are garbled together and I sound just as I did when I didn't have a tongue.

Ramsay studies my face for a moment and I know he understood what I said. Then he simply says, "No," and walks away.

"Bastard!" I yell after him. "You duplicitous, arrogant cock-for-brains bastard!"

He lets out a laugh and glances at me over his shoulder. "I understood that one too. You're not wrong. Now, if you'll excuse me, I have a captain I need to dispose of."

He leaves the room and I scramble to my feet, doing a hopping run toward the door wanting to escape but he closes the door in my face and locks it.

I let out a scream of frustration and bash my shoulder against the door, but it doesn't budge. We have no choice but to see what fate awaits us.

PART THREE

The Crossing

TWENTY-FOUR

Maren

I remember the day I discovered Aerik's true nature. Not just suspected that he was capable of cruelty, but actually felt it first-hand. We hadn't been married yet, but he'd proposed a couple weeks earlier on the long voyage to Denmark. I had said yes and it was the first word I'd been able to speak clearly.

Aerik was surprised. Not that I agreed to marry him but that I was able to speak at all. I remember thinking that his joy didn't seem genuine, that his smile didn't reach his eyes. At the time I thought maybe he didn't actually want me to say yes, but it turns out it was a little more complicated than that: He never wanted me to speak at all.

As we got closer to port, having just gone through the English Channel, I remember I told a joke. We were sitting at dinner with a couple of naval officer friends of Aerik's that stepped aboard from the south of England. They were coming with us for the final leg home.

Until that moment I had said only a few demure words to these men, since I didn't feel all that comfortable speaking yet. But one thing I had been good at was listening and reading people and I remembered a joke that Hodges had told Daphne. It was a joke about naval men and all the ports and women they visited.

I recall it had felt very off-color at the time, certainly a joke that

men would tell each other, and so for whatever reason, I felt emboldened to repeat it. I thought perhaps these men might find me funny or
interesting. I had never been considered funny or interesting before,
and while Aerik definitely doted on me more those first few months on
the coast of New Spain when I was a strange little creature, he seemed
to lose interest in me. I had hoped if others found me interesting that he
would too again.

So at dinner I opened my mouth and I told the joke.

The naval men found it hilarious. They were shocked at what came
out of my mouth but they laughed nonetheless. Despite their military
background they had an ease about them that I felt comfortable with
and I thought it was a great success.

But later that night, back in our cabin, Aerik yelled at me until he
was red in the face and practically foaming at the mouth. He told me
that I made him look bad. That they'd think he had an uncouth wanton
woman that would never be fit for the throne. It didn't matter that
Aerik was the third in line for it and would likely never be king and
never wanted to be king—he felt I humiliated him in front of his
friends.

When I tried to argue and tell him that they liked it because they
laughed, he told me that they *had* to laugh because of who he was, that
I wasn't funny at all, then he struck me across the face so hard that I
went flying off the bed, seeing spots. It was the first violence I'd felt
since my tongue had been cut out, and I never thought I would feel it at
his hand.

It's easy to look back and say I didn't see the warning signs. But I
did. I was a little too young to really know what they meant, for I had
no idea of the relationships between a man and a woman except for my
own parents, who were very loving and kind to each other (most of the
time). But I still knew what danger was and I knew when something
wasn't right.

I saw the signs and I stayed anyway because some part of me truly
believed that I would be exempt and that love would solve all my problems. I used to be a Syren that hunted men. In my eyes I was the

monster. I never imagined that men were monsters of their own, even after my mother disappeared.

As time went on I felt more and more trapped. The more he struck me, insulted me, spat on me, abused me, the more I determined I became to make our love work. I had sacrificed too much to be with him, I couldn't just leave and have all of that be for nothing. I filled my mind with all sorts of scenarios with why I couldn't, including that I would be alone and destitute.

The reasons were valid. Being alone doesn't sound like a death sentence, but it could have easily been. Staying with Aerik at times felt like a death sentence too. In the end I was caught between the devil I knew and the devil I didn't.

And now, now I feel like I'm caught between two devils and I don't know either one. There's Ramsay, who branded me, claimed me as his, promised to protect me from everyone but him. And then there's my life on my own. The world hasn't gotten any gentler to women, hasn't gotten any easier. Even if I decided to make my way back to the royal palace, I wouldn't be a princess. They wouldn't be my family. I would be cast out with nothing. The world of monarchy and politics has no room for sentiment. It's blood or nothing.

Which is why I find myself feeling envious of the Brethren at times. They're all together, from all walks of life, bound together by blood but not in the same way that it matters to humans. They've created their own family and let each other be who they need to be. Ramsay, until he decided to take my place for Nerissa, had been the glue holding them all together.

I sit back down beside Sedge, my hobbled legs too unsteady to stay on for long, and sigh heavily as I lean my head back against the wall.

What *is* Ramsay's plan? It's just him alone against an entire crew of the undead. I know he's a supernatural creature, part of this Brethren of the Blood, and can handle himself but I don't see how he can handle them all, especially if they're impossible to kill.

And then what happens after that? If Ramsay succeeds and he comes for us? I'm still bound and gagged. I'll be at his mercy.

I hate the way that deep, deep inside me I get a nervous thrill at the thought. The truth is, I'll worry more if he *doesn't* succeed.

BOOM!

Suddenly an explosion rocks the boat from above us, dust falling from the ceiling. Both Sedge and I look up just as another explosion happens further down the vessel.

Yelling and shouting erupts, a clatter of footsteps running back and forth on the deck above and then a yelp that seems to get louder. I look to the porthole just in time to see a skeleton go flying past, having been tossed overboard.

I get to my feet and hop to the porthole, looking out the best that I can. It's hard to tell from the angle of the ship but I don't see anyone swimming away.

After that, everything quiets down and then the boat fills with the groan of metal and the clanking sound of the anchor being pulled up.

This is either a very bad sign or a very good sign, I think, trying to convey the message with my eyes to Sedge.

He nods, looking unsure.

We wait.

A muffled sound comes from outside the door before the lock starts turning.

Both of us freeze.

Four skeleton crew walk in, looking relatively unharmed.

"We're taking you to see the captain now," one of them says, his jawbone looking especially loose as he talks.

I give Sedge an impassioned look. *Is this it for us? What does the captain want? What happened to Ramsay?*

Sedge gives me a patient nod in return, his way of telling me it will be alright.

But how?

The skeletons yank us to our feet and even though my nature is to thrash around a little and do some damage, I have no choice but to hobble along with them as we make our way out of the room and to the upper deck, the stairs especially challenging on my bound feet.

Once on the deck, I take in the sea breeze that brushes back my hair and flaps in the sails, noting how we're starting to pull away from the bay. There's quite a few of the skeleton crew up here all gathered at the aft deck, which is where we are swiftly taken.

I can see a captain's hat amongst the skeletons, a worn and battered tricorn with the jolly roger stitched across the front, and my heart slams against my ribs. Is the captain going to defile me with his bones? Pass his curse onto me like he did to Sedge? Submit me to a public flogging?

Or worse, discover what I truly am and drink my blood until I'm one of the skeletal Syrens in the deep?

An image of the crew suddenly swarming me and biting me with their skeletal jawbones puts a shiver down my back, my stomach filling with cold dread. The crew that's handling me dig their fingers into my skin and I'm shoved forward through the crowd, bones knocking with each other as they part.

And as the crowd parts it reveals the captain.

Captain Ramsay "Bones" Battista.

"Hello, my lovely *cearban*," he says to me, his brogue deepening. "That's quite the hook you have in your mouth." Then he nods at Sedge. "Sedge, my good man."

Relief floods my body and I exhale. "What happened?" I say through the chains, my throat drier than ever.

"I'm the captain now," he says with a grin. "I let loose a few grenades until I found their captain, who was quivering like a coward, knocked off his head, tied up his limbs with some iron and tossed him overboard. He'll be kept busy at the bottom of the sea for a long time now." He pushes at the hat on his head. "Took his hat and told the crew that I'm their new captain. Ain't that right boys?"

"Huzzah!" a cheer goes up amongst the skeleton crew.

How the hell did he win them over so fast?

He smirks at me, knowing what I'm thinking. "I told them we're in the business of hunting mermaids too. If we find one, she'll be shared equally amongst us."

Blast. I scowl at him. I knew there would be a catch. I also knew it would be me.

Then he winks at me, as if to tell me my secret is safe with him, but at this point I'm not sure what to think anymore or who to trust. I'll just keep trusting myself.

"And so now what?" I ask clumsily. I jerk my head at Sedge. "Remember you promised you would fix him."

"Such little faith you have," he says, his eyes gleaming. "We are going to get the *Nightwind* back. Turns out Nerissa abandoned her crew here for mine, and now Sterling has taken over as captain. I aim to get my boat and crew back and get these boys their witch back."

"You'll never catch them."

"But you remember that the gift of wind is for me," he says, and he nods his head toward the sails. "And she's filling the sails with all she has. Might take a few days but we'll catch the *Nightwind*, mark my words."

"With Sterling at the helm, they might not even be going to Acapulco anymore," I attempt to say.

He frowns and cups a hand to his ear. "What was that? Sorry, it's hard to understand you with that thing in your mouth."

"Aaaarrrrgh!" I roar, trying to lunge at him but bony hands shoot out and hold me in place.

"And that's exactly why I'll be keeping just as you are," Ramsay notes. He nods at the crew. "Take her back down to where you found her. Sedge is staying up here with me." He grins at Sedge. "You'll be my first mate now, is that alright with you?"

Despite how tired and awful he looks, Sedge nods, seeming pleased.

Me, however, I'm led away, cursing Ramsay to his grave.

The sound of waves smashing the bow of the ship wakes me from a fitful sleep, my body both numb and in pain from where the ropes cut into me.

I slowly sit up and look to the window where the sun is just starting to set, the sky shades of purple and pink. After the crew brought me back down here, I spent a good hour just bashing my shoulder against the door trying to break through or trying to break the porthole window to escape, though I know there is no chance that my ample rear would fit through that narrow space.

Then I fell asleep, exhausted beyond belief from the events of the day and night before. Even though I only had Sedge as a companion in this narrow hold for a few hours, I miss him already. I'm glad he's Ramsay's first mate for this voyage, but part of me wishes that I could be something more than just cargo and future provisions.

I shared my body with that man. I bared myself to him in ways I had never done before with Aerik. He spilled his seed inside me while I brought him to the highest levels of pleasure, and I did indeed see the heaven that he had promised me.

That meant something to me, and it shames me to admit it. He showed me how two people can truly unite in a physical way, enough so that it almost felt spiritual. Granted, I was soon aware right after that the man is not one that I can trust, and that he is still my enemy. But to put all of that aside for a few moments and experience a godly connection like that made me realize why Syrens sought out men for their own satisfaction.

It also made me realize why they kill the man when they've finished using them. Which is more or less what I had tried to do.

Had you done that to him, then you could never experience the pleasure of his cock again, a voice reminds me. I hate that the voice is right. There's even a chance that I might miss Ramsay's company, much like one could miss a mosquito in their ear.

But when the door opens and Ramsay steps in with a plate of food in his hands, both looking as delicious as ever, I have to tell that voice to shut it.

"Princess," he greets me as he closes the door behind him. "I have to say that even though you were a princess in your undersea kingdom, I'm not sure the term suits you anymore. You think of a princess and you think of someone stuffy and formal, one who looks down their nose at you. That doesn't seem to be you at all. Except perhaps that last part."

"What do you want?" I say through the chain, but my words are not only incoherent but barely audible.

He slowly walks over, his boots echoing and stops right in front of me before coming down into a crouch. I glance at the plate in his hand. It's a raw fish head and I know that wouldn't seem appetizing to many but it makes my stomach gurgle ravenously.

"I want you to be a good girl," he says.

I glare at him and try to take the plate from him but he holds it back out of the way. "That's not being a good girl, luv." He puts the plate behind him and then reaches out, grabbing my chin between his thumb and forefinger and I'm forced to meet his eyes.

"Did you know that one of the tricks we have as the Brethren is to compel humans?" he says in a low, smooth voice. "Some of us can make them do almost anything, at the very least we can get them to lower their defenses. Makes it so much easier to prey on them. But you, my luv, I never had that effect on you. I tried, of course, but it never worked. You would never yield. One of the many things I like about you, even if it infuriates me all the same."

I grumble at him, though I feel a burst of pride in my chest that I never succumbed to his supernatural manipulations.

He keeps a firm grip on me. "It's because you're a monster like me, not a creature of the night but a creature of the sea, and humans all around the world would fear us if they knew exactly what the both of us were capable of. Don't you think, then, that we belong together? We could rule the seas as leaders of a new empire—a dark empire. You were never meant to be a princess, Maren. You were meant to be a queen. Perhaps my queen."

I don't trust a damn word that comes out of his mouth.

Nice speech, I think, still glowering at him.

"Hmmph," he says, giving me a crooked smile as his eyes flit over my features. "I suppose you need time to think about it. We have a long voyage ahead of us, so there is plenty of time for that. And, so you're aware, I do know that Sterling is keeping course for Acapulco. Even without you to trade, they'll want to stick to our usual route for the galleons. Old habits die hard, so they say. It won't be long until I'm reunited with my ship and my crew. Which brings me to my next question…"

He lets go of my face and leans in closer until all I see are his eyes, the color of stormy seas. I know he said he doesn't have the power to compel me, yet I want to drown in his gaze all the same.

"Are you going to be a good girl?" he murmurs.

I snarl in response.

"Because if you're a good girl," he goes on, voice like silk, and he drops his gaze to my lips where I feel them burn, "then I can free you enough for you to eat. And then we can discuss my little proposition for you."

To hell with your proposition, I think. But the truth is, I am starving and thirsty and want nothing more than this chain to be removed from my mouth. I take a deep breath through my nose and try to soften my features, relaxing my shoulders. I try to submit.

"I know this must be hard for you," he says, his hands going behind my head to where the chain attaches. "To willingly give yourself to me and be sweet when you're such a vicious little monster. You have so much anger and rage and I know you wish to unleash it on me." He leans in closer still and my eyes flutter close, the intensity of his gaze getting to be too much. "I can't say I blame you either. But I promise you, if you're good, I'll let you take it out on me, all of it. If you play nice and fair, after you've had your food, you can hurt me. If you're good. Will you be good?"

I nod just as he undoes the chains and the metal is taken from my mouth.

I whimper. My jaw aches painfully as I attempt to close it. My mouth is parched, my tongue sore, my teeth feel brittle.

"Start with this," he says, reaching into his jacket pocket, a jacket that looks a bit too small for him and I assume belonged to the former captain. He pulls out a wooden flask with a scrimshaw Syren etched on it "The water on the ship I'm not sure I'd trust to drink, but I did find a bottle of rum in the captain's locker."

I'll take anything for my ravaged mouth so I grab it with my bound hands and tip it back onto my tongue, the rum flowing down.

I immediately start coughing, the alcohol burning my lips and throat, but there's immediate relief as well as it numbs me from the inside out. I drink more down, finding it both intoxicating and quenching, until I've emptied the flask.

"Impressive," he notes, and I toss the flask away, my focus now on the food behind him.

"Fish," I say, so hungry I can barely speak. "Now." The rum is already hitting me, making the room sway more than normal.

Ramsay watches me carefully, never taking his eyes off me as he reaches behind him and hands me the plate.

I immediately pounce on it, picking up the fish head with my tethered hands and biting a chunk out of it. It tastes like the sea, it tastes like home, and I'm barely swallowing it down before I'm devouring the rest of it, brains, bones, eyes, and all.

Before I know it, the fish head is gone, I'm a mess, and I'm barely satisfied. I want more than that. I want a lot more.

"That shouldn't have aroused me, and yet…" Ramsay comments, his Adam's apple bobbing as he swallows thickly.

If he's aroused then perhaps his reflexes aren't at their best.

I take the opportunity to attack but before I can even move a muscle and lunge at him with my mouth, my teeth sharpening in an instant, he reaches out with his hand and holds me back by my throat, choking me.

"Play nice," he warns, his grip tight and bruising as he presses me against the wall.

I manage to move my throat enough to spit in his face.

My spit lands on his forehead, a sliver of fish bone in it.

He grunts and reaches up with his other hand, wiping it away.

"Do it again," he whispers, eyes dancing darkly. "This time in my mouth, please." He opens his mouth, showing me his tongue, wanting it.

Damn it. Everything that's uncouth and repulsive about me he somehow loves.

He shuts his mouth and grins. "Fine. Just know I will be returning the favor one day."

Then he reaches down and grabs the chain from the floor.

"No!" I cry out but he starts choking me even harder, enough that I can barely breathe. "Please, not that."

"You did this to yourself," he says, the chain clanging in his hand. "I can't trust you not to bite my face off."

"Won't it just grow back?" I manage to say, my face going hot. "Your arm is fine." My gaze goes to his arm, which earlier today I had noted looked nearly healed even after I felt my claws slice him to the bone.

He gives his head a sharp shake. "I can't risk my face not growing back the same way. I'm nothing without these looks."

I curl my lip at him, as if I don't find him devastatingly handsome at the most inappropriate times.

"Now, luv, your disobedience has caused me to reconsider my proposition. Perhaps I will no longer open it up for your input but will force it upon you. I know you don't like that, you've had it with being told what to do, how to act, what to say, haven't you?"

I go still, just enough that he loosens his grip on my neck. "I'm listening," I tell him warily.

He gives me a stiff smile, though his other hand still grips the chain. "We need each other, luv, whether we like it or not. I have a feeling I like needing you more than you like needing me."

"I don't need you for anything."

He fixes me with a calm look. "You need me for my protection at the very least. Protection from this cursed crew who will gladly turn you into your sister, protection from the Brethren who will gladly put you in the hold with the dead bodies of your former servants, and protection from Nerissa, who is a sea witch and can't be trusted, especially not if she finds out what you really are. All that's stopping you from being torn apart is one word of truth: *mermaid.*"

I bristle at that. "You would never throw me to them."

His gaze goes cold, a wash of ice I feel along my spine. "Don't tell me what I would or wouldn't do," he says, his voice acidic. "You have no idea what I'm capable of when it comes to revenge. I will gladly sacrifice you in order to get what I want."

"And I will do the same to you," I retort, my steely tone matching his.

"You seem to believe you're in a position of power. You are not."

My teeth snap together and I grow silent and frustrated.

"Now, what I need from you, I think you already know," he goes on with a faint sigh. "I need your blood. I told you I wouldn't kill you for it and I mean it."

"But you'll gladly sacrifice me," I throw back at him, imitating his deep voice.

His mouth twitches in amusement. "Killing you and sacrificing you are two different things. But I'm not here to argue over semantics. I won't kill you, I'll barely even hurt you. You might even like it. Some people do. But I will feed from you, just a little bit every day, to build up my reserves."

"I think not," I grumble.

"In exchange," he adds, raising his voice, "I will keep you and your secret safe."

"You said that no one could hurt me if you claimed me," I point out, wishing he would let go of my neck.

"I can easily remove the brand," he says coldly. "Painful thing to go through. Wouldn't wish it on anyone."

The thought of him scraping my scarred flesh off in that still tender area makes me feel queasy.

"How about you think about it," he suggests. Then, before I know what's happening, he shoves the chain back in my mouth.

I scream and thrash but to no avail. He fastens it around my head and gets to his feet. "I'll come back for your answer tomorrow. Maybe you'll behave yourself better then."

TWENTY-FIVE

Ramsay

I'm having the nightmare again. It's happening as if I'm in the past and I'm awake and of sound mind.

The sea is dead calm. Not a cloud in the sky, not a hint of breeze. It's stifling and hot and nothing feels right. I'm about to say this to Sam when I hear that first thump.

The *Nightwind* shakes. The crew is thrown around.

My gaze goes to the side of the deck where I know Hilla will be standing with that smear of chocolate on her face.

But she's not there.

Instead it's Maren.

She's standing there with her back to me in a blue gown, a crown on her head as her black hair billows in the breeze. Her dress is wet, puddles of water forming underneath and flowing across the deck.

"M-Maren!" I try to yell at her, to warn her, because she's in my dream and she doesn't know what happens next, but her name is caught in my throat. I can't move either, I'm just frozen in place, forced to watch what I know will happen.

Another thump shakes the ship, causing people to cry out and then Maren starts to slowly turn around to face me.

I gasp, my heart sinking.

Though her eyes are as bright and beautiful as ever, her face has rotted away, barely any flesh covering the bone. She has succumbed to the curse and is crumbling away before my very eyes.

Then my gaze trails south to the hem of her gown where the water that was flowing is now turning red, tainted with blood, and the tip of a mermaid tail sticks out from under the dress. The tail slowly turns to bones.

"Maren!" I yell again, this time finding my voice. "Come here. I'll keep you safe. Choose me!"

But she doesn't move. Her eyes stare blankly at me.

And from behind her the great Kraken's tentacle rises high up in the air, the sun reflecting off a purple sheen, and then it comes crashing down toward her.

I yell and start to run to her, but the end of the tentacle is forced into her mouth and it pulls back like a fish hook, whipping her off the deck and down into the sea.

I wake up panting for breath, sweat making my hair stick to my neck. I nearly bash my head on the bunk above, remembering where I am in the nick of time.

I'm not on the *Nightwind*. No, this boat is revolting in its stench and dirtiness. Once upon a time she would have been beautiful, but a cursed crew would have different priorities than me, and keeping her clean wouldn't be one of them. In fact, the only place I found acceptable to sleep in was one of the officer's quarters, the only one with a working window to get the flow of air in here.

I look out the window at the night sky. The moon is out, just a crescent, bathing the water in fragments of silver, while tendrils of fog hover above the surface. The sea swells from earlier have died down, but the dream still sticks to me. I hate having a fear of the ocean but that's what those dreams do. They remind me that under this ship's keel is a world that I know nothing about, a world filled with monsters such as the Kraken.

Monsters such as Maren. I suppose that's why she fascinates me so. Both of us are monsters, creatures apart from humans, yet we still come from two different worlds. In all the time we've hunted mermaids—Syrens—I never thought that they would be something I could relate to. I never stopped to think that they could be kin. We're worlds apart and yet the same. There is so much to learn from her, if only she would let me.

I know she will be an uphill battle to win. She has been from the very beginning. I'll be the first to admit my tactics are rough and sometimes cruel and they are not the ones of an ordinary gentleman trying to woo an ordinary lady.

But she's also been dealt a poor hand in life. I see what disadvantage she's been at for a decade, and I also see how she lives in regret over her past. If I could just get her to trust me, I'd help her see her true potential. Right now she's this wild captured animal constantly lashing out, but if she could harness and focus that female rage, she'd be unstoppable.

We'd be unstoppable.

King and Queen of the high seas.

My heart changes tempo for a moment, becoming this foreign item in my chest. I haven't felt this way about anyone for a very long time, and the idea of Maren actually joining my side gives me a foolish sensation of hope. That all of this, this whole life over the centuries with all the pain and the losses, that it's not for nothing. That it's for something.

For someone.

Even though I said I would visit her in the morning, I know I've left her waiting for long enough. But if I need to convince her to let me feed from her, I have to at least attempt to win her over again.

I head up to the deck. The wind is steady in the sails and the ship is cutting smoothly through the sea, the dark night stretching beyond and mingling with traces of mist. By now I reckon we're getting close to the Kiri Islands from which we will be taking a northerly heading. I look over at the skeletons standing at the helm, the bosun and who I assume is the new quartermaster.

I wasn't sure how this crew would feel with me taking out their captain and taking over the ship, but once I told them that we could find more mermaids and that this would be the first they'd be chasing

Nerissa instead of the other way around, they were all for it. In any event, I don't think they've been allowed to sail this far across the Pacific, so they seem excitable and in good spirits.

Which, even though I was just battling them and chopping off their limbs and smashing in their skulls the other day (not to mention throughout the years prior), I do feel a responsibility for them now to keep them safe and happy. Being a captain of a ship isn't just about having control—it's about accountability and that's something I pride myself on.

I just hope the crew of the *Nightwind* still feels that way. I know how most of the Brethren regard me, especially my immediate family, but I don't know what Sterling has been telling them. The man has zero charisma and the brains of a gnat but that doesn't mean he won't strike a chord with some of them. It's impossible to stay in my position for so long and not acquire some resentment.

But I will worry about that later. I trust that Thane and Cruz will keep everyone as safe as they can and I'm hoping that Nerissa isn't causing too much trouble. When the cursed crew told me that she had left the ship for the *Nightwind*, I was surprised but, then again, the sea witches can be unpredictable and prone to following flights of fancy.

I bring my mind back to Maren. I know exactly what she needs and wants, even if she won't admit it. I go to the bench where I had laid some of the fish I caught earlier to ensure there are some left after Sedge and I cooked up dinner. Now that I know she'll eat one raw, it will be easy to keep her fed (though I shouldn't be surprised considering her appetite).

Then I go to one of the empty barrels that had been collecting rainwater, filled to the brim, and pick it up with a grunt, lugging it over to the stairs and below deck. There I rummage for anything clean, and finally find some old but acceptable linen sheets and a shriveled bar of lard and lye soap. On the *Nightwind*, we have bars of fragrant Castile soap that I am sure the princess is used to, but this will have to do.

I knock on her door as a courtesy and unlock it with the rain barrel sticking out first, just in case she feels like attacking me. It would be futile for her, but annoying for me.

But Maren is kneeling by the porthole and staring out the window at the moon and the sea and...damn it, it knocks the wind out of me. That's all she really wants. To go home. She doesn't want to be with me. She just wants to return to the sea.

Then I will help you get home, I think to her. *As soon as you help me.*

She slowly turns her head and looks at me. Tears have made her eyes wet and she blinks them away, her posture stiffening, becoming royal and composed again.

"I thought you might like a bath," I say, putting the barrel down, plus the sheets and soap. "If all goes well, I have dinner waiting for you upstairs. A whole damn fish all for you."

Her eyes light up now. I knew the way to her heart was through her stomach.

"What do you say?" I ask. "How about you let me bathe you while you tell me what you think about my proposition?"

That shine in her eyes grows hard. "How about you free me?" she asks. The chain garbles her words but I still understand her and I always understand her tone.

"It would be foolish of me to do that when the first thing you'll do is attack me. Perhaps I'm not as smart as those you've accompanied in royal circles, but I do know when a scene is doomed to repeat itself."

She doesn't say anything to that because she knows it would be a lie. But she does appear to relent a little. She gives me a slight nod.

I go over to her and pick her up so that she's on her feet. She's unsteady with her legs bound together and I figure at least I could loosen those for her. I bend down to untie them, keeping my focus on her face even though her breasts are largely in the way, until her legs are free.

"If you try and run you won't get far," I warn her. "I know you did earlier but the only reason I didn't catch you is because the skeleton crew caught you first. Believe it or not I watched the whole thing, the way you hung from that net. You were never in any real danger, Maren, I was always right there."

She gives me a look of disbelief. I don't expect her to believe me, but the moment I saw she was trapped, I stayed hidden in the bushes and followed them all the way back to the ship, planning for when I'd climb aboard and rescue her and Sedge. Though I suppose I'm not much of a rescuer if I'm keeping her hostage still.

I quickly crouch and scoop her up into my arms and she lets out a gasp of surprise. I carry her over to the barrel and then with my hands taking a firm grip of her soft waist, I lower her into the tub.

She winces slightly as her shirt billows around her, the water splashing over the sides of the barrel until it's just barely covering her breasts.

"I know it's cold but at least it's clean," I tell her. "And it's water. I figured that would be something you're missing. Raise your arms."

She stares at me for a moment with round, unsure eyes and I gesture for her to do it. She hesitates, then puts her arms straight up above her and I reach down to the hem of her shirt, pulling up over her chest and shoulders and head until the whole shirt is gathered at her wrists. I could take it off entirely but that would involve undoing her wrist restraints, and even though her hands and fingernails look normal at the moment, I don't trust those claws near my heart.

There has to be some sort of metaphor in that.

Naturally she's completely naked now and my attention goes to her gorgeous breasts, her nipples hard pink and breaking through the surface. I raise my gaze to meet her eyes and even with the chain in her mouth I can tell she's smirking at me. Either she likes that I'm admiring her body, or she thinks this is typical of me. Perhaps both.

I clear my throat and adjust my cock in my breeches, hard as iron and begging for release, then I pick up the soap. I wet it in the water, sensually rubbing my thumb over the bar again and again, creating a lather, and she's watching me do it with heat in her eyes. I know it reminds her of what my hands can do to her most delicate parts. Even submerged in water I can still smell her arousal.

With my gaze locked on her eyes I bring the soap up between her breasts, then glide it over her collarbones and shoulders, taking my time to wet her skin and wash her inch by inch. Her eyelids flutter closed.

"Have you had enough time to think about my proposition?" I ask her, my voice thick.

Her breath hitches while I slide the soap back down over her breasts, teasing her nipples with it, but she doesn't say anything.

"I could do it right here," I say to her, and just the thought of sinking my teeth into her neck causes lightning in my veins. "I'll be as gentle as I'm being right now. You won't even notice."

I bring the soap down into the water, smoothing it over her skin, down, down, between her legs, my arm fully submerged. I rub the soap against her in the same rhythmic motion I was doing earlier and her legs start to quiver, her breath quickening.

A low moan sounds from her throat and I take the soap away, using it as leverage. She gives me a dirty look, to which I smile. "Answer the question and I'll continue."

She thinks about that for a moment, her brows knitting together. Then she shakes her head. "No," she says.

Figures. "No, you don't want me to feed from you?"

Her gaze tightens on mine. Yes, that's exactly what she's saying.

"Alright," I say with a sigh. "If that's the way you want to do this. Either I feed from you, or everyone does."

She balks, the water splashing. "You're cruel," she manages to say angrily.

"I'm giving you a choice, Maren. Choose *me*," I implore. "Why can't you trust me?"

She gives me the most incredulous look. I suppose I deserve that.

"Listen," I say to her, coming around so that I'm at her back and I rest my chin on her shoulder. "This is the way it is and there's no getting around it. I need you. I really, really need you. More than I've ever needed anyone. And yes, this is a physical need in so many ways, but you drive me to despair, luv. You make me lose my reason. And I'm not going to give up on you giving in to me. I need your submission so badly that I feel the ache in my bones."

Maren relaxes slightly, leaning against the back of the barrel.

"This is for you too, my darling," I say to her, my voice lowering as I run the tip of my nose over her bare shoulder. "With your blood, I can defeat Nerissa *and* Edonia. Your revenge is my revenge. We both want the same thing, don't you see?"

I lower my hand again, this time forgoing the soap which floats in the water, and my fingers find her tender flesh between her thighs. I know exactly what to do to her body to at least have her submit to me this way.

Her legs part as much as they can in the narrow space and she takes in a sharp breath as I rub along her length, dipping into her cunt.

"I still hate you," she seethes through a gasp.

"You can hate me all you want with that brain of yours. But your body doesn't. No, your body loves me very much."

"Just your cock," she manages to say.

I chuckle. "Well, my cock happens to be my best feature."

With the fingers of one hand fucking her in the water, I lift her heavy hair away from her neck. She stiffens. She knows what I'm about to do. I can smell the metallic taste of her blood as it buzzes beneath the skin, all of her senses now coming truly alive as she straddles the line between predator and prey.

The lambs always know when the wolf is about to attack. They know it in their bones.

My canine teeth sharpen and I know there's a risk of me losing control with her. When I've fed from humans I never wished to hurt, more times than not I've gotten carried away and ended up killing them, either taking too much blood or tearing them apart. It's bloodlust and I've spent centuries trying to control it.

I don't want to lose it with Maren; I don't want to cause her any harm. I just hope that if I do, she'll be able to defend herself somehow. Though with the way she's tied up, she'll be as helpless as any lamb.

I swallow down my anxiety and hope and pray that I can keep myself in stride.

I bring my mouth to her neck where her veins sing to me the most. She shivers, gooseflesh erupting beneath my hot breath and I press my lips to her skin. She jumps and her heart pounds louder and stronger and I've never been so hard and hungry in my life.

Then I bite her.

I sink my teeth in through her flesh, piercing her neck deep and hitting the vein. She lets out a cry and my jaw tightens over her neck as the blood starts flowing into my mouth.

The effect is immediate. It had been some time since I fed from a human, as we were trying to ration the captives on board, plus we can go a while without feeding. But her blood, this Syren blood, goes straight to my heart. It feels like it's replenishing each vein in my body, like I'm being reborn as something smarter, faster, stronger. I've had their blood before and it was never so fast-acting as this. This time it all seems to go straight into my cock, a curious need to drink and fuck at the same time.

I let out a groan against her neck and she's starting to relax in the water and I remember to keep pleasuring her with my fingers. If I concentrate on that, I won't lose myself to the bloodlust.

And yet I can feel the bloodlust take over.

My vision goes red.

TWENTY-SIX

Maren

I've never been in such exquisite pain before. That's the only way I know to describe it. The moment that Ramsay's teeth pierced my neck and spilled my blood, it was excruciating agony that I felt so sharply in the marrow of me. And yet the moment he started sucking and drinking my body started to release me from the pain.

I started to get aroused.

And now he's touching me again, his fingers sliding over my womanhood as I'm sitting in this barrel of soapy water. I buck my hips up against his hand, trying to get more purchase, wanting him deeper, harder, everywhere. There's a part of my mind that wants me to remember that I am being drained of blood by a creature who drinks blood and kills to survive, and yet none of that matters much now that my body has taken over.

I want release. I want him inside me in every way possible. I want his cock rammed in me hard while his teeth penetrate my neck, I want him to fill me and take from me at the same damn time.

From those thoughts, from his long strong fingers, I'm brought to orgasm. I cry out in a wild moan as the orgasm tears through me, rendering me obsolete as he's fused with my skin in two separate ways. Water splashes over the edge of the tub and onto the floor and I can't control my body, can't stop writhing as he gives and takes and gives and takes.

My world is still spinning, my heart a racing horse, and though his hand has moved away, his mouth is still locked onto my neck. Now that clarity is returning a little, I wonder how long he's going to feed from me. Does he know when to stop? From his quick hot breath and the grunts he's letting out, it's hard to say what's normal and what's him getting carried away.

He promised he wouldn't hurt me, but I've never been one to take a man at his word.

"Ramsay," I try to say, trying to shift away from his bite. "Ramsay, stop."

But he won't stop. He doesn't even seem to hear me.

"I said stop!" I cry out, louder now. I yank my neck but all it does is create pain so sharp that I let out a scream, my vision going black.

"Stop it!" I yell, panic rising up and choking me. "Stop!"

My predator side unleashes. I can't move my arms a whit, not with the rope and shirt gathered around my wrists, but I do have more strength than normal and I am heavy. With a roar I use all my power to launch my body up and out of the tub.

I only make it halfway but it's enough for the tub to tip over, water spilling over the floor, and for Ramsay to lose connection with my neck.

As soon as I hit the ground and fall out of the tub, I roll over, ready to defend myself in any way that I can.

But Ramsay stays behind the barrel, his fingers digging dents into the wood. He's breathing hard, blood running down his chin. My blood. His eyes are darkened, the pupils wide and red, like a full crimson moon.

He looks menacing and monstrous and beautiful.

My gods, he is beautiful.

He swallows, the red in his pupils fading. I watch as his fangs disappear into normal teeth again, so much like my own do.

"I'm sorry," he whispers, his voice hoarse. "I didn't…I tried not to succumb to it."

"To what?" I ask warily, glad he's still keeping his distance.

"To the bloodlust," he says as he wipes his mouth and eyes the stain left on his hand. "We can lose control when we're feeding."

I give him a look like, *you don't say?*

"I must admit, it was harder than normal with you," he goes on. "Your blood is unlike any blood I've ever had. Your blood is…astonishing."

Even though the idea of bloodlust makes me uneasy, I somehow don't mind my blood being called astonishing. I think I'll take it as a compliment.

"I've never felt this powerful before," he goes on, stepping out from behind the barrel. "This unbeatable. Unstoppable. I feel like I could rip this ship right down the middle and then call up a maelstrom to devour the rest. I don't know what you've done to me, Maren."

He comes toward me, his movements graceful as always but reminding me of a fox about to pounce, everything so measured and controlled and deadly. My pulse kicks up again and I take a step back, away from him, knowing I don't have anywhere to go.

"I don't know what you've done to me," he says again, shaking his head slightly, awe in his gaze. "You're more than the answer to my prayers. You're the answer to prayers I never knew I had. You're an enchantment, a treasure, a powerful curse in its own right and I am one hundred percent under your spell."

He licks his lips, tasting my blood on them, then he gives me a wicked smile. "I have never desired you more."

Then in a flash he's at me, having moved in a blur of inhuman speed, and I let out a muzzled scream, prepared to fight, but then he's shoving me to the ground. I fall on my back and try to flip over, trying to defend my neck, but he's sliding down over my stomach and parting my legs and burying his head between my thighs.

I gasp at the intrusion of his tongue, the way his mouth clamps over me, sucking me between his lips, and I tense with worry that he might bite me there. Not that I wouldn't be opposed to anything rough but I don't want him to get carried away again.

But his teeth remain tucked away and he's all wet tongue and soft lips as he works me with his mouth, sucking and licking and ravishing me.

My hands go to his head, gripping his long soft hair as the shirt flops over his back and then I'm brought to orgasm again, so quick that it takes me by surprise.

By the time my moans fill the air and my limbs are shaking, my body convulsing from the inside out, he's tearing off his shirt and unbuttoning the flap of his breeches and I look down in time to see his gloriously thick cock placed in his palm, ready to unleash on me.

I expect him to shoot me one of his arrogant grins again, the one that tells me I'm in a lot of trouble and he's about to enjoy it, but there's a graveness to his face. His eyes are dark and crackling with intensity like a summer storm, his mouth parted, his jaw tense. He looks like he could either bed me…or kill me.

Instead he grabs me by the shoulders and waist and flips me over so that I'm on all fours. *Most immoral and sinful*, I can't help but think.

I can't help but like it as well.

He moves roughly and with urgency—a warm large hand pressed between my shoulder blades until I'm shoved to the floor, his hips coming up against my rear, fingers trailing through my hair, gathering it into a fistful.

One hand then goes to the tender flesh of my behind and runs over the curves of it in slow sweeping gestures.

SMACK!

I jerk as his palm strikes my arse, the pain sweet and swift.

"Did you just spank me?" I try to say through the chain, my skin stinging.

He merely chuckles.

SMACK!

And does it again.

"You should see your arse, luv," he says. "My palm will be on you for days."

Then I feel his shaft between my thighs, and he's pulling my hair back while the tip of him slides along where I'm still wet from earlier.

A gasp stalls in my throat and my whole body tenses and then he carefully pushes himself into me, his breath hitching.

My back arches and I feel the wind knocked out of me. My vision going out of focus as he works his cock into me, his chest pressing against my back.

Eventually, I relax enough and his cock slides deeper into me, sliding into my slickness.

"That's my good lass," he whispers into my ear. "Your tight little cunt takes this cock so well."

I feel my cheeks burn and I can't help but push back on him. He kisses the back of my neck, sinking into me slowly and I feel both of us becoming a part of one another. It's an intense feeling, nearly indescribable. There's pain but there's pleasure and I want to drown in it. I want to be consumed, but only by him.

His breathing is heavy by my ear and soon he's picking up the pace, thrusting in and out of me with hard slams of his hips, the sound of our skin slapping filling the space. The weight of his body holds me down as he grinds against my rear, his hands pulling my hair, feeling like I'm kept in one place for him, for his pleasure.

Except it's not just about him and his lust. As he pushes into the hilt, stealing my breath, he reaches around and finds me where I'm slick and swollen.

"This is what you want?" he asks, his voice rough and thick. "You want my fingers to play with you while you're getting rammed by my big cock?"

I try to answer but I'm too distracted by pleasure and I can only make a wild sound.

He touches me and caresses me, rubbing in the same agonizing pattern he did before, forcing me to orgasm. I suddenly feel my legs go numb, my thighs shaking as I'm driven over the edge and my body clenching over his shaft, my muscles spasm and squeeze as I'm brought to the peak of pleasure.

It takes my breath away, an electric storm arching my spine, pulling my legs apart.

When he feels me clamp down on him, he thrusts into me harder, tugging my hair until my back arches. Then he roughly takes his hand up until it's grabbing onto the back of the chain, pulling at my head like I'm a damned horse with a bit in her mouth.

I let out a growl, thrusting my rear back against him in defiance. How dare he degrade me to some animal?

But then his fingers don't stop and neither does his cock and before I know what's happening, I'm swept away yet again, my orgasm a violent, powerful thing that has me calling out his name over and over as I'm left shattering like glass.

"Ramsay!" I yelp, groaning. "Oh gods. Oh, fuck."

I hear him grunt in my ear, a sound of satisfaction mingling with exertion and then he's slamming into me to the hilt, his balls pressed against my arse, and his own orgasm comes in a burst of heat. He throws his head back and lets out a thunderous moan that shakes the planks around us, then finally lets go of the chain.

My head falls forward and hangs, my heart pounding so quick and hard that I fear I may die from it, my nose taking in as much air as I can with the chain still in my mouth.

"Maren," Ramsay says from behind me. "My Maren."

He plants a kiss on my spine, gentle and soft, then places a row of them down my back, whispering my name as he goes. "Maren, Maren, Maren."

He grips my hips and I feel him straighten up, exhaling shakily. "I've never had an addiction before," he says hoarsely. "But I think you'll be mine."

He clears his throat and then he pulls out of me and my entire body sinks to the floor, as if his shaft was the only thing keeping me on all fours.

"I'll come back with your food," he says, and I hear him get up, hear the shuffle of clothes being adjusted, then hear him walk toward the door before closing it shut.

But he doesn't come back.

TWENTY-SEVEN

Maren

I woke up angry this morning.

After last night I lay there, still bound in ropes and chains and wet from the bath, waiting for Ramsay to come back to me, waiting for him to bring me food. But he never showed up.

Now it's been several hours since the sun rose and I have let myself be swept into a murderous stew. I've had to use the bathroom in the corner of the room, which is humiliating, and my stomach is gnawing at itself so badly I feel I may starve. I ache between my legs where he fucked me so hard last night, the punishment from his cock was relentless in an area I was already tender.

Whatever waves of joy and bliss that man, that vile *creature*, brought me, I've forgotten all about it. Like it never happened. Instead I am back to hating him and plotting my revenge. How dare he use me like that? He took my blood without me explicitly saying that he could, then he defiled my body from behind, keeping me bound, going as far as to treat me like a horse under bridle. I'm surprised he didn't whip me, though I suppose he did with his hand.

I close my eyes at the thought, that sharp hit of pain at his palm meeting my flesh, the way he so thoroughly took me right after, as if he couldn't help himself, and my thighs squeeze together to stop the burst of pressure.

Stop it, I tell myself. *Figure out what you're going to do next.*

But I don't have time to formulate a plan, the anger inside me just simmers and boils over, my thoughts sluggish for it.

And then the lock jingles and the door opens and Ramsay steps into the room.

He's holding a bottle of rum and a plate of fish. I ignore the hunger pains and focus on the plate. I could break it and stab a shard in his heart, maybe that will do the trick.

"I have some apologizing to do," he says, locking the door behind him. "I know I promised you I would come back last night, and I broke that promise. I was so exhausted after what happened here, spent in a way I had never been before, that I fell asleep if you can believe it."

He walks over to me and goes into a crouch. He places the rum and the fish beside him, then grabs me by the shoulders and pulls me up to my feet.

"Don't touch me," I say.

He removes his hands as if I burned him then stares at me with solemn eyes, their color grayer, like the color of a gravestone. "I also made you another promise. I told you that if you're good, I'll let you take it out on me, all of it. That I'll let you hurt me. I'm here to honor that promise."

"I can't hurt you well if I'm bound," I tell him, tasting metal.

"I know," he says quietly. He reaches behind my head and to my surprise undoes the chain, tossing it to the floor with a heavy clank.

Again my mouth explodes in pain, a deep, sore ache from being forced open for so long, but already I feel my Syren teeth coming through. Power is shifting through me.

Is he really this much of a fool? I can't help but think as he goes to my wrists next, swiftly undoing the rope until my hands are free and my claws are out. They flex, my wrists stiff.

"Have at me," he says, calmly meeting my gaze, "Do your worst. I will not fight back."

I swallow hard, having a hard time thinking.

"I know you want to. I know you've been saving that urge, waiting until you can use it on me. I know your monstrous side will win in this case, because there's no way it can't win. I deserve your wrath, Maren. I deserve it, as do so many people who have tried to put you in a cage. People who have hurt you and overlooked you and ignored you. People who tried to make you into something you weren't. People who used fear to control you. Perhaps you can't hurt them all, perhaps you've already destroyed the one who hurt you the most, but you can hurt me. And I've hurt you, too."

You haven't hurt me, I want to tell him, my pride getting in the way. But the truth is, he has hurt me. And more than that, I'm angry at him. Angry that he put me in this position between wanting him and hating him. Angry that I want to trust him, that some deep warm spot inside of me *yearns* to trust him and yet I know I cannot.

"I will not put you back in restraints," he says, "and I will let you go free if you promise to unleash your fury on me."

Is this something else that arouses him, the pain?

But it doesn't matter what I think because I feel the anger rising through me, a vat of water coming up to boiling.

"Think of your sister," he whispers.

He killed your sister.

That pulls the trigger.

White hot rage blinds me.

The scream that comes out of my lungs belongs to a wounded animal. It shakes the air, breaks the glass on the porthole, and I attack him, claws out.

I go for his face, screaming. His beautiful handsome face. I slice my claws across it, cutting through his brow, his eye, slicing off the tip of his nose. I go for the other side, doing the same. I grunt and I cry and I shred him to pieces again and again until he looks worse than Sedge does. His face is hanging off in strips and he's no longer recognizable. He's just bone and muscle and bloody skin.

And I feel something come over me. I thought it would be shame, I *should* feel shame, I should be horrified, and yet there's still something so dark and defiant and evil inside me, a monster to beat all monsters.

I lunge at him with a snapping maw and take hold of his neck, much like he did to me last night, tit for tat. But where he just drank from me, I bite all the way through, tearing out a chunk of his neck, blood pouring to the floor.

You're done, stop, it's over! a voice yells at me from inside. *You will kill him!*

Ramsay sways on his feet, a mess of a man, and I wonder if maybe I went too far. Maybe he's not as invincible as he led me to believe.

"Are you still angry?" he says through shredded lips, his voice raw and inhuman. "Are you still full of rage?"

I start blinking back tears, a surge of emotions rushing to the surface.

"Yes," I say, barely able to breathe now. "I'm still angry. Gods help me, I don't want to be this angry."

He seems to think that over but I can't even see his eyes anymore, they are just bloody dark masses. "Then we'll try again, another day. Now if you'll excuse me."

He turns unsteadily and walks toward the door, his hands out in front of him as if he can't see at all, as if I've left him blind.

"I'll get Sedge to take care of you," he says as he pauses at the door. "Please, don't do to him what you did to me. I deserve all your wrath, Maren. He doesn't."

He leaves the room, locking it behind him, perhaps to keep me from destroying everyone else on the ship.

I stare at the door for a moment, terrified at being alone now, alone with myself, with this monster, and I look down at my shaking hands, at the strips of his flesh under my nails, wondering what I've done.

Wondering what I've become.

True to the captain's word, Sedge did come and visit me. He brought me a bucket, more fish, and another bottle of rum. I didn't say a word to him, I couldn't even look at him. The moment he left I took the bottle of rum and poured it all over my hands and in my mouth, trying to clean the flesh and blood from them. Then I took the bottle that Ramsay brought me earlier and I drank it down. I drank it until I was nothing but drunk and passed out on the floor.

My dreams weren't kind to me but, then again, they had no right to be. I dreamt of Edonia and the Kraken and Asherah. Of Ramsay and Sterling and Aerik. I dreamt I was captured by skeletal Syren and dragged down into the abyss. I dreamt I saw my father die of a broken heart and my mother was captive in a tank just like my sister was in.

I wake up feeling godawful. I crawl to the bucket in the corner and I vomit in it, the rum making my stomach churn, as well as the realization of what I did to Ramsay.

He wanted it. He wanted me to unleash my fury on him, he used those words.

And yet all I want to do is cry. The shame that grips me is so great. I want to embrace the monster in me, I want to be deadly and powerful so that no one can ever hurt me again.

But I don't want to do it by hurting him. Because even though he has done things to make me hate him, even though his treatment of me waxes between tenderness and roughness, swinging like the tide, I fear I'm starting to care for him. That when he told me that we could be a king and queen of the high seas, that a secretive part deep inside me swelled with joy. It wanted that, exactly that. To have a man that sees me as an equal, not someone to belittle or batter around.

Are we equals now? Ramsay has never been violent with me. The iron brand was harsh but he did it for my own protection. He'd never struck me or flogged me or purposely caused me pain that I didn't want or enjoy.

But *I* did. I hurt him, I ravaged him. And I don't think he enjoyed it. I think the madness I lost myself to, the rage that consumed me like a beast, I think I caused him a lot of pain.

And he just let me do it. He wanted me to do it. He didn't enjoy it, it was all for me, so that I could finally be rid of the anger inside me.

Only it didn't work. I'm still mad, this deep festering pit of fury inside me, and now I'm ashamed and scared. Scared because what if I broke something between us? What if I both scarred him and scared him? What if that thin line of respect we seemed to have for each other has been shredded the same as his face?

What happens then?

What happens next?

I spit on the floor and wipe my mouth with the edge of my shirt, then I crawl over to the broken glass from the porthole, picking up a jagged edge. Wind whistles in through the shattered window as I turn the shard of glass over in my hands. Once upon a time I thought this would be my way out, because I couldn't live with my regrets. Now I have another regret to add to the pile.

Then the door opens.

I hold my breath as Ramsay appears.

Before I have a chance to take him in, he rushes over to me in a blur of speed and plucks the jagged glass from my hands, grabbing me at the wrists, my hands upturned.

He stares down at them, brows furrowed, perhaps worried I'd hurt myself.

But I'm staring at him.

At his handsome, gorgeous, lovely face.

It's back to normal. It's covered in faint red lines, slightly raised in some areas, but his face has healed itself back together. His eyes are beautifully clear, the sea at dusk, and I can't help the smile it brings me.

"What were you doing?" he whispers harshly, his gaze pinning me in place.

I just shake my head, tears welling in the back of my throat. "You're okay," I say. "Your face…"

He manages a stiff smile. "I told you I would be fine. The question is, are you?"

I free one hand from his grip and place it at his cheekbone, fingers gently trailing along it, then down the hollow of his cheeks and over his strong jaw where his facial hair scratches my skin, to the faint groove in his chin. His eyes close and he breathes in sharply at my touch.

Then I move my fingers along to his lips, blessed lips that know how to please me so well, where he moves his head to the side so that he plants a gentle kiss on my palm. "I'm fine," he says quietly yet adamantly, staring at me now.

"I caused you pain," I say to him, and he raises my other hand to his mouth and kisses my wrist, the tender sensation causing a ripple in my chest. "I was a monster."

"I know," he says. "But you're my monster, Maren. My fierce little creature. You did what you were born to do and what I told you to do."

I raise a brow. "Always have to be in control, do you?"

"Aye," he says. "And I needed you to be free of the shackles that keep your monster in check."

I give my head a shake. "I don't want that. I don't want to be a monster if it does that to you."

He lets out a smile of reprieve, his gaze stalling at my lips. "I must admit that's a relief, because I don't want to go through that again. I've had my fair share of pain in this world but that one took the prize."

"I'm sorry," I wince, feeling a sharpness in my chest.

"Do not apologize again, luv," he says to me, taking my hand in his and giving it a squeeze. "What's done is done."

"It was a mistake," I say, ashamed.

"There are no mistakes. Just choices that took us on a different path." He clears his throat. "At any rate, now I've learned that you still might hate me, but you don't actually want me dead. And that, my cearban, is a relief."

"Cearban?" I say, trying to imitate his Scottish brogue. "You've used that word before. What does it mean?"

"Gaelic for shark," he explains. "Basking shark, to be specific."

I frown. "Basking shark? But they don't even have teeth."

"Aye." He grins. "But they have a very large mouth."

I laugh at that and he reaches out and touches my necklace. "I wanted to ask you about this," he says thoughtfully. "Was this from your shark friend? Nill, was it?"

I nod, pleased that he remembered his name. "The only part of that world I have left. Edonia let me keep it on purpose. A way to torture me I suppose, but this gives me faith when I seem to lose it."

"You do know that we are going to get our revenge, don't you?" he asks, eyes searching mine. "I promise you that."

I nod. "Only if you keep feeding from me."

He rubs his lips together, his brow crinkling in concern. "I will never do that again, Maren."

"Because what you have taken will sustain you."

"No," he says with a shake of his head. "While it felt incredible, the power it gave me only lasted through the rest of the night. I almost feel back to normal. It's a fair shame too because I could have used the extra healing power. I'm feeling quite ugly as it is." He gestures to his face.

"You could never be ugly," I find myself saying.

"Aye, you're probably still drunk," he says, eyeing the empty bottles.

"Feed from me again," I implore him, surprised at the words coming out of my mouth.

He raises his head back giving me a discerning frown. "I told you. I won't do it again. It's not fair to you and I almost lost control. I don't know what I'd do if you ended up dead because of my own lack of discipline."

"I don't care. I can defend myself against you, you know I can now. I can take it. If you truly need me to get your revenge—"

"*Our* revenge."

"Our revenge, then do it. Use me. Let me help in some way."

He runs his tongue over his teeth. "Let me think about it."

"If I'm giving you consent and I can handle it…"

A sigh escapes his lips and he runs a hand down his face, wincing a little as he goes over the fresh wounds. "My father and I had a complicated relationship, as I'm sure all lads do with their pa, but the one thing we saw eye-to-eye on was that we would never take blood if we didn't need it. He taught me those principles and I held fast to them. They are the same principles he gave to his crew of the *Nightwind* before they became my crew."

This surprises me. "Your father was the captain of the *Nightwind*?"

"Aye," he says. "Not for long, but the ship was originally his before mine. My father was actually born in Italy as the son of a sailor, Alberto Battista, then later he left home and became a privateer in Scotland where he met my mum. I grew up on a ship with Thane and my mother. Sailed everywhere you could imagine. It was safest for us out on the sea. In Scotland, we didn't have a good understanding of what we were. My father had started calling us the Brethren before we found out there were others like us aside from our own family."

I try to imagine Ramsay and Thane as young boys, running along the deck like Henry and Lucas do and I can't help but smile. "How did he become a pirate?"

He gives me a wan smile. "When you're already living on the fringes of society, it's not hard to take the leap into doing whatever is best for you and your family. Once he learned that there were treasures to be taken from ships, he was all in. Especially ships from England, you know, which was already enacting the statutes of Iona by wanting me and Thane to be sent to the Protestant schools in the south. He saw it as revenge on a king that betrayed him and he never looked back."

"That's an exciting childhood," I muse.

"You're right. Every day was an adventure. But you were a princess born under the sea, so I reckon yours wasn't too boring either."

I shrug. I want to know more about his past. "So he had the *Nightwind*."

"Nay," he says, his accent thickening when he talks about his homeland. "He had another ship first, but the *Nightwind* was the first galleon he captured off the Azores. After that, it became our main home."

"How did your father and mother die?" I ask, though I know it may be a painful subject.

He clears his throat and looks away. "My mother was human. So, you know. Old age got her. Though looking back, I see how painfully short her years really were. There was nothing *old* about it. Once you taste immortality, anything less than that is a right shame."

"And your father?"

Now his expression darkens, the gray becoming as hard as steel.

"My father was executed by a navy captain turned pirate hunter. Captain Ed Smith. After that, I became captain of the ship."

I blink. "Wait, how was he caught? Why was he killed?"

His gaze narrows sharply. "Captain Smith made it his life's work to hunt pirates, but especially my father. He had it in for my whole family. Not all of us who live by the blood share the same codes."

"He was one of the Brethren like you?"

"In name only. Yes, a creature like me, although I doubt his crew knows it. He's still out there to this day, still harboring an agenda. But now I harbor the same agenda for him. Edonia isn't the only one I want my vengeance against, luv. I've made my fair share of enemies in this life, and Ed Smith is one of the worst. Only problem is, if we're both hunting each other, it's rather hard to line up a plan of attack. But if I see him, mark my words, I will kill him and make him suffer until his last breath."

From the violence in his eyes, I don't doubt it.

Suddenly the door to the room bursts open and one of the skeleton crew appears.

"Captain!" the skeleton yells. "I reckon we've spotted the *Nightwind*!"

TWENTY-EIGHT

Ramsay

I glance at Maren, my eyes going between the remorse in her eyes and the nails on her fingers, knowing how easily they can turn into claws. I can either keep her locked in here forever or I can let her go free. I'm not as worried now that she may do further harm to me, but I am worried she might jump into the sea and leave me.

That's what you want for her, isn't it? For her to be happy? To return to what she is? If she doesn't go now, she will eventually.

She raises her brows at me and jerks her chin subtly toward the skeleton crew member. "The *Nightwind*."

I nod. "Aye. Come with me then," I say, grabbing her by the elbow and pulling her toward the door.

She seems surprised she's allowed to leave but she doesn't question it out loud. Instead she looks down at the dirty shirt she's wearing, stained with my blood. "Is there anything else on this ship that I could wear?"

I turn to the skeleton. "Do you perchance have any old clothes lying around? Stuff that's perhaps a little too big for you now?"

The skeleton tilts his head, seeming to think. "Yes, I suppose I do." He waves at Maren. "Come along then, see what we have. Slim pickings I think, definitely nothing for the likes of a pretty girl like you."

She looks at me for approval and I nod. "Go ahead. Meet me up top."

She walks off with the skeleton. At least I don't have to worry about her being alone with him. If anything, I worry for the skeleton.

I head up to the deck where the quartermaster and Sedge are waving me over from the forecastle. The skeletal quartermaster slaps a spyglass into my palm.

"Avast, there be a ship," he says.

I peer through the spyglass, having the feeling I've done this before, only it was when I was on the *Nightwind* looking at this ship. My god, that feels like ages ago.

And there she is, my glorious ship on the horizon. The sight of her makes my heart skip a beat, a very similar reaction I get when I look at Maren sometimes. There has to be some sort of analogy drawn between a captain's ship and his lover, but I'm not poetic enough to think of one.

All I know is that I am as obsessive and possessive about that ship as I am about Maren, and I would travel to the ends of the world to get the both of them back. They both belong to me. Luckily at the moment the *Nightwind* is in my sights and we are slowly but steadily catching up. As for Maren, I can only hope that her request for new clothes wasn't just a ruse and she's secretly escaping into the sea.

Oh, bollocks. That's what she was doing, wasn't it? She wasn't asking to get changed into new clothes, she wanted to be out of my reach and prying eye so she could clobber the skeleton over the head and jump off the back of the ship, knowing that by the time I'd clue into her duplicity she'd already be far gone in the middle of Pacific and impossible to find.

I sigh heavily, a coal of loss sinking in my chest. I—

"Did you spot her?"

I whirl around to see Maren standing behind me and staring at me with an open look, the skeleton at her side. She's wearing another over-sized white pirate shirt with a pistol holster around the small of her waist as if it were a leather corset, and wide black petticoat breeches. Her bare feet flex as I stare at them.

"You're still here," I say softly. "You didn't jump overboard."

She manages a quick smile. "Well, I have to admit the moment I saw you were willing to let me go, I did think about it. But I also figured I'll have plenty of chances later. I want to get back to the *Nightwind* too."

I grin with relief and hand her the spyglass. "See for yourself."

She stands beside me at the rail and peers through the spyglass at the horizon and I take a moment to drink her all in. With her pirate attire, her black hair blowing back in the wind, even those faint lines of gills on her neck, she looks so beautiful that there's a sharp ache in my ribs, a longing for her that has slowly been coming to fruition. She belongs here, right here beside me, with the ocean breeze in her hair and the sun on her skin.

Yet she also belongs at the bottom of the sea. How can she belong to both places, when only one of those worlds includes me?

Don't get attached to a caged bird if you only mean to set them free, I think.

"I don't see anything, just a dot," she says, frowning through the spyglass. She glances at me. "Are you sure that's the *Nightwind*?"

"Aye," I say, blinking my wayward thoughts from my mind. "My eyesight is better than yours. It's her."

I turn around to look at the remaining crew who have gathered on deck. "We have spotted the *Nightwind*!" I yell, pumping my fist into the air. "Keep this heading, bosun! The rest of you, you are not to harm any member of my crew except for Sterling McCoy, who has been calling himself captain. When we swarm the ship, go straight for him and lock him up in the hold until I know what punishment to dole out for a mutineer!"

"Huzzah!" the crew yells, raising their swords and muskets in the air. One of them is even lifting up a femur, possibly his own.

"Keelhaul him!" a skeleton yells. "Drag him under the ship!"

"Tar and feather him!" yells another.

"Maroon him," Maren says bitterly.

I glance at her curiously. "You think so?"

She nods. "What do they say pirates do? Leave them on an island with only one bullet? I know that won't put Sterling out of his misery, but that's the point, is it not? Leave him on a sandbar somewhere with a bullet that will do nothing for him. He'll spend eternity starving to death but never dying. No blood, no food, no water."

"I shouldn't be surprised at how sadistic you are," I say, grinning at her devilish brain. "Though eventually, given the nature of the world, he will get discovered and possibly rescued."

"Then chop off a limb and he'll be useless anyway. Those don't grow back, do they?" She eyes the wounds she left on my face.

"I've never known a Brethren to lose a limb," I admit. "But perhaps we can put it to the test."

She gives me a satisfied smile that makes my cock jump to attention. Always at the most inconvenient times.

With the wind steady in the billowing sails, the hull slicing through the water in rhythmic drops, we gain speed on my *Nightwind*. I know by now that this cursed ship would have been spotted by the preternaturally keen eyes of the crew. My crew. God help me, they will be my crew again. I can't imagine what must have taken place on that ship in my absence, but I know the ones that would have rushed in to defend me—Thane, Sam, Cruz—might be in some danger. They can take on Sterling, but Nerissa's the wild card. What does she even want with the *Nightwind*? Has she sided with Sterling? Does she plan to take over, or has she already? If she can't curse us Brethren to become the undead, can she do something else to us? And if so, why? Is she acting on behalf of Edonia?

My questions will have answers soon enough. The *Nightwind* has turned broadside for our approach.

"She's gone broadside," the quartermaster says to me. "Shall we prepare the cannons?"

I shake my head. "Not a single shot will be fired on that vessel."

"Even if they shoot at us, Captain?"

I grind my teeth together but hold fast. "Nay. We will take the beating and board. We will not fire upon the *Nightwind*, mark my words, or I will mark you."

The quartermaster lets out a groan of disappointment before yelling to the rest of the crew. "Hold steady, lads! Deadlight the windows! Hammocks in the hold!"

While many of the crew run down below to bolster the ship's sides against roundshots, Maren eyes me with a concerned frown. "You do realize we may have to battle with a sea witch."

"I'm realizing a lot of things, luv."

She leans in close, my nose filling with her sweet natural scent, something akin to ocean salt, sunshine, and jasmine. "Why not feed from me again?" she whispers, not wanting the crew to overhear.

With her so close to me and the heat coming off her neck, it's not just my cock that's hungry for her, but my stomach as well. "You shouldn't tease me so," I say gruffly. "It's dangerous for you and annoying for me."

"I'm not teasing," she protests, and I see the sincerity in her eyes. "Take me below and have your way with me."

I can't help but give her a crooked grin. "Are you threatening me with pleasure?"

She presses her hand against my chest and stares up at me. "I'm serious. Take my blood. You said it had already run through your system."

I grab the hand that's on my chest and squeeze it. "I also told you I made a vow not to take blood that I didn't have to. I don't need it to defeat Nerissa and Sterling. Let's save it for Edonia, for the both of us."

She doesn't seem so sure, but I meant what I said. Yes, I want her blood. Yes I want that incredible feeling that I got from it, that I was limitless and all-powerful, that I was a damn god on earth. I want that connection I felt to her as her blood mingled with mine.

But I know that not only could I get carried away at an inopportune time, but that it would drain her as well. I see it in her eyes now and she might think it's just from drinking all the rum, but I know the look of someone who has had too much blood taken from them. I can't weaken her now.

The *Nightwind* is now just a few hundred yards away. The bosun brings the ship so it's broadside against the *Nightwind*, a defensive position. Every time I'm able to view my ship from afar, either from a dock or the ship's boat as we're rowing away, it takes my breath away. She's a mighty ship, some might say even too big for a pirate crew such as ours, but she's ours all the same.

"She is stunning, isn't she?" Maren says as she admires her.

But now I'm looking at *her*, the pink of her lips, the softly upturned sweep of her delicate nose, her full cheeks sprinkled with freckles that seem to multiply by the day, and her dramatic eyes. "Aye. Beautiful and deadly all at once. The only kind of lady I fall for."

She gives me a quick, wry smile, not accepting the compliment. Then she frowns. "Where is everyone?"

I look back to the ship. I was so busy admiring her lines that I didn't stop to think how odd it was that there's not a soul on deck.

Dread forms in the pit of my stomach.

What has happened here?

"Ahoy there," I yell, my hands cupped over my mouth. "This is your former captain speaking. Permission to come aboard and cease fire?!"

But there is only silence in response.

"Now what?" Maren says. "Is it a ruse? If we board, will they ambush us?"

"Aye, it seems like a trap," the quartermaster says. "Proceed with caution."

I nod. "We can't just sit here and twiddle our cocks. If it isn't a trap, then my crew may need me, and fast."

"And if it is a trap?" Maren asks.

"Then we take it moment by moment."

And hope the moments are kind.

TWENTY-NINE

Maren

The sight of the *Nightwind* completely empty, her decks bare of crew, sends a chill down my spine. Where are they? What has Nerissa done with them? Or Sterling, for that matter? It doesn't seem feasible that any of the Brethren would listen to a big oaf like him, but I could be wrong. Perhaps there have been decades of festering resentment among the members, maybe even amongst his own family.

"Steady!" the skeletal quartermaster yells. "Get the plank ready."

Some of the crew bring out a long wooden plank and lower it over the rail until it slams against the rail of the *Nightwind*. Ramsay winces at the sound, not wanting any damage to his beloved ship.

Then he gives a silent command with his hand for the crew to board the ship, moving as quietly as possible. Not that anyone on board wouldn't have heard us already, but even so.

Ramsay looks back at me. "Maren, stay on the ship and guard it with the bosun," he says, dropping his voice.

I look over at the bosun and even though the crew's skulls seem to be grinning at all times, this one looks especially leering.

"I think not," I tell him and, before he can stop me, I'm pulling myself up on the plank and quickly running across it. Normally my balance is atrocious because of my legs but because it's the sea beneath me, the sea that I don't fear, I'm able to cross it with newfound grace.

I give Ramsay a defiant look as I join him and he just shakes his head in response.

"No point telling you to do anything, is there luv?" He reaches into his holster and pulls out a pistol, placing it in my hand. "Here. Just in case."

I relish the weight of it in my hands, though if it comes to it I'm ready to claw Sterling's face off, perhaps even the witch's too.

We head down the stairs into the dark and silent deck below, Ramsay first, followed by me, the quartermaster and the rest of the skeleton crew. Ramsay grabs a lantern and lights it with a strike of a match that he fished out from his pocket and this is the second time he's made fire easily appear. I have to wonder if this is some of the other magic that Venla gave him.

The *Nightwind* feels different now, like it lost its essence in the time that Ramsay was gone. He gives life to the ship and I know the ship gives life to him. Here in the dark gangways it feels sinister and cold, the shadows especially seeming to dance in the moving flame, and I see faces where there aren't any. Perhaps it doesn't help that every time I turn around I see skulls grinning at me.

We explore this deck, then the next, and each one is empty, dark as sin and quiet as the grave. I keep thinking we're going to be ambushed, as if I can feel things watching me from the shadows, and yet nothing happens.

Finally we go to the hold, with all its different rooms for storage. Down here it always smells awful because of the bilge but even more so now that it doesn't seem to have been emptied for a while and I know there are rotting corpses too. The air is thick with moisture that clings to your skin, the water sloshes against the hull. The captain of the *Elephanten* used to tell us that we were always three or four inches from death, which is the thickness of the planks of the vessel. I never felt it much until now, despite knowing that I can breathe underwater.

Ramsay heads straight toward the main hold where he had kept my crew and servants, the rest of us close behind him. The closer we get to it, the worse it smells, and I try to steel my stomach against the sight we may see. Even if the crew isn't in there, I don't care to see Hodges and the rest of the bodies.

With his lantern held out, he takes in a deep breath and puts his hand on the door.

Suddenly there's a scurrying sound, a scraping of the wood, and the quartermaster lets out a gasp as countless tiny black crabs come crawling out from underneath the door, heading straight toward us.

All of us yelp as they keep on coming, a stream of black writhing legs and snapping claws, hundreds of them fanning out across the deck, then crawling up our bodies.

I violently run my hands over my body, flinging them off, trying not to panic as they get in my pant legs, in my shirt, until finally the swarm of them leaves us and continues up the stairs to the rest of the ship.

"What in the blazes was that?" Ramsay says, panting hard. His body gives off an involuntary shake, thoroughly disgusted. "Skip is going to have his paws full."

I shiver, still feeling the crabs on me, even though they've disappeared into the darkness.

Ramsay puts his hand to the door again, steadies himself, and opens it.

The hold is full of bodies.

The bodies of his crew, piled high.

Dead.

I let out an ear-piercing scream and Ramsay stares in total shock, anguish and terror contorting his face in the light of the flame, while it shines on the pale, still faces of Sam, Henry, Thane, Cruz…

"God, no, god," he whispers hoarsely and starts to sway on his feet.

I reach out to steady him and there's a low rich laughter behind us.

We turn around to see Nerissa behind the skeletons who automatically part in fear of her. She's grinning at us maliciously, twirling a piece of kelp around her finger.

"I thought you'd come sooner or later," she says.

Ramsay tries to speak but he can't form the words and I watch in real time as rage takes over and he runs at her, lantern held high.

"Stop," she says, holding out her palm and Ramsay freezes in place, fighting against an unseen force. "And take a moment before you do something foolish. Look again at your dear crew."

I look behind me. They haven't changed position but even with the light fainter, I can see that Henry is breathing, his chest gently rising and falling.

"They're sleeping," she explains. "A bit of magic, hope you don't mind. They were so unruly and loud once I stuck them down in the hold that I needed some peace and quiet."

"You piled them on top of all the dead bodies," I say to her, aghast, when it seems Ramsay needs a moment to catch up. "As if they were disposable. That's cruel."

"That's cruel? Oh, my child. Goodness. *That's* cruel? That's exactly what they deserve! Don't you know that I am a great purveyor of justice? The reason there are corpses in there to begin with is because the crew of the *Nightwind* put them there." She gives Ramsay a look of disgust. "Your whole kind is remorseless, you bloodsucking lampreys of the land. It's about time someone taught you a lesson. See what it's like. Maybe you can change your ways."

"What do you want?" Ramsay asks, his gaze cold, his voice iron.

"Nothing," she says with a bright smile. "Now that you're both here, I have all that I want." She eyes the skeleton crew. "You must pardon me, my darlings, but I'm afraid I've grown weary of you. You're no longer part of my destiny. No, I've seen my destiny now in Thane's crystal ball."

Ramsay stiffens at that.

"And my destiny is here," she adds simply. "As soon as I saw the vision, I knew what my gut was already telling me, that I have business aboard this ship. Naturally, I slowed the wind. Perhaps you'll notice we were just sitting out here, waiting for you."

"You have no business here," Ramsay says with a jerk of his head. "Your business is with your skeleton crew on the *Norfinn*."

"*Bones*," she says, drawing out his nickname. "If I leave, then there will be no one to lift the spell. Your crew will sleep forever."

"Then wake them," he says, grinding out the words.

Her smile becomes coy. "You know how us witches work. We want a favor in return."

"Well?" he asks impatiently.

She tilts her head. "Last time we were at an impasse, you offered yourself. That won't do this time. I know what I want. The woman who wants to be a mermaid. You give her to me, and I give you your crew back. You keep her to yourself, and your crew will be at rest forever." Her gaze slides to mine, the copper in her eyes glowing, thoroughly enjoying this.

I gulp, feeling the weight of this decision. Ramsay is hesitating, panic and pain swirling in his eyes as he looks at me. He doesn't want to pick me over his crew, and he doesn't want to pick his crew over me. Last time we were in this exact predicament things ended in mutiny and I won't have that happen to the *Nightwind* again. My life is certainly not worth all the lives of his crew, especially the children.

"I'll go," I say quickly, looking Nerissa right in the eyes. I keep my chin up, my voice steady, and walk toward her. "It's fine."

"Maren, no!" Ramsay cries out, trying to reach for me, but Nerissa pins him in place with her gaze.

"She has volunteered and that is binding." She grins at me, a pretty but menacing smile. "Perhaps she's the one I wanted all along." She holds out her hand for me. "Come now, my raven-haired child. We have much to discuss."

"Wait," I say, looking behind me at the crew. "I'm not going anywhere until you lift the spell. I need to know I can trust you."

She sighs and then shrugs. "Alright, but when I lift the spell, it will awaken Sterling as well. He's hanging in chains around the corner, but he can be awfully loud."

"Who put him in the chains?" Ramsay asks.

"Your crew did. He's a mutineer, after all, and your crew is loyal."

Then she waves her fingers at the hold and both Ramsay and I watch with bated breath as they slowly begin to stir, limbs twitching, eyes fluttering.

"It will take them some time to come out of it," she explains, then reaches down and grabs my hand. It's surprisingly warm and soft.

But I pull back. "And I want another favor," I tell her. "Our mate Sedge fell victim to the curse. He's waiting on the *Norfinn* right now. I need you to reverse it. He didn't deserve it, not even a little."

She looks put-upon but she just closes her eyes and snaps her fingers. "There. Give it a few hours and he should be fine."

"What about us?" the skeletal quartermaster asks.

She laughs, rolling her eyes to the ceiling. "You? Why on earth would I reverse *your* curse?"

"Because it's been twenty years," one of them says. "Don't you think we've suffered and paid enough?"

"You know what you did," she says, voice hard. "You know what you deserve. I delivered justice."

Then she sighs, her shoulders softening a little. "I will free you from your curse," she says and as they all gasp in shock she raises her palm, tiny golden starfish etched on her skin, "*but* you will not be able to leave the islands to which you are tethered. Your ship will always keep you there, if another ship happens by, you'll just be brought back by force of the gods. You will live there for the rest of your lives, which are now painfully mortal and short. You will only reside on my island, which is still uninhabited, so people will be safe from your ways. I doubt you ever learned any of your lessons."

Then she closes her eyes and snaps her fingers again. "Now go," she says, eyes open and blazing with golden flames. "Go back to your ship and set sail before I change my mind. And make sure to hand Sedge back over to his ship where he belongs."

Though the skeleton crew doesn't look any different, they seem to believe her and accept the terms. They all start running for the stairs, clattering up them and to the top deck.

"Don't ever say I'm not fair," she says to Ramsay, then she looks back at me. "Come now. We have much to discuss."

She pulls me along toward the steps while Ramsay runs after us.

"Back!" she yells, whirling around with her palm displayed and Ramsay's large body is shoved back to the ground. Then she takes me up the stairs, all the way to the main deck and into Ramsay's quarters.

"What did the skeleton crew even do to you?" I ask her.

"They displeased me," she says. "Trespassed on my island. Plundered the villages, raped the women. They are bad men. They deserved this fate."

I can't argue with that.

"Into the cage," she says, gesturing to it.

I give her a pleading look. "I don't think you know how much time I've spent in there already."

"I will let you go," she says. "I just want to talk to you without you struggling or forcing my magic on you. It gets tiring and I'm already exhausted."

"And you think I should have sympathy for you?" I ask.

She just shoves me in the cage and locks it with a wave of her hands.

I turn around and grip the bars, hating that I'm back in here, even if it's not at the hands of Ramsay this time.

"What do you want with me?" I ask.

"What do you want with *me*?" she counters. "You know, Maren, there's something not right about you and I have a very good sense about people." She pauses, brushing her kelp hair behind her ear. "But you're not people, are you? Not human. And therein lies the problem."

I straighten my back, a chill in my veins. "What do you mean?"

"You know what I mean. I see those gills on your neck. I heard you asking to me to turn you into a mermaid. I saw you jump overboard to save Bones and stay under that water for an awfully long time. Not to mention what my cursed Syrens told me later." She takes a step toward me until she's right up against the cage. "They told me that you're one of them."

"They don't know what they're talking about," I say, wanting to mention that I kicked their heads right off.

"They do. They've heard the stories about a Syren who walks, who bargained with a sea witch. That she lives among humans, unable to return to her past form." She smiles at me. "That Syren is *you*."

A malevolent smile stretches my lips. "If that's true…" I begin.

My arm shoots straight out through the bars of the cage, not going for her heart this time but around her throat, my claws extending, my teeth sharpening as I bare them at her. "Then you have made a grave mistake."

Her eyes widen, her hands going to mine to try and pry my fingers off but my claws are digging into her neck, drawing metallic green blood that runs down in rivulets. She closes her eyes, trying to recite words, perhaps a spell and she's throwing around her hands but I won't let go. I squeeze and squeeze, feeling her drain beneath my hand.

"Maren!" Ramsay yells and I quickly glance at the door where he runs in.

"I've got her," I say, bringing my eyes back to the witch. "Grab her!"

He pauses. "I've got reinforcements." He says this in such a way that it takes me a moment to realize what he means by it.

My claws. My teeth. The crew can't see me like this.

I immediately let go of Nerissa, my claws disappearing into nails, and she falls to the ground just as Thane and Cruz run in, looking a little worse for wear. They run straight to her and grab her on either side, hauling her to her feet.

She looks consumed and barely struggles against their grip. She stares at me like she's hurt, as I've offended her somehow.

"Heigh-ho, Maren," Cruz says, staring at me in awe. "You certainly know how to defend yourself."

I can't even smile at that. I watch as Ramsay takes a key from his pocket and opens the door to the cage, then pulls me out of it while Nerissa is shoved in to take my place, falling against the bars. I watch as he quickly locks the door with that key and the three of them step back.

"How will that keep her in there? Won't she just use a spell?"

"Witches don't want you to know that their power isn't limitless," he says to me with a smirk. "She's used a lot of hers already. And at any rate, not every witch can undo every spell." He waves the key at me. "This key can open any lock and it can close any lock. My magic is equal and that cage is specially magicked to keep her from using hers."

"And that match I've seen you carry?"

He pats his pocket proudly. "Another piece of magic I was gifted. A set of endless matches that can create flames at any time."

"Fine," Nerissa says hoarsely, coughing as she presses her hand to her neck, the metallic green blood shimmering as it goes over her fingers. "Keep me in here. I told you I wanted to be on your ship anyway. Why not in the captain's quarters where I have the best access to Bones here?"

"I think it's time you shut up, harpy," Thane scowls at her.

Her eyes light up when she slides her gaze to his. "And *you*. My fate. I used your crystal, Thane," she says. "Don't you wonder what I saw in that purple light?"

Thane growls, making a move for the cage but Cruz reaches out and holds him back. "Don't bother with her," Cruz says. "I know witches, and she's unhinged like the rest of them."

"Oh, you call your own mother unhinged, Isaac?" she says in a silky tone, eyeing Cruz now. "I know that you left her back in Sierra Leone. I know that she was a witch herself, queen of the village. How much of her blood magic is in you, hey handsome?"

"I didn't leave—" he starts and then he gives his head a shake. He looks to Ramsay and Thane. "I think it's best that we leave her here before she tries to get in our heads."

They nod and we exit the room, Ramsay closing the door to his quarters as much as he can considering I shot the lock off.

"Will the cage keep her?" I ask. "Maybe you should put her down in the hold."

And out of your room.

"Don't tell me you miss the cage yourself?" he asks. "Not to fret, luv, you'll now be staying in one of the officer's quarters. A whole room to yourself."

His way of saying I'm sleeping alone.

But he's not.

THIRTY

Maren

A stream of sunlight hits my face, waking me from my slumber, and it takes me a moment to realize where I am. I'd never been in the officer's quarters on the *Nightwind*, so I wasn't expecting such a quaint space. It's a lot smaller than the captain's quarters but it's still tastefully decorated, with a narrow shelf lined with worn books, a small basin and bucket, a painting of some tropical island. The porthole window is above a small desk and I can't help but wonder who would have sat here before, penning letters or tallying things in a logbook.

I slowly sit up and smile when I see my trunk, having forgotten all about it. Though I am getting used to dressing like a pirate, I have missed my dresses, my own clean clothes that fit me like a glove and haven't been worn by a skeleton.

I get out of the bunk, careful not to hit my head, and go to my trunk, rummaging through it until I find my undergarments, a stark white chemise shift, petticoat and a pair of champagne stays. I forgo the panier since it only makes it harder to maneuver on the ship, then I decide to forgo the gown too. It's too hot for it, too stiff and clumsy, not to mention I no longer have a maid to help me with the pins. Why not just wear the shift? I know it would be seen as immoral to be seen in just your undergarments, but I don't have any shame left on this ship and I don't think anyone cares.

I decide to lace up the stays and the matching stomacher down the front, since my bust needs the support, but when I'm done I'm just in those, my shift, and the petticoat. I decide most of my shoes are too awkward for the boat with their heels and decide that if there's a pair of men's boots small enough for my feet then I'll be wearing them.

I don't have a mirror to look at my reflection but when I'm done I feel liberated and free. I feel like I'm still holding onto my Syren femininity yet I'm doing it my way, no longer boxed in to what society has been telling me how to dress.

I leave my new quarters, passing by the other rooms which belong to Lucas and Henry who share a room, Cruz, and Sam and Thane who share another. The rest of the crew sleeps before the mast in a large room filled with hammocks.

Then I head for the stairs, passing by the captain's quarters at the end. I feel a twinge of jealousy again at the fact that Nerissa is caged in the room. Why isn't she in the hold or the chains where Sterling is? Does he want her in there for other reasons?

I ignore that acidic feeling in my gut and go up the stairs to the top deck.

It's early, but everyone seems to be up and the sun is bright in my face, the salt air waking me up in an instant. I spot Ramsay at the aft deck sitting on a bench to the side of the helm beside Drakos the Greek who is whittling a piece of wood with a small paring knife that I always see in his possession, Henry watching Drakos as he works. Thane is at the helm with Crazy Eyes and Lucas discussing a chart and, occasionally turning around to see what Ramsay is saying.

I'm about to head up there when I notice Sam on the quarterdeck, waving me over. She's sitting on an overturned crate cross-legged, a tall mug of what I assume is steaming coffee in her hands, adorned in her usual attire with a tricorn hat on her head.

"Fancy some?" she asks and then pats the seat beside her.

I nod, feeling strangely shy all of a sudden. I'd become so used to dealing with all the men on board and their brash ways, but Sam intimidates me. Perhaps because she's so confident in her ways, owning who she truly is and not giving a rat's arse what anyone thinks. Plus I've seen her fight.

I sit down next to her and she hands me the mug. "Here, you have some of this brew. I can get more from Sedge later."

I give her a grateful "thanks" and take a sip of the coffee. "Strong enough to put hair on your chest," I say with a cough. "How is Sedge?"

"He seems to be alright," she says. "Nerissa reversed the curse so he looks more or less back to normal. He's happy to be here, though perhaps a little traumatized."

"I bet," I say.

"Might I say, I like the way you're dressed," she says, eyeing me up and down. "So much better this way, ain't it? Easier to move around without all those layers, not to mention cooler." She pauses, peering at me. "And you, are you traumatized?"

"Me?" I ask. "No, I've been through a fair bit worse than that. The skeleton crew were practically angels in comparison."

"I meant with Bones," she says in a knowing tone. "He told me that he fed from you."

I freeze, shoulders stiffening, before I carefully lower the mug from my lips. "He told you that?"

"Aye," she says, leaning back against the rail and adjusting her black shirt. "So you know all about the Brethren of the Blood now."

"Did he tell you...*why* he fed from me?"

She frowns. "Because he was hungry?"

What I'm trying to see without giving anything away is whether she knows that I'm a Syren or not. But from the way she's acting, I don't think she does. I relax a little and take another sip of the coffee. Ramsay had promised my secret would be safe with him and I have to trust him with that.

"Oh, he was hungry alright," I say.

"I bet," she says, her green eyes lighting up. "So how was it?"

I stare at her aghast for a moment. "You mean the feeding or...?"

"I'm meaning the plowing," she says salaciously. "Look here, I'm one of the Brethren, don't matter that I'm a female, I know what it gets like when you get the blood in ya. No doubt with Bones it led to the deed of darkness, aye."

I feel myself flush. "It's too early for this sort of talk."

"Then finish your coffee and wake up."

Laughing, I do as she says, finishing the rest of the mug. I've never had anyone to have this sort of "woman talk" with so I feel I should take advantage of it. I clear my throat. "You would not believe the abject filth that comes out of that man's mouth," I offer. "It's enough to make a sailor blush."

"Of course I can. Look at him," she nods her head up at the aft deck where he's seated. At that moment he's grinning at Drakos, looking both wicked and handsome.

"I have to admit, we were worried for a while there thinking he might never come back for us and the *Nightwind*," she adds, her voice turning grave.

"Were any of the crew seriously thinking of sailing under Sterling?"

"Nay. Not even close."

"So you really are like a family."

"Aye. I'm not just saying this as his sister-in-law, but we all trust him with our lives. Bones is doing what his father did and that's thumbing his nose up at the politics and privilege of the world. There was no place for them there and there still isn't. It doesn't help that we are part of the Brethren and distanced from society to begin with. Here, on the *Nightwind*, we are together and we are safe and we have our own world to govern."

"Even though Ramsay governs it."

She shakes her head. "As you've seen, it's a democracy. Can you say that about anywhere else where the kings and queens reign? The class systems that have been set up to make the rich richer and the poor poorer. They're even telling us now what religions we have to follow, what *god* to believe in. As if you can force belief onto some-one." She shakes her head in disgust. "Here we are equal. Bones leads us but we all need a leader and in the end nothing is against our will. We can be free out here to live the lives we want and be who we want to be. Do you think back in Glasgow I'd be allowed to wear these breeches!? My goodness, they'd hang me by my neck for being an outlier for that and everything else that makes me who I am."

I look back over at Ramsay, who has now borrowed the whittling knife from Drakos and is attempting to carve something out of a wood plank, laughing as he goes, Henry looking on in excitement to see what he will create.

"He's a good man, Maren," she adds with emphasis, leaning in to tap her shoulder against mine. "He may be rough around the edges, but pardon me for telling you this, I haven't seen him this happy in a very long time."

"Happy?" I ask, puzzled. "I assumed he was always like this." Not that Ramsay has been joyful all the time but he certainly doesn't have the seriousness of his brother.

"He can be brooding for sure," she notes with a smile. "Nothing like Thane, of course, he's a grumpy bastard by nature. However, before you came along, there was an inherent restlessness with Bones. The way we'd cross the Pacific over and over again. Always searching for the sea witch, as if that would bring him peace. The thing is, and I do hate to say it, but even if he finds her I don't think killing her will bring him peace. His daughter is gone and no revenge will ever bring her back."

I nod, though I don't want her words to be true. Will killing Edonia bring me peace? Perhaps not. But I don't even want her dead necessarily, I just want my fins back and my world back.

I still want that, don't I?

"She also has that book," I say. "The magic book that his witch wife wrote for him."

"Aye, that too. But he doesn't realize the book is pointless."

I look at her in surprise. "Pointless?"

She takes off her hat and adjusts a few strands of wayward red hair before putting it back on. "What is the book going to do for him?"

"Isn't it a way for him to access more magic?"

"It is. But what does he really want?"

"His wife back," I whisper, trying to ignore the knot in my stomach. "Can the book bring her back?"

She gives me a sympathetic smile. "No. It can't. And I know Bones has made peace with her death. It's been a very long time, Maren. He's let her go. He's moved on." She sighs. "But the book, he has not. His daughter he has not forgotten. His grief for her runs deep. For he knows that he can't get Hilla back, but he can get the book back and he thinks that it's the same thing. The book to him is his past. He needs to learn to let that go, too."

"And you haven't voiced this to him?"

Sam laughs. "Good heavens. You think he listens to me at all? He thinks the only reason I married his brother was to annoy him for the rest of his life."

"And that wasn't the case."

"No, just a bonus, if you will," she says with a smirk that causes a dimple in her cheek. "Though I will tell you, Thane wasn't my first choice."

My brows go up. "No? You wanted Ramsay?"

She nods. "Aye. I did. I had a wee crush on him, as did all the girls in Port Royal. Every time the *Nightwind* would come into port, I hoped I'd get Ramsay alone. I was a bar wench at one of the taverns, only came from Scotland a few years earlier. Had no idea that they were the same as me, the Dearg-Diulai, I only suspected it, the way you can sometimes tell where a person's from. We have this sheen, ya see? One night I stole upon the ship, thinking I would seduce Bones in his bed. I got the wrong bed."

"*No*," I exclaim in a hush, looking back over at Ramsay and Thane. They both share the same strong jaw, thick hair, build and height, but Thane is an inch or two shorter and a little more square in the face. Here Ramsay's hair is long and a deep dark brown, but Thane's is a little lighter and short, cropped close to the head. Though they both remain frozen at age thirty-five, Thane does somehow look a couple of years older, though perhaps it's just his mannerisms.

"One thing led to another and bam," she says, pointing to Lucas who is talking to his father about something. "I was with child. Soon as

Thane found out, we were married and I was the newest member of the *Nightwind*."

"And you never told Ramsay this?"

She tips her head back to the sky and laughs. "Oh, he knows. I remind him all the time. He was with Venla at the time anyway, it was a fool's game for me, but I was young and," she shrugs, "it all worked out, didn't it? Yet another reason I was grateful for the ship. You could get pregnant out of wedlock here and not be shunned and condemned. Can't think of a better place to raise our boy to be honest with you."

"He does seem like a good lad," I tell her. "Very polite."

"Aye and we all take turns schooling them too. Ramsay's especially taken a liking to Henry."

"I can see that," I comment, remembering the look on Ramsay's face when Aerik was threatening to kill him.

"So," she says, drawing out the word as she fixes her green eyes on me. "What are your plans for the near future? Since you don't seem to be a hostage anymore."

I run my fingers over the tooth on my necklace. "I don't know. To be true with you, I've never felt this free in my whole entire life, and yet…"

"And yet you feel a calling to this ship. You feel a calling to the captain."

I can't help but nod, wishing I could tell her the whole story. "I do. But…I had a family and a life before I met Prince Aerik. A life that I haven't been a part of in ten years. I'd like to go visit it while I can."

"I'm sure Bones will take you there."

I weigh that. "I think he would. Eventually. But what if I end up going where he can't follow?"

"Then it sounds like you're going to have to make a choice when that time comes."

Yes, but it's a choice that I can never come back from. If I get the spell reversed and my fins back from Edonia, I won't ever be able to live on land again. I won't have legs. I'll have to live under the sea and even though Ramsay can survive under there for a short time, I would never make any human—any *creature*—live that way in order to be with me. It would be cruel. Plus, to take Ramsay away from his ship, I could never. And he'd never choose that either.

You don't even know if he'd choose you at all, I remind myself. There's no point even entertaining the idea. Just because you bedded him a couple of times and he's had some of your blood doesn't mean the two of you are destined for something more than lust. Besides, he has a thing for witches and perhaps it's no accident that the gorgeous Nerissa is caged in his quarters and you're the one sleeping alone.

Suddenly I spot a movement of orange fur on the deck and I'm grateful for the distraction.

"Skip!" I call out to the feline who is padding along the base of the rail.

"Oh that cat never listens to anyone," Sam says under her breath.

But Skip looks at me, meows, and then starts sauntering over in that easy way of his. He's starting to remind me of Ramsay, self-assured and inclined to make you wait.

"Well I'll be," Sam says as Skip comes right under my hands and I lightly rake my nails over his back.

"Animals love me," I tell her, beaming, running my hand up the cat's silky tail.

"And that includes the captain," she says.

My heart skips a beat in my chest and I clear my throat, feeling something light growing inside me. "The captain loves his crew and he loves his ship."

"And he's capable of loving more things than that. Even a former hostage, former princess, former thorn in his side."

I roll my eyes and jab her lightly with my elbow, which makes her giggle.

Suddenly laughter peals out from the lads and we look over to see that Ramsay has carved what looks like a very giant phallic object out of the wood. They're all laughing as he holds it up, Lucas and Henry the guffawing loudest of all, while Thane just shakes his head in disappointment.

"Oh, dear," Sam says tiredly with a shake of her head. She gets off the box and then pulls me up to my feet beside her, holding my hand in hers as she leads me to the men and boys.

"You do all realize that you're showing off a giant cock in the company of a princess," Sam says as we stop below them and she holds up my arm, gesturing to me with flourish.

"Aye but she's a princess in her undergarments," Henry giggles at me.

Ramsay's mouth drops. "Henry," he admonishes him, trying not to laugh. "It's impolite to point that out to a royal."

Thane lets out a dry snort. "I wager the princess is no longer phased by such things," he says. "Every time I see her, she's one step closer to becoming a pirate. You best get her to come to our side, brother, or it will be harder to return her to proper society."

I lock eyes with Ramsay at that and he holds my gaze and I'm momentarily sucked into the storm in the dusky blue.

Do you want me on your side? I think. *Are we even on the same side?*

I can't read his eyes in response. But I know when he looks at me like this, with such intensity, he's seeing all of me, even the parts I'm used to hiding. And whether it's something I'm ashamed of or not, he sees it.

And I remember, once upon a time, that had been all I ever wanted.

THIRTY-ONE

Ramsay

"You're having a nightmare," a low voice says breaking through the dark abyss of my mind.

My eyes snap open and the nightmare fades, though the feelings remain lodged in my chest like black tar, slipping into my veins like invasive dread.

I look over at the corner of the room to where Nerissa sits in her cage, her eyes glowing in the dark like beacons, staring right at me. The skin prickles on my neck.

I clear my throat. "Sorry you had to witness that."

"Mmmm," she murmurs. "Wasn't just that I witnessed it, I experienced it. I was in your dream with you, as you."

I try to remember but I can't bring up the image of her there. I can't remember anything of the dream at all but I know it was the same as always. Only question is, was I dreaming about Hilla? Or was it Maren?

"Is that something you usually do?" I ask idly, swinging my legs out of bed. "Invade the minds of others?"

She scoffs. "I do not invade, Bones, unless it is an emergency. I was in your dream whether I wanted to be or not. You have a pull to you, as do all of your kind. Your minds can pull me in, similar to how you sometimes look around inside the minds of others." She pauses and from the moonlight coming in from the window, she smiles and her teeth glow. "I saw my sister in your dream. I saw one of her Kraken."

I swallow uneasily. "Who is your sister?"

"Edonia."

I feel like all the air has been sucked from the room. "You're Edonia's sister?"

She does one slow nod.

"Did you know about Venla?"

Another slow nod. "Venla was your wife. She was also my half-sister. I *loved* Venla," she says, her hands curling around the bars of the cage. "It broke my heart that she died. If she had been a full-blooded sea witch she would have survived."

I feel like this has to be a trick of some sort. "I don't believe you," I say through a harsh breath.

"You don't have to," she says. "But ask yourself why I'm here."

"I have been. I have been asking you and you keep saying it's destiny."

"It is destiny. And you don't need to believe me or believe in it, but destiny believes in you. In all of you."

I run my hands over my face. I feel like she's already getting in my head. Witches can't be trusted, and Venla was the only exception to the rule. "I need to get some air," I tell her, leaving the room. I can't lock it behind me because someone, and by someone I mean Maren, shot the lock off with a musket at some point in time, but I hope that the magic continues to hold her in the cage.

I go up to the top deck and immediately feel my heart calm down, my breath returning to normal. The sky is big and dark despite the moon and stars with low clouds coming toward us in the distance. It's quiet up here too, with only the murmurs of Remi and Horse at the helm, doing their middle of the night watch, the *gaurdia de modorra*. The steady beat of the wind in the sails and the sloshing waves are the only other sounds.

I sigh and stare up at the sky, feeling immensely helpless. It's not a feeling I curate, indeed it's a rare one. But I feel like there are complications in my life now where there weren't before and I'm not so sure how everything is going to turn out in the end. After Venla died, but especially after Hilla died, I lost one of my greatest assets, which was my positive attitude. In the before-times I was always optimistic that everything would work out. Even after my father died I still believed that everything would be alright in the end if you just kept going.

But then Venla died and I started to lose some of that faith. It didn't seem fair that she should die not long after my father, that I would have to deal with both.

Then Hilla died and I lost faith in the universe entirely. I lost the ability to assume that everything would be okay, because now I know there is no guarantee. Life doesn't pull any punches just because it's already beaten you to the ground. It doesn't let you breathe just because you're already drowning. There is no mercy there. I am an immortal and yet even I don't get to escape death. At times it's all around me.

The last few years, however, I finally felt a return to my old self.

But now…now…

I let out a heavy exhale, my gaze searching the stars as if I'll find answers there and then…

I do.

Up high in the crow's nest near the top of the mizzenmast is a woman framed by countless stars, her ink-black hair melting into the night sky.

"Maren," I whisper, wondering what the hell she's doing all the way up there. From the way she's standing so close to the edge of the platform, one hundred feet up in the air, she seems close to toppling over to what would surely be her death.

I sprint over to the mast and start climbing up the ropes that lead to the top, the ropes swaying as I go, trying to cover a hundred feet as quickly as I can.

Finally I reach the top, the wind whipping against my face.

"Maren," I say, pulling myself up onto the platform.

She whirls around to look at me, nearly going backward over the low rail and I quickly lunge for her, pulling her back in.

"What are you doing?" I whisper, my hand going around her waist and pulling her close to me so there's no space between us. She's just in her chemise, her black hair waving around her shoulders, her eyes wide with fear.

"I couldn't sleep and I've always wanted to come up here," she says softly. "I'm sorry."

I swallow hard, looking over her face. "No. Don't be sorry. You just gave me a fright is all."

"You thought I was going to jump?" she asks, her gaze resting on my lips for a moment.

I give her a small smile but it doesn't feel very assuring. "I saw you with that shard of glass the other day and I...I guess I'm thinking of the way we met."

"When I punched you in the face."

"When I rescued you."

She looks away with a wry smile. "You did not *rescue* me."

"You were drowning," I remind her, my grip tightening around her waist, one of my hands splayed at her back and keeping her pressed against me, as if letting her go now would result in letting her go forever.

"You were drowning and you weren't trying to fight it," I add. "And I don't blame you for it. All the abuse you've had to endure, the regrets that still poison you. It can lead a woman to madness. It can lead anyone to madness."

"Except," she says slowly, a flash of pink tongue coming out to lick her lips, "except now, I truly have gone mad." She glances up at me, a fierce look beneath her lashes. "Don't you think? What is madness if not rage? If not a monster?"

With one hand still holding tight at her waist, I put my palm at her cheek, cupping her face. Her eyes fall closed at my touch, her chest rising with breath. "Then perhaps the both of us are mad, if madness and monsters are one of the same," I murmur. "But we can be mad together. We can drown in our madness together."

Her throat moves as she swallows and I lean in, the tip of my nose brushing against hers. I can feel the heat of her lips radiate toward the heat of mine. In the distance thunder booms and the hair on my arms stand straight from the electricity in the air.

"Sometimes..." she whispers. "Sometimes I feel like I'm falling apart, slowly, then all at once."

"You are not falling apart, luv," I tell her, speaking so that my lips touch hers. "You are just falling into place."

"Is that place with you?" she asks, her mouth moving against mine, barely a kiss at all.

"What do you think?" I tell her, then I close the gap. I kiss her hard, I kiss her deeply, I kiss her with possession. My tongue slides against hers, her mouth opening wider to accommodate me, and my hands keep her in place, keep her right here with me as the kiss draws us both together in a way that is just as intimate as sex, perhaps even more so.

Her hands slide up my shoulders, gripping me there, and my heart does another flip, competing with my cock for attention.

I pull away for a moment, trying to steady my breath, steady my thoughts, and I rest my forehead against hers, cool from the night air.

"It's been so long since I've felt this way about anyone," I murmur, the emotions too buoyant to keep submerged any longer.

"What way is that?" she asks, her voice breathy, husky, hopeful.

"Like you're the moon and I'm the tides, and every thought, every need, every want, is drawn to you, Maren." I laugh to myself. "You're right, this is madness and I'm drowning and I don't give a damn."

This time she kisses me, her hands trailing down my back, holding me close, my cock rammed up against her hip, her thin shift providing no protection against my hard heat.

With a grunt I reach down and I bunch up her shift to her waist so that she's bare below then I pick her up in my arms and whirl her away from the railing so that she's pressed up against the mast that rises through the center of the platform.

"Let me drown in you, will ya?" I say before ducking down between her thighs while keeping her body pressed against the mast.

She cries out as my mouth finds her cunt and my lips and tongue start devouring her, savoring her taste, sea-water tonic. Thunder booms again, closer this time, but the only lightning I feel is the way her warm, slick skin melts against my tongue, sending jolts of need right to my cock.

"Ramsay," she says through a broken moan, her fingers digging into my loose hair, her thighs tightening around my head. I keep eating her, teasing where she's hot and swollen, circle after circle with hard flicks of my tongue, then sliding across where she's achingly wet and driving my tongue inside her. I fuck her this way, wild and messy and raw, until my jaw starts to ache and she's starting to tense around me.

Thunder rumbles, closer still, and then she's letting go, the tension in her snapping like a whip. She clamps around my tongue, her legs following suit around my face, and she's bucking wildly against me, her cries being swallowed by the wind that has picked up. Her hands tug at my hair, pulling me deeper into her and then when her limbs are shaking and my senses are flooded with the taste and smell of her, I straighten up.

I take my cock out with one swift motion, then keep her in place while I shove hard inside her. She's so damn tight it makes my eyes roll straight to the back of my head, my breath catching inside my chest, my body straining.

"Gods," she whispers harshly, and I feel like a god from the way I'm inside her, the way I'm able to make her look at me like *I'm* worth worshipping.

I feel the first drop of rain fall on my neck and the wind starts getting stronger, whipping our hair around, making my shirt billow. It's as if it's trying to match our wildness.

I've got her pinned to the mast, her leg hooked around my hip and I have one hand sliding down to her clitoris, surely still sensitive. But she only moans and starts driving her hips forward to meet my thrusts, and her mouth is on my neck, kissing me, biting me, licking me. The force of the wind is constant now, like several hands are holding us up from behind and driving us into each other.

"You still belong to me," I say gruffly in her ear, my cock so deep in her it's like she's squeezing on me like a glove that's a little too tight. "You'll always be mine."

"That remains to be seen," she says, then bites down on my earlobe, eliciting a low rumble from deep in my chest.

With a growl I reach down and grab her hip where my brand is. "You wish to see it? It's right here, luv," I tell her before I piston myself against her, feeling feral and unrelenting as I drive in deeper where she's hot and wet, tight and thick and just as owned as she's ever been in her life.

A flash of lightning cracks across the sky, followed by a deafening boom of thunder, and she cries out sharply as I start sliding my thumb against her, matching the driving pace of my hips.

Rain is falling harder now, lashing us, and she tilts her head back to the sky, her mouth open in a ravenous moan. I'm faster, deeper, and more intense than ever before and as I feel her tighten around me and the pleasure coursing through my veins, I know that this is where I belong, drowning in this madness with her. Two monsters that have found their souls in one another.

It's too late for me, I think as I sink in to the hilt, one hand cupping her breast now, pulling the neckline of her shift down so that I can suck her nipple between my lips. I can't pretend she's not what I want or what I've always wanted.

She lets out another deep moan and I'm vaguely aware that I do have crew that are one hundred feet below us on the deck and they might be hearing us, looking up at us, or perhaps we're swallowed by the thunder, wind, and rain. Either way, I don't have the capacity to care right now. All I want is for both of us to plunge into ecstasy together.

The storm whips me into a frenzy and I push in harder and faster, her slick heat wrapping around me like velvet. I can feel my orgasm building and I let out a low, deep growl as the pleasure takes over, my release coming on with fervent intensity. I slam her into the mast so hard that I swear the ship rocks beneath us.

"Maren," I cry out through a shaking breath, and I can feel her body quaking with her own release, her own senseless noises coming from her lips, the way she holds onto me like she'll never let me go.

I collapse into her, panting and trembling, completely satisfied while my emotions run high. We remain in that embrace for a long time, the rain washing over us, cleansing us, my cock still inside her. I don't want to break apart. I want to stay fused inside her.

"Ramsay," she whispers to me, and I raise my head off the mast to meet her eyes. Rain runs down her face in streams. "Is this the safest place to be during a thunderstorm?"

I laugh, still breathless. "Aye, I suppose it's not." I lean in and kiss her lips, hard and quick. "But I wager it was worth the risk, wouldn't you?"

She gives me a small, satisfied smile that agrees with the statement.

I pull out of her and take her up in my arms, gently lowering her onto the platform. Her shift is completely transparent, her nipples poking through, and naturally I'm hard again even as I'm putting my cock back into my pants.

She notices this, a dark brow raising. "Hard again already?" she asks.

"Have you seen how delectable you look?" I tell her, bringing her hand to my mouth and kissing the back of it. "Something about you being all wet gets me burning for you."

She beams at that and tilts her head back to the rain again, holding out her arms. "I've needed this."

"Are you talking about the rain or me?" I ask.

Her eyes flutter at me. "Both. I've needed both."

"Perhaps we can get dry in our quarters then," I say.

The joy in her face dissolves at once. "Not in your quarters. There's a sea witch in there."

"Ah," I say, remembering Nerissa. I don't even want to think about her and all the things she said before I left the room. "Well, your quarters are snug but perhaps you'd like some company."

But I can tell whenever I brought Nerissa into the picture her posture has stiffened, her face becoming more guarded. I don't like that look on her. I want that gleeful uninhibited joy to fill her face again.

"I sleep better alone," she says, raising her chin slightly.

I study her for a moment, trying to figure out her mood swing. I know she hates sea witches, and for good reason, and she'll hate Nerissa even more if she tells her she's Edonia's sister. I decide to bury that bit of information for now, especially since I suspect Nerissa is lying.

"Regardless of how you sleep," I tell her, "I'll be walking you to your quarters whether you want it or not."

She grumbles at that and turns and before I can offer any assistance she's climbing down the roped ladder like she's done it hundreds of times before. I watch her for a moment to make sure she'll be alright, then I start down after her.

By the time my feet hit the deck, she's already heading for the stairs down below. I pass by Remi and Horse at the helm who are snickering and giving out little encouraging hollers, and only give them an authoritative nod in response. I don't need for them to be bringing this up tomorrow with the rest of the crew.

I quickly follow Maren down the stairs to the main deck and she's just about to duck into her quarters when I reach out and grab her arm.

"You sure you don't want my company tonight?" I ask, lowering my voice.

She gives me a quick smile. "I think I've had what I needed."

Then she opens the door and closes it on my face.

THIRTY-TWO

Maren

"Where is Ramsay?" I ask Sam, shielding my eyes as I look around the top deck. It's a few hours before sunset, the sun lower on the horizon but still packing a wallop. I've gotten more sun in these last few weeks than I ever have in my life and my skin is starting to show it, freckles deepening and my pallor turning a light gold. With no more parasols to shield me or concerns from the queen about being as pale and flawless as possible, I relish the change in my skin.

"Bones should be reading to the boys," she says, playing backgammon on the bench with Cruz, otherwise known as Isaac. "He'll be in my quarters."

I nod and head toward the stairs.

It's been a week or so since Ramsay and I came together up in the crow's nest. I've been avoiding him since, just a little, trying to get my mind working in the right order. I feel his words are starting to undo the resolve that I've built up, they're threatening to unravel my agency, and everything is growing more complicated as the passage across the ocean stretches on.

From the moment I first stepped on land all those years ago, I knew I made a mistake and I have been trying ever since to find some way to rectify it. I was trapped but I still had dreams of returning to my home in the depths. When I was kidnapped by Ramsay, all those dreams started to become more of a reality. It was no longer something I hopelessly pined for, for now I had hope. A return to my true self and my old life was in my sights.

But while Ramsay gave me that opportunity, Ramsay is also the reason why everything is suddenly so complicated.

Because I don't want to leave him, yet I'm not meant to be a part of his world. I'm meant for the one I was born into. And if we're just destined to part ways at the end, then what good is it to have the feelings I'm feeling?

For I am feeling something. No, not something. I'm feeling *everything*. Everything from all directions and it lights up the darkness inside me, gives me a different kind of hope, makes all my regrets worth it if it leads to him in the end. When I look at him now, I ache deep inside, this constant yearning and longing for him even when he's right in front of me. I feel joined to him in ways I don't even understand and it has nothing to do with him claiming me.

I think I've already claimed him.

I worry my heart has already thought of him as mine.

And now he's opening himself to me and I'm drowning in his words, in our frenzied passion, in the way he makes me feel, and yet there's a witch in his room. And yet I will have to say goodbye. And yet we can't truly be together. And yet, and yet, and yet…

I don't want to ignore him anymore though. If I leave his world in the end for the one I'm meant for, then that means we only have so much time left together. I could keep my distance from him, as I have been doing, just giving him passing nods on deck and averting my eyes when he gazes at me for too long. But then I wouldn't be spending the rest of my time with him as I should.

I know now, no matter how I spin it, that whether I'm with him or not, it will hurt to say goodbye, cut me right down the middle. I can't pretend otherwise.

So now I want to use all the time I have left. Being out here at sea, with these nice calm days, life easy and the crew back to normal, we're covering a lot of miles and I know we're getting close to land, should be seeing the shore of New Spain any day now.

The journey is coming to an end.

I head down the stairs and pause by the door to the captain's quarters. If he's in Sam's cabin with the boys, then his chambers should be empty and I've been meaning to talk to Nerissa again.

I open the door and look around to see that no one is watching me, then I step inside.

Nerissa is standing up and leaning against the bars, staring right at me with calm eyes, as if she was waiting for me.

"I was wondering when you'd come back," she says in a low voice. "Was starting to worry that perhaps you didn't have a guilty conscience."

I walk over to her and eye the bandage around her neck. I feel the pang of guilt as if right on cue. "You assumed I was like the bloodsuckers," she goes on. "When I'm just a human. Well, a witch, but human still. And I bleed the same as they do, even though my blood is green."

"You expect me to apologize?" I say stiffly.

She grins at me. She really is pretty in an otherworldly way. "No, I guess not. Though perhaps you will when you realize that I am not out to harm you, Maren. I'm here to make all your dreams come true."

"Why?" I ask suspiciously.

"I know all about how you got your legs," she says. "You see, my sister told me how she tricked you."

My eyes go big. "Your sister is Edonia?"

She nods, her jaw going tight. "She is. Unfortunately."

I blink at her in surprise. "Unfortunately?"

"We aren't close. We never have been. I was closer to my sister Venla." She reads the dawning look on my face. "Oh, you know the name. Has Bones told you about her? Well good then, that saves us some time."

"Your sister was Ramsay's wife?"

"Half sister," she corrects. "When she died, it was like losing a part of my soul. When Hilla died, even more so. That was my niece, the closest that I'll ever have to a child. I watched her from afar, watched over her, and never did I think that Edonia would do a thing like that with her Kraken. That's when I knew that her appetite for evil really had no boundaries."

This sounds too good to be true. I can't for a moment believe that Nerissa isn't close with her sister. She can't be trusted. None of the sea witches can.

"Now I want what you want," she goes on.

"Which is?"

"Justice."

"For whom?"

"For Hilla. For you."

I give her a bitter look. "Me? You don't care about me. You don't know me at all."

"But I know what was done to you. If I can get the book back from Edonia, I can reverse the spell."

"I was thinking of getting her to do that anyway," I tell her, folding my arms.

She laughs. "And you think she would? Heavens, my little Syren. If Edonia sees you again, she'll kill you. You can't trust her for anything, you should know that. She will kill you for just having the audacity to ask."

"Did Edonia use Venla's book for the spell?" I ask.

She nods.

I think back. Even though I've replayed that moment in my head so many times, even though I still feel that knife through my tongue, sometimes it feels like a hazy dream. "Some men are resistant to a witch's charms," I say slowly. "That's what she said when I asked why she needed my tongue, my Syren song."

"Men such as Bones. Thinks a Syren song might lure him, though I suspect it won't. But it doesn't matter. Edonia hates him."

"I'm starting to think everyone hates him," I say under my breath.

"It's hard not to make enemies when you're a pirate, especially when you're one of the immortal, bloodsucking variety."

"Could say the same about witches too," I remind her.

"And Syrens," she counters, giving me a look of satisfaction. "You see, we're all warring with each other but in reality we're all very much the same. Different types of monsters united by being outcasts from the world."

"So what do you want with me then?"

"I want you to help me get my vengeance," she says, lowering her voice. "When the time is right, and you'll know when it's right, I want you to free me. I can fix everyone's problems at once. I can deliver justice and make right all the wrongs."

I frown at her confidence. "You know I don't trust you, do you not?"

"I know you don't," she says with a smile. "But I pray in time you do. Before it's too late. I have seen our destiny, Maren. I have seen it, and gods help us all if it gets more grim than that."

I want to ask her what she's seen but I have a feeling it will only mislead me.

I nod at her and leave, closing the door to the quarters. Once I'm away, I take in a deep breath and try to shake off our conversation. I want to trust her, I do, because to trust means to hope, but I can't let myself fall for her tricks. If she's Edonia's sister, she's bound to be just as slippery as she is.

Though I wanted to talk to Ramsay, I don't want to interrupt his teachings with the boys. Still, I'm ever so curious and find myself heading toward Sam and Thane's quarters. The door is half-open and I don't hear much but the scratching of pencils. I nudge it open a little and look inside, smiling at the scene. All of their backs are to me and I watch for a moment as Ramsay stares over the shoulders of Henry and Lucas as they write down in their notebooks.

"That's the way, Henry boy," he says to him, giving him an affectionate pat on the shoulder. "I before E."

"Except after C," Henry says proudly.

"But only then when the sound is eeeee," Lucas finishes.

"And I'm sure there are even more exceptions I don't know about," Ramsay says. "But this will get you far enough. Now if you'll excuse me boys, you stay and fill the rest of that page, then run along upstairs to get your exercise with your pa. I have an onlooker to attend to."

At that Ramsay turns around and gives me a dashing smile. The boys turn around too, to see me, surprised. I guess their senses won't be as heightened as Ramsay's until they turn thirty-five.

"She's still in her undergarments," Henry whispers to Lucas who giggles.

Ramsay shoots them a dirty look before walking over to me.

"Maren," he says to me, his expression warm yet guarded as he folds his arms across his wide chest. "To what do I owe the pleasure of your company?"

"I was wondering if I could talk to you," I tell him. "In my quarters," I quickly add.

His brows raise but he only nods. "Alright."

I nod, hating this distance between us, distance that I put there, and walk to my cabin, feeling his immeasurable presence at my back. What a fool I was to think that this type of space would change my feelings for him in some way. If anything, I'm feeling quite desperate, which was the feeling I had been trying to avoid in the first place.

I step inside my cabin and sit down on the bed, the top of my head just grazing the bunk above. He stands in the doorway, looking around.

"Do you like it in here?" he asks idly.

"Very much. I do wish there was a mirror above the basin. I'd like to see how I look before I start the day."

"I can be your mirror," he says, leaning against the doorframe. "And I'll be the first to tell you that you look prettier than a peach. So, what can I help you with?"

Suddenly I feel very small and very awkward. I point at the seat at the desk.

He's about to sit down but I jerk my chin toward the door. He goes and closes it then sits down across from me. Now that guarded blasé look on his face fades a bit and his brows come together in concern as he leans forward, elbows on his thighs. "What is it?"

"I wanted to apologize for acting strangely lately," I say, staring down at my hands in my lap, wincing at the dirt under my fingernails. "I know I've been short with you and I just wanted to say I'm sorry."

"Maren," he says, waiting a beat. I glance up at him and he gives me a smile that's both soft and lopsided. "I really don't like it when you apologize. In fact, I'd wager you apologize entirely too much." I open my mouth to say I'm sorry but he raises his finger. "Ah, see. There you go. Please, do stop that. There is no need, especially not with me. You understand that, don't ya?"

"I do," I say, warmth flooding through my chest, making me feel lighter. The idea that I don't have to say sorry to this man is liberating. Not that I will listen, not that I won't need to, but compared to my years of apologizing for even breathing, it feels like a tonic to the soul.

"But what I do want to know is why you were short to me to begin with. Every time I looked your way, luv, you acted like I wasn't even there. Just a ghost on the ship with you."

I chew on my lower lip for a moment, trying to figure out how much to say, if anything at all. With his gaze on me so intensely, it makes me feel that much more vulnerable. "I guess I've been..." I start, still avoiding his eyes. "I've been scaring myself."

"How so?"

I manage to look at him, caught in his gray gaze. "You told me many wonderful things the other night."

"Aye," he says, running a hand over his chin, his beard grown in and making a scratchy noise. "I don't know whether you found them wonderful or not but I did. And I meant it, too, if that's what you're worried about. I make no false claims when it comes to you, luv, you belong to me body and soul, heart and spirit." He pauses and gives me a breathtaking smile that makes my stomach flip. "Monster, Syren, princess, and pirate."

I feel my cheeks going red.

"And now I've made the lady blush," he says. "How I've missed that particular color of pink. Same as your nipples and your cunt when I've had my tongue on them."

My skin burns even hotter now and I have an urge that I've never had before.

A sinful, deviant urge.

I get off the bed and down on my knees.

I crawl to him.

Ramsay eyes me in surprise as I make my way between his legs.

"Don't tell me you're teasing me, luv, I couldn't bear it," he says roughly.

"I'm not teasing," I tell him, my heart starting to beat louder. I reach for the waistband of his breeches. "I've been wanting to pleasure you this way for some time now."

He swallows hard and blinks, his strong hands sliding over mine and holding me in place for a moment. "Promise me you won't be using those teeth," he says. "Unless I happen to like it," he adds, clearing his throat.

"I promise," I say, giving him an innocent smile. He lets go of my hands and I undo the buttons at the flap of his breeches, my hands shaking slightly with excitement. While his member has been inside me numerous times, I've yet to handle it with my own hands, let alone my mouth.

I glance up at him and he's staring at me with so much raw energy that I feel lightning crash down my spine, my nerves crackling throughout.

I take in a deep breath and reach into the flap, my hands closing over his hard length, and I pull him free.

I gasp. I can't help it. I feel the heavy, warm weight of his cock in my hand, surprisingly soft, and absolutely menacing looking.

He lets out a low hiss, his shaft twitching in my hands, making me grip him and I swear he gets even harder under my touch.

"Oh, my luv," he whispers hoarsely, his head going back.

I can't help the smile. I love that I can do this to him, that I have this effect. Perhaps this tickles the seductive Syren part of me, but it's different, because it's not my pleasure I'm after right now, I'm after his. I want to watch him with his cock in my mouth, watch him give himself over to me, so that he's as vulnerable as I feel.

"Why don't you feed from me?" I ask him, running my palms over his stiff length, enjoying the hot velvet feel of him.

"Cearban, it looks like you'll be feeding from me," he says, his voice husky as I continue to stroke him.

"I mean it," I tell him, holding out my wrist as an offering. "Why not take my blood right now? You never know when you're going to need it," I add, thinking of what Nerissa said about our grim destiny.

"Because you're going to need both hands while you work me," he says, his eyes pinching shut as I squeeze him near his glistening tip.

I dip my head and lick the moisture off of him and he jerks, his hands gripping the edge of the chair, letting out a deep moan that seems to fill the room. "Christ, woman, you're going to make me come already."

I just lick him again, tentative passes of my tongue over his swollen dark head, enjoying the salty flavor of his essence.

"If you like the taste of that then you better start sucking me, luv," he says through a groan. "Let me fuck your mouth until I coat your throat with my seed. I know you can take me, even if you choke on it."

I know I can too. I open my mouth wide enough to fit his girth and with a tight grip I slide him in through my wetted lips. He cries out and thrusts his hips so that his shaft goes straight to the back of my throat and he's right, I am choking on him.

But then he pulls back and when he tries to pump inside my lips again, I have control of his length, sucking him in at my own pace, my tongue swirling around all the hot ridges. His cock feels warmer now, like fire barely contained.

"Maren," he grunts, his accent growing thicker. "Fuck. Maren. I lose it with ya, I fucking lose it with ya."

I try to tell him to orgasm but I can't when he's taking up all of my mouth. Instead I push him over the edge, keeping tight control with my fist while letting him pound into my mouth, the tip of his cock sliding along the roof of my mouth, my tongue sucking him deep.

"Christ!" he bellows, "I'm coming. I'm coming, luv. God, your throat is just as tight as your cunt, darling. I'm going to fill you until it's spilling on the floor."

I nearly choke as he says that and then his hips are bucking and his cock spasms and I feel wet heat shoot through my mouth, landing on the back of my tongue and down my throat. I swallow it quickly. Despite what he said, I don't want any of that on my floor.

Finally, when he seems to still, his breath ragged and quick, I pull him out of my mouth, a trail of spit between my lips and his spent head, and I look up at him shyly.

"I've never seen a more beautiful sight," he says, his sated gaze pinned on me. "I've never experienced anything like that before, my luv."

I delicately wipe my lips and fold my hands in my lap, like a lady.

"Captain!" someone outside of the door yells.

He straightens up, shaking his head and tucks his cock back in the flap. He clears his throat as I quickly get to my feet and head to the door, opening it when I see Ramsay is decent.

Cruz's tall frame fills the other side of the door.

"Captain, we've spotted a ship. You're going to want to see this."

THIRTY-THREE
Ramsay

F rom the apprehensive way Cruz is looking at me, not even
paying attention to the thick tension in the air and the way I'm
sitting, I know that this is important.

I quickly get to my feet, adjusting my worn-out cock, which Cruz
pretends not to see, and then we leave Maren's quarters. She follows
me, which I don't mind. I'd like it if she were at my side for all of the
day and the night, even though there's an uneasiness in my belly about
this ship they've spotted.

Up on the top deck everyone is gathered at the forecastle and when
I approach Thane looks grim.

"It's the Royal Navy," he says, handing me the spyglass. "She's
heading right to us." A beat, his eyes flash bright amber. "It's Ed
Smith's."

My heart stills, lodged somewhere in my throat, and I look through
the spyglass. I let out a harsh breath of air. There she is. There is the
Pembroke, a 60-gun ship that flies under the flag of Great Britain, and
is currently commanded by Captain Edward Smith. Someone who is a
member of the Brethren but definitely not of our crew.

"There should be other ships," Thane mutters. "Where are the other
ships of the line?"

I bring the spyglass along the horizon but there's nothing, not even a hint of a mast. There is only the *Pembroke* and she's sailing dead for us.

"They see us," I say. "They're coming for us."

"We can outrun them," Cruz says.

"No!" I snap at him. "We are not outrunning them! We stay and we fight!"

"*Captain*," Thane says. "With all due respect, they have sixty guns and most likely sixty gunners. We have forty guns, and only a handful of crew at them."

"You know this ship will not sink," I tell him.

"Only because we know when to evade."

"He's in our sights, brother!" I say, suddenly spurred by frustrated rage at having waited for this moment for too long, and I turn, grabbing Thane by the collar. "We need to avenge our father. We need to do this for pa!"

Why doesn't he have the need for justice that I do? Why isn't he frothing at the mouth to destroy this man?

Thane's stoic expression softens. "Our father would not want us dead if it meant vengeance. You can't let it control you like it has been. You need to learn to let it go."

I shake my head, blinking at him, unable to come to terms with what he's saying. "You say we should flee with our tail between our legs? We have fought naval ships before."

"And in the end the wind always takes us away. Even if the *Nightwind* can't sink, *we* can. We're not all at our best and Smith knows exactly how to kill us," he says imploringly and his gaze goes to Maren behind me. "And we already have people on board that may not survive this."

"Don't worry about me," Maren says with a growl of determination and my heart sings at her loyalty to me. "I say we do as the captain says. We fight. We destroy that ship and the man who killed your father. What kind of pirates would we be if we ran away every time things got a little hairy?"

My god, I think I might be in love with her.

"This is a great democracy on the *Nightwind*, is it not?" I yell to the crew as I let go of my brother's shirt.

A cheer rises up from them.

"And since this is a democracy, I say we put it to a vote. Those who oppose the fight, who thinks we should evade and run, say aye."

"Aye," says Thane, Cruz, and Drakos. When Sam doesn't raise her hand or speak, Thane gives her a look of quiet disdain to which she shrugs.

"Everyone else?" I yell. "Do we fight like the pirates we are? Like the Brethren of the Blood?"

A cry goes up, the majority of the crew siding with me.

"Then the democracy settles it. It has been put to the vote. Now I must ask my quartermaster and my first mate, will you be helping me with this or shall I put the ship's boat down for ya?"

Thane just scowls at me and slaps me on the shoulder. "You know we're here for you, Captain," he says begrudgingly. Then he turns and starts barking orders at the crew and the deck erupts into controlled chaos.

My blood pumps hot in my head, my skin feeling as if tiny pins are being pricked upon it and my senses are becoming clearer than normal.

The battle has begun.

"Ramsay," Maren says worriedly, pulling me to the side of the chaos. "Feed from me," she whispers.

"There's no time, luv," I say looking at the *Pembroke* quickly approaching. I wave my hand at the sails above me to make sure we slow down so we don't collide at high speed. "I must make sure everything goes as plan on deck and god help me if I lose control again."

"I won't let you lose control," she says, tugging at my arm. "Come on. It won't take but a second."

That's what she thinks but it's far more complicated than that. To feed would mean I have to leave the deck where I'm needed and disappear with her below, not the best look for a captain. Besides, I need to keep her Syren identity a secret and this won't help.

"Maren," I tell her sternly, grabbing her by the shoulders. "It's too late now. And it doesn't matter a whit anyway. I'm going to go kill that man and I don't need any help in doing so. You go and take the boys and Sedge and hide them in my quarters."

"With Nerissa?" she asks in surprise.

"She won't touch them, they'll be safe with her," I tell her, going off of pure instinct now, "and there's a lot of weapons in there."

"Okay," she says, fearfully. "But I'm coming right back here with you."

"I know I can't stop you, you stubborn little shark," I say, pulling her in for a hard kiss before letting her go again. "Hurry!"

She runs off and I turn my attention to the deck, making it as clean and clear as possible, hauling ropes to the side and helping the bosun in storing the sails.

Cruz pulls out his violin and strikes up a tune to get everyone's hearts going and their nerves ready, then Drakos runs around giving shots of rum. I know I need to give my usual inspiring speech but right now I'm buzzing with so much nervous energy that it's making me sick.

Somehow though I manage to compose myself enough to give them a short one: "We're all together in this, lads. We are the Brethren and we do not back down from a fight. We're doing this for all the pirates around the world, for the sinners and the outliers and everyone else who has to take to the sea to find their home. And this man will not take our home! Nay, we will take his and his life!"

The crew responds raucously, a battle cry that rings out through the ship, and I notice Maren coming up the stairs, a cutlass in her hand. God, I hope that she knows how to use that thing enough to defend herself. At the very least I hope she has the good sense to throw it to the side and use her teeth and claws instead. Yes, the crew would see she's a monster of some kind but in a life-or-death situation it may be her only way out.

"Gunners, prepare to fire on my mark," Thane yells, taking the route of shooting first. Our rounds do have a little extra magic to them that help them hit harder and shoot farther, something that the naval ship lacks, so being proactive is the best line of attack when they have more artillery.

"Fire!" Thane yells and the gunners below set off the canons which go off with a bang, shaking the ship. They smash clear into the side of the *Pembroke*, the kind that will send oak and shrapnel into their crew.

"Fine shots lads!" I yell. "Once more! Then switch to chain-shots to the mast! Lothar, Matisse, clear their deck!"

The cannons fire again from below, more clean shots, while Lothar and Matisse raise their flintlock muskets and fire at the deck, their sharpshooting skills honed as buccaneers able to shoot dead the helmsman and another crew member before needing to reload.

I'm trying to see if Smith is anywhere to be seen on the top deck but I don't spot him and then they're firing from the cannons at their portholes.

The shots come all at once, at least twenty of them slamming into the broadside of the *Nightwind*, shaking the ship violently. Maren falls to the ground but I reach out and grab her in time just as their own chain-shots attempt to destroy the rigging. They manage to hit the fore-mast, taking off the top, and the sail starts to fall toward the deck, prompting me to haul Maren out of the way.

"Perhaps now you should go below," I tell her as the sails slam into the deck behind us, narrowly missing some of the crew.

"Perhaps I'll just stay out of your way," she says, moving back toward a barrel, brandishing the cutlass in her hand.

I curse at the fallen mast. Lothar will make quick work of it as the ship's carpenter, but for now he's busy reloading the musket and picking off more of the navy.

We fire more shots and the navy ship responds in kind, some going right into the *Nightwind's* hull, making more work for Lothar. I hear a cry from below and know that either Remi or Horse has been hit and that hopefully they'll be okay. Sterling was our main gunner but at the moment he's tied up in chains. I spend a moment wondering if he's worth freeing but decide against it. In his state, he'd probably sabotage our ship and side with the Royal Navy.

"Sam!" I yell for her. "Go to the gun deck, we may need rein-forcements."

She nods and runs just as a bullet goes flying toward her, striking her in the shoulder.

"Ahhh!" she yelps, holding onto her shoulder and grimacing in pain but then she keeps running, not letting the bullet stop her. The woman is made of iron.

But while she can survive any bullet, Maren cannot. I glance at her to check that she's behind the barrel still, but now she's brandishing the pistol I had given her a week ago and trying to aim it at the navy ship. I want to tell her to save the bullet for close combat but she fires it and manages to hit one of the navy crew in the neck.

She turns and grins at me, delighted at her shot, and my chest grows tight with want for her.

"That a girl," I tell her, even though she can't hear me over the din.

BONES.

Suddenly I'm doubling over, my hands over my ears as I hear Nerissa yelling from inside my head.

BONES HE HAS THEM.

"Are you okay?" Maren cries out as she runs over to me, her hand on my back just as another roundshot fires through the deck below, making the *Nightwind* shudder like a beast, and a bullet whizzes over my head, striking a barrel of tar behind me.

"Nerissa," I manage to say, keeping low as I look around through the carnage, the air filling with smoke. "Where is she?"

"She's still in your cage, of course," she says, sounding confused. "I put Henry and Lucas and Sedge in your quarters like you said, told them to block the door with something heavy after I left." She searches my face fearfully. "Why? Is she going to hurt them?"

"It's not Nerissa I'm worried about," I say, gently pushing her aside and running across the deck for the stairs just as another explosion rocks the boat and I have to dive to the planks, the wood splintering beneath my impact.

I lift my head, ears ringing fiercely, and look back to make sure Maren is okay. She's getting to her feet and limping over to me, waving at me with her hands to get going. The rest of the crew seem fine, though Matisse is holding his own hand from a bullet wound to the palm and Cruz is on his back groaning from the latest cannon round.

I can't worry about them right now. I push myself up and we run to the stairs and stagger down to the main deck and straight to my quarters.

"Henry!" I yell, trying to open the door but despite there being no lock, it won't open, something heavy has been pushed against it. "Lucas! Sedge! I'm coming!"

I look around for the boarding axe that we use to smash through the locked doors of conquered ships but there's none to be found, then I run a few steps back then launch myself at the door with my shoulder, the door almost coming off the hinges and something toppling over on the other side. I pull back and throw myself against it again, this time the door splintering under my weight and I burst through into my quarters.

I see Ed Smith standing before me, the balcony doors open behind him from where he must have climbed up.

He has two pistols in his hands aimed at the heads of Sedge, Lucas, and Henry, who are on their knees in front of him, facing me.

And I'm having a most awful case of having lived this moment before. But while then it was with Prince Aerik and he had the marline-spike against Henry's head, I knew that somehow we would prevail, and we did thanks to Drakos. This time I'm not so sure. I feel so unsure that I can't even feel the planks beneath my feet, as if none of this is happening and I'm not even here at all.

BONES.

I hear Nerissa's voice boom in my head from over in the cage but I don't dare look at her, nor do I look at Maren who I know is behind me, gasping softly at the scene before us.

I tried but I couldn't stop him, Nerissa goes on. *I can't work my magic from the cage. I'm sorry.*

I ignore her. I focus on the boys, on the crew, and I try to manage the unfathomable hate for this man before me before it swallows me whole.

Ed Smith looks the same as he ever did, as is the case with us

Brethren. But while he may have not aged, evil has done something to his features, hardened them into something reptilian. His nose is more pointed, his narrow mouth twisted into an arrogant, ruthless leer, and he's wearing a red periwig that brings out the red in his brown eyes, making him look positively demonic. His ship *Pembroke* has only been under his command for the last ten years, before that it was another, and before that was another. I wonder if he switches his names out as often as he switches out his wigs. It's not easy to evade notice when you're in the public service and yet you never age.

The rage licks me from the inside out, a red-hot inferno that I feel spreading to my mind, rendering me into something raw. I've never wanted to murder someone more. Make him watch as I rip off his head and shit down his neck.

"Captain Battista," Smith says in his haughty accent. "Or should I say Captain Battista *Junior*. You seem surprised to see me."

"Let them go, Smith," I tell him, my words coming out like knives, "and there won't be any trouble for ya."

He sneers. "I invite your trouble, Battista," he says. "It reminds me of how bad you are it. Once I got wind from my fleet that you were out here on your course to land, well, I had to set course for you. Knew you'd be coming to Acapulco, naturally, knew that with your tricky sails you cut straight across the ocean, the trade winds be damned. I just figured it was better to deal with you out here instead of closer to shore. Much tidier that way, isn't it."

He waves his pistols at my crew. "Honestly, I'm not even here to kill you, Battista. Eventually, yes, but I merely want to make you suffer first. You see, what you should have done after I killed your father was give up the ghost. Give up this immoral lifestyle. Hang up the jolly roger and call it a day."

His eyes narrow. "And yet you didn't. You saw what happened to your dear old father and yet you decided that you should become captain of the *Nightwind*. You made it even worse by having a wife, a daughter, on board. These ships are no place for children, don't you have any decency? You know what you went through, you and your useless brother, seeing your own father executed at my hands, and yet you didn't think about the risks in raising them here?"

His fingers twitch on the triggers and I'm staring into Henry's eyes. They're so open and full of fear and hope that I will save him and of course I will save him.

Of course I will save you, I think, before looking to Lucas, who is trying so hard to brave but his chin is trembling, and then to Sedge who shows no emotion on his face, only determination. *I will save you all or die trying.*

"They're safer here than they ever are on land, and you know it," I say, my voice hoarse with contempt. "Does your crew know what you are? Do you hide it? Do you keep one human to feed from? Is he sworn to your secret? Even you know that on the ship you have freedom you could never have on land. The high seas are very good at harboring secrets, that's why we keep our secrets here."

He scoffs, raising his chin and staring down his nose at me. "Spare me your sermon. Your words only exist to make yourself feel better. But mark me, you'll only blame yourself after this, *Captain.* Their deaths are on you."

I know what he's about to do before he does it.

"No!" I scream and I launch myself through the air at him just as he pulls the triggers. Even though I'm flying at him as quick as a flash, everything slows down. I see the bullets both fire from the muzzle of the pistols, a burst of flames and gunpowder, one shot a second behind the other and going to the back of Lucas's head. The delay has him leaning toward Sedge, the bullet just grazing the tip of his ear in a spurt of blood.

The other bullet fired quicker.

It went right in the back of Henry's head.

A horrible burst of red sprays up.

I feel I am dead of a shattered heart before I even hit the ground.

In this case I hit Ed Smith, taking him down with my hands around his neck. We tumble backward and onto the balcony and I bite his neck, trying to tear him apart like a rabid animal.

"I can save him!" Nerissa yells from the cage. "Let me out before it's too late!"

"Ramsay, the key!" Maren screams and I bring my jaws away from Smith to see her running to Henry's side, collapsing to her knees beside him, tears of horror streaming down her face, while Sedge comforts Lucas who is screaming in pain and holding onto his head.

I reach into my pocket for the key and take it out, about to throw it at Maren, when Smith knocks it from my hand. I watch as the key goes sailing over the rail and down into the sea below.

God almighty. This can't be it.

"I've got it!" Maren yells. She gets to her feet and runs at us and for a moment I think she's going to attack Smith too, but she's leaping over us and over the railing, diving over the edge to get the key.

I hear her splash below and in that distraction, Smith flips me over, nearly knocking over the railing, and strangling me with one hand while he reaches for his knife. "Let's see how quickly I can remove your heart. As fast as I removed your father's head?"

He holds the knife above my chest and I hate how equally strong we are, hate that I didn't listen to Maren and take her blood earlier, hate how quickly my life just fell apart again, and I fear that perhaps he is going to end me here, that I'll soon be joining my father in whatever place the mortal immortals rest.

Then Sedge staggers over, hovering over us, looking bloodthirsty as I've never seen him, holding up a blunderbuss aimed right at Smith's face.

Smith has the audacity to smile at him and it's while he's smiling that Sedge pulls the trigger. The muzzle fires, the case shot hitting Smith, obliterating his face and the force of it causes him to crash back through the railing.

A choked scream sounds while Smith falls to the sea below.

I quickly look over the edge to see him sink into the waves and disappear. Maren is also nowhere to be found and the surface is littered with the bodies of the naval members that fell victim to my crew.

Sedge drops the gun and puts his arms under my shoulders, helping me to my feet and I turn around to see Henry still motionless on the floor of my quarters, Lucas beside him, holding up his head, covered in his blood. His own blood pours down his face from his ear, mixing with the tears as he bawls, rocking back and forth.

It's only then that I realize that I'm crying too.

I look to Nerissa in the cage, my vision blurred. "I'm sorry," I whisper to her, the words choked. "I don't know how to get you out without the key. And I can't otherwise undo the magic that's keeping yours at bay."

She's gripping the bars so tight that her knuckles are white and she nods, her attention going to Henry. "I wish I could help you, my child," she says to Henry, her voice low and strained. "I can only wish that the gods take your hand as you go."

"No! We must do something!" Lucas sobs uncontrollably, holding on tight to his dear friend. He stares pleadingly at us with his tear-streamed face. "We have to make him better. Please make him better."

But Henry is dead.

My poor boy is dead.

Sedge goes to his knees beside Lucas, putting his hand on his shoulder, trying to comfort him and I feel frozen in place, a dread so sharp and cold that I don't think I'll ever feel warm again.

This can't be.

"Ramsay!" I hear Maren yelling my name from outside. "Ramsay!"

I stagger out to the balcony and look over the edge where the rail is broken. She's in the water below between the two ships and she waves the key at me. "I have the key!"

I look over my shoulder at Nerissa but she only shakes her head solemnly.

"His soul has left us," Nerissa says softly, her copper eyes welling with tears. "It is too late to bring him back."

I look back at Maren but can't bear to say the words.

But from the way her face crumbles in sorrow, I know I don't need to.

She knows.

Henry is gone.

PART FOUR

The West

THIRTY-FOUR

Maren

It's just after sunset, the sky a watercolor painting of moody lavenders and blues. A few stars are starting to appear, announcing their arrival by dancing. Though we can't see the land yet—least I can't with my somewhat ordinary eyes—you can tell it's near. You can smell it, the vague scent of vegetation and earth in the air.

Sorrow hangs in the air, too.

We had our funeral for Henry this morning, before the sun rose. Ramsay has been beside himself with grief, so Sam and I took the boy's body and Lothar fashioned a raft from planks and wreckage from the *Nightwind's* many wounds. We put Henry on it and adorned it with all the trinkets and toys that he liked, little dogs and bears whittled out of wood by Drakos, plus his favorite items of clothing and his favorite books. Sedge took what was left of the coffee beans and scattered it around him like petals, since Henry had only recently taken a serious liking to the drink.

Many a tear were shed. They may be pirates, but the crew of the *Nightwind* are an emotional bunch, always wearing their hearts on their sleeves. Even the normally unmoved Thane was brought to tears and hugged Lucas and Sam extra tight.

And poor Lucas is grieving as much as Ramsay is. He seems to be doing alright after being shot at, though the top of his ear is gone and his head bandaged, but he lost his best friend, and to see him die in front of him like that—to have nearly died himself—will be a hard thing for him to get over. I doubt he ever will.

So with Cruz playing a heartrending tune on his violin, Henry was lowered into the sea and the raft was set alight. We watched as it drifted off into the rising sun, the flames growing as it rose over the horizon, bathing us all in glowing light.

Then he was gone.

The only one of us who wasn't present at the funeral was Nerissa, but it wasn't because she was in her cage. After I dove down to retrieve the key from the bottom of the ocean, thankful that we were over a seamount which meant I didn't have to dive for thousands of feet, we decided to let Nerissa go free. Ramsay seemed to have given up entirely, not caring if the sea witch wanted to wreak havoc on his ship. As for me, I was starting to believe that Nerissa was someone we could trust. I know she would have saved Henry if she had been able to, or at least she would have tried, and from what she said, the moment she saw Ed Smith crawl in through the balcony, she had tried to contact Ramsay using her mind, the only thing she was able to do.

So now she's staying elsewhere on the ship, having found herself a corner there, and the crew avoids her like she has the plague. I don't blame them, considering Henry's death and her arrival are probably tied in their minds, but I know there's no correlation. Naturally, Ramsay has told her she's free to go but she's determined to stay on the ship, at least until we reach the Bay of Banderas, which will be our first contact with land.

The thought of that, of reaching New Spain and Acapulco, and being closer to Limonos, has my heart in knots, more so than it already was. How do we even find Edonia? Will Nerissa help us? What if she doesn't want to be found?

The bigger question is, can the crew go through another battle like that again? The *Nightwind* took a savage beating from the navy ship, but she's still standing. In the end, the navy ship was destroyed and nearly all their crew was killed. Thane took a few prisoners alive and put them in the hold as sustenance for later, and Ed Smith was never to be found after Sedge shot him in the face. It's possible that he's swimming somewhere in the middle of the ocean, but we would have left him far behind by now.

But while cannons and guns are one thing, the Kraken and magic are another. Unless the *Nightwind* can physically fight back, the Kraken can take down a ship this big without a care. It can tear apart the Brethren with its tentacles, all at Edonia's doing. We may have lost Henry with this round against the Royal Navy, but we still won, we still survived. Next time might be the death of us all.

Which is why I've decided that I will need to seek Edonia on my own. Maybe Nerissa will help me, maybe she won't, but I can't let my need to fix my regrets endanger anyone else. This is between Edonia and I and no one else.

If you're even going to go through with it, I remind myself as I slowly walk along the deck, staring up at the sky as more stars appear.

I sigh and make my way down the stairs. I should go to my room or perhaps pester Sedge to make me something to eat, but instead I need to check on Ramsay. All he's been doing is keeping to himself, locked in his head, and I've been giving him space, but I know that grief isn't something that is dealt with in a day.

I knock on his door and wait to hear if I can come in. Lothar welded a new lock for him and I try it with my hand, even though there's only silence.

It opens and I step inside and see Ramsay rolling over in his bed to face me.

"Maren?" he asks quietly, voice raw.

"It's just me," I tell him, closing the door behind me. "I only wanted to check on you and see if you needed anything."

I walk over to him and stop by his bed. In the dim light of the cabin I see that his eyes are bloodshot, his hair a mess, and my eyes briefly trail down over his bare chest, the rest of him covered by his blanket.

"You," he says hoarsely, holding out his hand for mine. "I need you."

I place my hand in his and he pulls me into the bed on top of him. He puts his hands on both sides of my face, fingers into my hair and gazes up at me. "I need to escape this hell, Maren. I don't want your platitudes."

"I don't have any," I tell him. "I'm just here to be with you, to listen. Nothing I can say will give you comfort, I know this."

"Then kiss me," he says.

I lean in and press my lips to his and he immediately envelopes me in his kiss, wet and open and hungry. I'm pulled in, like he's reaching up from the depths I've been too afraid to swim in and I can't stay afloat any longer. He's the undertow and I'm powerless against his pull.

"You are delirium personified," he rasps against my mouth, his hands in my hair, giving my strands a sharp tug. "You're a fever in my soul, for which there is no cure."

He releases my hair with a groan and reaches down, trying to undo my stays. "I need to feel your skin against mine," he says with urgency, his fingers grabbing hold of the ribbons. I quickly reach back and try to help him but in a fit of desperation he rips them in half with a great tearing sound and tosses my stays across the room.

Then my shift is pulled over my head and he's pushing back the blankets, taking me by the waist with a bruising grip and placing me on top so I'm straddling his muscular thighs, the hard, thick length of his cock sticking up along his stomach.

"I need you to help me forget, luv," he says, his fingers pressing into my skin as he stares up at me. "I need you to be with me like this."

I feel completely on display riding him but for once he's entirely nude as well. I take a moment to rake my eyes over his body, his smooth skin a light gold and without flaw, I suppose due to the fact that his skin doesn't scar. His muscles are well-honed and taut and he vibrates with strength and virility. There's scattering of hair at his chest, then down a narrow path over his tight abdomen to where it gathers at the base of his cock.

He does the same to me, staring at me with reverence as his heated gaze drinks me in, wordless and rapt.

Then he picks me up and moves me over his shaft and shoves up into me and he's so thick, so stiff and immovable, that I feel the breath being pushed out of my lungs.

"Look at you, you miracle of a creature," he murmurs, his brogue getting thick. "Look at how you take me so well, how well you ride my cock."

My back arches, thighs trembling already, and I feel him so deeply that I can't even think straight.

"I need to take from you right now," he says, his nostrils flaring as he raises my hips up with the thrust of his. "And I need you to give. Can you do that for me, luv?"

I nod, closing my eyes. He doesn't realize that as much as I'm giving, I'm taking too. I concentrate on the movement of my hips, letting him guide me where he wants me, gasping with pleasure every time the root of his shaft slides against my most sensitive area.

He adjusts himself for a moment and then his cock goes in deeper, pressing against some aching part inside of me that I didn't know existed.

I let out a thin sound of need, stretched to the breaking point.

I want so much of him, too much, the feeling like a vice around my heart.

My hips start moving in small circles above him as he thrusts up, my legs shaking as I start to increase the pace. He moves his hands to my hips and holds me tight, keeping me in place.

"I won't last too long if you keep doing that, luv," he warns.

Then he's suddenly pulling me off of him and flipping me so that I'm on my back underneath him. He grins at me before kissing me deeply with a searching tongue as he spreads my legs with one hand and pushes his length back inside me, somehow thicker than before.

I let out a harsh moan, relishing the feeling of his hard, heavy weight on top of me, the feeling of hot skin pressed against hot skin. I reach up and feel along the muscles of his rock-hard arms, his broad shoulders, his taut back, always wanting to touch him this way, exploring the smooth and rigid planes of his skin. His body is just as magnificent to feel as it is to see.

"Keep touching me," he whispers, nibbling along my jaw, then down my neck. "Keep your hands on me, luv, I've been dying to be worshipped by you."

I do as he says, my palms coasting over every part of him, especially enjoying the feel of his rear, the tight firm muscles flexing under my touch as he uses them to keep plowing into me. Damp with sweat, he grunts with every hard shove, every circular jab of his hips making the bed creak beneath us. His arms are flexed, mouth open slightly as he stares down at where his cock disappears inside me. I do the same for a moment, mesmerized at the sight, of how thick he is, how tight I feel, the slick sound of our meeting filling the room. I feel like we're animals in heat, and perhaps that's not too far off base when it comes to creatures like us.

Then he pulls out with a grunt and I'm gasping, feeling bereft and hollow and aching without him, and he quickly rolls to the side and thrusts back inside me. He reaches down and hooks his arm under my thigh and starts fucking me hard from behind as we both lie on our sides.

He brings one of his hands to his mouth where he spits on his fingers before reaching down and placing it on my clitoris, even though I'm already drenched enough. While he gives my swollen slick skin a hard pass with his fingers, circling and circling, his other goes to my breasts where he pinches my nipples until I'm crying out.

"Oh, cearban," he gasps into my neck. "You sound like you want more, you greedy little creature. Come for me, my luv."

I'm more than ready. I want the hard clench of it, I want to be violently shaken and let loose into stardust. The need to climax claws up my spine, threatening to destroy me and I brace for an orgasm.

"Let go," he says, biting my neck but not piercing the skin. "Now."

"Aye Captain," I manage to say which brings out a huff of amusement from him, his breath hot on my neck.

It takes another hard rub from his fingers to set me off and I choke on the noises rising up from my throat. Heat prickles across my body like an electric storm and I'm gasping for breath, calling out his name, seeing stars.

"Fuck," he grunts in my ear.

His muscles tremble, his sounds growing louder and he's driving in deeper and faster, until I feel like I'm being fucked to death in a wild, messy fervor. He hammers into me as if he's lost to madness, as if he'd die without spilling his seed inside me.

Then he's brought to completion and I feel his hot spurts inside of me, his hips slowing down into three hard shoves.

And he stills, holding my body against his, his breath short and ragged. I collapse against the bed, against him, and he pulls out as we both lay on our backs.

I swallow, my heart beating like butterfly wings in my chest, and stare up at the wood planks of the ceiling. With my body slowly returning back to normal, my mind does too. It returns to the sorrow. It returns to the future of unknowns.

"Maren," he whispers, brushing the hair off my forehead and kissing my cheek with such tenderness that my heart skips a beat. When he's this soft it completely disarms me.

"Yes?"

"We'll be anchored in the Bay of Banderas soon," he says. "I don't know what you wish to do."

I think that over, sucking my lip between my teeth.

"I know we both have our revenge," he begins. "I know you deserve to get yours. But I worry. I worry that by doing that, I'll lose you to her. Lose you to the person you once were. And I don't know if my heart can take anymore loss, my luv."

I swallow hard. His words, these words, they mark me.

"Stay with me," he whispers. "Don't go back to the deep. Stay with me at the surface. With the sun and the moon and the stars."

I close my eyes and relax against him, resting my head on his chest, hearing the steady slow beat of his heart beneath, and I can't help but imagine that it belongs to me. By nature, Syrens crave the hearts of men, but I only want his heart to love me.

"If I don't get revenge, then who am I?" I ask in a hush. "All I've known as an adult is trying to return to the creature I once was. To the girl I was. If I let that go, then I have to make peace with what I am now."

"So then you make peace with it," he says, pressing his lips against my head. "As long as you know that the path to peace is a hard one, perhaps as hard as the one you'd take for vengeance. But it's the right one, and that's what counts in the end."

I take a moment to think that over. He's right, of course, but it's always easier said than done. There's something so passive about acceptance that bucks against my personality, perhaps because for so long that's what I was. I just sat back and took what was dealt my way in the way of Aerik and my life as a princess. The fact that I finally have been given an opportunity for agency and to take action and I'm turning my back on it, it feels like I'm giving up.

"I'm just afraid that I'll make a mistake, yet another one I won't be able to live with," I say.

He stiffens. "You think I'm a mistake?"

"No," I say quickly, looking up at him. "You are not a mistake, Ramsay. You are a choice and, what you've said before, a different path to take."

"So do you choose me, luv?" he asks and I've never seen him look so vulnerable. It causes a dull ache in my chest.

Because this is the question, isn't it? Do I choose him and my legs and this life above the sea? Or do I say goodbye and go back to living under the water, back in a kingdom without my father, mother, or sister, with my other sister elsewhere?

The latter was all I had ever wanted for the last ten years.

The former is all I've ever wanted over the last few weeks.

"You don't need to answer me," he says, giving me a squeeze. "We still have time."

I don't need to look at an hourglass to know that time is running out.

THIRTY-FIVE

Maren

"Sedge," I say as I stand in the entrance to the galley. "Could I get two mugs of coffee?"

He gives me an amiable smile and nods, putting the kettle on the flames. Even though Sedge doesn't speak, I enjoy coming down to the galley and talking to him. It's not just that he's a good listener, although I have noticed his mind wanders a bit, but I understand him. He may not vocalize words as language but there is a language he communicates with and that I think most of the crew know how to read at an innate level.

"Are you doing alright?" I ask, even though I've asked him this a lot over the last few days. We've all been traumatized, and though he is back to normal in the sense that the curse was reversed, what he witnessed with regards to Henry was horrific, not to mention how he might feel about blasting another man in the face with a gun. Granted, he knows how the Brethren are and that he probably didn't kill Ed Smith, but even so it had to have been a gruesome sight.

He nods again, giving me a quick, reassuring smile. *Yep*, he seems to be saying. *No worse than the last time you asked me that.*

I take that as a hint to stop asking.

"Can I tell you a secret?" I then say. "Even though I know you've probably made some guesses already since we were held together on the cursed ship."

He nods eagerly as he puts the beans in the grinder and turns the handle.

I look around the galley. It's quiet and I know it's just the two of us here.

"I'm not one of the Brethren," I begin quietly. "But I'm not a human like you either. I'm actually a Syren, or a mermaid, as you come to know it."

His eyes widen though he doesn't seem too surprised nor scared.

And so I launch into the story of my life, how I was once a little mermaid under the sea and how I traded it all for the heart of a prince. Other than Ramsay, I've never had the chance to tell anyone else this story without fear of reprisal, and I have to say it feels terribly good to let it all out like this. I've wanted to tell the rest of the crew this too but I know it probably won't go over very well, considering what mermaid blood does, but Sedge seems to be a good place to start.

By the time I'm done talking, Sedge has made the coffee, already poured into the mugs, and his eyes are as wide as saucers.

Wow, he seems to say and I realize I really do have quite the story to tell. Perhaps I'll write it all out one day.

A slow clap and jangling noise comes from behind me and I turn to see Nerissa standing there, smiling at me coyly, her hands pressed together, her pearl and shell bracelets rattling.

"I thought I knew your tale, but I didn't think it would be quite like that," she says. "Do you have my coffee?"

I nod and grab the mugs from Sedge, handing her one. When I had passed by her earlier she had seen me drinking coffee and there was such an envious look on her face that I asked if I could get her one.

"Shall we go for a walk?" she asks me.

"That sounds fine," I say, knowing walks up and down the top deck were a common way for the crew to let loose excess energy. That and swordplay.

"I have much to discuss with you," she says. *In private.*

That last part makes me flinch. It came directly inside my head.

It's okay, child, she goes on with a secretive smile. *You can answer back too.*

I glance at Sedge but he's gone back to chopping vegetables for supper.

You can hear my thoughts? I think.

She scrunches up her nose. *Maybe try again, really project to me.*

Can you hear me now? I say, thinking harder.

She grins, her teeth glowing white. *Loud and clear. Come now and walk with me.*

We go up the stairs to the top deck, our hair blown forward as the wind meets our backs. The scent of land is stronger now and it feels like the wind is pushing us faster toward it.

The crew looks up as we pass. I notice now that they revere me with respect and warmth, I suppose because they're both used to my presence and it's obvious now that the captain and I are having an affair. The hostage is no longer here against her will.

But while they look at me like I'm part of their family now, a feeling I enjoy very much, they look at Nerissa with suspicion still. Even with her free to roam the ship and the fact that she stays out of everyone's way, they haven't been able to let their guards down. Especially Thane and Cruz. Seems she's rattled them both to their core.

If she's bothered by this, she doesn't show it. When she walks, she walks like a goddess with her head held high, her perpetually wet ivory gown trailing behind her.

"What seems to be the matter?" I ask her.

She gives me a dry look for already forgetting the whole speaking-inside-of-our-heads technique.

You know I saw things when I looked into Thane's crystal ball, she says. *Things I am not allowed to repeat, just so we are clear.*

Did you see Henry's death? I ask.

She gives her head a shake, her mouth set in a grim line. *I saw a death. I saw it at the hands of that man. That Ed Smith. But I did not see who it was.*

But you knew someone was going to die, I say looking at her in surprise. *And you didn't say anything.*

I did. And I tried to tell you the best I can.

Why can't you just come out with it? What happens?

It is hard to explain. It's like I am physically unable to.

So you can only give us clues and hints, then?

Yes, she says, giving Sam a polite nod as we pass her by. Sam smiles at me but only scowls at Nerissa. The sea witch sighs in response, her expression crestfallen.

What?

Sometimes you know there is a fate that you cannot change, she says, giving Sam a strained look over her shoulder. *At times I see many futures, many paths, but other times, no. That is set destiny. That is the fated. That is when I know nothing can be done, no warning can be made.*

Are you trying to warn me of something now?

She nods.

My heart jumps. Oh gods. *What?*

She just shakes her head. *I cannot tell you what. But what I do know is that perhaps it is time, Maren, for you to tell the crew who you are. Tell them you are a Syren.*

I frown. *Why? They'll want to eat me.*

Her brow raises. *And maybe you should let them. Do you understand my saying?*

My eyes widen in fear. *You think I should...*

Tell them what you are and give them your blood, she says. *That's all I can say. But I promise you it's not for nothing.*

I swallow hard and stew that over as we reach the forecastle and turn around, slowly walking back. I see Ramsay at the aft with Thane and Crazy Eyes and I wonder what he would say to that.

Don't worry about Bones, she adds hastily, following my gaze. *He doesn't get a say in this. He may have claimed you as his, but you are still your own true person with her own agency. Take his feelings into account but don't let it sway you.*

I find myself nodding. *Alright.* I glance back at Nerissa. *Can I ask you something?*

Of course.

Is my future with Ramsay? Or is it not?

She gives me a small smile that makes her metallic eyes dance.

"You already know the answer to that."

I don't sleep well that night. I'm in Ramsay's bed and that alone should lull me to sleep, especially in the comfort of his strong arms, but I can't stop thinking about what Nerissa told me. How I need to give the crew my blood and how they need to know what I am. I'm terrified that this fate before me is set in stone, made worse by not knowing what it is that Nerissa saw in that crystal ball.

I get up and Ramsay reaches for me in his sleep, his arm slipping around my waist. He mumbles something and I just slide out of his grasp, then lean over and brush his hair from his forehead, kissing him there.

"Go back to sleep," I whisper, smiling at the sight of him.

He mumbles something again, eyes still closed, and rolls over, breathing deeply in moments. He's been having nightmares lately, where he wakes up in a cold sweat, whimpering, and I don't need to ask what it's about. It's impossible not to have nightmares after what just happened to Henry.

I get up and leave his quarters, going up the stairs to the top deck, hoping the fresh air will bring me clarity. I walk along and look back at the helm to see it totally empty. There should at least be one person on shift tonight. Then I hear a low groan and I look toward the bow. I squint and realize I can see a figure using the head on the bowsprit, thankfully he's more or less obscured at this distance. I'll be avoiding that area at any rate.

I'm about to turn around when suddenly I feel a presence at my back and a smelly hand goes across my mouth. I immediately know who it is.

"All claims are off," Sterling sneers in my ear, his other hand starting to hike up my shift. "You're mine for the picking now, strumpet."

In an instant I feel my teeth and claws sharpen and I open my mouth against his palm, biting down.

Hard.

He lets out a loud yelp as I chew through bone and sinew and nearly bite his hand in half.

"Bitch," he growls, letting go of me, though now I'm not letting go of him, my claws digging into his arm, my jaw locked like a rabid badger, tearing at him.

He winds up his other arms and punches me square me in the face.

My face explodes in pain and I fall backward to the deck, hearing Crazy Eyes in the background wondering what's happening. I quickly flip around and try to scramble to my feet but I'm disoriented and he's fast and he's grabbing hold of my legs and yanking me toward him, pinning me down from behind. My shift is pushed up again until my rear is exposed and I'm trying so hard to turn over and fight, my jaws snapping at the air like a piranha, but he's too strong and now I'm screaming, hollering for help.

I hear Crazy Eyes running along the deck toward me saying, "What's happening here? Princess? Sterling!"

And I'm staring up at him, my hand outreached, asking for help as Sterling's about to violate me in the most horrific way possible. But Crazy Eyes comes to a standstill, his shocked gaze caught on something beside me.

I hear a familiar roar of male fury that fills the air, then a *whoosh*. There's the sickening thick sound of metal through muscle and bone, and I feel a splatter of hot blood at my back and the weight of Sterling collapsing against me.

I try to turn over and can't and Crazy Eyes has my hands now, pulling me out from under Sterling.

I manage to flip over to see Sterling on the deck with an axe sticking out of his spine and Ramsay behind him, holding onto the handle, his eyes wild with rage, his breath hard and uneven. My lover's gaze goes to mine. "Did he hurt you?"

I try to speak but I can't. He didn't hurt me, but he was close, he was so close.

"Did he hurt you!?" Ramsay repeats, sounding feral now, a vein throbbing at his temple.

I shake my head. "No," I say, my voice trembling, just as Sterling starts to rise from the deck.

"Arggh," Sterling lets out a cry, cradling his arm and hand that are still torn savagely by me.

"No," Ramsay says to him, absolutely seething as he pulls the axe out of Sterling's back with a wet sound. "No, you aren't going to live through this one, mate. The lady you just tried to take, my lady, had been kind enough to consider marooning you. You won't be marooned now. Now you're going to eat your own cock before I chop your head off. The taste of your own shortcomings is the last thing you'll know."

Sterling hollers and tries to get to his feet, but Ramsay kicks him over onto his back and looks over him with a manic grin. "I see Maren has already left her mark on you. How does it feel to be so thoroughly hurt by a woman?" Ramsay brings out a knife from behind him. "Never you mind, I'd rather not hear your answer."

Ramsay drops to his knees and I look away quickly, burying my head into the arms of the bosun who is swearing up a storm of Irish curses under his breath. I hear the tear of fabric, the swift cut of Ramsay's knife, then Sterling's ear-splitting scream. His scream seems to go on forever until it suddenly becomes muffled and I know Ramsay is doing exactly what he said he would.

I lift my head, peeking around the bosun's arms enough to see blood everywhere and Sterling attempting to spit out his own severed shaft that has been stuffed mercilessly inside his mouth.

Then I see Ramsay raise the axe, spit on Sterling's forehead, then bring the axe down on his neck. His head splits cleanly from the rest of his body with a final crunch.

I hold the bosun tighter, overwhelmed by the violence even though I know I'm capable of such myself. Had I been able to fight back a man of his size, I would have done the same to Sterling. But even so, I am shocked and shaking.

Ramsay throws the axe to the ground, breathing hard, his focus now on me. He seems a little unsure, as if he lost control and went a little too far and doesn't know how I'll react.

"No one touches you," he says, wiping the sweat from his brow. "Ever."

By now there's a crowd gathered behind him, gasping at the bloodshed at his feet.

And Crazy Eyes looks down at me in his arms. "Looks like the princess can take care of herself," the bosun says, frowning at me. "What in god's name are you, lass?"

THIRTY-SIX

Ramsay

I stare down at Sterling's decapitated body and the only remorse I feel is that we didn't get rid of him sooner. I don't know how he escaped from his chains but us Brethren can pull up extra strength at times and perhaps it got loosened during the battle with the Royal Navy. Had we done what Maren suggested and found some atoll and left him there, this never would have happened.

But it did happen. And though I know Maren can defend herself, she's better on the offensive, better when she's the one attacking and not the other way around. Sterling had her, he…he almost broke her. Thank the lord that when I heard her get up and tell me to go back to sleep that I didn't stay asleep for long. I had this niggling feeling in my gut that something wasn't right.

And now Sterling is dead and we have a lot of explaining to do, not least of which is to answer the bosun's question of "what are you?"

I go over to Maren, a little unsure if she'll think differently after I brutalized Sterling like that in front of her, but I also don't care if she thinks it's an overreaction. I'd warned him once that I would kill him if he touched her again. I only followed through with the threat. Besides, I am on edge these last few days. The loss of Henry has had my rage a lit fuse. It was only a matter of time before it all came out like this in explosive violence.

I reach down and take her from the bosun's arms, giving him a nod to thank him for taking care of her, then I hold her against my chest. Her arms go around my waist and she grips me tight. I kiss the top of her forehead. "I will always protect you," I say against her soft hair. "No matter what."

She nods against me and sighs, still shaking slightly. Then she cranes her neck back to look at me. "We need to tell them."

I glance over at the crew, most of them awake and chattering amongst themselves and wondering what's happened, Cruz poking Sterling with the tip of his boot. "Uglier in death," Cruz comments with a grimace.

Maren pulls away from me and clears her throat, facing the crew.

"There's something I need to tell you all," she says. She sounds so strong, her voice steady, though I hate the fact that she's telling them this way and not on her own time.

I grab her hand and give her a squeeze for support.

She takes a deep breath, looking into everyone's curious eyes.

"I'm…a Syren," she says. "A mermaid."

A hushed cry goes out among the crew, nearly everyone squinting at her bare legs expecting to see fins appear.

"I *was* a mermaid," she clarifies. "Though we call ourselves Syrens. And once upon a time, I lived under the sea in the Kingdom of Limonos. When I was sixteen, I fell in love with a prince and, well, you know how that ended. But in order to gain his love, I had to sell my soul to the sea witch, Edonia."

Several people gasp, knowing full well who Edonia is and what she's done to me.

"Edonia had me trade my fins for legs and my tongue so that she could have my Syren song. I don't know why, I was never a very great singer to begin with," she adds with a smile. "But I digress. She promised me things that she knew weren't true and I, being young and brash, fell for it. So now you can see what I've been for the last ten years. I have had legs. Eventually my tongue grew back. But I could never return to the sea." She pauses. "That is, until I saw my sister, Asherah, the mermaid in the tank."

More gasps and murmurs spread in the crowd, followed by someone, Drakos I think, saying, "I knew it!" But of course he couldn't have known that.

"As Asherah lay dying, she kissed me and that kiss gave me some of my abilities back. I became more of a monster, if you will, though I still have legs." She sticks one of her legs out. "So, that is everything there is to know about me."

Thane steps forward, giving Maren an inspecting look before looking at me. "Why didn't you tell us this sooner?"

"Because I didn't want you losing your bloodthirsty minds once you found out she had mermaid's blood," I tell him.

"But," Maren says forcefully, "now that you all know, I am here to offer you my blood."

"Maren," I growl, pulling her to me, my hackles raising. "What are you doing?"

"I want to give them my blood," she says, her brows knitting together. "It's the only way we can defeat Edonia."

"We don't even know if we'll see Edonia," I tell her, a coil of molten possessiveness forming inside me. "I don't want to share you."

She narrows her eyes at me. "It's just blood. It's not sex." Then she pauses at that, frowning. "Good gods, I hope I just didn't offer everyone sex."

"No," I tell her firmly. "It's out of the question."

"Bones," Nerissa's low voice rings out across the deck, "keep your jealousy under control."

Everyone turns to look at her at the back of the crowd. "If Maren thinks they should have her blood, then they shall," she says.

"They'll drain her," I stammer.

"For heaven's sake, Ramsay," Thane scolds me. "Do you really think your motley crew lacks that sort of control and finesse? We don't have to feed directly from her, you arse. You can siphon her blood into a bottle and we can pass it around. You know only a little bit will do."

I think back to when I fed from Maren. It had hit me so fast and I had so much of it, I felt like I could lift the *Nightwind* clear over my head. It also faded by morning, though there were still some residual effects. Even a little bit would suffice for the short term. A little bit amongst the crew might be enough to have a solid fighting front.

But even so.

"No," I say firmly. "Absolutely not. She's mine and her blood is mine too."

"My blood is my own," she cries out. "It's mine to do what I wish."

I ignore her and look to the crew. "I forbid you all from drinking her blood and, as captain, that's an order."

They all sigh and grumble amongst each other, turning around and heading back below deck and to their quarters, waving their arms in a dismissive motion. All of them leave except Crazy Eyes, who steps around Sterling's body and takes his position back at the helm, and Nerissa who lingers and gives Maren a long knowing look. If I didn't know any better, I'd say that information was passing between them silently.

"Pray tell, what are you doing?" I ask. "Maren?"

Maren finally tears her gaze off Nerissa who walks off below deck, then looks at me with a scowl. "You say you own me Ramsay, but you only own my heart."

I go still.

"Only?" I repeat, feeling the stillness fade as a wave of strange emotions crashes over me and I hold her closer. "Only your heart? Your heart is everything to me, luv."

Is she saying I own it? That she's giving it to me freely?

She swallows hard, her lip pouting. "You know what I mean."

"I don't," I tell her, my chest growing hot. "You have my heart, Maren, but do I have yours? Do I truly claim you in that way, more than just a brand on your hip, more than my possessiveness, more than just the way I join with your body? Are you willingly claimed? Do you give your heart to me in return?"

She reaches up and touches my face lightly, a sweet smile on her lips. "Yes, I give you my heart, Ramsay."

"Truly?" I whisper, afraid the truth is no. I pull her hands to my mouth and kiss her knuckles.

"Truly," she says.

"Because I've fallen in love with you, cearban," I tell her, holding her hands tight. "I've fallen for you, drowned in this pure delirium of what you are, this fever dream that won't let me go. Your heart, soul, body, and spirit. Oh, how I love you fiercely." I kiss her delicately, passion rising up through me like a spring. "I love you as fiercely as the fierce little creature you are."

She grabs hold of me, kissing me back, and I feel like we're both being pulled to the stars above.

"And I love you," she whispers against my lips and I feel like the stars are raining down on us now, sinking into my veins. "My feral pirate lord."

My god, how I love the sound of that.

Then we break apart, her chest rising and falling, and her eyes are defiant.

"But though I give you my heart and my body and my soul, though they now belong to you," she goes on, breathless, "my blood is still mine to give. Let me give it to your crew. Let me help in some way." She pauses and gives me a heartsore look. "They're my family too."

I shake my head. "I'm a stubborn man, Maren, you know this by now. You can do what you want, but they won't be drinking it. Your blood is yours and mine and that is it. I do not share, not in any way."

She lets out a huff of disappointment but frankly I don't care because she had just told me that her heart belongs to me. She just told me she loves me. After all that I've lost—my father, Venla, Hilla, Henry, I still found someone that loves me for me, and someone that I love back deeply. I love her and I'm never letting her go.

Nothing else matters now.

W hen I wake up in the morning, I find that Maren is gone. Again.

I immediately panic, springing out of bed, the image of Sterling forcing himself on her last night still ingrained in my head. There's been so much violence and horror as of late that I don't trust the world anymore. I'm waiting for the rug to be pulled out from under me every second of the day.

I slip on my breeches and rush out of the room, calling her name, then hear her answering from down the length of the main deck, so I hurry along past her room and the officer's quarters until I find her in the galley. She's sitting on the wood counter with Nerissa standing beside her, looking like two peas in a pod at this point. Beautiful creatures of the sea.

But then I'm looking at Maren's arm which is bandaged up, then I'm looking at Sedge standing to the side of her, holding a roll of gauze.

"What's going on here?" I ask. "What happened to your arm?"

Maren gives me a faint smile and I realize she looks paler than normal. "Nothing. I just nicked myself while I was helping Sedge chop onions for the pages' breakfasts."

I try to swallow down the lump in my throat that comes with the fact that Henry won't be having breakfast as usual. I dissolve the sorrow with a shake of my head and look back at her arm, then at Sedge who just shrugs innocently. Finally I eye Nerissa, who also shrugs, although she's doing it with a demure smile.

I squint at them. "If I find out there's been some misbehaving…" I warn them.

"Then I volunteer Maren for the spanking," Nerissa says wickedly.

"Hmmphf." I make a disgruntled noise. "Well, you're up terribly early considering the night that we—"

"Land ho!" Thane's voice booms from above on the deck above. "Land ho!"

We all exchange a look of shock, this moment coming sooner than I thought, and then I'm running out of the galley and flying up the stairs to the top deck. The crew is gathered along the rail pointing to the distance where the sun has just risen. I run over and follow their direction. I don't even need a spyglass to see it, there's a line of low haze on the horizon and just beyond that, the peninsula that sticks out at the north of the Bay of Banderas.

I don't know what I feel, to be honest. During every voyage across the Pacific, land has represented a change from the monotony at sea. Personally I don't mind that monotony, the sea means freedom to me and the land is just a place to get in trouble. But the crew loves it when we pull into the harbors. There are fresh victims for us to feed on, fresh cunts and cocks to fuck, and fresh treasures to steal. The Brethren aren't like Maren, we aren't sea-going creatures to start with, and even I will admit there's a sense of grounding there that you don't often get floating above the waves.

It also represents the start of the pirate raids for us. We go up and down the Pacific coast of New Spain, from the Bay of Banderas to Acapulco, looting galleons from their wares, whether it's gunpowder, silk, ivory and jade coming from Manila, or heaps of silver coins, wine and weapons just setting out from Acapulco. Either way, the galleons are always loaded and even with their convoy with them, things get chaotic close to land and easier for us to take over.

Now, however, our purpose isn't the same as it was when we left Manila. When we left we had a hold full of treasure to spend and barter with when we got to this side of the ocean. We also had a prince and a princess to hold for ransom. But the prince is long gone, the princess is now a pirate—even if she doesn't think so herself—and the treasure we have in the hold doesn't seem as important as the chance to fight Edonia. We all know she lives somewhere along this coast, and so even though getting to land is imperative for the crew, it's not the end of the battle for me.

Maren appears beside me, squinting at the horizon.

And she's another reason why the sight of land is bringing forth so many conflicting feelings. Our voyage together is coming to an end. I love her and she loves me and yet I don't know if that love is strong enough to prevent her from returning to her home if given half the chance.

"Wow," she whispers. "I never thought land would look so strange."

"Strange?" I ask.

She nods, and I'm noticing she looks a little unsteady on her feet. "Yes. The last I saw it were the islands, and it was good riddance to that creepy place. But so much has changed between then and now, between here and there. I thought I knew what I wanted the last time I saw land. Now that I'm seeing it again, I'm not sure what I want."

What you want is me, still, isn't it? I want to ask.

I just put my hand at her lower back and she leans into me, falling over slightly.

"Are you alright, luv?" I ask, peering down at her. She still looks pale and when I glance at the bandage around her arm, I can see a hint of red peeking through. The sight of blood stirs a primal hunger in me, which I bury deep for now.

She nods and makes a faint noise of agreement. "I'm fine."

God almighty, she didn't do what I think she did...

"Maren," I say, grabbing her shoulders and forcing her to look at me. "Look me in the eyes."

She slowly opens them, swaying. The color of them is the pale blue of a shallow shoal, barely any pigment in it left.

She's been drained.

My jaw tightens. "You didn't give them blood did you?"

She gives me a tired smile. "It's all in a bottle. Thane has hidden it. Please don't be mad."

"Mad?!" I explode, livid. I quickly look around for Thane. I'm going to kill the bastard. "Thane!" I yell. "Where are you?! Where's the bottle?"

But when I spot Thane he's standing by the helm on the aft deck now, staring down at the water.

I let go of Maren and march over to the steps to the aft deck, running up them until I'm at his side.

I push at his shoulder to get him to look at me. "Thane," I growl.

But he just stares down at the water with horror in his eyes. It's a look that makes my own blood run cold.

"What?" I ask and I peer over to see what he's staring at.

At first the ocean looks normal, a deep blue, richer than it's seemed all voyage since we're getting closer to land now. Then I realize there's something moving under the surface. Something dark, very dark, and impossibly large.

A hint of yellow eyes.

I suck in my breath and yell like I've never yelled before.

"It's the Kraken!"

THIRTY-SEVEN

Maren

"I t's the fucking Kraken!" Ramsay yells again, and panic spreads across the deck like a virus.

"Get the bottle of blood!" Cruz yells at Thane from the forecastle.

Ramsay shoots me a look of terror that I feel from across the deck, though I'm not sure if it's because of the Kraken or because now my blood is being called into use.

But then he yells at Thane. "Aye, get Maren's blood! Pass it around to everyone! One shot will do ya!" And I now I know that he's on board with the idea, finally.

This morning I got up early, emboldened by Nerissa's idea that I ignore Ramsay's possessiveness and just give the blood to the crew anyway. So I snuck into the kitchen and she joined me, then I asked Sedge to cut into my vein to bleed me. He hesitated, of course, but he also understood, and soon my blood was draining out of me and into a cup, which was then tipped into an empty bottle of wine.

Now that bottle of wine is verily coming in handy.

But while it's being passed around so that the crew can fortify themselves, I don't know what to do. My blood doesn't have that effect on me.

"Stay away from the sides!" Ramsay yells. "You all know how far those tentacles reach!"

"Maren!" Sam yells at me, holding up a cutlass. "Avast!"

She chucks the sword my way and it's only luck that I manage to catch it by the handle. "You're a true pirate now, lass!" she calls out. "You're going to need to hack away at those tentacles, unless you think your teeth and claws might do."

"I reckon I'll try all three!" I tell her, gripping the sword tight. My experience with the Kraken has been shallow, so to speak, but I saw what those tentacles tried to do to Nill.

But then of course, if the Kraken is beneath the ship right now, wouldn't that mean Edonia is controlling it?

Blast, I swear. *Where is Nerissa?*

I don't want to leave the top deck in case the Kraken strikes and an extra sword is needed in defense, not to mention there could be more than one of them. But Nerissa should be up here with us. If she can somehow talk to her sister or the Kraken, then perhaps we need not fight at all, least not the whole ship.

I decide to chance it and run down the stairs to the main deck, looking around for Nerissa.

"Have you seen Nerissa?" I ask Sedge as I burst into the galley.

He shakes his head.

"Alright, well we have company in the form of the Kraken, and I don't know where the best place is for you and the boys. I know it's asking a lot to get you to step back into the captain's quarters again, but in the event the ship starts to sink, at least you can escape through the balcony."

Sedge just tilts his head as if to say, *the ship can't sink.*

Gods, I hope he's right. *Nightwind* might be able to handle some roundshots and grenades and the fiercest storms, but if that sea beast decides to tear apart the ship plank from plank I don't see how it would be able to put itself back together. It's not like it's part of the Brethren itself.

"Will you do that, get the boys for me and keep them safe?"

Sedge nods emphatically.

I let out a breath of relief and then I start running through the rest of the decks, calling out her name. The only people I find are Remi and Horse in position at the cannons, one on either side of the deck. They give me a terrified look.

"I heard it was the Kraken," Horse says. "Is it the Kraken, truly? We're waiting for the command to fire."

"Maybe we'll get it right in the mouth," Remi adds with put-on bravado.

"You wait for Thane's command," I tell them. "You'll be alright." I pause. "Have you seen Nerissa?"

They shake their head in unison. "No, milady," Horse says clumsily. "Haven't seen her since...since..."

He trails off, his mouth going slack, eyes locked in terror on something behind me. I whip around to see the open gun port on the other side of Remi. Instead of looking at the blue horizon, all I see is a giant yellow eye peering at me.

"Kraken!" I scream. "Fire! Fire the cannons!"

I don't care that I'm not Thane and neither do the gunners. They strike a match and light the back of the vent and the shot is fired with a deafening *BANG*, smoke filling the air.

The cannon recoils with great violence, pulling back at the ropes that hold it in place and the roundshot fires straight into the Kraken's eye.

It lets out an otherworldly bellow that shakes the whole ship, that sounds like it's come right from the bowels of hell and the ruined eye starts to fall from view but now the tentacles are slamming into the side of the hull, shaking the ship.

Screams and cries come from the deck above and I know I need to help them. I look at Remi and Horse, at the fear on their faces. They don't look like this when they're battling the Royal Navy, but the Kraken is an entirely different fight altogether, one that could spell death for them all.

"Did Thane come by here with the bottle earlier? No, he didn't have time," I answer myself, hoping that bottle is still getting passed around up top.

I take hold of my arm and rip off the bandage, the motion opening up the wound from earlier. My blood starts to flow and I quickly jam my arm up into Remi's face. "Suck!" I yell at him, aware of how it sounds, also aware that Ramsay has been very adamant I don't share my body with others. But when it comes to a life-or-death situation and not a hypothetical one, I don't give a whit what he thinks.

Remi delicately sucks back the blood, giving Horse an unsure look, and then I see his pupils turn red and he's biting me.

"Ow, damn it!" I cry out, "you didn't have to bite me."

"Remi," Horse chides him, pushing him off my arm, droplets of my blood gathered in his thin mustache, then Horse begins to feed. He shows a little more restraint and doesn't bite me, but Remi already made it easier for him.

Then Horse's pupils go crimson and I know he's starting to get carried away so I kick him in the shin until he stops.

"You feel it now?" I ask them and they nod vigorously, their eyes growing large with verve. "Then fire again!"

They jump to it, moving so fast now that they're a blur.

I turn and run out of the gun deck and to the stairs until I'm face-to-face with the carnage up top. The Kraken's tentacles are wildly thrashing the ship, one pulling down the foremast, another slamming through the railing until the shards go flying across the deck, another pounding the deck like a fist.

"Help!" Crazy Eyes screams as a tentacle grabs hold of him, squeezing him like it means to cut him in two, and then Cruz is there, slicing through the tentacle with a broadsword, wielding the giant weapon like it's a toy.

The more I look at everyone, the more that I see they've all had my blood. They're moving faster, they're stronger, they're thinking two steps ahead. I don't know how long a shot of it will last in their systems, but it might be enough to destroy the Kraken.

And what about Edonia? I can't help but think. *If she's here, where is she? Why doesn't she show her face? And where did Nerissa go? Has she abandoned us already?*

Dread shocks my system.

What if Nerissa led Edonia right here? What if this was all part of her master plan? What if there is no destiny but something that she controls?

I'm thinking that over in horror, refusing to feel betrayed, while I watch as the crew keep hacking away at the Kraken's tentacles. It's a massive beast the size of the ship, yet with the cannons firing into it from below and the strength of fight that the Brethren is showing, it seems to be giving up.

I run closer to the edge of the deck, stopping beside Matisse who gives me an up-and-down look of approval. "Thank you for the blood, by the way," he says in his French accent. "You taste magnificent."

I just shrug off the strange compliment while Thane yells, "It's retreating!"

"Fill the sails!" Ramsay yells from the aft deck. "Let's outrun the beast!"

"Aye!" the crew shouts as they start running to and fro.

"All thanks to Maren!" Sam says, stepping up on the crate beside the rail. She raises the nearly empty bottle of my blood in the air. "Thanks to your mermaid—"

A purple-black tentacle rises up from the other side, right behind Sam as she stands there at the edge. I open my mouth to yell her name but the tentacle curls back for a moment then strikes so fast that I choke on the sound.

The Kraken punches a hole straight through the middle of Sam, obliterating her heart.

"Sam!" I finally manage to scream. I run toward her, my cutlass raised, and start hacking away at the tentacle that is sticking straight through her body. I stab and slice and cut, tears rolling down as she falls off the crate and lands face first onto the deck.

The tentacle then retreats, with Sam's heart still pulsing in the suctioned tip.

"No!" I scream, aware that the others are running toward me now, yelling for Sam, yelling for me, horror taking over the ship.

Then another tentacle appears, and as the one with Sam's heart slides back into the sea, the other one goes straight for me.

I try to leap out of the way, but the tentacle is fast. It curls around me like a fishhook, the slimy suctions sticking painfully to my skin, then it raises me in the air and starts pulling me overboard.

I twist around, trying to free myself, and the last thing I see is the deck of the ship, Ramsay running to the tentacle with his sword raised, Thane kneeling on the deck beside Sam, and Sam lying there in a pool of her own blood, dead.

Then I'm pulled straight down into the ocean.

Straight to Edonia.

THIRTY-EIGHT

Maren

The Kraken who has me moves quickly but it's not alone. When I turn my head to look back at the surface, I see another one still battling with the ship, though it seems weakened from the fight.

It continues to swim down, taking me as a hostage, and at first all I see is the dark blue of the deep rising up to meet me, that infinite abyss that stretches on forever. It doesn't take long before I spot the bottom, a dark red reef that reminds me of blood, and in the middle of the towering reef, in a circle of sand, is Edonia.

The Kraken's grip on me tightens, as if it knows I'd try and squirm away. I try anyway, attempting to loosen myself from the suctions but they cling on to my skin so hard that I'm afraid they might tear my skin right off.

"Here she is," Edonia calls out to me in her smooth, malevolent voice. "How I've been waiting for this day."

I stop my struggling to gape at her as the Kraken delivers me, holding me out like a hard-won prize.

Edonia looks more or less as I remember, but even more powerful and menacing. She seems taller, her shoulders wider, and her white hair is longer, turned into pearlescent writhing eels that snap at the water.

The red in her eyes is no longer a bright coral but dried blood, bordering on black, and they seem to take up her whole eye so there's no white left in them.

She smiles at me and her teeth rival mine, sharp as knives.

I compose the look of awe on my face and give her nothing back.

"I know you've been waiting for this day too," she says with a knowing tone. "My sweet ink-haired girl, I remember it like it was yesterday when you called upon me, only miles from here if you can believe it. So fresh, so young, so full of innocence. It's hard to believe that you're the same Syren at all, and it's not because you have legs. You seem so much…older. And I know, twenty-six is not old, not down here in the deep, but up there…"

"If you're trying to insult me it's not working."

"Insult you? Gracious, no." She grins at me and small fish dart out of her mouth. The white eels of her hair snap at them as they go, eager for a snack. "But it is the truth. The world up there has been most unkind to you, hasn't it?"

"I've managed," I reply curtly. I try to straighten myself but it's impossible when you're engulfed by a giant tentacle.

She gives the Kraken a nod. "Release her."

The Kraken lets go of me, the suckers releasing with a *pop pop pop*. I gasp and sink to the sand, holding onto my aching skin where they had sucked at me.

"So I heard you want me to reverse the spell…" she says.

I struggle to my feet, feeling strangely unbalanced despite being underwater. "Who told you that? Nerissa?"

"My sister? Goodness, no. As if I would ever listen to her. Barely even a sea witch, if you ask me, but every family has to have a black sheep."

She takes a few steps toward me, her movements smooth and measured. Her black diaphanous gown floats around her like silk and I realize it's made of Kraken ink. "I'm no fool, dear, though I certainly am curious. I don't make bargains with Syrens like you and assume that everything has worked out in the end, not with so many variables in life. For I believe in accountability."

I snort at that and she gives me a steady look as she continues. "I am a fixer, Maren. A life-changer. A wish-maker. I need to know how my...clients...have adjusted to their new lives. You were never truly alone, princess, no, I was always there in some way. I have creatures below the sea and above that checked in on you from time to time. I liked to keep an eye on you to make sure all was well."

Indignation flares in me. "All was well?" I repeat, the phrase a bitter taste in my mouth. "Then clearly you saw that for the last ten years, nothing has been well!"

"You made your choice, dearie," she says with a patronizing tone, walking around me, her white eel hair shining like pearls as they swirl in the current. "And it was your choice. You've forgotten that *you* were the one that came to me. *You* asked me. *Begged* me. I gave you what you asked for. You've rewritten the story to make yourself the victim here but you're only a victim to your own foolish choices."

I open my mouth to rebuke that but shut my mouth into a tight line. Because she's right. She's pure evil. She was in the wrong, she persuaded me to continue by telling me the lies I most wanted to hear, but I am the one who asked for it. I am the one who made the choice in the end. I've known that too, of course I have, and I've hated myself for it. That's why this mistake has weighed so heavily on my soul, because I know that in the end, I am the one to blame.

I close my eyes, remembering Ramsay's words, that we don't make mistakes but choices that lead us on a different path. This is the path I chose. But it's not the one I have to stay on.

"What are you thinking, I wonder?" she muses and I open my eyes to find her gone. A shadow passes over and I look up to see her swimming above me, moving like a shark, the sun a faint glimmer behind her. Before my eyes her legs come together and turn a smooth seamless white, a shark's tail at the end.

"Are you envious of what I can do?" she says, swimming down now and circling around me. Now she's no longer Edonia but a great white shark, a ferocious-looking beast with her red eyes. "Do I remind you of your friend?"

She doesn't. Nill was smaller and a smooth bronze-gray color with long rounded fins, the tips bright white like they'd been dipped in paint.

"Do you wish that you could do as I do?" she asks idly and in a moment she transforms back into herself, though her teeth still look like they belong to a shark. Her eyes go to my necklace. "You kept it throughout the years. Every time you touched it I hope it reminded you of what you lost."

"What I lost doesn't exist anymore," I tell her stiffly. "My sisters are gone, my mother, my father. I don't know who is left in Limonos."

"Oh, well I could fill you in on all the gossip," she says gleefully, placing her hands together. "Asherah went across the Pacific while I believe Larimar might have gone south to the poles. Your sisters left after your father died of a broken heart, all because of you. With them gone, there was no one left to rule the kingdom and they all," she gestures with her hands, making the eels in her hair twitch, "scattered. All the Syrens left Limonos. Now it's a barren sea surrounded by barren land. Amazing isn't it, what one girl's selfishness can do?"

I glare at her. "I'm tired of feeling badly for my choices."

She gives me a mock sympathetic look, pouting. "Oh, I bet you are. Isn't that why you're here?"

"You had your Kraken pull me down here!"

She wags her finger at me. "Only because I know that's why you came all this way. Everything led you right to me, just as you wanted. It's destiny, dear. And now, I will be so gracious as to grant you your wish and reverse the spell. Don't say I never do you any favors."

She gestures to the sand with a wriggle of her fingers and the grains starts to rise and swirl like a maelstrom, around and around, until a book surfaces out of it, a worn leatherbound manual, the pages flipping as it comes through the water.

"That's Ramsay's book," I say.

"Yes. The one his *wife* wrote for him," she says, an edge to her voice. "I knew Venla was a traitor to her kind when she married that bloodsucker, yet I didn't think she'd go so far as to write a book of magic for him so that he could learn the spells and use them for himself." Her eyes narrow into crimson slits. "Our magic is for witches only. We don't share with humans, and we especially don't share with the Brethren. They're our one true enemy, gracious, we don't give them the only weapons we have! That's punishable by death."

I stare at her, aghast. "You didn't kill Venla, did you?"

"I didn't," she says with a raise of her pointed chin. "I wanted to, but she was still my sister. Half of her was, anyway."

"You killed his daughter though," I glower.

She smiles coldly. "I did. I wanted the book. That book didn't belong in his hands, it belonged in mine. Killing Ramsay's little girl was a distraction. Besides, she would have grown up to be half-witch and half-bloodsucker and the world doesn't need the likes of that. There are too many Brethren now as it is. The world is becoming uneven."

She sighs, giving her head a shake, and the eels sigh with her. Then she tilts her head to face me and fixes me with a satisfied eye. "But now the book is in the right hands, my hands, and with it I will transform you back into what you desire."

I find myself shaking my head, my pulse quickening. "No," I say, swallowing hard. "No, I don't want that anymore."

She stares at me, eyes rounding. "You don't want what anymore?"

"I don't want to return to my full Syren state," I tell her, feeling conviction for the first time. "I want to stay as I am."

"A monster who dwells on land," she says with contempt.

"Who is in love with another land-dwelling monster," I say boldly. "Ramsay and I are the same. He is my blood and I am his. I won't return to this world if I can't be with him in it."

Her expression turns even more venomous, enough that I get chills. "Even though he's the reason your whole world crumbled to begin with?"

I frown. Her words put me on edge. "What do you mean?"

"Life is made up of sequences, darling. Your mother was taken from you, which meant your father ignored you because of his grief. So you left him behind for good, which killed him in the end. With no queen and no king and no princesses left to rule Limonos, the kingdom crumbled. And you're turning your back on it again because you say you've fallen in love with the very man who captured your mother."

It sounds like the world goes deathly quiet for a moment. I don't even hear my own heart.

"What?" I whisper harshly, my chest filling with ice.

"You heard me," she says. "Ramsay captured your mother and killed her. That's what they do. Those pirates, those Brethren. They love their mermaid blood. You might think that they'll view you as crew, perhaps even a new family for you to call your own, but in the end they just want to use you and discard you. They did the same to your mother and they'll do the same to you. You're just fish to them."

"No," I say, shaking my head. "I refuse to believe that."

"Fine," she says, staring at her nails. "But tell me why you've never found who took her. Ramsay is no idiot. Not entirely. He knows that the truth would ruin what trust he's built up between you."

I keep shaking my head, not wanting to let the words sink in. It can't be true.

"No. No, I asked him if he had ever taken a mermaid who was a mother," I manage to say.

"And what was his answer?"

Not that I know of. That's what he said. It wasn't a lie. He didn't even know I was a Syren at the time.

"I see," she says, reading my face. "No matter. What's done is done and you're lucky that I'm on your side."

Her hand shoots out and the book that's been floating in the water comes straight over to it, the pages flipping until she holds the tome in her hand and stabs the pages with her finger.

"Ah, here we go. How to reverse a spell," she says. "Though I should let you know that there are costs that come with this reversal. They're necessary so that I don't spend all my days undoing what is asked of me. The cost of doing business, as they say. Though perhaps it would be better to tear out the page entirely."

"What costs?" I ask, then I shake my head. "No, I don't want it, it doesn't matter."

"The cost," she goes on, tearing the page out from the book, "is that you will get your fins back, like you never lost anything at all. You will return to the way you were in every way possible. Isn't that what you've wanted? These last ten years, isn't a return to the girl that you were, isn't that all you dreamed of and wished for?"

"It was," I admit, my heart hammering in my chest. "But I don't think I can go back to her. I don't think I want to."

"Oh you do. You know you do deep down. And I will give you that. A return to yourself in all ways...all except one."

"Which is?"

"I remain in possession of your soul."

"You never had my soul to begin with!" I tell her. True, I often thought and said I sold my soul to her but that was always just a figure of speech.

Wasn't it?

She gives me a dry look. "Semantics, my dear. But I will thoroughly possess it now."

And at that she waves her fingers at me, ink shooting out from her palms and making the world go black.

THIRTY-NINE

Ramsay

One moment I'm staring at Sam as the Kraken stabs the heart right out from her, the blood of a fellow Brethren spilling onto the deck.

The next moment I'm watching as the Kraken grabs Maren like a hook, hauling her off the ship and into the air.

I'm moving toward her before my mind has a chance to catch up, racing with my broadsword drawn, ready to slice the Kraken's tentacle in half and free my love, but the tentacle retreats back into the sea, taking Maren with it.

"Maren!" I scream, watching as they disappear into the deep, waves closing over them.

"Ramsay," Cruz says to me, his voice low and poignant. I turn to see Thane on his knees with Sam's head in his lap, the blood spreading out from under her like an opening rose. She stares up at the sky, lifeless, gone.

For a moment I don't know what to do. The Kraken—I'm assuming there are more than one of them now—is attacking the other side of the ship still, its tentacles smashing the *Nightwind* in places, though its movements are weak and sloppy, and Lothar and Matisse are working hard with their swords to keep it at bay.

Sam Battista is dead, my dearest sister-in-law, my brother's beloved wife, and I know he's in such immense shock and pain that there is no coming back from this, not for a very long time. I've been there, I know the journey that lies ahead.

And I know I can't do anything for him. Just as no one could do anything for my losses. I can't do anything but avenge Sam's death now, as well as Hilla's, and go and get Maren before she becomes like them too.

"I will get our justice, brother," I announce to Thane, holding up my sword. "I give you my word."

He looks up at me, tears streaming down his anguished face, and my heart breaks with the loss. He nods.

I don't wish to abandon my crew, but Maren needs me and it seems like everyone is holding their own, thanks to her blood. I am eternally grateful that she decided to go against my wishes and follow her own will. I will never try and prevent that again, though even if I did, she still wouldn't let me. One of the things that I love most about her is her tenacity.

If she's even alive, I think and the idea strikes me to the core.

I go to the railing and climb up about to dive over into the sea with my sword.

"Bones!" I turn to see a seagull flying in the air toward me, a seagull I'm fairly certain just called out my name. I frown. Perhaps it's normal to hallucinate at a time like this.

"I'm going with you," the seagull says and right before my eyes it sails over my head and then shifts into the curved brown body of Nerissa, diving straight into the water without even a splash.

Just then the Kraken strikes the ship again, making it shudder and knocking me off-balance so I fall into the ocean too.

I land with a splash, nearly losing my grip on the sword and I start kicking down after Nerissa, following her kelp-like hair that glitters a lighter green in the dappled water. She's fast, a natural at this, but because of Maren's blood I have all the energy and strength in the world and I'm able to keep pace with her.

Down we go, into the drowning deep, until Nerissa suddenly

reaches out and grabs my arm, pulling me to the side in another direction.

This way, she says inside my head.

How do you know? I ask. All of the ocean looks the same from here.

Because I do, she says. *I know my sister.*

I swallow hard. *So it is her. Not just the Kraken.*

Of course it's her. The Kraken are just creatures under her spell. She controls them, and I'm afraid right now that she may be controlling Maren.

That's impossible, I think. *No one controls Maren. She's one hundred percent her own woman.*

And so is a sea witch, she reminds me. *Come now, see the edge of the cliff there? It will give us coverage.*

I stare down at the dark red and gray reef that's built up along the top of a bank, the side of it giving away to the abyss. I swallow uneasily, hating the fear that the darkness of the ocean gives me. It seems a silly thing when you're a sailor, when you're afraid of the deep, but it's not something I think about until I'm staring face-to-face with it. The seafloor drops off so steeply that it's dizzying, as if I'm about to get sucked in and fall forever into the great below, so many monsters hidden in these dark depths.

But the monster I need to face the most is Edonia, so I follow Nerissa as we swim along a narrow canyon created by the reef, my broadsword heavy but gripped tightly in my hand.

We swim like this for a while, passing by fish of different colors, barracudas, even a few dolphins who eye us curiously from afar, when suddenly Nerissa pulls us to a stop and ducks behind a tall mound of coral.

This is where I leave you for now, she tells me, her eyes flashing darkly. *You need to deal with my sister alone.*

I nod, not wanting her help anyway. *This is between me and Edonia, no one else.* I brandish my sword, even though it moves far too sluggishly through the water. *Any words of advice?*

She's a liar, she says emphatically, her kelp hair swirling around her bronzed face. *She'll have told Maren lies to get what she wants. Whether what she really wants is you or Maren, you can't believe a word out of her mouth. Just know that no matter what's happened to Maren, it doesn't have to be that way. You get the book and you can change things.*

The book. Of course she would still have that blasted book.

I give Nerissa a final hard look and then I swim off, continuing along the canyon until I hear a beautiful unearthly voice echoing through the water. It's a haunting song, high and as transparent as glass and from the way it stirs something in me, a longing, a dizziness, a sharp lance right into my soul, I know it's no ordinary song. It's a Syren's song. Maren's stolen song. And by the grace of god, perhaps the grace of Maren for letting me have her blood, I am able to remain invulnerable to it.

At least I know I'm on the right path and it's not long before I see the Kraken, its dark massive size stretching outward, seeming to blend with the abyss behind it, its yellow eyes especially piercing.

In front of the Kraken is Edonia, looking much more impressive than I remember her being. Her white hair wriggles around her, and the longer I look at it the more I realize it's made of shimmering eels. Around her neck is a necklace on a chain of tiny bones and hanging from it is a small potion bottle with purple smoke swirling inside.

And beside her is Maren.

I stop swimming. My mouth drops open, water filling it as I gawk at her in awe.

Maren is upright in front of me, no longer just a woman but a god damn Syren. From the top she looks the same, with her long black hair flowing with the current, her full breasts, her stays and her undergarments that she's been wearing as a dress.

And beneath the torn hem of her skirt protrudes a gloriously long and powerful fish tail, the scales a shimmering teal that taper into shades of purple near the fin, the color shifting when it catches the light.

With her teeth and her claws and that stunning tail and her

gorgeous face she looks like a dream and a nightmare all at once, a creature torn between a goddess and the devil.

"God Almighty," I swear, bubbles rising from my mouth. "You are the most stunning monster I have ever seen."

She's also on a leash, a collar of writhing fishbones around her neck, the rope leading back to Edonia. The expression on Maren's face could be made of stone.

"Maren and I have made a new deal," Edonia says. "She wanted so badly to return to her life under water, and I was feeling gracious enough to grant her the request."

My heart sinks at that. I stare at Maren, trying to get her to see me, really see me, but her eyes are so blank and indifferent. *Did you still want this after all?* I think to her. *Did you choose this in the end and not me?*

"Naturally, it came at a cost, and well, she belongs to me now," Edonia drones on. "Isn't she a feral little pet? Like a wolf turned into a guard dog."

"Maren isn't a pet," I grind out, my hand flexing over the sword's hilt. "She deserves to be set free."

She shrugs. "Perhaps." Then she raises her arm and the Kraken reaches forward with one of its tentacles and places a book into her hands.

And it's not just any book. I'd know that leatherbound tome anywhere. I've been looking for it for twenty-two years.

"You have a choice Ramsay. Either you take this monster as she is, or you take the book." She wriggles the leash with one hand and raises the book with the other. "It's your choice."

I think about what Nerissa said. About how Edonia lies. If I choose the book, there's no chance that she'd actually let me have it, especially as I could undo the spell and set Maren free. There's also no telling what she'd do to Maren.

I stare at the book, remembering how Venla spent hours writing in it in her quarters, the same quarters that Maren has taken up in. She'd sit at her desk and craft me all the spells she thought would be useful for a Brethren, even ones she just thought were fanciful. She thought a book of magic would be a way to unite both of our kinds, to show the hidden world that unity and understanding can be found in the most unlikely of places.

When Edonia first took that book from me, it was all I'd wanted since. I couldn't bring Hilla back, but that book was a tangible thing that could survive through time and it was something that once belonged to me and should belong to me again. It was my possession and I'm very passionate when it comes to my possessions.

But I finally realize now that getting the book back in my hands won't bring anything back. It won't give me my daughter again. The only thing it could give me now is Maren. And Maren is the only thing I want. Other than that, the book is the past.

I have to let the past go.

"I choose Maren," I tell Edonia. "I still choose her."

"She's a monster, Ramsay," Edonia spits out the words, her eyes flashing with anger at my choice. "She's a ferocious creature of the deep."

"Aye," I say firmly. "And I don't love her in spite of it. I love her because of it."

"You are about to make a grave mistake," she glowers.

I lift one shoulder. "It's just a book."

Her nostrils flare and she sneers. "Fine! Your choice will be your last." She yanks back the rope until the fish bones around Maren's neck break apart and Maren is suddenly loose. "Bring me his heart, my pet," Edonia coos.

Maren comes at me with a savage roar, teeth bared, claws out, her tail propelling her so fast that she's just a blur. Even with my lightning quick reflexes I barely have enough time to drop the sword and reach for her arms, grabbing her at the wrists.

She lets out a high-pitched scream that sends shockwaves through the ocean and then I'm flying back down against the sand and she's above me, snapping ferociously with her teeth.

"Hello, luv," I grin up at her. "Am I ever glad to see you."

However she is not glad to see me.

She snarls and writhes and she's strong, she's so terrible and so strong and she's pushing me back deeper into the sand, the sand starting to fill in around me, burying me. She wildly claws at the water, her wrists snapping back and forth, and it takes all my strength to hold her back. Even so, she's pushing me down so I sink even further, the sand now covering my torso and my arms are starting to shake from the strain, my hands sore from gripping her forearms in order to keep her claws away from me.

"Maren," I manage to say. "You don't remember me do you?"

"Oh she does," Edonia says smugly, watching the whole thing. "She's not completely deranged. I just told her that you murdered her mother, so she's particularly angry. Her rage is a blessed thing."

"Her mother!?" I exclaim, staring up into Maren's eyes. They're all white now, the blue faded, and I don't even know if I see her soul in there. "Maren, I didn't kill your mother." What in god's good name is she even talking about?

"Something you'd have a hard time keeping track of, I have no doubt," Edonia says mildly.

"Maren," I repeat, her claws now touching my shirt and tearing through the fibers, millimeters away from piercing my chest. "I swear to god I didn't kill your mother."

But when I stare in those eyes I know she doesn't hear me. Because I'm realizing her soul, that ferociously stunning complicated soul that I've grown to love, it isn't there. It's as if this isn't her at all. All she is, is her rage personified.

"What have you done with her!?" I cry out, turning my head to look at Edonia as I sink deeper into the sand. "This isn't my Maren."

"It's just the shell of her, but that's all a man wants from a woman anyway," she says, and she touches the bottle around her neck, the purple smoke swirling inside of it. "I'm keeping her soul safe, right here."

I look back to Maren in horror. Her body is being used to kill me while her soul is in Edonia's necklace, perhaps watching the whole thing.

"No," I tell her, pleading. "No, don't do this. Maren, luv, princess, I know you can hear me."

But her claws are now piercing my skin, stinging me, the blood rising up in the water and Edonia is laughing and laughing, about to watch my heart get ripped out and eaten right in front of me by the woman I love.

And then Edonia's laughter stops.

Maren keeps digging her claws in me, not tiring in the least, but I turn my head as the sand starts to spill over my neck and look to the sea witch.

There's another sea witch behind her, holding the book in her hands.

"What are you doing here?" Edonia cries out when she sees her.

"Righting some wrongs," Nerissa says to her and then opens the book and begins to read in Latin.

Edonia cries out, "No!" and lunges for the book, but a pack of barracudas come out from behind Nerissa and fire into Edonia like bullets, peppering her body with sharp stabs of their mouths, keeping her at bay.

"Maren animam tuam liberabo!" Nerissa shouts hastily, snapping her fingers.

Edonia lets out a panicked scream, trying to grab her necklace but one of the barracudas snatches it in its mouth and it dangles from its jagged teeth as it brings it over to Nerissa.

With Maren still trying to kill me—I can feel her claws wrapping around my heart, ready to rip it out—Nerissa quickly takes the necklace and uncorks the tiny bottle, the purple smoke turning to liquid and leaving the vessel, heading straight for Maren.

"Hang on Bones!" Nerissa yells at me.

"Not as easy as you think," I manage to say, gasping in agony as I feel the tips of Maren's claws graze the wall of my heart.

I'm not prepared to meet my end.

FORTY

Maren

I'm about to rip Ramsay's heart out.

I had watched the scene unfurl from the captivity of Edonia's bottle, trapped for what was supposed to be an eternity, unable to do a damn thing about it. I watched as Ramsay showed up, swimming out of the reef like a knight in shining armor, his broadsword at his side, stark determination on his handsome face, and I'd never felt more in love with him than I was in that moment. I knew the things that Edonia told me about him killing my mother could have been true. I knew that Ramsay has had a ruthless past when it comes to killing people, Syrens or otherwise. But at that moment, none of that mattered. I loved him, truly, madly, deeply.

But the body of the creature I was, the one that Edonia controlled, was fueled by my rage and for the first time in my life, I became separate from that inferno that always bubbled inside me. I was able to watch my rage as something else, something I couldn't control, and I realized that it should never be separated. My rage is a part of who I am, not something to bury and not something to blindly let loose either. It's something to make peace with, a part of being human.

And yet in those moments, all I wanted was to rein it in. It looked like the mindless killer that Edonia created, the product of my own rage unfettered, was about to pull Ramsay's heart out of his chest and eat it.

Then Nerissa appeared, taking the book from Edonia when she wasn't looking, when she was too focused on Ramsay's demise, and she recited the words that set my soul free.

But now, back in my Syren body, I'm horrified that it might be too late. Ramsay is beneath me, staring up at my face in agony, blood rising up from the wounds I've created, my claws sunken in all the way through his chest, ready to pull out his heart and...

In an instant I soften. Love softens me. My claws dissolve back into nails, my teeth dull, and the rage that was driving me thaws to where I'm able to wrestle it aside.

"Ramsay!" I cry out, removing my fingers from the gaping wounds I created in his chest. I stare down at my fingers, my breath catching, as I make sure his heart is still where it belongs. There's only his blood on my hands, nothing else.

He lets go of my arms and then grabs my face, pulling me down toward him. He kisses me with desperation, holding me against him so tight that I can't move.

"I'm sorry I tried to kill you," I manage to say, pulling away, my lips moving against his.

He grins, that beautiful, utterly handsome grin, letting out a burst of laughter that escapes into bubbles. "If I have to go, I'd rather it be by your hands, my luv."

I kiss him again, then I hear a growl that echoes through the water and snaps us out of our reunion. I straighten up, then pull Ramsay out of the sand.

Nerissa and Edonia are grappling with each other, their hands around each other's necks as they roll along the sand, plumes of silt rising up around them. Barracudas dive and peck at Edonia, drawing blood and pulling at the eels in her hair, while the Kraken has a tentacle wrapped around Nerissa's legs, trying to yank her away.

"I still want my vengeance," Ramsay says with a growl. He picks up his broadsword, turning it over in his hand, and stalks over to the battling witches.

"Step aside, Nerissa," he commands, sword raised. "Edonia's death is mine."

Nerissa cries out and with a final burst of strength she manages to flip Edonia over on her back and then lets go of her, allowing the Kraken pull her backward through the water, the bottle necklace still in her grasp, while another tentacle is holding onto the notorious book.

Nerissa and the Kraken disappear from sight, swallowed by the deep blue, and I want to swim after her, to help keep her from being torn limb from limb by the tentacled beast but Ramsay is my only focus now.

Ramsay who takes the broadsword and holds it above Edonia's heart as she screams beneath him.

"You will never not be a monster!" she yells, teeth bared, ugliness personified.

Before she can duck out of the way, Ramsay pushes the sword down, piercing it through her heart.

"Then so be it," he says, twisting the sword with emphasis.

Edonia's scream makes the water ripple, flowing outward, all the fish and creatures swimming away from her in a hurry. She keeps screaming, blood filling the water, until the last pearlescent eel on her head stops writhing.

All is still.

The witch is dead.

Ramsay pushes the sword in further with a grunt, until she's impaled even deeper into the sand.

Now she's exceptionally dead.

Then he's throwing the sword to the side and swimming over to me.

"Maren," he whispers, pulling me right into his arms again. "It's over, my luv. It's over."

But I can only shake my head, my whole body starting to tremble. "It's not over, Ramsay," I say, my voice broken. "Look at me. *Look* at me."

He lets go and steps back, his gaze raking over me and I don't think

I've ever felt so worshipped and adored. "I'm looking at you, Maren. And I'm in love with what I see."

"I'm a *Syren*," I cry out softly. "Don't you know what this means? I can't be turned back to a human again. The spell was reversed. I'm stuck like this."

He frowns, his eyes sliding over me again, taking in the width and length of my tail. "Is this not what you wanted?"

I shake my head. "I didn't choose this, Ramsay. Edonia pulled me down here."

"I saw," he says grimly.

"I told her I didn't want my fins back but she did it anyway. She reversed the spell and then said my soul belonged to her forever."

"The last part isn't true," he says, taking my hand and holding it tight. "Your soul is yours. You are free."

"But not if I'm like this," I cry out softly. "I spent so long wanting this and then I realized what I had wanted all along was *you*. It was always you, Ramsay. From the very beginning I wanted to be heard and understood and seen, and you *see* me. You see me for all that I am, princess, pirate, monster, Syren, whatever I am, it doesn't matter. You see me and somehow, no matter what…you actually love me."

"Of course I love you," he says, his dusky eyes searching mine intently. "You're bloody impossible not to love."

His words break me, shattering like glass. I close my eyes and try to wrestle with the hopelessness of the situation. "Except now I'm doomed to live my life in the water, never to go on land, never to be on the *Nightwind* at your side."

"It doesn't matter, cearban. I will live down here with you."

I blink at him, my chin jerking inward. "You can't be serious. You can't give up a life on land for this one. I don't care that you don't need to breathe much, this isn't your world."

"I will make it my world," he says gruffly, hand at my face now, finger-tips pressing into my cheekbone. "Aye? I will make it my world for you."

"I can't ask you to do that."

"And I'm not taking direction either," he says. "You are the choice

I'm making. Besides, what good is being a pirate when I've already got the treasure?" He gives me a crooked grin.

"I'm serious," I tell him.

"So am I," he says, running his thumb over my lips. "We will make it work somehow."

But I don't see how we can. He's one of the Brethren, he can't live a life under the water with me, even if drowning is impossible. More than that, I don't want him to give up his ship or his family. What I want is to have my legs back, to go up to the *Nightwind* and keep the life I had. I never realized how much I liked being part of his crew, part of his life, until it was taken from me.

I gaze at him, sorrow wracking through me. I understand all that he's been saying, but this still feels like goodbye. I'm not ready to say goodbye.

He reaches out and gently trails his fingers over the smooth scales at the side of my tail. "My brand," he says quietly. "It's gone."

I glance down. He's right. There's no trace of the jolly roger with his initials inside. That mark had become one of my favorite parts of my body.

"It doesn't matter," I tell him. "It's still there, even if you can't see it. You've branded my heart, Ramsay."

You've claimed me for life.

"Kiss me," I whisper. "Lay with me. I want to feel you from the inside."

His eyes widen and he looks down at my new body, his hand going up to my waist while the other cups my jaw. He kisses me deeply, a kiss that seems to take a hold of my heart and squeeze it, making my fins twitch.

He pulls apart, confusion in his eyes. "I'll admit, my luv, that I am not a hundred percent certain how this course of action could, well, happen."

I'm relieved that he doesn't, to be honest. That would mean he's lain with a Syren before. Yet I'm not entirely sure either, given that as a Syren I had never bedded anyone. But I am still familiar with this body, even though it's an adult one now, and I know what part of me aches for him, where I need him in deep.

"I'll show you," I whisper, feeling both nervous and emboldened. I'm finally the one showing something to him for the first time instead of the other way around.

I lie back on the sand staring up at the surface that looks a million miles away. I'm aware that Edonia's dead body is nearby, that the fish are already making quick work of her as she's tethered by the sword. I know that elsewhere there is sorrow on the *Nightwind* with the death of Sam, and there's sorrow in my heart too for her. I know that Nerissa has been dragged by the Kraken into the deep and I might never see her again.

But for all that is happening elsewhere, my mind and heart are here with him. My body is especially here with him.

If he'll have me like this, in my complete Syren form, I think with trepidation.

There's a chance he won't want me at all. That he'll think I'm too strange and different in this form.

But from the heated look in his gaze, the way he's swimming over me, pinning my wrists over my head with one hand, undoing the flap on his breeches with the other, I know my worries might be unfounded.

"You're beautiful, Maren," he says to me, leaning in to give me a deep, fin-curling kiss. I look down to see him bring his thick hard cock out, his obvious desire for me on display, and I soften with relief.

Then he glances down, hesitating. From the way the iridescent scales of my tail all come together, you wouldn't really know where my womanhood is. It's fairly invisible at first glance.

So I reach down and his gaze is glued to my hand as it slides over my torso and down over the start of my tail until I'm a quarter of the way down, at more or less the same place where my legs would come together.

Slowly I slide my finger along the scales, parting them, the sensation already slippery and then my finger dips down inside to where I'm hot and slick.

I gasp, the sensation so incredibly new to me, like I'm being touched this way for the very first time, and my back arches on the ocean floor. I let out a moan, the bubbles rising to the surface above, and I'm lost to my own touch already.

"Lord help me," Ramsay says, his voice raw with lust.

At that he pushes his cock inside me, sliding in past my fingers and I'm so impossibly tight, even more so than on land, that I let out a holler that fills the sea. His cock doesn't seem like it'll fit, but then I'm so slick and he's thrusting in to the hilt, my back is being fused to the sand.

"Oh gods," I cry.

I try to move my hands to grip him, wanting to feel those tight muscles of his arms, of his shoulders, of his back, hold on to this man that I would do anything for. But he has my wrists pinned and he's fucking me so hard and deep that my brain is rattled, foggy, and I'm swept away by sensations that are both familiar and foreign. I've never had a man like this, never had Ramsay like this, and it's like sleeping with him for the first time. Every slide of his cock, every touch of his fingers on my breast, of his lips on my neck, and I feel like I'm some land being discovered.

I feel conquered.

And he's staring down at me with such rapt focus, watching my face for each gasp I make, each time my eyes roll back, each time I arch my neck, that I've never felt so idolized and studied before. It's like he's committing me to memory with every hard shove of his hips.

Perhaps he is. Perhaps he knows that this is all we have left. That there can't be anything more for us. Two monsters who belong to two different worlds being put back in their proper places. He, the king of the high seas, me the queen of the world below.

Except now I'm a queen without a kingdom.

And I'll soon be a queen without her king.

"Stay with me," he whispers, nostrils flaring as he tries to rein himself in. "Be with me here and now, luv."

I nod and let out a low moan as his hips circle in just the right way, bringing my thoughts back to him, back to this moment, where he's so deep inside that it's hard to imagine ever being without him.

It's not long before that focus in him starts to waver, the look in his eyes being replaced by the equally intense look of wild abandon. He looks like a feral man, moves like a savage creature, fucks me like an absolute monster.

"Ramsay!" I cry out, my orgasm coming for me like the tides, getting closer and closer.

"Come for me, my beautiful creature," he grunts, thrusting his impossibly hard cock in quick shallow movements before driving in deep enough to make me scream.

"Oh gods. Oh my gods." My chest is tight and hot and I feel like if I let go, I'll let go of him forever, and I'm trying to hold on harder and harder.

But he just feels too good and he's too good at uncovering my feelings, like shells revealed beneath the sand.

I cry out, my hips bucking up to meet him and I'm spiraling out of control, my body convulsing as the climax rocks through me, shaking me to my core. I feel this howling creature inside of me, one that wants to claim him in every way possible, wants to keep him inside her forever.

He succumbs soon after. The determination in his brow cracks and I watch as his orgasm rips through him, rendering my strong man into something soft and free. A heavy gasp escapes his open mouth, his neck taut with the final push of his hips, his muscles shaking from the strain of thoroughly bedding me under water, and then he stills. He falls against me, just for a moment before the buoyancy of the water lifts him off me so that we're barely touching.

"Maren," he says softly, reaching down to touch my cheek. "That was—"

"Incredible?" I fill in but as I do so a wave of emotions comes crashing over me, wanting to drown me in the deep fear of what's next for us. I press my lips together, willing myself not to cry and I look past him to the surface, unable to look at the adoring expression on Ramsay's face.

But as I look I notice something.

High on the surface a ship plows through the water.

Then there's another one to the left of it, and another one to the right, and then behind, and they're all heading in the direction of the *Nightwind*.

"Ramsay," I whisper, and it takes him a moment to raise his head and look up.

"Oh, bloody hell," he says. "It's the Royal Navy."

FORTY-ONE

Maren

"The Royal Navy?" I repeat as he pulls himself out of me. "Are you certain? How can you tell from down here?"

"Well I ain't certain," he says, giving me a furtive look as he tucks his cock back in his breeches. "But when you see ships of the line like that and moving at that speed, I'd wager that's what they are. At any rate, I have to return to the *Nightwind*."

"I'll take you," I tell him, "You won't be able to swim as fast as those ships, but I can."

He gives me a wry smile. "Are you sure you don't have dolphins we can ride?"

I manage to laugh at that. He doesn't know what bastards dolphins actually are. "I'm faster than a dolphin." I hold out my hand for him. "Come on. I'll show you."

"You've already shown me a great deal, luv," he says. "I'm not sure how much more I can take."

"Really? Here I was thinking you were able to handle me."

"Oh, I can handle you," he says gruffly, his brows coming together.

"We'll see," I say and I start swimming, my tail moving as fast as it will go and I'm holding on tight to his hand, yanking him along through the water.

"Christ!" he swears, his words drowned in the water as I speed him along. I haven't swam like this in a decade but it's like second nature. I reach top speeds fast and it comes so easily to me that I'm actually smiling as I go, delighting in the feeling of being so lithe and nimble. While I love being above the water on two legs, I'll never have the balance or the coordination in my legs to be especially graceful. But here in the deep, with the body I was born with, I take great joy in movement. It is the one thing I'll be grateful for in this new life underwater.

But I push those thoughts out of my head before I have time to dwell on them. Right now, the crew of the *Nightwind* are potentially in trouble, and whether it's the Royal Navy or a galleon fleet that are heading in their direction, the pirate ship will be a sitting duck.

It's when we get closer to them that the navy ships start to slow and we see the looming shape of the *Nightwind* further down. It has turned broadside, ready to fire against their attackers and taking the defensive position.

"What are they doing?" Ramsay exclaims, his voice becoming clear as I slow down. "The *Nightwind* needs to outrun them! They'll never survive an attack like this."

I glance back at him, terror dawning on me. "You're not there. You're the wind in the sails, Ramsay. You're not on the ship."

His eyes widen and I start swimming again pulling him with me until we're breaking through the surface at the aft of the *Nightwind*, out of the way of the battle. The *Nightwind* has taken its first shots at the nearest navy ship, splinters of the boat falling into the water, but then it's seconds later and the navy is firing back, a BOOM BOOM filling the air, smoke rising.

"I need to get up there," Ramsay yells over the noise as he stares up at the sides of the *Nightwind*, gasping for breath as we tread water. "We need to get the ship moving."

I gulp, unsure of what I'm supposed to do.

"I'll come back for you," he tells me, pulling me to him and holding my face in his hands. "I promise I'll come back for you."

I nod and he kisses me hard. "I'll be here," I tell him, trying to sound brave.

But what if you can't find me? What if I can't find you?

The ocean is too large, too deep, and now too dark.

His expression crumbles for a moment as he looks at me, perhaps wondering the same things that I am. "I love you, don't forget that."

I swallow the tears in my throat. "I love you." I nod up at the ship. "Go protect your crew. I'll help in any way that I can."

He nods curtly and then starts swimming for the ship. He brings two marlinespikes out from his holster and starts stabbing them into the sides of the wood, climbing up the ship that way, until he reaches an open gun port and crawls in.

I watch, not sure what to do. The *Nightwind* and the closest navy ship are still firing at each other, the navy ship taking on far more damage. The constant boom of the roundshots deafen my ears and the smoke gets thicker.

But as the smoke parts I notice that on the deck of that navy ship is a silhouette that looks verily familiar.

A cold pang stabs my gut, followed by the heat of anger.

Captain Ed Smith.

The bastard that Sedge shot in the face survived and he's come back to finish the *Nightwind*, this time with the rest of his company.

I can't just leave now. Even if the *Nightwind* sails away, I need to do something to this man. This man deserves an awful death and I want to be the one to give it to him. After all, I'm already quite good at it.

I dive under the water and start swimming to his ship until I'm right under it, trying to figure out if there's a weakness. Perhaps if I tried hard enough I could pull off the planks from the hull. After all, everyone on the ship is only three or four inches from death.

I swim up until my hands are running over the planks. Unfortunately they're coated with tar as waterproofing, with barnacles making their home there too. My claws extend and I start trying to pry them off, but even with my strength as a Syren they don't budge.

Maybe if I start at another part, I think and while I'm swimming along I hear a splash into the water.

I look over to see a naval man has fallen in and is attempting to swim. He's not very good at it, barely able to keep above the surface.

I grin to myself and slowly swim over to him.

I poke my head up right beside his, giving him an awful fright.

"Hello there," I say to him.

"Hello?" he says, spitting out water, his wig floating beside him. "How did…Who are…?"

He glances down into the water and sees my tail flash in the sunlight.

He gasps, his eyes wide. "Mermaid," he cries out, starting to thrash in the waves.

"Syren," I correct him.

Then I lunge.

I bite into his neck while my claws start tearing at the rest of him. Blood fills the water and he chokes on his screams and I start ripping him apart, swiftly removing his organs, eating my way through his liver, his kidney, and finally his heart.

Then I let him go and he starts to sink in the blood, and I should be satisfied by having eaten so much of him but I'm still ravenous.

I wait, circling below the ship like a shark, just by the curve of the hull so I'm not spotted, though from here I have a clear view of the *Nightwind*. I see Ramsay on deck, who has clearly spotted Captain Smith, and instead of the ship turning tail and leaving with the wind, it's staying in place. No doubt Ramsay wants his final piece of revenge.

I want it too.

I get started by tearing apart every naval man that falls into the sea from the cannon explosions. I rip them limb from limb. I shred their skin, remove their organs, and at this point I'm just tossing them aside as fish food because I've had my fair share and I'm saving my appetite for one man.

But now that the *Nightwind* isn't leaving, the other naval ships close in, coming around the pirate ship from all directions. I'm enjoying being a predator, but in the end I'm not helping much, just killing those who would probably die anyway.

I wish there was something more I could do.

"Maren."

I gasp and whirl around to see Nerissa treading water behind me.

"You're alive," I gasp.

"You have blood on your mouth," she notes, a sly smile.

I quickly run my hand across my lips. "I'm so happy to see you. I thought you were gone. I thought the Kraken would have torn you apart."

Her smile deepens as her kelp hair flows in the water around her. "The Kraken are free, my child. Edonia is gone." She reaches into the waves and pulls out the bottle necklace around her neck, the one that my soul was kept in. Now there's green smoke swirling about. "Well, I suppose she's not too far gone."

I frown. "Is that…is that her soul?"

Nerissa gives me a haughty look. "She is my sister, after all. It would be unkind to leave her completely dead, wouldn't it? This way I can have her at my side for all time, and I'll never have to hear a word from her."

She looks back to the ships and the cannon fire, now coming from the others in the fleet. "Looks like your side might need some help," she says, nodding to the *Nightwind*.

"I'm not sure if that's my side anymore," I tell her. "I'm no longer part of their crew, if that wasn't obvious." I gesture down to my tail. "I'm no longer a part of their world."

She makes a tsking sound as she swims closer to me. The waves reflected in her copper eyes make them glow like the sun. "You, my dear," she says to me, placing her hands on both sides of my cheeks, "are one in a million. And you can make any world your own."

Then, while still holding onto my face, she starts reciting words in Latin, her eyes falling closed.

I don't want to interrupt what she's doing because I'm sure it's some sort of spell and I have to trust that she has my best interests at heart now, but at the same time the world is falling into chaos around us. The *Nightwind* is withstanding shot after shot, some of the round-shots penetrating clear into the hull, others are double-head and chain-shots that smash through the rigging, the foremast already having taken a beating from the Kraken. But the more the *Nightwind* takes, the more it seems like Brethren can't possibly win. There are cries and screams of pain and fright coming from the crew and I fear that more people than Sam may be dying today.

Finally, Nerissa opens her eyes and stares at me.

"You love him?"

"Love Ramsay?"

"Yes."

"I do. I love him with all my heart," I tell her, feeling my very heart swell.

"Then that is all you needed to say," she says.

Before I know what's happening, she's leaning in and kissing me lightly on the lips, the same way that we Syrens do with close kin.

"What was that for?" I ask when Nerissa pulls away, swimming backward.

She just does her usual devious smile. "You'll find out."

"I'll find out?" I repeat with a scoff. I gesture to the war happening in our midst, just as one of the naval men fall screaming toward the ocean, lit on fire. "Perhaps now is a good time."

"I will tell you one thing," she says to me. "You can control the Kraken."

Then she stares at me with gleaming eyes before her head disappears below the surface.

What on earth?

I duck my head under but Nerissa is swimming down, down and then she's just a barracuda, darting away into the shadows.

I burst back up through the waves and look around. I can control the Kraken now? Why would I want to do that?

Then it dawns on me.

I nearly squeal with giddiness and then dive back beneath the water. I swim deeper, in the same direction as Nerissa went, until I'm far enough away from the noise of the battle, the cannon balls sinking through the deep like lead.

I open my mouth and start singing my Syren song.

I start calling for the Kraken.

FORTY-TWO

Ramsay

There are times in a captain's life when he knows he has to make an important decision for the safety of the crew, a decision that may be at odds with what the crew wants. Other times the captain will have to make a choice that essentially picks the crew over any treasure or bounty that may be promised to him.

I've had to make two such decisions in a very short amount of time.

The moment I climbed up the *Nightwind* and stole back on board was one decision made. I had to leave Maren in the water to tend to the ship, to put the wind back in the sails. I knew she would be fine and safe in the ocean, that there was no fiercer creature than her in that wide endless sea. But I didn't know how and when I could return to her. I knew I would—I promised her I would—but there are so many unknowns that it breaks my heart to even think about it.

Then when I got on deck, much to the delight of the crew who thought I had abandoned them forever, or worse, thought I was dead, I had to make another choice. Because though it was easy to put the wind back in the ship's sails and retreat, that plan of action came to a halt when I realized *who* was on that other ship.

Captain Ed Smith.

Though he was far away, I could still make out his hawkish face, that revolting sneer of remorseless evil, and the injustice of it all started to claw at me from the inside out.

Here he was, having come back to finish the job, and this time he brought the naval fleet with him. He knew we were cornered.

He also figured I was such a selfish prick as to pick my vengeance over the safety of my crew. He didn't realize that being selfish isn't in my nature, not when I truly know what's at stake. I have made mistakes in the past, but I've learned from them. I was not going to stay and fight him no matter how hard he taunted me.

I was going to flee. Get the wind billowing and leave him and his fleet in my wake, sailing us to safety.

But while turning tail and getting the hell out of there was what I wanted, despite my need for justice, it turned out that my crew's need for vengeance was greater than mine. Well, perhaps not greater, but it certainly had more weight considering I was now the only one who wanted to leave the scene.

Everyone else wanted to fight, all of them emboldened by the driven vengeance of Thane and their love for Sam and Henry. They wanted to stay. They wanted revenge. Justice. They wanted Ed Smith to die at their hands.

And so I had to make a choice. Either I ignore my crew's wishes in order to keep them safe or I give them what they want while putting the lives of everyone on board at risk.

In the end, it's a democracy on this ship and the people have spoken.

We were to stay where we were and fight.

To the death.

"Crew of the *Nightwind*! I need you all to listen up, and listen well!" I bellow. Normally Thane would be giving some of these orders but from the way he's still cradling Sam's lifeless body, albeit moved out of the way of the action now, I decide to let him be. I just hope he knows to look out for himself, but even if he doesn't, I'll be sure to look out for him. Brothers will always have each other's backs.

"Cruz!" I bark. "Go to the swivel guns and clear the decks of those nearest ships over there. Matisse, you and Lothar keep picking them off with your muskets. Don't fire unless you get a clear shot."

"Aye, aye," they chime, scrambling in different directions.

"Bosun!" I yell, picking up a musket and tossing it to him. "Keep the boat steady, shoot when you can."

"Aye, cap'n," he says, catching the rifle and going back to the helm.

"Drakos!" I yell just as a roundshot blasts through the ship, causing a barrel of tar to explode and all of us to hit the decks. I cry out as my shoulder strikes the edge of an iron cleat, then I'm quickly getting to my feet to survey the damage. There is tar and oil everywhere, but the rigging still stands.

"Drakos!" I yell again and he appears beside me, panting, soot marks under his eyes. "Go down below and recruit Sedge, John, and Bart. Lucas needs to stay in his room in the center of the ship, but the other boys, it's time for them to play. Get them to help Remi and Horse, we need more cannons firing from both sides of the deck now."

"As you say it," Drakos complies and starts to run off.

"And when you're done, join Cruz at the swivel guns!" I yell after him.

He nods at that and disappears below deck.

I look around, trying to figure out the next move. Ed Smith is standing right over there, just a few yards from the ship, and while we're holding our own and pummeling the devil out of his ship, it's the other ships that have us in a chokehold. The *Nightwind* has never stayed in place and fought an entire fleet before. That's forty guns against hundreds and those ships are getting closer. No matter what we do, we'll never be able to outgun them.

We're not going to win this, I think, and the realization hurts like hell. I always thought that when my time came that I would make peace with it, but there is no peace here. I can't die at the hands of Ed Smith, I simply won't allow it. Normally there's always a way to escape for us Brethren since we're so particularly hard to kill. Humans assume they shoot or stab you and that's it. There was even a time when Cruz was captured and taken to the gallows, but he just played dead and when night fell and everyone was gone, he removed himself from the noose and walked away. Complained about a sore neck for a few days, but that was that.

But Ed Smith is one of us. He's the worst kind of Brethren and he knows exactly how to kill us. If we end up in his hands, each one of us is going to die a horrible death. He will make sure of it. He will torture us for days and he will torture me the most of all.

I'm just glad that Maren isn't here to see it. That she's safe in that ocean where she will remain the top predator. I just hope that by some small bit of luck that Smith might take a tumble into the sea. Then he'd surely be torn apart. Oh, how I wish that's something I could see.

"Looks like I'll be joining her soon."

I turn around to see Thane behind me, red-eyed and covered in his wife's blood. He nods at the ships. "There's no way we can survive this. Doesn't matter how blessed we are."

"We can always outrun them," I suggest. "We can always put wind in the sails."

"Aye," he says with a slow nod. "But don't you get tired of running sometimes?"

I sigh. "I do. But sometimes I get tired of fighting too."

We stand beside each other as the cannons blast from below us, as our gunners pick off as many crew as they can, and everything the navy ships fire back deliver twice the impact.

We don't have much time before the *Nightwind*, our unsinkable ship, finds her grave at the bottom of the sea.

"It's been nice serving with you, brother," Thane says to me. "Our father would be proud of you."

I feel a prickle of tears at the corner of my eye and briefly put my arm around Thane, squeezing him.

"I know he'd be proud of you too," I say.

Meanwhile on the other ship Ed Smith smiles gleefully at us, awaiting our demise. I abhor that he's going to see it.

But as I'm thinking that, on the other side of his ship, large black tentacles start rising out of the water.

"Oh my goodness gracious," Thane mutters.

"Jesus Christ!" I swear. "It's the Kraken."

This is exactly what we need right now, though I'd rather the Kraken kill us at this point than Smith.

But when the Kraken brings its giant tentacles down, it brings them down on Smith's ship, smashing the railing off.

And then cries start filling the air, screams of terror and horror as we look around and see more Kraken appearing, all of them coming up out of the deep to the other naval ships, starting to destroy them. Their tentacles bash into the sides, they sweep the decks of their crew, they grab the masts and twist them.

They're attacking everyone but us.

Then the Kraken that hit Ed Smith's ship rises from the deep, looming over the naval captain like a yellow-eyed leviathan.

And riding atop the beast's domed head, with the biggest smile on her face, is Maren.

My Maren.

My Maren, the Syren, is riding the Kraken.

I can scarcely believe my eyes. I have to blink several times to make sure it's not some sort of dear death hallucination.

"Oho, that's your woman as a mermaid," Crazy Eyes says with wonder, appearing beside me with the musket in his hand.

"Yes, that surely is," I say, beaming at her as she shouts a command to the Kraken, causing it to smash another tentacle onto the ship, sending men flying.

"She's riding the Kraken."

I grin at him. "Have you ever seen such a glorious sight?"

He grins back. "No, sir, not in all me years." He takes off his hat and holds it to his chest, as if paying my Syren his respect.

If I still had my hat, I'd do the same.

Now the rest of the crew have stopped fighting and are watching Maren in awe, murmurs of surprise and adulation rising from the *Nightwind*. The Kraken she's on top of keeps pummeling Smith's ship, right down the middle, while the other Kraken are doing the same to their respective ships, some of them already destroyed and being dragged down to their watery graves.

And then there's Ed Smith. We all suck in our breath as he emerges from hiding behind a barrel, as if that would protect his cowardly soul.

"Get him, Maren," I seethe under my breath, my fists clenching. "Destroy him for us."

"Tear him fucking apart!" Thane growls.

"I'm so glad she's one of our crew," Drakos says joyfully, shaking his cutlass in the air.

"Aye, that she is," I say, though I don't know how it will be possible with her as a full Syren now. But no matter what happens, she will always be part of our crew.

She will always be mine, even if she doesn't wear my brand anymore.

The Kraken she's riding now focuses its sights on Smith, its yellow eyes gleaming, and Maren is telling it something that we can't hear over the sound of the splintering wood and screaming men.

Two giant tentacles shoot out, one of them grabbing Smith by the neck, the other grabbing him by his legs. Smith cries out and the Kraken raises him off the deck and holds him in place.

Smith writhes, and even from this distance we can all see the terror plain on his face. He knows there's no escape from an awful death, no way out of this.

"Please," he begs Maren as she stares down at him with icy contempt. God Almighty, does she ever look like a queen. "Please let me go. Let me reason with you, mermaid."

She doesn't say anything and he whimpers like the pitiful fool he is while all of us Brethren watch on with bated breath.

Vengeance has never tasted so sweet.

FORTY-THREE

Maren

"Syren," I tell Ed Smith, watching him squirm from my lofty position from up on top of the Kraken's slippery head. "I'm a *Syren*. Mermaids are mythical creatures that you men made up, as if there were swarms of females in the seas just waiting to worship you." I let out a mirthless laugh. "Syrens, on the other hand, we don't want to worship you. We want to *eat* you."

"Lower me to him," I tell the Kraken, "I want to get close."

It takes a free tentacle and gently wraps it around my waist, taking me off his head. It lowers me down toward Smith, holding me out right in front of him, close enough to touch.

"I know you don't know me," I tell Smith, watching the fear swimming in his eyes as I bare my teeth at him, "but I know you and I've known men like you. I know who you are and what you've done. You're a pathetic, lily-livered coward, a sorry excuse for a man and an even sorrier excuse for a Brethren. You've spent your life hiding the creature that you are and attacking others who have the audacity to live life on their own terms. You resent their freedom, their willingness to shun a society that has already shunned them, and you envy their closeness and connection, something you never had and never will have.

You will die here, you will die now, and you will die knowing you've never lived a true day in your ugly little life."

Then I hiss at him and strike him with my fist, my claws coming out and plunging into his chest. I grab hold of his beating heart and rip it right out of his chest, leaving nothing but a gaping hole.

I hold his pulsing heart in my hand and keep my eyes on his as I bring it to my mouth and tear into it.

He lets out a gasp of dying air and I chew on a piece of his heart for a moment before I grimace and spit it back out, the chunk landing on his forehead.

"Even your heart is rotten," I tell him, tossing the heart behind my shoulder where it splatters to the deck.

Suddenly the air fills with cheers and hoots and hollers and I look over to see the motley crew of the *Nightwind* jumping up and down, their swords all raised in the air. I see Ramsay most of all, the proud look on his beautiful face, his dark hair blowing back in the breeze, and all at once I feel how free he is, how free all of them are, no longer tethered to revenge.

I look to Ed Smith, his eyes fluttering closed as he dies slowly, but his head is turned toward the *Nightwind* and he sees them. Sees them celebrating his death, sees that in the end he lost and they won.

I make the Kraken continue to hold him up until he's almost dead and then I say, "Tear him apart!" and the Kraken pulls its tentacles in opposite directions, tearing Captain Ed Smith of the Royal Navy in half, ripped right down the middle.

The Kraken releases Smith's body parts and they tumble to the deck in a gruesome bloody thump.

"Bring me over to them," I tell the Kraken, pointing at the *Nightwind*. "But remember not to touch a hair on their heads."

The Kraken understands this. I can communicate with it in an innate way, not hearing voices per se but just feelings. The Kraken comes off of the ship, leaving it to sink on its own, and then glides over to the *Nightwind*. With its great size, we're up against the pirate ship in a matter of seconds.

The crew all back up from the rail, looking wary, their swords and pistols ready. I don't blame them.

"Don't worry," I tell them. "The Kraken won't harm you anymore."

They relax, just a little, and I tap the tentacle with my hand, asking it to put me on the deck. I know that because of my tail I'll feel completely useless and helpless once I'm on the ship, but I want to hold Ramsay again. I want to kiss him and tell him that now, *now* it's over.

The tentacle gently lowers me to the deck but Ramsay steps out with his outstretched arms and takes me in them. The Kraken releases me and I wrap my arms around Ramsay's shoulders as he holds me up against him.

"Hello, luv," he says to me, grinning from ear to ear.

"Hello, Captain," I say, staring up at him with a silly smile on my face.

"I told you I'd come back for you," he says.

"Technically I came back for you," I tell him. "But I won't hold that against you."

He chuckles softly at that and leans in to kiss me, a soft, sweet kiss that feels like butterflies and sunshine. A kiss that feels like I'm coming home.

A gasp rings out amongst the crew and I think that they're all enamored with our public act of affection, enough so that I deepen the kiss, pulling Ramsay closer to me.

But then Cruz says, "Princess, uh, your tail…"

I open my eyes and break apart from Ramsay's kiss and look down expecting to see my tail propping me up in some manner against the deck.

Instead I see a pair of pale legs from underneath my shift.

I let out an astonished cry. "Gods!"

I stumble backward but Ramsay's arm is there, holding me back. He stares down at my legs with the same amount of disbelief. "Maren? What the devil?"

"I don't know." I gasp, shaking my head. I hold out one leg, then the other. They're both wet, faint traces of shimmery scales left on my skin that seem to slowly evaporate into the air. I flex my ankles, toes, stretch my calves. They feel weak, perhaps even more so than before, but everything seems to work.

"My legs," I say quietly as I marvel at them. "I have legs again."

But even though I'm overjoyed to have them back and more so with what having legs represents for me, I do have a faint pang in my chest over losing my tail. I feel like I didn't really have a chance to enjoy it again. But I suppose you can't have the best of both worlds, something I've known from the very start.

"Was it the kiss?" Ramsay asks, looking so hopeful that I almost laugh. "True loves kiss, right?"

"Don't be daft," I tell him, trying to bite back my smile at the crestfallen look on his face. "We've had plenty of those so far."

Then I think to what Nerissa said.

You can make any world your own.

"Wait a darn minute," I tell him, sliding out of his grasp. "I have to check something."

"Maren?" he asks as I start running across the deck, hope rising in my chest. My strides are short, my gait uneven as always, and I can't move very fast but still I run across the *Nightwind* until I'm to where the railing has been smashed away by the Kraken.

I take in a deep breath and I jump off the side of the ship, diving straight down into the water below, the Kraken having already disappeared into the depths.

I dive deep and the moment I do so I feel a current of electricity around my body. My gills start to work again, rising from my neck and when I look down at my legs, I watch as they fuse together, turning into a tail. Into *my* tail.

I let out a squeal of joy in the water and start swimming for the surface just as Ramsay launches himself overboard and into the waves. He lands with a splash and swims over to me and I flip around, raising my tail in the air for him to see.

"Behold!" I cry out, laughing, making the sun shimmer on my scales, shifting them from teal to lavender and back again.

He laughs too. "What does this mean?" he asks, pulling me into a kiss.

I press my forehead against his, my tail swishing beneath me. "Nerissa gave me another chance, another spell."

"You saw Nerissa?" he asks, his dark brows raised.

"How on earth do you think I was able to control the Kraken?"

He lifts his shoulder in a shrug. "Maybe a Syren thing I wasn't privy to."

"Well, now that Edonia is dead, they've been released from her spell. They're free agents, they just happen to listen to me now."

"And they did a lot of your dirty work," he says as he treads water, kissing me on the head. "For which we are all fucking grateful, in case you couldn't tell."

"Oh, I could tell. And best of all, Ed Smith could tell too. Your cheers were the last thing he heard. Well, aside from me telling the Kraken to tear him apart."

He gives me a devilish grin that makes his eyes gleam. "I have never wanted you more." He kisses me again, deep and hard, then pulls back. "But this still doesn't explain your legs and your tail."

"Nerissa had chanted some kind of spell when she found me," I tell him. "Then she kissed me, as if that sealed the deal. She wouldn't tell me what it was, other than that I could control the Kraken now, but she did say that I could make any world my own. I guess this is what she meant." I wave my tail around for emphasis. "She gave me the ability to live with you above and in the sea below, able to choose which ever world I should want."

"And do you still want mine?" he asks, his brows shadowing his eyes.

"I want yours and I want you," I assure him. "That is always a given, Ramsay. But isn't it delightful that I can return to being a Syren any time I wish? I don't have to give up that part of me anymore."

"Of course, cearban," he says to me, a look of heat coming across his face. "And I don't have to pretend I didn't want a chance to bed you on the ocean floor again." His expression hardens slightly. "What about the book?"

I think about that. "Perhaps she has it. Last I saw it was with her and the Kraken. But fret not, Edonia is gone. Her soul is in the bottle around her sister's neck."

"The bottle should be destroyed," Ramsay grumbles.

"You know how family can be," I say, somewhat understanding why Nerissa would want to keep part of her sister close, no matter how horrible she is. My sisters came looking for me even though I'm the one who left them behind.

At that thought my heart clenches and I say, "I hope I see Larimar again."

He gives me a faint smile. "I'm sure you will, luv. You've only just got your fins back and it's a mighty big ocean."

"And this is just the Pacific," I agree, gesturing to the wide horizon beyond the graveyard of Kraken-smashed ships. "There are more oceans and seas on the other side of the world where she could be. The North Sea, the Atlantic, the Mediterranean, the poles. She could be anywhere."

"Luckily for you, you also possess a ship that can take you wherever you want to go," he says, and I gaze up at the *Nightwind*, suddenly aware that the crew has been staring down at us and watching with rapt attention. Even Skip has jumped up on the railing, staring down at me.

Ramsay goes on. "So I suppose the question is this, princess: Where do you want to go next?"

FORTY-FOUR

Ramsay

THREE MONTHS LATER

Of all the battles we fight, grief is the one that we cannot win. There is no winning and there is no losing. Grief makes a home within your bones so that you'll carry it for all time.

It's been three months since we lost Henry and Sam. I thought that grief was done with me when I lost my father, and Venla, and Hilla, but that was a wishful and foolish thought. Loss and tragedy don't stop more loss and tragedy from occurring and grief will always follow you, like a shadow you don't want.

In that time, there has been a lot to be grateful for. I have the rest of my crew, I have Maren, and I have my ship. After the battle at the Bay of Banderas, the *Nightwind* headed south toward Acapulco, but since the demolition of an entire fleet of naval ships, the British Government had a price out on our heads. Granted, we actually didn't do anything to the ships except fire a few cannons and take out some of their rigging and crew. But we didn't actually sink those ships.

Be that as it may, since the waking world doesn't believe in the Kraken, harkening the monsters to tales a drunken sailor would tell, they jumped to the conclusion that we somehow destroyed an entire naval fleet. I have to say, even though it meant a bounty on our heads, I didn't mind that we added to our already fearsome reputation.

However it meant that we needed to lay low. We bypassed Acapulco and took the ship down to Panama City, a place that was uneasy about pirates since Henry Morgan burned the original city to the ground last century, and therefore fearfully respectful of us. We've been here ever since, the crew stretching their legs for the last while, renting estates and living in villas on land, spending our treasures, eating the local food and drinking the local people.

But while this time has been a respite from life at sea, it's also been full of hardships. I miss Henry terribly and there isn't a day that goes by that I don't think of him. Sometimes I'll think of the future and all that I thought he would grow up to be, and it destroys me to think he won't ever grow up, in the same way it hurts to think about Hilla. But while there is pain, there is a slow and steady acceptance of it. Maren has been exceptionally patient with me when I've wanted time alone to brood and drink, when I've been short with her, when I've been acting like I don't have my head on straight. She's stayed by my side, a steady, comforting presence.

I miss Sam too, her good-natured personality, her sass and wit, her ability to put me in my place. She was more than a sister-in-law, she was like a sister to me, and her absence in our lives is markedly notice-able. Most of all I miss the way she made Thane and Lucas feel. They adored her and she was the glue holding them together.

But for all their struggles, my brother and nephew have managed to hold tight to each other. Lucas I feel for most of all, having lost his mother and his best friend in such a short amount of time, and I'm grateful that Maren has stepped in to try and be there for him when he's willing.

My brother has been a tough nut to crack. He's taken to drinking, as we all do when times get rough out here. It's the pirate life, after all. But tomorrow we set sail, heading back north to Acapulco where we hope to raid a galleon before heading back across the Pacific to Manila, and I've decided to drop in on Thane at the local tavern before he gets carried away.

The tavern is located just a stone's throw from the beach where we've purposely stranded the ship, setting the beast on the sand so that the locals we've hired can do repairs to the hull, scrape away the barnacles, and add more tar to waterproof it. It's also part of the inn where Maren and I have been renting the top floor, while Thane and others have rooms below.

I find Thane sitting outside at a table, drinking his rum and staring off into the night sky, the waves gently lapping the shore.

"Brother," I say, sitting down across from him.

He just grunts at me in response and slams back his drink.

"Look here," I say to him. "I know the toll these last few months have taken on you and you deserve every bit of escape that you can get from the cards that life has dealt you. But tomorrow we set sail for Acapulco and after that we don't know the next time we'll be on land again. Might be months."

"What's your point?" he says gruffly.

"The point is that we are a family. We are the Brethren. And when we come together on that ship there, on the *Nightwind*, we need to act as a unit. You know I've turned a blind eye when it comes to Crazy Eye's drinking habits, or Lothar's mood swings, but for the sake of us all, because you're the quartermaster, the one with all the real power, you need to be at your best."

He lets out a derisive snort and gazes at me sharply. His amber eyes are bloodshot.

"My best? I don't have a best anymore, Ramsay."

"You do. And you know you do because you put on your best for your son. For Lucas. He's lost as much as you, maybe more, and he's young. He's just a boy, Thane, he's mature and he's seen a lot, God Almighty has he ever, but he's still just a boy. And he needs you to be his father, just as much as the crew needs you to be their quartermaster. And try as you might, you won't be able to be those things when you've got this much drink in you."

Thane eyes me with sorrow, his brow crinkling. "Do you think your words will make my grief go away? Do you wish to fix me? Does it make you uncomfortable that I'm feeling this way?"

I reach out and put my hand on his, giving it a squeeze.

"Nothing will make it go away," I tell him bluntly. "No words. Not even time. I'm just here to remind you that you still have duties more important than your grief."

He doesn't say anything for a moment, his attention going back to the *Nightwind* and the crabs that scuttle nearby, their shells gleaming in the moonlight. Then he nods. "Aye. Lucas."

I sigh inwardly with relief. It's not in Thane's character to lose control for so long. He's always had such a handle on his emotions.

Silence falls over us. Crickets chirp from the jungle.

"I know Sam initially wanted you, brother," he says, his voice so low it's barely audible.

I frown. "Pardon me?"

"You heard me," he goes on. "I know she wanted you."

"We joked about that all the time," I remind him. "It was comical."

"Was never comical to me, though," he says. "The fact that I was second best. I'm always second best to you, *Captain*."

I balk at him in surprise because that has never been the case between us. "Second best? What the devil are you talking about? Are you a bloody idiot? I suppose you are. You were the sacred child growing up. The oldest. Mum's favorite. Pa's too. It should have been you leading the *Nightwind* from the start, not me."

"Because I didn't want the job," he says. "You were always better at being a captain. You unite people."

"And you get those people to listen to you. They respect you a hell of a lot more than they respect me."

He shrugs. "All I'm saying is that Sam wanted you. She settled for me. And I'm afraid I was never truly able to give her what she wanted in the end." He fixes me with an impassioned gaze. "I loved her, I did, I was never able to give her the love she needed, the love that she originally wanted from you."

I swallow, wishing I had stopped by the tavern's wench to get a drink myself. I wish I knew all the right things to say to him.

"You were a good pair," I tell him. "You complimented each other. And regardless of how you think she felt, or how you felt, in the end it doesn't really matter because of Lucas. Because you produced a son whom you love very much. A son who needs his father more than ever."

He spins his glass around in his hands and gives me a thoughtful and surprisingly sober look. "Are you going to be a father?"

The question catches me off-guard.

"Again, I mean," Thane adds.

"There is no again," I tell him sharply. Then I loosen my shoulders. "Meaning, though Hilla is gone, I'll never stop being her father. That doesn't stop with death. She will always be my daughter."

He nods and waits patiently for me to go on.

I sigh. "But I know what you're meaning—with Maren."

"Aye."

"To be honest with you, Maren and I haven't really discussed it. I have thought about it, of course, of what that could possibly be like. Half-Syren, half-Brethren? The child would be an outright monster, but our monster of course."

Thane manages a slight smile. "Aren't all children monsters at some point?"

I laugh. "That be true, they can be. But you know, I don't think it's vital to our relationship. I believe Maren has great mothering instincts but being a mother isn't at the forefront of her mind. Perhaps in time."

"Perhaps in time."

"Though I will say, from the amount of seed I'm spilling in her on the daily, I'm rather shocked she hasn't fallen pregnant yet."

Thane lets out a groan and gets to his feet, leaning against the table for balance, a look of disgust on his face. "Alright, I think it's time for bed. I don't want to hear another word about your *seed*."

I laugh and watch as he staggers away. "You sure? I have countless salacious stories I can regale you with!"

He gives me a dismissive wave of his hand and disappears around the corner.

I watch him go, heading up the stairs and into the inn, not into the tavern, and I relax, happy that perhaps I talked some sense into him. Then I turn in my seat and lean back, breathing in the heady scent of frangipani in the air, watching the moon on the water, the silhouette of the *Nightwind* resting at the foot of the waves. I know she's eager to return to the sea and continue on, just as I am.

I sit there for some time, wishing I had a cigar, when I hear heels on cobblestone behind me.

"May I join you, Captain?"

I turn and smile at Maren who walks to my table. Her ebony hair is piled high on her head, more out of need to deal with the stifling heat and humidity here rather than what's fashionable, and her dress is far more elaborate than the one she wears on the ship. Its rich teal color and silk purple threading at the bust and stomach remind me of her Syren tail and that's probably why she picked it.

My heart beats faster than hummingbird wings, a sensation that happens whenever she's around, and I pull out the chair for her and gesture for her to sit down.

"Princess," I greet her.

She gives me a small, chiding smile. She doesn't appreciate the moniker anymore but when she looks the way she does, I can't help but call her that.

"I saw you had what looked to be a heart-to-heart with Thane," she comments.

"Aye," I say. "As you know, I've had my concerns."

"And?"

"I think I've gotten through to him. Just had to remind him that while wallowing in grief is fine, even healthy, he still has a boy to look after."

"Good," she says, her gaze raking over the ship. "I have no doubt Thane will take your words to heart. He's a good man and a good father."

With her words on that tangent I clear my throat.

"Have you had any thoughts about getting married?"

She jolts then slowly turns her head to look at me, an incredulous look on her face. "Are you proposing?"

"No."

Her nose crinkles in consternation. "I don't like your game, Captain Battista."

"But if one day I were to propose," I go on, leaning across the table to her. "Do you fancy you'd say yes?"

She raises her brow, giving me a steady, discerning look. "I don't know, Ramsay. I suppose I would have to think about it."

"Hmmphhf," I say. "Still waiting for an even taller and richer pirate to sweep you off your feet then?"

"I doubt such a man exists," she says. "What I'm waiting for is a ring."

"I'm getting you your ring, princess," I tell her. "Just have to wait for the right ship to plunder."

"Is that a euphemism?"

"Maren, I think I've plundered every hole on your body. Nay, I'll know the treasure when I see it."

She laughs at that. "Figures my engagement ring would be something you've looted."

I grin at her. "I can't help what I am."

"And what are you again?" she asks in a coy tone, a brazen look coming across her bright blue eyes.

"A Brethren," I tell her, getting to my feet. "A pirate," I say, walking around her chair until I'm in front of her. "Your lover."

I drop to my knees and start running up my hands up her calves. "Your worshipper," I go on.

She gasps and looks behind her at the tavern, the lights are still on and patrons are still drinking inside. "Someone might see."

"Let them see," I tell her gruffly, my cock already painfully hard at the thought. "The whole world should know how dearly I make you come."

Then I flip up her dress and her petticoats and bury my head between her legs.

She lets out a loud gasp which she tries to cover up with a cough and I attack her savagely, my fingers on her thighs in a bruising grip, spreading them apart, my mouth meeting her cunt with hunger.

"Oh gods," she cries out softly and bucks her hips up to meet my face.

"Such a hungry little monster, aren't ya?" I growl into her, my tongue sliding up and down in hard quick passes, from her swollen heat down into the wet depths of her. I eat her like I'm a starving man and the truth is I'm always ravenous for her. She's never not on my mind, never not being craved by both my heart and my cock.

I'm beyond lucky to have found this creature, this woman, this soul that belongs to my soul. She and I are the same, two worlds come together until we've created one of our own, a world we carry with us no matter where on the seas we go. We will never be apart, we will always be one.

And I will always make her see the damn stars.

"Ramsay," she says, panting. "Oh, I'm going to come."

I grin into her, making sure to thoroughly work her now, my fingers getting involved and fucking her deep while my tongue and lips suck her clitoris into my mouth and then she's pushed over the edge. Her body jerks and trembles, thighs squeezing the side of my face and if anyone is watching at this moment they'll see a lady of high standing acting as if she's been possessed by the devil.

But nay, it's not the devil.

It's just me.

Captain Ramsay "Bones" Battista.

FORTY-FIVE

Maren

It feels amazing to be back on the *Nightwind* again, out on the open sea, the blue water churning in the ship's wake below the aft balcony where I'm bent over the railing.

It also feels quite amazing to be thoroughly taken by Ramsay from this position.

My dress is hitched up around my waist and he's completely nude, gripping my hips and thrusting his cock in me from behind, buried into the hilt. The sea air whips my hair back as his balls press against me, our skin hot.

"Such a gorgeous view," he rasps, the raw lust in his voice making me even wetter than I already am. "Your arse, the ocean, I'm not sure which one I love more."

"It better be my arse!" I tell him and I attempt to look behind at him but he raises his palm and lays a hard SMACK against my rear.

I cry out, stiffening from the shock of pain. He certainly doesn't hold back when he thinks I deserve a spanking, and I often deserve quite a few.

"What have I told you about talking back," he mutters playfully.

"You told me it gets you hard."

"Aye, that it does." He pauses before laying another WHACK of his palm on my rear. "But what doesn't?"

Another smack lands down, my skin stinging, and then he's pushing himself in deeper, his grip on my hips becoming a vice as I'm thrust against the railing. With the railing freshly rebuilt, there's a chance he might fuck me right into the ocean, but given that's my second home and I can swim as fast as the ship, that'd be fine with me. So long as he doesn't leave me on the edge of climax.

"Come for me, luv," Ramsay murmurs into my neck, picking up on that thought. He slips one hand around the front of me and under my dress, fingers sliding over my sensitive flesh, creating currents of heat that radiate outward.

He is so exquisite. How I love this man.

I let out a groan. "Gods, I—"

"Merchant galleon!" I hear Thane's voice boom from the deck above, interrupting Ramsay's urging. "Fresh for the taking! All hands on deck!"

Ramsay pauses mid-thrust. "They've spotted a galleon already? We're not even that close to Acapulco yet."

I expect him to stop fucking me at that but he keeps going instead, his pace quickening, driving in deeper, harder.

"If you don't come right now, I'll make you come," Ramsay threatens me.

"So then do it and quit talking about it," I retort.

He growls at that, nipping at my neck, just enough to draw blood.

I moan louder. I adore it when he feeds from me. He won't do it often, in fact he'll only do it when he's put in chains so that he won't get carried away with his bloodlust. But everyone now and then his teeth will pierce me and he'll take a little taste, especially if we're about to head into potentially violent situations like raiding a Spanish galleon.

"Suck me back," I tell him, encouraging him to take a bigger drink. "You get so much bigger when you do."

He lets out a low, guttural sound of want, biting harder now, drinking me down and I feel his cock swell inside of me to the point where I might break in two. Then the swift pass of his fingers takes me over the edge.

My orgasm sweeps through me, making my knees buckle, claws coming out and digging into the wood of the railing to keep myself up, and he climaxes even harder, removing his fangs from my neck and letting out a long bellow that I'm sure will be heard throughout the whole ship. Perhaps they'll think it's his battle cry, though by now they're all used to the noises coming out of his quarters at all hours of the day.

"Did I hurt you?" he asks once he's calmed down, his breath still heavy as he pulls out of me.

"From your palm or from your teeth?" I ask, straightening up and pulling down my dress as I lean back against the railing. "Neither but how does it look?" I tilt my head, baring my ravaged neck to him.

"Just two puncture wounds," he says with an apologetic smile. "I am getting better at this."

"Yes, you are." My gaze drops down to his half-hard cock, his purely masculine body on perfect display in the bright daylight. If we didn't have some adventuring to do, I'd be tempted for another round.

"Bones!" Cruz yells impatiently from somewhere on the deck. "You're needed up top, Captain!"

We get going, Ramsay pulling on his wide breeches and black shirt and I help him strap on his holster, slipping the pistols and cutlass in them. Then we run out the door and up to the deck where the crew has gathered at the forecastle. In the distance, near the shore, is a lone galleon.

"She's a sitting duck," Ramsay says, rubbing his hands together with glee.

We go right over to Thane who is barking out orders to everyone. He gives us both a disappointed look at our approach.

"Taking your time, *Captain*?" Thane notes. "It's only your ship."

"It's *our* ship, brother. And as quartermaster, you know exactly what to do in my absence."

Thane mumbles something under his breath. I didn't catch it, but

Ramsay did with his superior sense of hearing, giving his brother an obscene gesture with his hands in reply.

Thane bursts out laughing at that, probably the first time I've heard him laugh since Sam died. Then he turns to the rest of the ship, his expression quickly sobering.

"Alright lads, we want this to be our treasure ship before we cross the mighty sea, so let's make this one count."

"Let's take what's ours!" Drakos shouts, the rest of the crew cheering.

"Give no quarter!" Thane yells, raising his cutlass.

I lance the quartermaster with a sharp look. "We'll be giving *some* quarter, if you please," I tell him. "The days of ruthlessly murdering everyone on board are over."

Thane glares at me then looks to Ramsay, utterly befuddled. "What the devil is she going on about?"

This is the first Thane's hearing about this. Over the last few months, since I officially joined the crew as Ramsay's lady, I've had a lot of time to think about my life and what I wanted from it. Though I will follow love to the ends of the earth, Agency is still a god to me and one that I will always revere. I want to live a life, a product of my own free will, where I can not only be free from the restraints of society but have a good conscience too. I know what I am, I know what Ramsay is and the rest of the Brethren: we're monsters. That's something that will not change and I will never feel shame for harboring a dark, monstrous side.

But monsters do not need to be tethered to their impulses. I don't want to be a puppet to my rage. I tend to my anger like a garden, I keep it pruned and watered so it's healthy, so it gives to me instead of taking. And because of that, I know I have what it takes to separate right from wrong, to flirt between moral and immoral, saint and sinner, princess and pirate.

I told Ramsay that if I were to be a pirate at his side, especially a pirate bride one day, then we would need to change some things.

I just don't know whether the crew is on board for those changes.

Ramsay eyes me and then looks to his brother with a shrug. "I figured we try it her way this time. Attack on the ship, plunder the loot, but instead of slaughtering everyone we let some of them go and take only who we need."

"To be bloodletters," I finish.

"Bloodletters?" Cruz asks and I realize all of the crew are listening.

"Aye," Ramsay explains. "They'll be bloodletting for us. Give them a choice. It's only fair. Ask them if they want to die or become a bloodletter. If they agree to being a bloodletter we keep them on board but only for our voyage. We let them go on the other side."

"Don't you think that's a wee bit cruel, cap'n?" Crazy Eyes says. "I think they'd all rather die than be kept in the hold."

"I've fixed up the hold," I tell them. "Sedge and I have spent the last few days disposing of the bones and washing it down. We've put in hay for bedding, blankets, and we have plenty of food and water now from Panama City. We can keep them in there for the voyage, only taking blood when you need it. It worked when I gave you my blood, straight in the bottle, it can work with them."

"That goes against our nature," Lothar says darkly to which Matisse nods. "I don't want to drink human blood from a bottle. That's what wine and rum are for. I want it direct from the source." His teeth sharpen before my eyes and he bares his fangs at me.

I bare my fangs right back, hissing at him, then I put on a demure smile. "Your nature can be unnecessarily savage."

"Says the woman who eats hearts for breakfast," Ramsay says under his breath.

I smack him against the chest as I give him a dirty look. "Come now. You're supposed to be on my side."

"I'm forever on your side, luv. But let's take one thing at a time, shall we? We'll go and get the bloodletters and put them in the hold. Maybe their blood will go into bottles, maybe we'll all end up drinking from the source, but I agree that perhaps we can rein in our ruthless-ness…some."

Thane sighs, running a hand over his face. Even though I know he's a broken man inside, it's nice to see his grumpy self is back. "Alright. Captain's orders everyone. We attack, we pillage, we take…

bloodletters. Leave the rest to tell a tale that no one will believe." He clears his throat. "Hammocks up, chests down!"

"Aye, aye!" the crew shouts, running about.

Cruz brings out his violin and starts playing a lively tune.

"Set fighting sail!" yells Thane.

"As you say, quartermaster," replies Crazy Eyes as he runs to the aft.

"Batten down your hatches!"

"Aye!" Remi and Horse retort in unison, disappearing below.

"Hoist the colors!" Ramsay bellows, raising his pistol in the air. "And be quick about it!"

"Aye, Captain!" the crew cheers and we watch as the red flag with the jolly roger gets hauled up the mast, flapping gloriously in the breeze.

"Hoist the colors!"

FORTY-SIX

Maren

"Are we there yet?" Ramsay asks me, holding his hand out for the bottle of wine.

I take another swig of it, the beautiful Madeira grapes tasting lovely, and hand it to him. "You're the captain. You tell me."

He chuckles before taking a sip. "It's your kingdom, Maren, not mine."

We're sitting side by side up on the crow's nest, our legs dangling over the edge of the platform. The sun is low in the sky and bathing us in streams of gold, the sea breeze blowing salt and the perfume of the nearby land in our faces. It already smells like home.

We were supposed to be heading across the Pacific already, but I asked Ramsay if we could have a little detour to the Sea of Cortez. Growing up, the sea had a different name but now that I've seen the charts, I realize that the Kingdom of Limonos is at the bottom of that sea, not too far from the village of Loreto, under the Viceroyalty of New Spain.

Ramsay agreed—it doesn't take much to convince him to do anything, especially when I use my feminine wiles—and so the *Nightwind* set sail toward the gulf. We've been cruising up along the coast, the dry rocky landscape with its craggy coral-hued mountains and prickly desert plants looking so achingly familiar. The water too, with its many shades of blue and green, calls to me, beckoning me to come in.

But I've been waiting until I know for sure. The gulf is large, feeling like it stretches on forever, and even though I roughly know the spot, I don't want to go in the water until I'm certain. I know that the *Nightwind* has places to go, indeed now that we have bloodletters on board, so we don't have a lot of time to explore the sea looking for my lost kingdom.

From one hundred feet up the mast with Ramsay, however, I sense we're getting closer. I can just feel it.

"What will you do when you get there?" Ramsay asks me, his eyes flicking over my face as he studies me. He's curious but there's a hint of trepidation in his voice. I know why. He thinks that once I see Limonos I won't want to leave.

I shrug. "I really don't know. I just want to see it so that I can say my goodbyes. I reckon I need the closure." I reach out and put my hand on his, my skin now bronzed from the sun and a shade darker than his that never seems to take on any color. "I'm coming back to you, Ramsay."

The corner of his mouth lifts, his eyes dancing with determination. "You realize that if you don't, I'm getting in the water and hunting you down. I don't care how long it takes, I will find you and bring you back to your real home." He picks up my hand and places a lingering kiss on it, his gaze locked on mine. "Your home with me."

Butterflies flutter in my stomach and he lowers my hand from his mouth. Another wary look darkens his dusky eyes and then he's reaching into his shirt pocket with his hand and pulling out something.

A ring.

My eyes widen, mouth falling open as I stare at it in his fingers.

The ring is beautiful, silver with a crescent moon hugging a dark blue stone, the same color as the sea.

You are the moon, I am the tides, he had once told me.

"This is for you," he says, clearing his throat. "Maren, will you do me the honor of becoming my wife?"

My chest tightens, like I have too many euphoric feelings at once, and I steal a glance at his face. For once Ramsay looks positively boyish. Younger and unsure and there's something so achingly vulnerable about him that in this moment you'd never think he was a bloodthirsty pirate who—

I stare back at the ring.

"Wait now, whose dead body did you lift this from?"

His vulnerability fades and his glower returns. "I'll have you know, Princess, that I had the ring specially made for you while we were in Panama City. I just wanted to wait until the right moment to give it to you." He pauses. "And the right moment happens to be right before you turn into a fish and that brand on your hip disappears. So that you remember you belong to someone."

I glare at his use of the term *fish* but I can't stay mad at him for long because the ring is absolutely beautiful.

"Can I put it on you?" he asks.

"I didn't say yes yet," I tease him.

His face radiates impatience as he stares at me, waiting. "Well? If you're going to tear my heart out and eat it, Maren, at least make it quick."

I laugh, the joy escaping me. "Yes," I tell him. "Yes, you dirty pirate. Yes, I'll marry you."

He slips the ring on my finger and then laughs, grabbing my face and pulling me into a long hard kiss that reaches every inch of my soul. When he's done, we're both breathless and he rests his forehead on mine, my face still cupped in his hands.

"You are the moon, I am the tides," he whispers.

"I love you," I whisper back.

Then I glance down and admire the ring on my finger.

"By the way I am not a *dirty* pirate," he scoffs after a moment.

"I know you're not dirty, but I'm also not a fish."

He chuckles at that and shrugs and then a familiar scent wafts over me, like sea salt and something deeper, muskier.

"We're here," I say anxiously, quickly getting to my feet.

"Are you certain?" he asks, getting up beside me.

I look around and then point to a small narrow island. "See that island? See the tip? I know that land. I used to haul myself up on shore all the time and look for ships." I look back at him excitedly. "Limonos is right there."

"Belay the ship!" Ramsay bellows to the crew below, then he waves his hand at the sails which deflate considerably.

I start climbing down the rope ladder as fast as I can and, as soon as my feet hit the deck, I'm running to the rail, shucking my stays and dress off until I'm completely nude.

"What the devil?" Cruz says as I run past him naked. He looks to Ramsay for an explanation.

"I don't know," Ramsay says. "I asked her to marry me and this was her reaction."

I laugh at that and I'm still laughing as I launch myself over the side of the boat, swan diving into the sea.

The minute I hit the waves, my body transforms and I sigh with relief. Even though my teeth and claws have always come at will, my tail and gills never materialize until I'm in the water.

I use them both to my advantage and start swimming down as fast as I can, both eager and terrified to see what's left of Limonos. But the deeper I go, the more my smile fades. There are some ruins of what was, coral formations and rocky caves and sea mounts, but there's not a soul to be found.

"Hello?" I call out. Then I try calling from inside my head. *Hello? It's me, Princess Maren. Is anyone there?*

I swim and stop, listening. All I hear is the snap of shrimp and other creatures. Somewhere in the distance is a song, but it's the song of a gray whale, not of a Syren.

I start swimming again, hoping to see something, anything. I go to where the kelp forest is and while I see friendly seals and octopus, they don't seem to know what I'm talking about when I mention Limonos. I swim to the coral gardens and that too is home to schools of fish and the occasional sea turtle passing through. Finally, I swim over to the arches where my father used to reside on his throne, shafts of sunlight coming through the rock formations and lighting up the empty spot.

Because it is empty.

My father is gone.

Every Syren is gone.

There's only me.

Asherah and Edonia told you it would be this way, I think to myself. I knew that, deep down, I just wanted Asherah to be wrong and I wanted Edonia to be lying.

I exhale, my heart feeling waterlogged, and rest my tail on a patch of pink sea anemone, trying to think. I glance up at the surface, at the dark shape of the *Nightwind* as it waits for me.

That's where I belong now anyway and I know it. Up there with Ramsay. I didn't even think I'd find much down here, I just wanted to say my goodbyes if there was anyone to say them to.

But all the Syrens have left. My family is gone. And the family I do have is up there on the *Nightwind*, waiting for me.

I look around once more and then start swimming up toward the ship.

I see movement from the shadows out of the corner of my eye and I stop swimming, my heart leaping in my throat as I turn to face whatever it is, hoping it's a Syren.

But it's not. It's a shark, heading straight to me.

I put my hands out as a way to warn the creature.

But it's not stopping.

It's coming faster and faster and it's almost upon me when I recognize the white tipped fins and the bronze-gray body of Nill.

No. It can't be.

But it is.

"Nill!" I exclaim, exploding with joy.

The shark comes right up to me, practically running me over, and I throw my arms around his body, holding onto him tight. "Nill, Nill, it's me."

I know it's you, Nill says. *I have been waiting for you all this time.*

I'm crying now, tears disappearing into the sea. "I'm so sorry," I sob, so many emotions running through me. "I'm sorry that I never came back for you. I couldn't."

I know, the shark says. *But I had to wait for you, even when the last Syren left.*

I pull back and look into his black eyes, seeing my reflection in them. "You must have been so terribly lonely here."

I had faith that you would return, he says simply.

I look around at the emptiness around us. There's plenty of sea life here, perhaps even more than there was when the kingdom was inhabited. Maybe us Syrens did more damage to the local population of sea creatures than we thought. We were their biggest predators, after all.

"Are you happy here?" I ask him. "It feels so strange."

At times, he answers. *But I can find happiness anywhere.*

"You know, I have a new home now." I point up at the *Nightwind*. "It's on that ship. I know this sounds far-fetched but we journey across the oceans with magic wind in our sails. Would you like to come with us?"

Nill's lower eyelid blinks. *I am your sworn protector, Princess Maren. I made a grave mistake by leaving you the last time. I will never be leaving you again.*

"You sound just like Ramsay," I say, grinning at my oldest friend.

Who?

"You'll meet him," I say, letting go of him. Then I show him my necklace. "See, you never left me at all."

He wags his tail back and forth in response.

I pause before I ask my next question. "Have you seen Larimar?"

Nill nods. *But not for a long time. I have faith that we can find her again.* He looks up at the surface. *Show me your ship*, he says.

I smile and turn and start swimming for the surface, the shark right behind me.

When I surface, the sun nearly setting, making the surface glow a metallic orange, I look up at the *Nightwind* and see Ramsay staring over the railing at me, Skip perched on his shoulder.

"There you are," he says, looking relieved. "I was just about to jump in and…uh, Maren, I do say there's a shark behind you."

I glance behind me to see Nill's dorsal fin slicing through the water.

"I found Nill!" I shout up at him. "He's going to come with us."

Ramsay frowns, probably trying to figure out the logistics of it all.

"He can swim as fast as the ship," I assure him. "He'll be our convoy."

He nods, perhaps not loving the idea of a shark always circling the ship, but he'll get used to it. Pirates are nothing if not adaptable.

"Do you need help getting up? We can lower the net," Ramsay says.

I shake my head. "No, you go and get the wind blowing again. Nill and I will catch up."

"Are you sure?" he asks.

I wave at him. "You sail into the sunset, I'll swim after you."

He nods. "Alright, luv," he says. "But when it gets dark, I'm coming down into that water and fishing you out myself. I'm not letting the future Mrs. Battista out of my sight."

"That's a deal," I tell him, waving my engagement ring at him.

Ramsay beams with pride, Skip still on his shoulder and waving his tail. Then Ramsay winks at me before turning to the crew. "Wind in the sails, boys! Let's set course for Manila!"

"Aye, aye, Captain!" the crew responds.

The sails fill with the wind, billowing out in a dramatic fashion, and the *Nightwind* begins to move toward the sunset with speed.

I glance down at Nill, who is just below the surface. "Shall we?" I ask him.

He wags his tail in response.

Nill starts swimming and I start diving up and down through the waves, laughing as I go, following the *Nightwind's* wake, following the man who has my heart, and the life I had once only dreamed of.

THE END

T hank you for reading A Ship of Bones and Teeth! If you enjoyed the book, I would be honoured if you could leave a review (and please give me a follow on Instagram if you want to stay in touch for future releases).

If you want more books in a similar vein, I can thoroughly recommend BLOOD ORANGE (a gothic dark romance retelling of Dracula) and RIVER OF SHADOWS (a dark fantasy based on Finnish mythology). Both books are available in Amazon KU and in paperback! Turn the page for a sample of River of Shadows.

Read a sample of River of Shadows

River of Shadows is the first book in the dark fantasy romance series Underworld Gods, a spicy Beauty and the Beast and Hades/Persephone-inspired series based on macabre Finnish mythology.

The ground drops beneath me.

I'm falling.

I scream for a moment and then I stop, as if caught in mid-air.

Then I realize I *am* in mid-air, suspended.

I just ran off a cliff, right into a giant spiderweb that must stretch thirty feet across a rocky chasm. I'm on my stomach, the sticky webs strung across my face, staring at a babbling brook forty feet down that's half hidden by ferns.

Oh god. This isn't good. This really isn't good.

I groan and try to push myself up onto my back but it's impossible. I can barely lift my head off the web, the silky threads sticking to my face until they finally snap back into place.

Okay, don't panic. Don't panic. Just because you're in a giant spider's web, doesn't mean there's going to be a giant spider. I mean the web might be huge but the spider could be small. Or maybe it's like a family of small spiders. Oh god, no, that's worse. Don't think about that. Don't think about anything, just calmly get up, and climb out onto the cliff.

I take in a deep breath and try to push myself up. It's like doing pushups while being attached to the ground. Every single muscle in my arms and back are straining to the max, causing me to shake, the threads refusing to yield.

"I wouldn't do that if I were you," a rich low voice says from above me, now horrifically familiar.

I pause, still shaking, trying to swallow.

"And why not?" I manage to say.

"Because," Death says smoothly, "you're trembling. I must admit I'm impressed by your strength. You may have the face of an angelic fairy but you're built like a warrior, and even I can admire that. But you're also painfully stupid."

"Excuse me?" I exclaim, though I immediately regret it. This isn't the time to be insulted.

"You don't even know me and yet I already get under your skin," Death says. "Don't know what that says about me, but I think I like it. At any rate, you're stupid because you've obviously never seen a spider web before. Even in your world they work the same. The spider waits in the corner for the prey to fall on the web and then once it's caught, the vibrations from the prey's struggles are what alert the spider to come and feed. In this case, it's a wrathspider, which has earned its moniker for reasons you will soon find out."

Oh my god.

I have to get out of here.

I go back to pushing myself up, but the web shakes even more and out of the corner of my eye I see something gigantic and black step onto the web. It's not Death—he's somewhere on the cliff behind me—but it's dark as sin and about the size of a fucking hippo.

Not including the eight thick legs which stretch out from it like oars.

Fuck! I swear. No, no, no, no. This can't be it, this can't be how I die. Not here, not now, not so close to finding my father.

Not by a giant spider.

"I'll make a bargain with you!" I cry out.

Death sighs, and though I can't see him, I feel like he's bored. "I'm tired of bargains, to be honest. The more that I make, the more this world tilts off-balance. Eventually there will be a reckoning."

"I don't give a fuck about your reckoning," I spit out, feeling the web shake now as the spider gets closer in my line of sight. "I want you to free my father."

Death laughs dryly. "I figured. And so what's your bargain?"

"Me for him," I tell him without hesitation. "You save me from this spider, you take me as your prisoner, you let my father go."

Silence falls. The web continues to vibrate.

"Or," he muses, "I could just let you die. Do you know what happens when a not-dead mortal dies here?"

"I've been told," I say, my voice trembling now, the fear starting to eat me alive.

"I could just let you die," he goes on. "And keep your father. And maybe one day when I tire of his company, I'll bring him here and feed him to my new spider friend and you both will share the same fate."

"No!" I scream, tears rushing to my eyes. "Please! I will do anything. Anything you wish, anything at all, just let my father go. You don't even have to save my life, let me die here, but please let my father go."

Another weighty pause. My heart is pounding so hard that I can't tell if it's shaking the web or the spider that's slowly getting closer, its massive shape starting to block out the light.

"You would really do anything for him?" he asks carefully.

"Yes!" I cry out adamantly. I knew from the beginning that if my father was in this situation, where he was taken by Death and still alive, that I would trade my life for his. I would trade my soul. I would take his place and let Death do his worst to me.

"I promise you, I will do anything you want. I will endure anything you wish. I will cook you meals and clean your house, or you can chain me up in your basement, keep me in a cage, you can torture me, have your way with me, give me to others, make me your bride, treat me like a dog, beat me, spit on me, I don't care. I will do it all, if you just let him go."

The spider is almost on me now. I see a glint of fangs, about as long as my forearm, and my spine starts to prickle at the nauseating thought of getting stabbed there.

"*Please*," I add pitifully.

"Hmmph," Death says slowly, too fucking slowly. "A trade."

Fuck. I'm going to die. This is it.

"You did list off a lot of things, some of which aren't relevant, some which are intriguing," he continues. "I really don't like the idea of letting a shaman go, though. It's not good for them to have too much power. You saw what happened to your redheaded boyfriend."

He's not my boyfriend! I think and then almost laugh, because this is probably going to be my last thought before I die.

The spider is right above me now. I manage to turn my head to finally look at it, getting a glance of its leg and the five iron claws at the end. Of course this thing has claws, made of iron no less.

It stops and rears up on its back legs like a horror-show horse, the fangs glinting, and hundreds of red eyes gleaming like balloons of blood.

Hell.

Death sighs dramatically. "Fine."

There's a pause, a swooshing sound, and then the web violently shakes. The spider crashes to the sticky threads, one of its giant hairy legs narrowly missing me, and I realize that Death jumped on top of it.

The spider immediately goes still, dying instantly.

I crane my head up to look at Death as he gets off the spider like he's dismounting a horse, and makes a show of putting one of his armored gloves back on his hand, and for a brief second I see his bare skin, which is covered in lines of pulsing silver.

Then he walks over to me, balancing gracefully on the web. He looms over my body, his figure larger than life, his cape black and flowing behind him, hate burning in the depths of his unseen eyes, and I realize that perhaps it would have been better had the spider ended me.

I'm about to find myself on another web, Death lurking in the shadows, waiting for me to tremble.

Afterword

Dear reader,

I hope that ASOBAT took you on a wild ride across the Pacific —
it certainly was one of the best times I've ever had while writing and
the two months it took for this book to come together were some of the
most enjoyable I've had in a very long time. If you follow me on social
media or through my newsletter (by the way you can find me on Instagram HERE or my newsletter HERE), you will know that I have had a
hellish two years full of loss and pain and this book has made me fall

in love with writing again and let me trust my creative soul, something I thought I had lost. So while I am glad that you've read it, I'm even more glad and relieved that I was able to write it.

This isn't fan fiction (I've actually never written fan fiction before, aside from when I was 19 and I wrote a story for the X-Men where a new mutant and Logan fall in love in a definite bully/enemies-to-lovers romance, all scribbled longhand in notebooks while I traveled across Australia by myself on a bus, and now I'm wondering if I should ever publish it haha) however ASOBAT is a retelling of The Little Mermaid and is definitely influenced by Pirates of the Caribbean especially in terms of the combination of gothic horror themes, action and humor. In fact, a seed of this idea came from me riding the Pirates of the Caribbean ride in Disneyland in December 2022 and being struck by a vision of a shimmering blue grotto and feeling the need to make that into something. I didn't know what but I wanted to capture that feeling on the page. Fast forward to March of 2023 when my husband and I were in Loreto, Mexico for the first time and I was staring at the Sea of Cortez from our balcony, and had the sudden urge to write a re-telling of the Little Mermaid but with pirates, something dark and sexy and fun. Voila, A Ship of Bones and Teeth was born. The idea arrived fully formed and I was off and running with it.

Now at the time readers had been expecting my third book in the Underworld Gods, my dark fantasy series about the God and Goddess of Death in Finnish Mythology, but I wasn't ready to start it. I had just come off of Black Rose, a book that took a lot out of me to write and had high expectations from readers who had read the first book, Blood Orange, and I just wanted a chance to breathe. A chance to just write whatever I felt like instead of forcing it, preferably something different and fun with zero expectations from the audience, and most impor-tantly, something that was a total standalone, with no relation to other books and a complete story.

Now, if you have a keen eye and have read my vampire books, you'll notice that the Brethren of the Blood are the same as my other vampires and that's because it is part of the same world. There are no shared characters (unless you count that book, in which ASOBAT is its origin story) but the Brethren are vampires, though back in the first half of the 18th century, the term vampire wasn't used often. Thus they called themselves the Brethren. Which I like more.

Anyway, if you haven't read those books and you want more like ASOBAT in the vampire sense, I suggest Blood Orange or Black Sunshine by yours truly.

And if you want a book that has killer mermaids I suggest Into the Drowning Deep by Mira Grant. It's not romance, it's pure horror, but it's so clever and scary and well-done and I really insist you read it soon. Another, albeit much shorter, killer mermaid book is The Salt Grows Heavy by Cassandra Khaw. And of course if you need a dark historical pirate romance (with no fantasy elements) Pam Godwin's Sea of Ruin is amazing (just be warned it's far darker than this book).

Finally I must plug Scott Mackenzie's book Uncharted Waters. It's a standalone adventure set at sea with some romance, intrigue, suspense and danger with a major twist that will have you reeling.

Acknowledgments

Much thanks goes to Scott Mackenzie for his unwavering belief in me. Thanks again to Betul E. for your thoughtful input as my beta reader, Laura for literally editing this despite going to the hospital, Michelle Moras for all your hard work with this release, Becca Syme for your encouragement and keeping me guessing, and Hang for this gorgeous cover!

About the Author

Karina Halle is a screenwriter, a former music & travel journalist, and the New York Times, Wall Street Journal, & USA Today bestselling author of River of Shadows, The Royals Next Door, and Black Sunshine, as well as 70 other wild and romantic reads, ranging from light & sexy rom coms to horror/paranormal romance and dark fantasy. Needless to say, whatever genre you're into, she's probably written a romance for it.

When she's not traveling, she and her husband split their time between a possibly haunted 120 year-old house in Victoria, BC, their sailboat the Norfinn, and their condo in Los Angeles. For more information, visit www.authorkarinahalle.com

Find her on Facebook, Instagram, Pinterest, BookBub, Amazon and Tik Tok

Printed in Great Britain
by Amazon

9d84024b-fc85-4c65-8cb0-52a6025081b5R01